Citadel

CITADEL

Philip G. Williamson

LEGEND

Published by Legend Books in 1995

1 3 5 7 9 10 8 6 4 2

First published in the United Kingdom by

Legend Books Limited
20 Vauxhall Bridge Road, London SW1V 2SA

An imprint of Random House UK Limited

London Melbourne Sydney Auckland
Johannesburg and agencies throughout the world

First published in Great Britain in 1993 by
Random House UK Limited

Phototypeset by Intype, London
Printed and bound in Great Britain by
Mackays of Chatham PLC, Chatham, Kent

ACKNOWLEDGEMENT

The author wishes to thank Jane Siberry for her songs and music, for calling angels, illuminating the Well and suggesting the way to some of the Citadel's more distant regions. Whatever *Citadel* may be now, it would have been less without her.

Citadel is dedicated to everyone on the road.

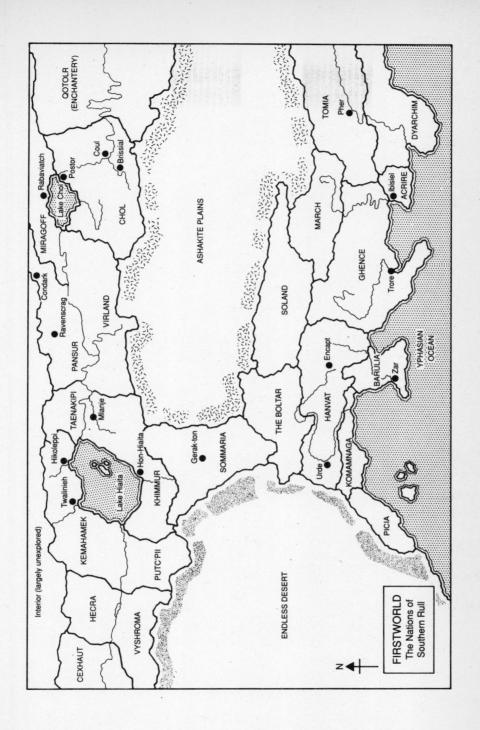

FIRSTWORLD
The Nations of
Southern Rull

N

Interior (largely unexplored)

QOTOLR
(ENCHANTERY)

TOMIA
Pher

DYARCHIM

Coul
Brissial
Rabaviatch
Postor
Lake Chol
MIRAGOFF

Ibisiel
ACRIRE

CHOL

MARCH

Condark

Ravenscrag

VIRLAND

GHENCE

ASHAKITE PLAINS

Trore

PANSUR

SOLAND

YPHASIAN
OCEAN

TAENAKIPI

Hikoleppi

Mlanje

Encapt

BARULIA

Zar

Twalinieh

Lake Hiaita

Hon-Hiaita

Gerak-ton

THE BOLTAR

HANVAT

KEMAHAMEK

KHIMMUR

SOMMARIA

Urde

KOMAMNAGA

CEXHAUT

HECRA

PUTC'PII

VYSHROMA

ENDLESS DESERT

PICIA

I

MY INITIAL REACTION upon hearing news of my passage
through a place I had not been was one of curiosity
mingled with a little concern, but I had no reason at that time
to suspect anything particularly sinister. It was disconcerting
and somewhat unsettling to learn soon after that I had in fact
been accused of gross crimes there. But to discover subsequently
that I had been arrested, tried, found guilty of said crimes and
executed left me with a unique and haunting sense of unease.
After all, I could demonstrate beyond any shadow of a doubt
that this was not the case, for here I was, palpable and conscious, and there I quite definitely had not been. Yet the reports,
reaching me in the manner they did, commanded belief, and in
one case emanated from a source I deemed utterly reliable.

This is not to say that I had never visited Anxau. I had, on
numerous occasions. It is a wild and largely inhospitable land,
lying far to the west of Khimmur, beyond the shimmering grassy
Urvysh Plains. It is bounded to the north by the Great White
River; its southern perimeter lies in the arid dustlands of the
Endless Desert, merging unnoticeably into its great wastes like
valley mist merges into overlying cloud. Sparsely populated in
the main, Anxau is home to motley of rude peasant stock,
rough, ill-mannered mountain types, erstwhile nomadic wan-
derers and scabrous settlers from afar. They are an unruly lot,
given to superstition and conflict and, no matter their back-
grounds, tend to be leery of foreigners. On the whole, Anxau
is considered a risky place in which to ravel.

An extension of the major international trade route Wetlan's
Way spans the country, and upon this Anxau's fledgling capital,
Dehut, has congealed. A sprawling ramshackle city, uncoordi-
nated, riddled with petty intrigue and corruption, it was held

1

under shifting sway at the time of which I write by a trio of upstart rival lordlets. Here were no-goods, scoundrels and thieves in their swarms. 'Trust no one' would have been an apt motto for this place. Dehut was a rat-hole, make no mistake – but from time to time I had done good business there.

Though not in recent months.

Yet all accounts made it more than plain that I had been seen there only weeks earlier. And, as I was to learn, my arrest, trial and appallingly cruel death had taken place only days before the first report of it filtered through to me.

Given the choice, I would have dismissed it as a joke – indeed, I tried. I tried to assure myself that it was of no importance, but circumstances quickly contrived to persuade me otherwise, in ways that I could hardly ignore. My nature is such that, once my curiosity is aroused, I become bound to pursue a matter through to its satisfactory resolution. Thus a point was reached where I could do little but investigate for myself those queer rumours from afar.

I would come to rue this. Many times I would berate my decision to leave Khimmur for Anxau and search out the truth behind the hearsay. In fact I would wish all manner of things before the business was done. So much was now to be decided by my actions. I am not keen at any time to risk my life if it can be avoided but, I would quickly learn, much, much more than my life was at stake here. The road to Anxau and beyond was a deception-ridden trail. leading me to terrors and wonders I could scarcely have imagined and into perhaps the strangest mystery I would ever encounter. No, by choice I would not have gone – but that is my excuse: in the end I had no choice.

I have leapt ahead of myself – a fitting turn of phrase, as it happens, conjuring as it does an image of *I* jumping out of *me*, perhaps taking a few brief steps then turning back to gaze upon myself. Bewildered, unnerved, seeing myself standing there and wondering, 'Which am I? How can *I* be sure?'

Let me retrace my steps, then, and describe the beginning of this business, at least as I experienced it. I could not see it at the time, but it started with a note delivered to me at my warehouse on Hon-Hiaita wharf.

2

The messenger was a boy, unknown to me. He entered with a cocky gait, identified me without hesitation, placed the stiff, sealed paper in my hand, accepted the coin I proffered, and was gone. I withdrew to my office and prised open the seal.

'*Bring it tomorrow. We can wait no longer. Sermilio.*'

It meant nothing to me.

I looked at the reverse, imagining it to be a mistaken delivery. But no, the words 'Master R. Dinbig, Grand Merchant, Hon-Hiaita, Khimmur' were clearly written there in the same hand that had penned the message. I scanned the message again. Bring what? Who was it who was so pressed? The name, Sermilio, was unfamiliar.

There was one other item on the page. A symbol or emblem of some kind, placed after and beneath the name 'Sermilio' and formed in the same ink. It consisted of a bulbous stem supporting two curving outstretched limbs, their tips downturning. A solid ovular form rested within the crutch of the limbs. Somewhat thus:

I stepped quickly outside, wanting to recall the lad who had brought the note. It was mid-morning. The sun glittered off the harbour waters and off cobbles dampened by earlier rain. A long low cog was made fast to the wharfside, several longshoremen working to unload its cargo. They sang in rhythm as they hefted bulging sacks and sealed wooden crates and bore them in file to their respective storerooms.

I scanned the harbourside. A few folk could be seen about the shops and taverns, some clearing forecourts and entrances of the debris of the previous night's excesses, others making for or coming from unknown assignations. Fishing-boats moored further along the quayside attracted litters of mange-ridden cats. Hon-Hiaita's cluttered rooftops scaled away into the distance towards the inclinations of Far Prospects and the Gell. King Gastlan Fireheart's great palace rose majestically upon the Gell's sheer granite height, a mighty sentinel above the town, surveying the meadows, rugged hills and forests beyond and the great inland sea of Lake Hiaita which lapped, or oftimes foamed and broiled, at its bedded feet.

For a moment I savoured the mingling multitude of smells borne on the cool moist air: oil, grease, water, mud, weed, the damp, cleated boards of boats, thick hemp rope and netting, fish, ale, grain, the waft of warm bread and sizzling meats, the sweat of men and animals, woodsmoke from the Gell, faint traces of a score of different perfumes imported from lands near and far. It felt good, just then, to be alive. My eyes fell upon a merchant some distance off in conversation with a pair of slouching militia-men. Beyond them a horse-drawn cart rattled slowly up Mags Urc't, Hon-Hiaita's main thoroughfare, towards the great Sharmanian Gate. A tethered ass waited patiently beneath an arch as two men haggled over what it was to carry. All this and much more, but no sign of my young messenger.

I returned indoors and called my assistant, Minyon, to me, thinking that he had perhaps made some arrangement in regard to the sale of my goods of which I had not yet been informed. But he declared ignorance upon seeing the message.

'Ah, well, whatever it is he wants, this Sermilio, he is not going to get it. At least, not today. Perhaps tomorrow, in his disappointment, he will show his face and explain the mystery.'

I folded the paper and pushed in into a pocket inside my robe, and for the moment forgot about the episode.

That evening I took off to the taverns around the harbourside, in particular to The Laughing Mariner, a favoured haunt of diverse folk and a place where information flows as readily as wine – for those with the knowledge and means to elicit it. I was keen to rendezvous with a Sommarian silk merchant named Sorias Bon who had arrived in Hon-Hiaita that afternoon with four wagons laden with silks from the far south. I knew well that ladies in Hon-Hiaita and Mlanje, Khimmur's second city, would pay handsomely for such fineries, and was confident, too, that with a little haggling and smart trade I might make a profit in lands to the north as well.

We ate and drank to near-excess and eventually arrived at terms pleasing to us both. Bon then expressed a desire for entertainment and I, being well acquainted with the pleasure houses of Hon-Hiaita and wishing at the same time to keep him from the company of my business rivals, offered to act as guide. He readily accepted and we prepared to leave.

There was a fellow I had noticed earlier in the common-room. He was an ill-dressed, unwashed varlet with a very mobile tankard who gave the impression of having drunk far more than was good for him. For the last few minutes he had been sprawled on his back in the middle of the floor among the sawdust and slops.

I recognized him. He was called Buel, known as Buel the Vile. I knew him for what he was – at least to some degree. When I first entered he had caught my eye and given me a sly wink. I had returned him a measured glance. In the company of the Sommarian merchant, Bon, I was not especially keen to have contact with such as Buel. But as we made for the door Buel rolled towards us. Before I could sidestep him he had wrapped an arm around my shin and hauled himself to sitting.

'Mashter Dinbig! You are back already! Did you be changing your plans?'

I frowned down at him, in puzzlement rather than annoyance. His face was smudged with grime, the dark hair and beard matted and unkempt. He grinned, showing blackened teeth.

'Back?' I queried. I had in fact returned the previous day from a week-long trip to Mlanje. But I could see no reason why it should have been of interest to Buel. 'Yes, I believe I am. But to what plans do you refer?'

'You shaid you did not exshtec—exsh*pect* to return to Khim-mur in the near future.'

'I said? When was this?'

'About two weeksh pasht.'

I studied him curiously for a moment, then raised a scented handkerchief to my nose as I crouched at his side. Buel's toler-ance of his condition never ceased to amaze me, but I knew better than to dismiss him as feeble-minded. 'And where?'

'Dehut, Mashter Dinbig.'

'Dehut? In Anxau?'

Buel nodded. There was a gleam of keen intelligence in his eyes. I could see that he, too, perceiving my puzzlement, was now curious. He hawked and spat upon the floor.

I lowered my voice, though it was hardly necessary. Our exchange could not be heard above the hubbub of the tavern, and no one except the Sommarian merchant was paying us any heed. I quickly glanced his way. His look was bemused but I felt I could gamble on his patience holding for a few moments.

'Are you saying you saw me in Anxau two weeks ago?'

Buel nodded again. 'Does your memory fail you? It was not I as I, of course.'

'Of course.' I took a moment for swift thought. 'We must talk. Can you visit me at home later?'

Another nod.

'I trust you will bathe beforehand?'

'For you, Mashter Dinbig, no exshesh be too great!' He coughed raucously. As I rose he released my leg and slumped back to the floor.

I returned to my home sometime after midnight, having left Sorias Bon happily and sleepily ensconced in one of Hon-Hiaita's choicest bordellos. As the evening had worn on and his happiness increased, I had successfully lowered the asking price for his silks even further, and departed with a firm arrangement for an exchange of other goods at my warehouse early the following morning. I was, I should say, solidly en route to becoming a wealthy man; only the previous year I had purchased a comfortable four-storey villa situated just a little way south of the select Far Prospects quarter of the town. My youth had been marked by oftimes grinding poverty and toil, but with diligence, perseverance and sheer hard work I had built up a respected trading business with interests both at home and abroad.

My success in the area of foreign relations has been an achievement in which I take great pride. For generations Khimmur had been virtual no-go region for outsiders. With some justification it was held to be an unstable nation of semi-barbarians, given to brigandry and internal conflict. Our king, Gastlan Fireheart, had actively striven to resolve the disputes and ages-old feuds which fragmented the kingdom, as had other sovereigns before him. He had met with some success, though several *dhoma*-lords remained intractable. Still, I had always seen the potential in encouraging open trade with other nations, and after lengthy discussions with the king and his advisors I had been permitted to travel abroad to establish links with our neighbours to improve Khimmur's image and invite foreign trade.

At the age of twenty-two I was a well known and influential man. I had also, two years earlier, successfully completed my neophyte training in the secret schools of the *Zan-Chassin*,* bound my First Entity and become an Initiate of the First Realm. This bestowed significant honours and privileges upon me, and further opened the way to knowledge, power and influence both at home and abroad.

I had my heart set on purchasing a manse in Far Prospects within the next few months. Here, proximal to the Royal Palace, the movers and notables of Khimmurian society resided. To be sited among them would be indelible testament to my ascent.

This night I sat at my desk in my study, not yet ready for bed, awaiting my visitor. My thoughts ran over the brief, odd conversation I had had earlier with Buel the Vile. I knew him to be a sharp fellow, no matter his appearance, and his claim to have met me in Anxau two weeks earlier had greatly intrigued me.

I summoned a servant and ordered aquavit and sweet and salt biscuits in anticipation of his arrival. Moments later there was a quiet knock at my study door. The same servant entered and announced my visitor. 'Viscount† Inbuel m' Anakastii of Kemahamek, sir.'

The man who strode into the room was quite tall, well built if a little slim, with pale skin, dark, closely curling hair and a short, neat beard. He was young, no more than a year or two older than I, and garbed in travelling gear of good quality and cut: blue hose, a white puff-sleeved shirt and padded blue velvet

---

* See Appendix.

† The full and proper Kemahamek title for the individual referred to is 'Pelòp-antator-tenda', designating him the scion, or perhaps sibling, of a high Kemah-amek noble of acknowledged rank, who has achieved, or is destined to achieve, rank and distinction in his own right. 'Viscount' – given here to avoid confusion – is the closest familiar designation, though it fails to convey the subtle specificity of the Kemahamek honorific.

waistcoat, high, soft leather boots and a short cloak. A narrow sword hung from his waist.

He entered with an assured gait, smiling broadly, his brown eyes twinkling with merriment. 'Ah, Sir Dinbig! Well met! How are you?'

He spread his arms wide, stepped forward and embraced me warmly.

'Inbuel, it is good to see you.' I returned the embrace. 'How are you? You look and smell better, I am pleased to say.'

'Ha, yes! Indeed, I am in fine shape and good odour – at least for the next few hours!'

I poured aquavit as he seated himself, and after a brief exchange of pleasantries I said, 'Now what of this claim of yours to have seen me in Anxau? I take it it is no jest?'

Inbuel looked surprised. 'Jest? Why, no. Why would I jest about such a thing? Yet you seem concerned.'

'Perplexed, certainly.'

'Why so? I gathered in The Laughing Mariner that you did not wish to speak of it in company, yet my only query was as to why you had altered your plans.'

'I did not alter them.'

He frowned. 'Then why have you returned to Khimmur?'

'I have not.'

'Ah, Sir Dinbig, now it is you who jest.'

'Not so, I assure you.'

'Then what—?'

'Inbuel, I have been away, but to Mlanje, which as you know lies to the east. I have not left Khimmur for many weeks. The last time I was in Dehut was almost a year ago. And, unless my memory serves me ill, I have not seen you for several months either.'

'But this is absurd. We met. We spoke.'

'In Dehut?'

'Aye.'

'Then I was there without my knowledge!'

I rose from my chair, suddenly irked, and replenished my goblet from the carafe of aquavit, offering more to Inbuel – who declined, setting his goblet upon a small table at his side.

I paced the room. 'Plainly you have met an impostor. My question is, why?'

Inbuel was shaking his head, a frown of consternation upon his brow. 'He was no impostor, Dinbig. Do you think I would not know you?'

'But I was not there, I tell you!' I stared at him. His transformation was remarkable. It was not easy to identify him with the odious varlet in the tavern. He employed that guise quite regularly, finding it a useful means of gaining information. People spoke freely in the hearing of one they deemed slack-witted and hardly warranting acknowledgement as a living being. Buel the Vile possibly knew more of Hon-Hiaita's secret life than all the king's domestic spies put together. Indeed, he had more than once traded me sensitive information about Khimmur's internal affairs which I had later corroborated at official meetings at the palace.

'What guise did you adopt in Anxau?' I asked after a pause.

'I was there as myself.' He gestured with both hands towards his breast. 'Viscount Inbuel, a noble and High Merchant of Twalinieh in Kemahamek.'

'You were there on business?'

'Business of a kind.' He flashed a curt smile which told me it would be impolitic to enquire further. I assumed his business had been, at least in some part, official. Like myself, Inbuel travelled with his nation's interests in mind.

'And what were the circumstances of our "meeting"?'

'We came upon one another by chance in Culmet's Bazaar. It was late morning, if I recall correctly.'

'And we spoke?'

'Briefly. You were fatigued after a long journey, preoccupied with some business which you were anxious to resolve quickly that you might away to catch up on lost sleep.'

'So we spoke for just moments?'

'Indeed, and then you were off.'

'Mystifying. It is, to my knowledge, the first time I have ever taken part in a meeting at which I can confidently say I was not present.' I returned to my seat. 'I say again, then, you found yourself in the company of an impostor, albeit one of unsurpassed skill.'

9

Inbuel slowly shook his head. His look was sombre now. He spoke with seeming reluctance. 'I am lost for an explanation, Dinbig. You were not your usual bright self, it is true. You were tired, a little drawn, monosyllabic and perhaps a touch under the weather. Yet I know you well. I would never have believed, and I do not believe now, that after all we have been through together I could be fooled by some impudent ruffian attempting to impersonate you.'

I sat back in my seat, surveying him long and hard. It was true that we were confederates. We had worked profitably together on many occasions over several years, had aided one another's rise in our respective countries, had had numerous adventures together and, indeed, had on a couple of occasions been instrumental in saving one another's lives. We had become firm friends and I trusted him implicitly.

'Then I have no explanation, either,' I said.

Inbuel sat pensively, one forefinger crooked beneath his nose. At length he said, 'Two possibilities occur to me. Both are somewhat delicate, but I must put them to you. Sir Dinbig, is there something you are not letting on? Have you been engaged in some secret business on your king's behalf, something you are not free to discuss? Was our meeting an embarrassment to you, bringing you to my attention when you would have preferred that no one be aware of your presence in Anxau?'

'If that were the case I would have confessed already, Inbuel, in preference to this tedious rigmarole. No, I was engaged in no secret business, for King Gastlan or anyone else. That I can assure you of.'

'Well, my other question, then. I know little of sorcery, as you are aware. But you are skilled in the arcane art. Have you, or perhaps your *Zan-Chassin* associates, by some means, and for some purpose undeclared, contrived to have a semblance of yourself manifest in Dehut? Again I appreciate that this may be a matter you are not at liberty to discuss, but you have called me here for an explanation and I have complied as best I can. Indicate to me that I have touched upon something approaching the truth and I will enquire no further. The matter will be closed, you have my absolute promise.'

I shook my head. It is commonly believed that the *Zan-*

10

Chassin possess powers far exceeding our actual capabilities. I could not cause my person to manifest in the flesh in any location other than the one I currently occupied, and to my knowledge such a feat was beyond the capabilities of even our most advanced adepts. (I made a mental note to question the Hierarchy on this matter at the earliest opportunity.) I did not say as much to Inbuel. *Zan-Chassin* activities are not revealed to the uninitiated, and it does no harm if people in Khimmur or elsewhere allow their imaginations to exaggerate the powers we command.

'Were it so, I would not hide it from you,' I said. 'But it is not. I was not in Dehut, Inbuel: it is as simple as that. Yet by your account I was. Thus I am guilty of having been in two places at once – what's more, without knowing it! It is preposterous, and more than a little troubling.'

Inbuel shifted in his chair, hanging one leg over the other. 'This is a fine mystery, then. I am most intrigued to learn the secret of your duality.'

'I too.'

'Would that I could emulate it.'

'There is little point if you are not conscious of doing it.'

I offered him another drink, which he accepted. 'You say I was uncommunicative,' I continued, 'so we spoke but briefly, then parted. Did we exchange any more words, other than those you have recounted?'

'None. I told you that I was leaving the following day and making for Khimmur before returning to Kemahamek. I suggested we meet here in Hon-Hiaita. You said that would not be possible: you were occupied with other business and would be unlikely to return home for some weeks. That is the sum total of our conversation.'

'I gave no indication of the business I was engaged upon?'

'None.'

'Hmph. Well, we could talk all night but I do not think we will discover anything more.'

We spoke of other matters for a short while, then Inbuel rose, indicating his intention to leave. I enquired as to his lodging, offering my own guests' chambers, but he declined. 'I have made the acquaintance, as it happens, of a wealthy young widow here

11

in Hon-Hiaita. It is to her welcoming bosom that I should go now, before the night is over.'

'And how long do you remain in Hon-Hiaita?'

'Just tonight. Tomorrow I take ship for Twalinieh.' His eyes alighted in passing upon an object on my desk. 'May I?'

I nodded. He lifted it carefully, an irregularly formed chunk of rare green amber, and held it up in the candle-light. 'This is a most attractive piece.'

I was a little distracted and made no comment. Inbuel inspected the amber for some moments, then replaced it upon the desktop, commenting again upon its unusual attraction. 'Go well, my friend,' he said, embracing me.

'And you.'

After he had gone I brooded awhile beside my desk. It was an unsettling notion, that someone unknown was impersonating me, and so expertly. To what end? And how was such an apparently perfect imposture achieved? I mused upon this for some time but made no more progress than I had when talking to Inbuel. Eventually I returned to an awareness of myself and found I was gazing down at the piece of amber which he had admired, and upon which the tips of my fingers unconsciously rested. It was a fascinating object, gleaming with a warm citrine lambence – shot with a greenish tinge – which reflected the candle-flames in the room. I had seen a number of similar pieces over time, brought as curios from distant lands. Trapped within them were little insects, perfectly preserved. They were relatively rare – and green amber was the most sought-after of all – and I had sold them profitably to wealthy folk with an eye for the unusual.

Certain scholars reckon them to be ancient, even thousands of years old. They profess the belief that the amber stone was once liquid; that it by some means hardened instantaneously to trap its hapless guests forever. It is true that the preserved insects are sometimes alien to any species known; this gives weight to the argument that they are of a type which no longer dwells upon this world, or even that they are magical creatures or things of another world entirely.

I lifted the stone and peered into its translucent glassy depths. It was cool and solid in my fingers. Tiny bubbles hung motionless in deep yellow, suffused in places with that strange greenish tinge. A cluster of minute winged creatures were held inside, scores in all, a veritable swarm. They were difficult to make out in any detail; I could see slender dark bodies and fragile wings which gave an impression of deepest black and crimson. I had not seen their like before, and for that reason had kept the stone for myself. I was fascinated both by the insects and by the thoughts their mummified existence engendered. Many times I had gazed into the amber and mulled over what I saw: life preserved in stasis, in death; the irretrievable retrieved yet untouchable; the past held forever prisoner in the present.

It was only as I was replacing the green amber that I recalled how I had acquired it. I had bought it, along with numerous other articles, from a trader I had met the previous autumn at a caravanserai beside Wetlan's Way. I had enquired as to the provenance of the piece; he claimed to have bought it in a small mountain village he had passed through. He had jerked his thumb over his shoulder, indicating west and the Urvysh Plains. I had paid no attention at the time. Now the thought came to me that there were no mountains in the Urvysh. Travelling westwards, there were no mountains until one entered Anxau.

I chided myself. I was making associations where there were none. It was the merest coincidence – in fact, not even that. I gave it no more thought. Snuffing the candles I locked my study and made my way to bed.

2

THE FOLLOWING MORNING, as I was preparing to leave for my warehouse, I received another letter. The messenger this time was one of my own men, Bris, a stalwart fellow who had been among the first to enter my employ, more than four years earlier. I opened the letter quickly and read:

I would have preferred to have delivered this in person, but time and tide wait for no man. I therefore entrust it into another's hands, knowing you hold him reliable and wholly above reproach. Nonetheless, assure yourself upon receipt that the seal is unbroken.

After leaving you last night I was struck by a chilling thought: when we next meet, whenever or wherever, how will I be sure that I am talking to the real you? Perhaps I have the impression of making light of the Dehut incident. The truth, as you must surely be aware, is that it has potentially sinister implications. Prudence is advisable, then, until the facts are known.

I suggest a code. When I see you next, no matter my face, I shall greet you with the words, 'Fortune is in the air, so I hear.' Your reply must be, 'With every breath comes change.' Thus will I know whom I face.

Go well and safely, and be certain of yourself.
Your friend,
Inbuel

'Be certain of yourself'! It was a pointed warning. The manifold implications of those hastily written words came at me now in a sudden shocking rush. A cold shiver rived my gut and I felt a queer and unnerving sensation that the ground was about to give way beneath my feet. *Somebody else was pretending to be me.* By that very fact, certainty – certainty of self – was the one thing I was denied.

By all the gods, this could indeed be a sinister business.

Or was I making too much of it?

In the night I had awoken from a dream in which this person, this malevolent impersonator, had brought himself to Hon-Hiaita, had successfully passed himself off as me, had worked his way into the confidence of friends and associates who had no reason to suspect that anything was afoot. He had begun to take control of everything that was mine.

I had started from my sleep with the awareness that my life was in ruins, that everything I had ever striven for had been taken from me and put into the hands of this other, whose identity and ultimate aims were undeclared. As I thought these things in the dead of night, his hired assassins silently entered my chambers, coming like phantoms, like the shadows of vampires. They fell upon me, and though I struggled I was helpless in their hands. I was spirited away to some lonely, hellish locale, and there my life was taken.

I had lain for some time breathing fast, in a cold sweat, not knowing what was real and what was not. The horror ebbed slowly, and the recognition came through, little by little: it had been only a nightmare, something conjured out of my deepest fears, brought to the surface by Inbuel's news. What I had dreamed could not actually happen. This impostor, whoever he might be, was far away. He had done no harm. He was, more than likely, nothing worse than a prankster.

The *Zan-Chassin* discipline teaches mental techniques for overcoming fear and dispelling unwanted thoughts. I was not yet a master of the art but I knew enough to clear my mind and allow myself to sleep again undisturbed till morning.

Now I applied my mind once more to calm myself. Bris stood waiting at my side. I re-read Inbuel's letter.

No, I was not making too much of it. Quite the contrary, in fact. Inbuel's words impressed that upon me. His precautions were commendable and wise. If anything, I was guilty of not having taken the matter quite seriously enough. I should report the incident without further delay. Any man who could successfully pass himself off as me, fooling someone who knew me as well as Inbuel did, had to be taken seriously. His accomplishment declared him a master of his art, and his art, put to wrongful use, was pernicious. My nightmare had told me what might ultimately be achieved. I could afford to take no risks. Measures similar to those proposed by Inbuel in his letter would have to be taken with my other close and important associates.

I questioned Bris. 'Who gave you this letter to deliver?'

'Viscount m' Anakastii, sir. He came hurriedly to the warehouse at dawn. He was sailing within the hour on a Kemahamek cog, the *Star of Twalinieh*. He bade me bring you this message with all urgency.'

'Then he has sailed now?'

'Aye, he will have been at sea this past half-hour.'

I felt a twinge of annoyance at myself. Inbuel's letter had had the secondary effect of reminding me of the note I had received the previous day, from Sermilio. I did not imagine a connection between the two incidents, but Inbuel, his experience of the world being as encompassing as my own, might have known who Sermilio was, or failing that might have identified the mysterious symbol upon the page. There was nothing to be done now; I had not thought to show him the note, and it might be months before we next met. Today, of course, was the day Sermilio was so anxious to gain whatever it was his letter referred to. Would I become better-informed as the day progressed?

Memorizing Inbuel's code, I crossed the room and dropped his letter into the flames of the hearth. I watched until it was consumed, curling into flaking fragments of black, then turned back to Bris. 'Go immediately to the home of the Chariness, Hisdra. If she is not there you will find her in the *Zan-Chassin* catacombs within the royal palace. Tell her I seek an urgent audience, with her or with others of the Council of Elders. Bring me her reply, and do not tarry.'

Bris was gone. I made my way down through the near-empty streets to the wharf. The early-morning air was chill and sharp, with just the lightest of breezes beginning to play down from the hills beyond Morshover Vale to the south. At the quayside I gazed across the mist-wreathed waters of the inland sea, Lake

16

Hiaita. The breeze gently stirred the mist, ruffling the mirror of the water. The cog, the *Star of Twalinieh*, which carried my friend Inbuel was visible no more than half a mile away. Clearing the breakwater and the hidden shoals beyond, she had shipped her oars and unfurled her single sail, which began to swell now as it took the breeze. With a favourable passage she would be home within three days.

The Sommarian merchant, Sorias Bon, arrived. His eyes sagged in dark circles and he complained of a throbbing head, but he had enjoyed the night's entertainments and was in overall good humour. In my office we drank steaming dark cocoa laced with plum spirit and he came to life, extolling the skills and virtues of Hon-Hiaita's whores. We conducted our business swiftly and amicably, and Bon made ready to leave. On an impulse, as his wagons were being unloaded and restocked, I asked him whether he was familiar with the name Sermilio. He said he was not. Folding the stiff paper so that he might not read the message thereon, I revealed to him the strange symbol.

'Does this mean anything to you?'

Bon shook his head. He had never seen its like before.

'Ah, well,' I said, replacing the letter in my robe, 'it is of no great account.'

One of Bon's assistants entered to tell him that the loading was done. I had seen the fellow before, though I did not know his name. He was a thickset swarthy man, aged about thirty, a veteran of the trade roads. He had ridden guard for other merchants with whom I had done business in the past. He acknowledged me with a nod of the head and a curt grin, and said something which struck me as curious. 'They let you out then. Master Dinbig?'

The full significance of this remark would not strike me until later. Even so, I felt it warranted some explanation. Bon's man was already half out of the door, anticipating no more than the briefest of replies, if any.

'What was that?' I called after him.

He turned back, a vaguely quizzical expression on his face.

'Would you repeat what you just said?' I asked.

He did so.

'To whom do you refer?' I asked. 'Who let me out? And out of where?'

The man was mildly perplexed now. 'Feikermun's beasts.'

'Feikermun?'

'Feikermun of Selph.'

Something seemed almost to fall into place, a feeling both of understanding and, simultaneously, of being further confused by events. It was like a weight descending, a cloud falling upon my spirits, and again the sensation that the ground was crumbling beneath me. Feikermun of Selph was one of the three thuggish lordlets who held sway over Dehut in Anxau.

Rising from my seat behind the desk, I approached Bon's man, extending the full strength of my personality in the manner I had learned over years of *Zan-Chassin* training. The fellow was bigger than I, and stronger, but with satisfaction I saw him quail before me. ' What in Moban's name are you talking about?'

'It's just something I picked up, Master Dinbig. I didn't mean any offence.'

'I am not offended, simply mystified. Explain, please.'

'Well, word is that Feikermun wanted you and that his beasts had caught you and were taking you back to Dehut.'

'Where did you hear this?'

'From a Putc'pii herder we met on the road some days back. He said you'd sold Feikermun bad goods or something. Feikermun wanted your blood.'

Was this it? Did I have an answer? Was my alter ego at work bringing my name into disrepute in Anxau? If so, it was a dangerous course. In fact, by this account he might already have paid the price.

But the question still lingered: Why?

'What's the name of this herder?'

'Fol Hostromn, sir. He said he'd heard it in The Goat and Salmon Pool, in Riverway. Everyone was talking about it, he said. Seems they thought it was the end of you. Feikermun's not a merciful man.'

No, he was a sick-hearted monster. A man who reckoned himself untouchable; a murderer, torturer, despot . . . wholly devoid of any shred of decency. I had done business with him once, and had no wish to repeat the experience. I had emerged the poorer, but at least I had kept my life. To better Feikermun was to invite a blade between the ribs, or a slit throat as one slept at night. He had no respect for status. That I was in effect a roving ambassador of my country was of no account in lawless Dehut.

Feikermun had ruled unopposed until a few years ago. His henchmen were beasts indeed, and through them he had held the city in terror. Then his brother and former right-hand man, Gorl, had attempted to assassinate him. The attempt had failed, but Gorl escaped with his life and gained control of part of the city, leading to split rule and bloody street warfare.

At about the same time a third party sprang to prominence. A mysterious figure known as the Golden Lamb took advantage of the chaos and seized control in Dehut's relatively affluent western quarter. Tripartite conflict had continued ever since, but the place was minimally less bloody these days, as each of the three had something of a curbing effect on the excesses of the other two. Feikermun and Gorl were as bad as each other. Little was known of the Golden Lamb. His reputation spoke of a stern ruler who commanded a loyal following, but it appeared he inclined somewhat less towards indiscriminate bloodletting than his two adversaries.

When engaged in business there, I, like most, endeavoured to avoid direct contact with the three or their immediate henchmen. The central marketplaces offered reasonable opportunities for trade, and generally one could do business there unmolested.

Recently rumours had filtered out of the death of Gorl, Feikermun's brother. He was said to have been slain by his lover, a woman named Malibeth, who now ruled in his stead. Whether this was true or not I could not say.

'And what is your name?' I demanded of Sorias Bon's man.

'Mursa, sir. Gillin Mursa.'

'Well, Gillin Mursa, should further such scurrilous tales reach your ears you may inform the rumourmongers that they are unfounded. You are witness to the fact that I am alive and in good health. I have had no contact with Feikermun of Selph, or his beasts. Nor have I sold him, or anyone, substandard goods – and he does not seek my blood. Do you have that?'

19

'Yes, sir. I'm sorry.'

'You may go.'

Mursa glanced sheepishly at his employer, who nodded, and he went back to his business.

Soon after this Bon departed. I remained for a while at the warehouse, attending to a few matters of business, then took myself off to a quayside tavern to enjoy a breakfast of pickled eels and herb potato flakes, with more hot cacao. Bris found me there, and brought the news that the Chariness expected me at noon in her audience chamber in the *Zan-Chassin* catacombs. This left a few hours in which to find diversion. That business should be a pleasure is one of my most basic tenets, and with such in mind I returned to the warehouse and had a boy load a barrow with some of Bon's new silks, plus a few other choice items of jewellery, perfumes and ornaments. With boy and barrow in tow I set off for Cheuvra, the Hon-Hiaitan manse of Lady Celice of Selaor.

Lady Celice was seventeen and a rare beauty. She had recently wed the Orl Kilroth, *dhoma*-lord of Selaor. He was arguably the most powerful of Khimmur's nobles and, fortunately for King Gastlan, a man fanatically loyal to the Crown. Kilroth's seat was Castle Drome, in the central province of Selaor, but Celice, who had a taste for the finer things in life, found the place without charm. She was Selaorian born and bred yet, since her betrothal, had succumbed to a quite mysterious and debilitating malady which affected her most notably when she was obliged to spend time in her home province, particularly within the chill walls of brooding Castle Drome. Hon-Hiaita, on the other hand, with its choice company and diverse entertainments, she found far more appropriate to her health and temperament. Celice had therefore moved herself into the splendid manse, Cheuvra, within days of her wedding. For the most part the Orl's time was taken up with matters of duty at his beloved Drome.

Eager to contribute to and sustain the young Lady Celice's sense of well-being and enjoyment of life, I had paid a number of visits to Cheuvra. On this occasion I arrived unannounced, and was shown in by a footman who disappeared upstairs to inform Celice of my arrival. She, as it happened, had returned to Hon-Hiaita from Castle Drome just a couple of days earlier, having been engaged in formal duties with the Orl which she simply had not been able to avoid.

She appeared at the head of the stairs, garbed in a bright, elegant carmine gown, gathered tightly at the waist and cut low at the breast, its split bodice laced with criss-crossed twin velvet thongs. I recalled having brought it to her some weeks earlier.

She was a vision, it has to be said. Slim, of average height, auburn-haired, slender-waisted, and blessed with a bosom of such youthful bounty as to cast a man into a swoon. That the orl should opt for the wild scapes of Selaor over the sweet abundances of lovely Celice was something I could not begin to comprehend.

Her beautiful young face broke into a delighted smile at the sight of me – in fact, it was more than delight. She appeared surprised and overjoyed, clutching her hands together beneath her chin and giving a little jump at the head of the stairs. It was a greeting rather more effusive than I had expected. Her first words explained why, and at the same time filled me with misgiving.

'Dinbig! You are safe! I was so worried!'

Somehow I knew then that the revelations of the last twenty-four hours were going to continue to haunt me, even here. 'What do you mean?' I said, gloomily anticipating the broad tenor of her reply.

Celice descended three steps, then halted. Her cheeks were flushed, her eyes dewy, but I saw now that she fought to restrain herself in front of the household staff. 'I heard the news of your terrible adventures in Anxau.'

I nodded. 'Ah.'

'I was told you were dead – and worse!'

'Worse?'

'I was told you had suffered such . . . such . . . But I see the reports were exaggerated, for here you are – and I am so pleased – neither dead nor mutilated.'

'Indeed, that is correct. Well, Lady Celice, in my livest and most unspoiled manner I have brought new goods for you to inspect. Perhaps, as you cast your eyes over them, you might care to tell me precisely what it is you have been told.'

I hoped my tone of voice and expression conveyed my desire to speak to her in private.

'Of course,' agreed Celice. 'Please have the goods brought upstairs to my apartments. I shall inspect them there.'

The boy, helped by one of Celice's servants, unloaded the barrow and together they took my goods to Celice's chambers. She ordered mulled wine and cakes to be brought, and we ascended. She ran her hands over the silks with expressions of delight, quickly examined the ornaments and jewels, and sampled the perfumes. Her manservant arrived with the refreshments on a silver platter and poured sparkling amber wine into two goblets.

'I do not wish to be disturbed,' said Celice.

The servant bowed and withdrew, closing the door behind him.

As soon as we were alone Celice seized my arm. 'Oh, Dinbig, you don't know how I have been! I was sure you were dead.'

Her slender arms slipped around my neck and she hugged me fiercely, pressing her warm cheek to mine. I breathed in the lush scent of her, and savoured the sensation of her yielding body against my own.

'Now what is this?' I murmured. 'What is this strange tale you have been told, and from where did it come?'

She drew back slightly. I gazed down upon the swell of her breasts, the deep, inviting shadows of her cleavage, inhaled her warm perfume, and my ardour rose.

'I was told you had been executed,' said Celice. 'You were picked up for rogering the wife of some Anxau warlord. You were tortured . . . horribly. Mintral said that before killing you they . . . they hacked off your pizzle and made you . . . made you . . .'

'Made me what?' I said, shuddering.

She screwed up her face. 'Made you *eat* it.'

I shuddered again.

'They didn't, did they, Dinbig?' Celice's hand slid downwards over my breast and belly, to press itself warmly against the accused, who by this time was impressed stoutly against the

22

inside of my trousers. 'Aah,' she breathed, and smiled and gave me a tender squeeze.

'You see, it is all foul rumour with not an iota of truth. I am very much a whole man. It was Lord Mintral, you say, who brought this news?'

Celice nodded. 'He was here, the day before yesterday. He was convinced it was true.'

I felt a moment of concern. Lord Mintral was *dhoma*-lord of Beliss, Khimmur's most westerly domain, which bordered upon the Putc'pii plains. His castle lay no great distance from Hon-Hiaita. I was not happy with the thought that Mintral might have been here, in this house, doing what I was about to do. I would question Celice further, both about the nature of Mintral's visit and the exact details of his report in regard to my supposed activities, but now was not the time.

'Did you roger a warlord's wife, Dinbig?' Celice asked, a slight tremor in her voice.

'Of course not. I have not been in Anxau.' I kissed her. 'Did Mintral mention the name of the offended warlord?'

'Oh, he did, I think. But I can't remember it.'

'Feikermun?' I offered. 'Of Selph?'

'Yes, that's it.' She frowned, pouting. 'How do you know, if you haven't been there?'

'Because Feikermun's name has already come up once today in connection with myself – again, on bogus premises.' I kissed her again, a long, deeply intimate kiss. 'I take it your husband is still away?'

'At Drome, as was I. He has organized a grand hunt with his local lords, commencing today. He says he will decorate the banqueting hall with a dozen vhazz heads.' She gave a grimace of distaste. 'I don't want hideous vhazz heads on my walls.'

The vhazz are strange creatures, dog-like but partly human, semi-intelligent. They are considered savage, wicked and vile, known to take human babies from their cribs and feed them to their young. The vhazz are hunted remorselessly by men.

'Ah, good,' I said.

'Good?'

'I mean good that he is not here to disturb us, not good that he intends to mount hideous vhazz heads upon your walls.' As

23

I spoke I unlaced the velvet thong fastening Celice's bodice and eased the material aside to free her breasts. I drew my breath at the marvellous sight, and slipped my hands upon them both. 'The good orl will not be back for at least a week, then?'

'At least . . .' She sighed and bent back her head. I lowered my lips to kiss the smooth soft flesh and gently circle a pert rosebud nipple with my tongue.

'Ah, Dinbig, have you brought your magics?'

'Of course,' I murmured.

'Then cast them now.'

I had used certain minor raptures before as enhancements to lovemaking. The practice was not, strictly speaking, approved of within the *Zan-Chassin* Hierarchy, but I do not imagine that I am the only one to have employed it. I picked Celice up in my arms and carried her through to her bedchamber. Laying her down, I invoked the raptures. In a haze of erotic magic I slowly removed her clothing and she slowly removed mine. There were more than two hours before my meeting with the Chariness. That time would be filled to the utmost as I steeped myself in the inimitable lovelinesses of Celice.

3

IT SEEMED TO me that Hisdra, the Chariness, had always been old. My earliest childhood memories of her were of a withered crone, more ancient than I could imagine. Now I was an adult, and she remained as impossibly aged as she had always been. It was as if she had been old from the beginning of time. I could not conceive of her bones ever having been strong and clad in firm, youthful flesh; I could not imagine her in the arms or the bed of a lover, nor see her dancing, running, playing. She was for me the perfect living embodiment of ancient wisdom – and wiles.

She sat before me now, her body tiny and frail, her chin wispily bearded, her pallid, wrinkled pate visible beneath thin wreaths of sparse grey hair. She wore an informal robe of sombre damask embroidered with blue-and-silver edging. She could barely stand, or even sit, without support. Her limbs were bony and bird-like; they shook incessantly, outside her conscious control. By my estimation she had known at least nine decades of corporeality. A possible contender in the age stakes was Lord Gegg, grand patriarch of Gegg's Cowm in Selaor. He had fought for and against more Khimmurian kings than any other living *dhoma*-lord, had lost an eye and a leg in separate battles for the effort, had spawned sons and grandchildren beyond counting, and was now partially deaf and half-crippled with inflamed joints. Sagas were composed about Gegg, but I believe Hisdra had at least a decade on him.

Her physical infirmity aside, she was the most accomplished and powerful member of the *Zan-Chassin* Hierarchy, our Sacred Mother, an Adept of the Sixth Realm. Few before her, and none among the living, had advanced so far.

It was in Hisdra's eyes that one could perceive something of

25

her true nature and strength. Sunk within bald bony sockets and skin that was cadaverously shrunken and desiccated, the eyes shone with a disarming vigour. Her gaze was keen, alert, perceptive, bright with the light of knowledge, the humour of understanding, the quiet energy of achievement. Also, unmistakably, she emanated an aura. One gazed upon her and saw a frail wisp, clinging to life; yet one instinctively sensed more, and recognized, without knowing quite how, that here was an old woman of rare and exceptional qualities.

'Feikermun of Selph has been an object of interest to us for some time, Dinbig,' she said, seated almost like a rag doll upon her carved-oak ceremonial chair. We were in her chamber deep within the *Zan-Chassin* catacombs beneath Khimmur's Royal Palace. Her feet hung from her robe, well above the stone floor; there was a small wooden step beside the chair to help her climb on and off. 'It is curious that you should come to me now, mentioning his name in connection with your strange circumstance.'

'In what way has he attracted the Hierarchy's attention?' I enquired.

'His state of mind is a cause for some concern.'

'How so?'

'He is almost certainly insane.'

'He is not so far gone that he cannot command loyalty among his followers.'

'And fear among his adversaries. That is so.'

'And his connection with myself, or my double, seems purely coincidental. If the stories that have reached my ears are true, it is my imitator who has caused offence to Feikermun and has thus drawn himself to his attention. Feikermun has not been the instigator.'

Old Hisdra's head swayed slowly back and forth upon her scrawny neck as she contemplated this. 'That is how it appears at present, I grant you that.'

'And, insane or not, why should he be of interest to the *Zan-Chassin* or Khimmur? Feikermun may be considered a mad nabob in his own domain, but on an international scale that domain is small and of paltry significance. He commands a rabble – albeit a murderous one – not an army. His influence barely extends beyond Dehut and its immediate environs, and any plans he may harbour for expansion are thwarted by the presence of his two opponents there.'

'It is Feikermun's interests that draw our attention, Dinbig. We believe that for some time now he has been engaged in illicit research.'

'Research? Of what kind?'

'Magic, in some form.'

I pondered this. 'And has he met with any success?'

'This is where our concern lies, but our precise knowledge is vague, as we have been unable to get close to him. We do know that limited magic has been his for some time. For instance, he is sensitive to the presence of magic and is able to employ limited but reasonably effective means to detect and negate its use against him. For that reason we have been unable to spy upon him from the Realms or with out-of-body techniques. Apart from this he has, until now, had no access to any but the most minor of rapturous effects.'

'Until now?'

'Firm evidence is lacking but we have good reason to suspect that Feikermun had made significant advances in recent months. It is possible that he is on the verge of achieving mastery of a major discipline.'

'Has he a teacher?'

'We do not know.'

I considered this. *Zan-Chassin* magic is unique to Khimmur, and its use has always been carefully monitored and controlled. Other magical forms exist elsewhere, but they are likewise jealously guarded. The Simbissikim priesthood of Kemahamek, for instance, has developed its own discipline, but like us the Simbissikim reveal their secrets only by degrees, and to candidates who have undergone long and arduous schooling. Similarly with the shamans of the tribes of the Endless Desert, of whom virtually nothing is known, for they resist all contact with the world beyond their sands. Renegade magicians crop up here and there, it is true, but they are infrequent and generally not particularly powerful, and tend to employ their magic purely for their own ends.

Powerful magic has been known in the past. During the

period of the Great Deadlock some one and a half centuries ago, the Hecran king Moshrazman III somehow mastered the secret of summoning vile Gneth. These monsters he then used to drive Kemahamek invaders from his soil, but later paid the price when the Gneth turned upon him and his troops, destroying them and reducing Hecra to a wasteland. Gneth roam Hecra in some number still, and men avoid the country, but the secret of their summoning has long been lost.*

All magic is believed to have derived from mysterious Qotolr, known as Enchantery, which lies far to the east. Millennia ago beings with the powers of gods warred there and distorted the land and its very air with their magic. Men have been fearful of magic ever since. Enchantery strikes an even greater chill into men's hearts than Hecra, and none go there – or, if they do, they do not return.

Magic, then, is a potent and unpredictable force, of apparently illimitable scope. Its spread outside the known disciplines, as well as its development within, has always been a matter of great concern. The idea of its having fallen into the hands of a madman like Feikermun hardly bore contemplating.

I said, 'Are you suggesting there is a connection between Feikermun's possible acquisition of the power and the appearance of this mysterious double of mine?'

Old Hisdra fixed me with a clear gaze. 'We do not know, Dinbig. Certainly your situation must be judged worthy of investigation. Would you not agree?'

'Quite so. I am eager to get to the bottom of it.'

Hisdra nodded. She inclined her body forwards a little, and with two hands shakily lifted a blue faience bowl from a small table placed beside her chair.

'Drink, Dinbig,' she said, and brought the bowl to her lips. 'It will restore depleted energies.'

Without great enthusiasm I took up a similar bowl which had been placed beside me. Steam rose from a greenish-brown liquid within. A pungent, earthy aroma reached my nostrils. It was a herbal concoction and I knew its taste to be foul, but I

* These events are detailed in *The Firstworld Chronicles I: Dinbig of Khimmur.*

could not refuse her. I raised the bowl to my mouth and sipped. The brew scoured my palate and seemed to coat the inside of my gullet with fur as it slid down. I felt not the least bit invigorated, nor encouraged by the fact that most of the tea still remained to be drunk.

'For some time we have wondered about placing an agent in Dehut,' old Hisdra said, setting down her bowl, 'to try to ascertain the degree of Feikermun's development – if he has any – and at the same time to keep check on his rivals, lest they entertain similar ambitions.'

I nodded slowly. 'It is perhaps wise, given the circumstances you have described. But immensely difficult. An agent would need to gain Feikermun's trust, but Feikermun trusts no one and is as likely to execute a friend as an enemy. I would envy no one that task.'

'Certainly it would require a person with unusual talents.'

'What of this "Sermilio", Sacred Mother?' I asked. 'Does the name mean anything to you?'

Hisdra picked up the paper which I had given her upon my arrival, and studied it for the second time. She shook her head. 'Unknown to us.'

'And his symbol?'

'Again, unknown, though I shall check the archives, for it may be recorded there. Perhaps you will learn more today. But, as before, one is drawn to wonder whether it is purely coincidence that this missive should arrive, with all its apparent urgency, at the same time that you receive such unusual news from abroad.'

I nodded again, unhappy at the notion of a possible link, and tried to hide my disappointment that nothing more had been revealed. I sensed that Hisdra was studying me intently, and grew a trifle uncomfortable under her gaze.

I broached the question that had been worrying me since Inbuel's visit. 'Sacred Mother, do you or others known to you possess the means to project your physical selves, or a convincing image of your physical self, from one place to another?'

She paused before her reply. 'There are secrets known to the highest *Zan-Chassin* adepts which I cannot reveal to you until the proper time – you know that, Dinbig. But if your question

29

is "Have we created this other you?", the answer is most manifestly "We have not".'

'But might others have done it?'

'We are not so well versed in all magical forms as to be able to know precisely what can and cannot be achieved by others, though we wish it were otherwise. However, we do not know of any existing magical form that can accomplish such a feat – outside of Enchantery. But plainly it would be foolish for us to ignore what has happened.' Her scrutiny of me was undiminished. 'Dinbig, it is apposite, is it not, that this strange matter of your double and a connection with Feikermun of Selph, however tenuous, should arise just at this time?'

'In what way, Sacred Mother?'

'For the reasons I have just outlined.'

There was an inflection in her voice, a subtle but definite shift of tone that I could not miss. I stiffened slightly, abruptly aware that I was being addressed by a superior. A hollow feeling was beginning to form in my gut.

'As I said,' Hisdra continued, 'we have for some time been considering the possibility of placing an agent close to Feikermun.'

The hollow feeling gaped abruptly to become a chasm which had opened beneath me and into which I found myself falling – a sensation that was becoming horribly familiar. I heard myself replying, 'Sacred Mother, you are not saying—?'

'You are under no duress, Dinbig' – in a voice that made it plain that in truth I had little choice. 'It is a thought, that is all. Were you to elect to further investigate this matter personally, you would almost certainly want to travel to Dehut, would you not? I do not see how you could do it otherwise. That being so, you might indeed wish to consider our interests and that of Khimmur in regard to Feikermun. We would place every possible assistance at your disposal, of course.'

Which would be next to nothing, I thought miserably. The power of the *Zan-Chassin* lies mainly in the ability to interact with the Realms beyond the corporeal and with the entities that inhabit them; effective intervention on the physical plane is limited – unless there are indeed great secrets that I have no inkling of. In this case it would be worse than limited: Hisdra had just admitted that Feikermun possessed the means to detect and even repel magic. I would be alone in Dehut, then, surrounded by murderers, thieves and lunatics. I would be far from home, without friends or allies when I most needed them. I felt suddenly horribly depressed. I didn't want to go.

But I was caught. I knew it. I should have seen it coming. I knew old Hisdra's wiles, and her power. I respected her utterly, but was fully aware of what she was capable. She had been constructing her web quite openly before me, had even elicited my assistance. And still I had flown straight into it, a hapless insect, a winged ingénu.

I cursed silently, and fumed at myself. I could hardly decline the commission, no matter the politic manner in which it had been couched. Even so, I thought desperately for a way out.

'I do have many commitments at the moment, Sacred Mother.'

'I understand. As I said, you are under no duress. Drink more tea, Dinbig.'

We repeated the little ritual. Having replaced her bowl Hisdra linked her gnarled fingers in her lap and allowed a weighted silence to pass. Presently she said, 'Dinbig, your advancement as a First Realm Initiate has been pleasing.'

'It pleases me that you should find it so, Sacred Mother.'

'We do see great potential in you.'

'I am honoured.'

'We would all like to see you rise to join the Hierarchy, and eventually the Council of Elders. We perceive tremendous ability in you, partly latent as yet, but with the proper training...'

'I strive always to be a shining example by which the Zan-Chassin may be glad to be judged.'

'The king himself takes a great interest in your progress.'

'Then I am doubly honoured.'

'You are keen to advance, aren't you?'

'Most decidedly, Sacred Mother.'

'That is good.'

The silence resumed. Everything had now been said. The Chariness had brought the wind around, had caused it to blow at her beck. My plans for advancement were at stake, my

31

progress both as a *Zan-Chassin* initiate and as a rising political star and advisor to the throne.

'I will go, gladly, Sacred Mother.'

'Excellent.'

I knew that I had already chosen to investigate the matter of my double anyway – I could do little else. And I acknowledged that a journey to Dehut would almost certainly be required. I believe that the Chariness knew this too. But to spy upon Feikermun was something of a wholly different order. This was certain peril, and my stomach griped at the concept. As I have already said, I am not one to endanger myself unnecessarily: I have a love of life and of adventure, and if ahead of me the two seem to clash uncomfortably I will endeavour to seek out a more amenable road.

Now all alternative roads had been blocked. I felt deeply uneasy with myself, filled with foreboding. I was unable to meet Hisdra's gaze.

Swallowing drily I said, 'I must make certain preparations before I depart. And I would like to interview Lord Mintral.'

'Of course. I shall see to it that he is informed, and will therefore expect you at Castle Beliss. When will you go to him?'

'Tomorrow.'

'Return here the following morning. We will have made our own preparations and conducted all possible research on your behalf. Everything that is known about Feikermun, and anything else deemed pertinent to your task, will be made available to you.'

'Thank you, Sacred Mother.'

'It is an intriguing thing, Dinbig, to be riding into another land, effectively in search of yourself. But, if your reports are accurate, it does raise certain problems. For instance, if your double has already suffered execution at Feikermun's hands it will excite controversy to have you reappear suddenly in his midst. You will be seen as a ghost, or a demon. Feikermun, being what he is, will probably have you killed again immediately, which would be an unfortunate and premature curtailment of your mission. At the same time, your imitator – if he still lives – is unlikely to operate freely if aware that you are close by.'

32

I nodded. 'I shall adopt a disguise.'

'We will discuss this in greater detail upon your return from Castle Beliss. Why do you smile in such a grim way?'

'I was simply contemplating the paradox, Sacred Mother. I am to ride into another land in search of myself, but to do it I must pretend to be someone else.'

'Ah, yes, that is fascinating indeed.'

Her face showed no emotion. I said, 'I would request as a further precaution that a code be established, now, before I depart the catacombs. Thus when we next meet you will be in no doubt that it is I with whom you speak.'

'Dinbig, an imitator may fool the flesh, but the soul-personality, externalized, has its own unique resonance. You need only exit your physical form so that we may identify you.'

'Even so, I would feel further reassured.'

'Do you have a suggestion?'

'When I return I shall greet you, or whomsoever of the Hierarchy or Elders I encounter, with the words: "The mirror has been broken. The image was my own." If I fail to use these words, be wary that I may not be what I seem.'

She nodded. 'It is apt. All relevant persons will be informed.'

I felt suddenly a profound and almost paralysing fear. I was struck by the full force of what I was about to undertake. It seemed that something had been taken from me. The realization that, to others, I might no longer be deemed trustworthy, that no one could accept me for what I was, was shocking. I felt that I had lost control of my own existence. I was being manipulated from all angles. How might *I* be sure of myself, when no one else could? What was I? How could I know?

'Is there something the matter, Dinbig?'

I shook my head. It was pointless to attempt to express the inexpressible. Our audience was over. I stood, feeling that I was still falling into the dark chasm that had opened under me. I bowed, and withdrew.

Most of the remainder of the day was spent attending to mundane matters, informing employees and associates of my impending absence, making the necessary arrangements for travel. In regard to my journey I was presented with a problem.

It was unsafe to travel long distances without a strong body-guard, particularly outside my own country. Ordinarily, travelling as a Master Merchant with two, three or more wagons, I would take a guard of from three to a dozen men. But now I was not to be Ronbas Dinbig of Khimmur. To travel with men known to be Dinbig's employees might attract the wrong kind of attention, might encourage persons to look a little more closely at me than they would normally have done, and perhaps see through my deception.

It was a vexing point, for I was reluctant to travel alone. Nor was I keen to employ strangers, effectively placing myself in the car of men whom I might not be able to trust. I considered taking Bris, with perhaps one or two others. We could masquerade as a band of peddlers, pilgrims or labourers seeking work. If Bris or the others were recognized and the association with Ronbas Dinbig made, they could explain that, following Dinbig's incarceration or death, they were in the unhappy position of being obliged to seek employment abroad.

But no. Everything as yet was hearsay. I lacked firm evidence that the bogus Dinbig was dead, or even a wanted man. And, if either condition did apply, then Bris's very association with him – with me – might place my trusty servant and the others in danger from Feikermun and his thugs. On the other hand, if my double continued to operate freely, then the merest whisper that employees of mine were known to be in Anxau might be sufficient to drive him underground.

I gnawed upon the problem for much of the day. My sense of disorientation, of isolation, deepened. I cursed old Hisdra again. She was not the spider, I saw that now. Nor was I the hapless insect. I was in fact spider and fly and more; she had allowed me to trap myself in a web of my own construction. I had become all three, fly, spider and web, and she was something other, a mysterious force, a numen which hovered beyond. She saw and understood what I did not. She acted impersonally, for greater ends, ensuring that the three elements brought themselves together. And when they did they became transformed almost magically into a single entity which could do nothing except her bidding.

But it was pointless to blame Hisdra, or anyone. I was simply involved in a mystery I could not comprehend, which had begun to assume proportions far greater and more profound than I could have foreseen.

The day passed and neither Sermilio nor anyone claiming to represent him made an appearance.

That night I had a strange dream. I found myself in an unfamiliar place, yet one in which I felt, inexplicably, I had been before. It was a place imbued with a feeling of the unnatural, of extraordinary magic, of a reality which manifested in ways ungrasped by the minds of mortals.

All was silent there; nothing moved. I stood upon a flat area of baked yellowish mud, and a road stretched away before me. A little way off, beside the road, was a building. It appeared to be a temple of some kind, its interior open to the skies. Its frontage was characterized by seven tall, ornately carved pillars set at the head of wide stone steps.

I turned my face upwards to gaze upon a sky that was startlingly black. Not the black of night but blackness of another quality. It made me feel that I had never known black before.

But there was illumination, though I could identify no source. Everything stood out with exaggerated, hallucinatory clarity. In the stillness and the silence I feared it might all vanish before my eyes. That fear, a sense of the loss I would suffer, struck me more deeply than I could explain.

I looked at the temple again. A man had been placed upon the steps; I was certain he had not been there earlier. He wore grey – a tunic, close-fitting hose, soft ankle-boots and a hood – and his posture was extraordinary. He rested motionless upon one foot, the other raised and supported lightly against the upright knee, the leg crooked. His arms were lifted above and before him, the fingertips touching as if in supplication, or perhaps celebration. His head was cocked to one side and slightly upturned. I could make out little of his face, but his gaze seemed to be upon something distant, overhead, perhaps within his own mind, and his shadow was long and slender, draped darkly across the steps at his back.

I stepped down on to the road, thinking to approach the man. (Only now did I realize that I had been positioned upon

35

a low stone platform.) Somewhere a baby cried, breaking the strange silence, the sound seeming to breathe life into the eerie tableau. Small gusts of wind whipped up dust on the road. I heard the soft patter of tiny particles of grit blown against the stone. The baby cried: I heard a voice, so sweet, as the mother sang. From high above there came the sound of bells.

The man on the steps moved, slowly lowering his upraised leg and arms and rotating his head and body to face me. I turned away. I was weeping – I did not know why. The road stretched before me and I stepped out, one foot then the other, so heavy, so heavy. I barely moved. I looked back: the man had gone. All was silence again but for the wind. I was alone.

Ahead of me, beside the road, there stood a strange figure silhouetted against an ocean gilded with the fabulous hues of sunset overhead. The figure's back was to me. I approached, infinitely slowly, hampered by the heaviness of unfamiliar flesh. The figure was clearly visible, yet it seemed a lifetime, an eternity, before I reached his side.

He was a young man, garbed in a loose white kirtle and blouson with a fine golden cincture binding his waist, from which hung a short sword with a bright blade so slim as to be hardly more than a stiletto. From his back there sprouted a pair of magnificent wings, huge and gleaming – even folded – their plumage a lustrous black banded with deep red. I moved around him so that I might see his features. He was gazing upon the sunset with a rapt expression, and he turned slowly to face me. He looked at me for a long time, then smiled. 'You have come.'

'Why?' I asked. 'What have I come for? What does this all mean?'

'You do not know?'

I shook my head. 'It's almost . . . if I could just . . .' I fell silent, for there were no words.

He turned slightly, pointing down the road. The breeze whispered through the feathers of his gorgeous wings. 'Go to the well,' he said.

There were other buildings before me now – a cluster of small houses, another temple-like structure – all supported by the yellowish dust suspended within the embracing black. The winged youth spoke in my ear. 'From the well all things come. Out of the well comes the truth.'

He stepped back and spread his wings wide and rose from the ground. 'We need you,' he said, and rose higher and higher to become an oddly familiar form against the sky, then a dot, then nothing.

I gazed upon the sunset, filled with such a feeling of love and intensity as I had never known before. If only . . . if I could just break through . . . understand what this all meant. I tore my eyes away, my face wet with tears.

I was among the buildings. A narrow grassy path led off down a gentle incline, and at its base was a strange well. I approached it slowly, with trepidation, but no longer hampered by the heaviness of before.

I arrived at the well's rim, which was surmounted by a low circular stone wall. A line of dark trees stood nearby, bending and shaking in the breeze. I laid my hands on the warm stone of the well's wall and inclined by body forward to peer into the hollow depths.

Utter dark. Then I heard a fluttering sound far below, a faint echo, the rustle of feathery wings, a splash of water. My heart pounded in my chest. I was afraid. Something was in there that I did not want to have to face. I heard screams, then saw – or thought I saw – a staggering figure, covered in blood. Others came behind, likewise bloodied, clutching their heads, moaning and wailing in distress.

Then the vision ended. The baby cried again. I cried out, something wordless, an expression of what I could not express. The bells rang, resonant and profound. And the mother sang, and her voice was the sweetest sound I had ever heard. My tears streamed from my face and fell glistening into the warm blackness of the well.

Behind me I heard the beat of powerful wings. A rush of air stirred my hair and clothing as the winged youth alighted beside me. His beautiful face was contorted with anguish.

'Save us,' he cried, imploring, and fell back as though struck by something unseen.

I stared at his body, the wings draped wide upon the ground. 'What has happened?'

37

I awoke then, still weeping. My pillow was wet with my tears, and for a long time, as the grey light of dawn seeped slowly through the shutters of my room, I was too overcome to move.

Not for some while would I understand anything of the true significance of that dream.

4

MY VISIT TO Castle Beliss bore no great fruit, though something which would later prove to be of relevance did come to light.

I rode there with Bris and another good fellow, Cloverron. The day was bright, if chill, and our journey uneventful. We arrived a little before midday.

Lord Mintral received me cordially in his private apartments. 'The hospitality of my house is yours. Please avail yourself fully of anything you require. How long will you rest here? Shall I have rooms prepared?'

'You are kind, my lord, but that will not be necessary. I am returning to Hon-Hiaita this afternoon.'

'Then you will take luncheon with us?'

'That would be most agreeable.'

Mintral was in his early thirties, of about average height and with a build tending to slight underweight. His pale brown hair, parted at the centre, fell to his collar and was bound by a slender circlet of gold. His face was rather long and oval in form, with a prominent nose and eyes of deep blue. Drooping eyebrows, pendent moustaches and darkly sagging crescents beneath the eyes gave him a somewhat mournful look. He had elected to follow scholarly pursuits rather than a purely military career, and had acquired an impressive collection of rare books. By all accounts he passed much of his time locked in his library at Castle Beliss, engaged in silent discourse with philosophers, artists, poets, historians and others, the topics roaming over present and past, far and wide. I wondered that Mintral had never entered the *Zan-Chassin*; he seemed to me an ideal candidate. Perhaps he had, and had for some reason been found unsuitable – I did not enquire. His love of academic knowledge notwithstanding, Mintral commanded loyal and disciplined troops. He pledged his unrivalled allegiance to the Khimmurian Throne and had in the past proved himself a more than capable commander.

He was elegantly and a touch flamboyantly attired in a long, richly textured robe of dark blue velvet with flared and scalloped sleeves hemmed in gold satin. It had not been purchased from me, I noted. His fingers were adorned with a number of gold and silver rings studded with precious stones, and soft boots of blue calf's leather covered his feet.

Though his manner was welcoming he seemed just a little wary – a not uncommon response from one visited unexpectedly by an initiate of the *Zan-Chassin*. He showed me to a chair set before a blazing log fire which warded off the spring chill penetrating the ancient stones of Castle Beliss. As he seated himself opposite me I said, 'You show no great surprise, Lord Mintral, at receiving into your presence one whom you believed to be gone from this world.'

Mintral produced a wry smile. 'Ha! Well, I was informed yesterday of your coming. The message came from the highest level of the Hierarchy, and stated that you wished to interview me. I took it as given that I was not to be interviewed by a corpse. Might I add, Dinbig, how pleased I am to discover you alive and well and apparently – *ahem!* – in one piece. But how in Moban's name did you escape?'

'I didn't.'

He appeared nonplussed. 'Then, what—?'

'I was never there,' I said testily. These endless references to my having been in Anxau, deriving from so many sources, were rapidly becoming tiresome.

Mintral eyed me narrowly.

'Lord Mintral,' I said, 'would you be good enough to repeat to me exactly what you heard in regard to myself and my so-called misadventures abroad?'

'Of course.'

His account of the indignities served upon me by Feikermun and his beasts accorded more or less accurately with Lady Celice's version.

'And the stated crime that I had committed?' I enquired when he had done.

'That you had unwisely bedded one of Feikermun's concubines.'

'And from whom did you hear this?'

'The news was brought to me in the first instance by my head steward. He had received it from a trader who was passing through here and had stopped to sell a few items. I immediately went down to speak to the trader and get the details from the horse's mouth, so to speak.'

'I see. And this fellow related to you the tale of my misfortunes as you have just recounted them.'

'Precisely. And I would add that his account was convincing. He claimed to have been present in Dehut when the word went out that you were wanted, and to have seen you subsequent to your arrest, bruised and bloodied, being led by those monstrous thugs of Feikermun of Selph. Plainly, I must now conclude, he was a low fellow intent upon spreading malicious gossip.'

'Yes, plainly.' Lord Mintral had obviously heard nothing of my double, and I thought it expedient to remain silent on that subject.

'I apologize most profusely, Dinbig. It shames me to learn that I have been nothing more than a propagator of scurrilous rumour. However, I would add that the same news was brought to me quite soon afterwards by others, coming out of Putc'pii. They had heard it in Riverway, and seemed equally persuaded of its veracity.'

I gave this thought for a moment. 'This trader who brought the news initially, Lord Mintral: do you recall his name?'

Lord Mintral closed his eyes briefly. 'Aah, no. It escapes me. Harand is sure to know it, though.'

He stood and pulled upon a blue tasselled cord suspended beside the hearth. Presently there was a knock at the door and a tall, somewhat aged fellow with long dark grey hair entered.

'This is Harand, my chief steward,' declared Mintral, and turned to the man. 'Harand, what was the name of that sly merchant who passed through here some days ago, bringing the tragic and bogus news of Master Dinbig's death?'

'Wirm, sir,' replied Harand without hesitation. 'Wirm of Guling Mire.'

'Are you quite sure of that?' I asked.

Harand levelled a haughty glance at me. 'Quite, sir.'

'Does the name have some relevance to you?' enquired Lord Mintral.

'No, not especially, though I have heard it before.'

In fact Master Wirm of Guling Mire was known to me. He was a specialist merchant – the speciality being twiner-meat, which he farmed – though like any trader of reasonable acumen he was willing to deal in diverse goods providing they brought him a profit. He was a man of questionable integrity with, from what I had heard, a background that spoke of achievement by sometimes underhand means. Most significantly in the fog of my present situation, Wirm of Guling Mire was the man who had sold me the chunk of green-tinged amber that currently adorned the workdesk in my study in Hon-Hiaita.

Mintral dismissed his head steward. I gathered my thoughts and said to him, 'Having gained this news about me, you brought it straightway to Hon-Hiaita. Is that so?'

'I happened to have urgent business with one of my tenant-farmers the following day at Little Nestor. As the village is hardly two leagues from the capital I took the opportunity to go there and report the news. This was, mmh, just four days ago, I believe. You were absent, which though not unusual seemed ominous under the circumstances. My time was limited, so I left a sealed letter at the palace.'

'Did you speak of it with anyone else?'

'Mmh . . . I had occasion to pay a brief call upon Lady Celice. She had just returned to Cheuvra from a sojourn in Selaor. I mentioned it to her. She seemed rather upset.'

'I heard that you had called' – not for the first time, I wondered about the nature of Mintral's business with the Orl's beautiful young wife – 'yet I was not told about your letter.'

'You were not? Well, one assumes that the palace was better-informed than I in regard to your immediate state of health, and thus took scant heed of my words.'

It was a reasonable enough explanation. I had learned a little, but not sufficient to shed any positive light on the mystery. I dined, then, with Lord Mintral and his family, and afterwards returned to Hon-Hiaita.

Dusk was closing in by the time we arrived; the hills deeply blue, the evening sky a tarnished silver-grey lit with pale colour in the low west. As we rode up Water Street towards the Sharmanian Gate, the sea had merged with the sky to become a void at the city's back; the River Huss beside the meadows glowed with a dim phosphorescence.

The night guard was taking up its post as we rode through the gate and entered the town. I dismissed Cloverron but had Bris accompany me to my home. During the day I had given additional thought to the nature of the disguise I would adopt and the manner of my journey to Dehut. I had decided upon a compromise. Bris, and Bris alone, would accompany me as far as Riverway in Putc'pii. But he would not know that it was I who rode at his side. By means of this simple subterfuge I could thoroughly test the effectiveness of my disguise.

At Riverway I would leave Bris, who would make his own way home. I would hire an escort of perhaps two or three men to take me the remainder of my journey to Dehut. These need not be total strangers. At Riverway's main inn, The Goat and Salmon Pool, there would likely be men willing for a fair salary to throw in their lot with a traveller. I had passed through there enough times to know faces and reputations, at least to some degree. All things considered, this seemed the most acceptable option.

'Some time within the next couple of days you will be sent for,' I told Bris. 'A messenger will come to you asking you to meet a man who requires a strong and reliable fellow to accompany him into Putc'pii. He is a person well known to me – indeed, he is very dear to me. He asked for my recommendation in regard to a trustworthy companion to ride as his escort. I had no hesitation in giving him your name. He will treat you well and pay you generously. Does the commission interest you? It will take only a few days.'

'It does, Master Dinbig. But what of my work here?'

'As I said, this man is a close friend of mine. I am happy to give you leave to accompany him.'

'You are kind, sir. What is his name?'

43

'He will tell you that when he sends for you, if he so chooses. Do not be offended if he speaks little to you. He is a taciturn fellow, and suffers moreover from a painful scourge of the throat.'

This last I added as a precaution. My physical features I might well alter so that Bris would not know me, but it would not be as easy to disguise my voice. Silence would be a great virtue.

'When he dismisses you, return forthwith to Hon-Hiaita. I wish you to take charge, with Minyon, of matters here, as I shall be taken up with other business pursuits for some time.'

'Do you not need me with you?'

'It is more important that I have men I can trust to oversee the day-to-day running of my affairs here until my return.'

I felt again that clutch of fear in my innards as I said this: the thought that I might not return – *or that the person who did return would not be me.*

Bris left, and I climbed the stairs to my study. I sat for some time brooding as the darkness closed in and stole the features of my room. A servant entered to rekindle the fire and light neglected candles. I found myself gazing again at the lump of rare green amber that I had acquired from the travelling merchant, Wirm of Guling Mire. I picked it up and held it before me, rotating it back and forth in my hand. It was a queer shape, as such pieces generally are. It was irregular, angular, assymetrical. No attempt had been made to smooth its edges or faces, as is often done. I stared at the tiny, still creatures trapped inside.

I am like one of them. The thought came dismally. *Trapped in circumstances over which I have no control.*

I could move, yes; I could make decisions and act upon them. But it felt more and more that I was no longer the master of my actions. Whatever I did it seemed I was obliged to do, without real choice of free will. I felt restricted; I felt trapped; uncomfortingly I felt myself to be a victim, my movements and choices determined by others, hardly more free than these insects trapped in amber.

I did not like the feeling.

'Feikermun is dangerously unstable. His behaviour is erratic; he suffers grim delusions. He feels himself persecuted and trusts no one. He rules with an iron hand and murders indiscriminately and unquestioningly on the merest suspicion of a plot against him.'

'A charming companion, then,' I said. 'What else can you add to his list of delights?'

It was Eldana who was addressing me. She was a fragile young woman, calm and perceptive, with a tranquil, sensitive grey gaze and a smooth porcelain complexion. Already, at the age of twenty-one, she had attained the office of High Sashbearer and was a member of both the *Zan-Chassin* Hierarchy and the Council of Elders. She was being carefully groomed for advancement, and would almost certainly be Chariness one day.

Her solemn expression did not change. 'This is virtually all we know of him with any degree of certainty.'

'It tells me little that I was not already aware of, or at least suspected.'

'We know. But the point is that an acquisition of power combined with that instability is a terrifying prospect.'

Terrifying for whom? I thought indignantly. *You are safe. It is I whom you are casting to demented ogres.*

Disconcertingly, Eldana replied as though she had read my thoughts. It was a trait I had perceived in her on previous occasions, and it left me feeling a touch uneasy. 'Such power would represent a threat on an international scale. There is no doubt that Feikermun would forcefully extend his influence, were he able.'

I knew it, and she knew that I knew it. I had already discussed the issue with old Hisdra; but I was being reminded now of my role in the greater game of politics and foreign relations, the balance of power between nations and influential groups.

We were assembled in a convocation chamber deep within the *Zan-Chassin* catacombs. Hisdra was there, as was her daughter, Crananba, who seemed almost as old as she. Also present were Lord Yzwad of the *dhoma* of Tiancz, who was of the Hierarchy, and Mostin, the king's High Chamberlain. The stated purpose of the convocation was to avail me of all that was known about Feikermun and his two rivals in Dehut. Precious little had so far been revealed. Even so, I liked what I was hearing less and less.

'He is addicted to *gidsha* root, which as you know promotes visions of strange intensity,' Eldana continued. 'This no doubt exacerbates his madness and his tenuous grasp on reality. The visions it invokes may help promote his mastery of power.'

This *was* news. *Gidsha* is the sacred drug of the natives of Tanakipi, a wide tract of deep forest which lies over the White River to Khimmur's northeast. They are an inoffensive lot once you understand their strange ways. They spend their entire lives in the dream-state the drug induces. They alone are believed to know the secret of its cultivation – for, improperly prepared, the *gidsha* root is poisonous.

Before I could make further enquiry, Mostin spoke. 'He also greatly enjoys drinking the blood of his victims, chosen often at random on the spur of the moment. He believes sacrificial blood, human blood, to be the source of great power, the source of life. He frequently opens the veins of a member of his company simply to slake his thirst and renew his vitality.'

I looked at him sharply. There was a thin, sardonic smile upon his pale lips, and his gaze was glassy and cold. He was a silky-voiced, stoat-eyed little man, a few years older than I. He occupied a position of great power and privilege, being perhaps the closest confidant of the king, and had recently attained Second Realm and showed himself adept in certain aspects of *Zan-Chassin* magic. He bore me no great affection, being ruthlessly ambitious and perceiving in me a rival, I believe. Mostin was not a man to whom I would willingly show my back on a dark night in a lonely place; and I knew that he, for one, would shed no tears were I to fail to return from Anxau.

I chose not to respond, and addressed Eldana once more. 'From where does Feikermun acquire the root?'

'That we have been unable to determine.'

'One of your tasks, Dinbig, will be to attempt to discover from where or whom Feikermun acquires the drug,' said Hisdra. 'If it comes out of Tanakipi, the people should be informed. It is their fetish, their god, revered by them, the key which provides them access to lands inaccessible to others. They would not normally permit it to fall into the hands of an outsider. If it derives from a source other than Tanakipi, we wish to be apprised. It could do much to enhance relations were we able pass such information on to them.'

Possibly, I thought. In my experience the Tanakipi have no interest in relations outside their own clans. They are a stupefied race, barely aware of the existence of others. You could walk among them, doing as you wished, and you would be ignored. Pillage their homes, ravish their women, disembowel their children – the chances were they would be oblivious and would take no action against you. To acknowledge your existence they would have had to have previously dreamed you. Were that not the case they would be unaffected by your presence, no matter the atrocities. To the Tanakipi natives the dreams, the visions and the sacred root are the only true reality; the world as we experience it is a non-place, illusory and insubstantial. Life has no reality; it is insignificant, nothing but a dream.

In many ways, I suppose, theirs is an enviable state.

'The *gidsha* root may also be your way into Feikermun's confidence,' Hisdra continued.

'How so?'

'We have given much thought to the manner in which you should approach Feikermun. The perfect way is to offer him what he desires most.'

'You have *gidsha*?' I had not expected this. The treated root is jealously guarded by the Tanakipi, the one thing they value. It is not easily acquired.

'A small amount. A sample, specially alchemized by ourselves. You will offer it to Feikermun. We believe it will please him more than the root extract he presently ingests. He will be eager for more.'

'And there I am undone, unless you are able to furnish me with a regular supply.'

'You will carry sufficient for several doses. Have Feikermun understand that you can acquire more, but that it will take time. In effect you will be bartering for your own sure survival. Keep the root ever like a carrot dangling before him. As long as he believes in you, I think he will not do you harm. But you will be reliant upon your own judgement to determine when he begins to suspect that the carrot does not exist.'

47

'At which point?'

'Get out. Fast.'

I was not reassured. The whole thing seemed calculated to place me at ever greater risk. My spirits, already sunken, plummeted to subterranean depths. 'And in that time I shall be expected to have determined the degree of mastery of Feikermun's power, and the means by which he has acquired it?'

'That is your primary task. There is one other thing.' Hisdra spoke evenly, her old eyes levelled unblinkingly upon me. 'If Feikermun has acquired the power it will make him an extraordinarily dangerous foe. It would be expedient, therefore, if he could be eliminated.'

My blood ran suddenly cold. 'You want me to assassinate Feikermun?'

'Assess the situation, Dinbig, and keep us apprised. We will let you know what is required.'

'Keep you apprised?' I was, to say the least, bewildered. Was I being offered a ray of hope? Was I not, after all, to be entirely alone in Dehut? 'How?'

'You may, if you judge it safe, establish contact with us via your Custodian.'

'But you have already told me that Feikermun is sensitive to the use of magic.'

'That is so. You must select your moments with extreme care. If you believe yourself at risk, do nothing that might reveal your talents. But it takes mere moments to summon your Custodian and have him relay a message to us, and a summoning is not like the casting of a rapture. It leaves no subtle residue.'

I considered this. The Custodian is the Realm Entity or allied spirit bound by all successful First Realm initiates. Its role is to take charge of the initiate's corporeal body when he or she chooses to leave the physical world and journey in the Realms beyond. In addition the Custodian can be instructed to communicate with other Realm Entities, or with the spirit-bodies or bound-servants of other *Zan-Chassin*.

'We shall remain vigilant for your Custodian's coming at all times,' Hisdra continued.

Again, I felt the numbing fear. I was to inform upon Feiker-

48

mun's state, and if the Hierarchy did not like what they learned I would be ordered to bring his life to an end.

'But what of the status quo?' I said, hopefully. 'Should Feikermun be removed, Gorl – or Malibeth – and the Golden Lamb will gain.'

'If Feikermun has attained the power he will crush them effortlessly. That is what he craves. The fact that he has not done so is almost certain proof that he cannot, yet. That is why we must act now. It will not end there, of course. He will establish himself as absolute ruler of all Anxau, and then his gaze will focus beyond. This must not happen.'

I brooded wretchedly, then asked, 'What of the other two? What do we know of them?'

'Gorl is dead, of that we are quite certain,' replied Eldana. 'Malibeth, his lover for some years, has succeeded him. We were concerned at first that she might be in Feikermun's employ, that Gorl's death might be an act of revenge for his betrayal of his brother. But that seems not to be so. Gorl's followers support Malibeth, and she opposes Feikermun with a hatred and zeal that equals, and even surpasses, Gorl's.'

'You can perhaps make use of that, Dinbig,' said Hisdra.

'Malibeth is considered to be a beautiful woman, and as ruthless and dangerous as Feikermun himself,' Eldana said. 'Take care in your dealings, Dinbig, should your paths cross.'

I looked at her and she met my gaze. I tried to read her face, for I thought I had detected something more than a detached relating of facts in her voice. There was the briefest dimpling at the corners of her mouth, the faintest smile, and her eyes held, just momentarily, an expression of concern.

'And the Golden Lamb?' I asked.

Eldana lowered her eyes. 'We have learned nothing of this person. He appeared at a time when the conflict between Feikermun and Gorl was at its height, and he used it to his advantage to gain foothold in the town. This he quickly exploited, establishing himself in strength in the western quarter and refusing to be dislodged.'

'But who is he? Where has he come from?'

'I am sorry. We have no physical description, though we suspect he is not an Anxau native. His troops are seasoned,

49

disciplined fighters, with a cohesive organization suggesting trained professional soldiers.'

'Foreign soldiers?'

'Or Anxau mercenaries, schooled in foreign armies.'

'Once more, Dinbig,' Hisdra interposed, 'we would welcome reliable information. We need to know the precise situation in Dehut, and whether intervention is required.'

'I do not anticipate that my time in Dehut will be long, Sacred Mother,' I replied. The words held a hollow ring, imbued with a fatalistic note I had not intended.

She nodded her old head. 'But you will do what you can.'

I said, 'Sacred Mother, you were going to research the archives in the hope of shedding some light on the symbol I showed you – the one on the back of the note from Sermilio.'

'Yes. That symbol is associated with an ancient mythical race called the Avari.'

'The Avari?' I racked my brains. The name was distantly familiar.

'The Tutelary Spirits,' said Hisdra. 'The Companions of the Soul.'

Now it came to me, out of the blur of a long-forgotten past. I knew the Avari as creatures of folklore, things of childhood tales, ghostly spirits said to walk unseen at the shoulder of every individual throughout life. They came at birth, one for each newborn child, and their role was to be protectors and guides, communicating with us by subtle, subliminal means, striving to ensure that we each passed through life without undue hazard or suffering, without succumbing to the grosser temptations of the physical world. The Avari, for those who believed, were the guardians of the innermost being, protective spirits of the soul. At the end of your life, it was said, if your Avari had remained with you throughout – that is, if you had not wandered so far from the path of goodness that your protector had lost sight of you – then your Avari would embrace your soul as it slipped free of the body, and escort it safely to a higher realm beyond.

I did not recall the origins of this belief: it derived from a time long past. Elements of the Avari story could still be found in some form within numerous religious and spiritual doctrines. *Zan-Chassin* discoveries of the Realms beyond the physical had broadened our perception of existence. We had found entities there as diverse, fickle and unpredictable in their own strange ways as we were in ours. But we had not made contact with the Avari, and nor did we expect to. They were considered powerful mythical figures, elemental figments of an ancient imagination.

I put this to the Chariness, wondering again whether there were things that I, as a lowly First Realm Initiate, had never been told. She hesitated momentarily before giving her reply. 'There is no evidence for the existence of the Avari outside the minds of the fanciful and those inclined to a specific form of worship.'

'Then Sermilio's note . . .'

'The symbol upon the paper is the insignia of a secretive group known as the Arch of the Wing. They were believers, fanatics even, who attracted converts through claims of a transcendent knowledge and exclusive understanding of the ways of the Avari. The Arch of the Wing has not been heard of for many hundreds of years.'

Lord Yzwad spoke for the first time. 'The Old Religion which was the source of the Avari myth describes another phantasmal race, the Scrin. The two were said to be mortal enemies, for they were complete opposites. The Scrin were evil, scuttling things whose task was to drag men's souls into darkness and depravity from which they might never know redemption.'

Old Hisdra nodded. 'Perpetual war raged between the two races, so it was said, in a dimension beyond our own. Life and the continuance of existence were believed to be held in the balance by their struggle, and the need to prevent the Scrin from corrupting the souls of men.' She paused and shrugged her frail shoulders almost dismissively. 'These are things of childhood tales, drawn from a time beyond telling. They are stories passed to us by our parents and grandparents, who had them from their parents and grandparents, who had them from theirs . . . So it goes on.'

She said more, but I did not hear, for I was aware of the stir of individual memories long buried beneath the sediment of the river of my greater memory. I recalled the only description I had ever been given of an Avari. I could not remember who had

51

told me this – my mother, I assumed, or my father; perhaps my childhood nurse. Certainly it was an image that harked back to my earliest infancy. But it filled my inward vision now, blotting out all other perceptions, for it was a powerful image, suddenly strangely familiar.

It was a youthful figure I envisioned, unclouded by time. A person of rare and exquisite beauty, male or female – an androgyne, I should say, embodying qualities of both genders. Its hair was golden, its eyes crystal-clear, almost devoid of colour. The figure wore a loose white kirtle, and from its back sprouted a pair of fabulous coloured wings.

I remembered my dream of the previous night – the winged youth gazing intensely upon a sunset, the youth who had directed me to the strange well, who had made a plea for my help and then fallen back dead upon the ground.

And it came to me that, as the Avari had risen into the air, its diminishing figure with its wings partially outstretched against the vivid sky had seemed vaguely familiar. I saw now what it resembled. The symbol on Sermilio's note: a birdman.

'The Avari were winged humans, were they not?'

'That is how they have generally been depicted. You seem troubled by this, Dinbig.'

'Not troubled, but curious. As you yourself said, Sacred Mother, one cannot help but wonder whether the arrival of this note at this time is purely coincidental.'

'Have you learned something you have not told us?'

I shook my head, deep in thought. 'It occurs to me that I might benefit from speaking with the spirits of the ancestors, for perhaps they can tell me something more of the Avari.'

Ancestral spirits may be summoned to an ethereal meeting-place, to which a *Zan-Chassin* may also journey, leaving his body in the charge of his Custodian. It can prove a useful means of gaining information or guidance, specifically in regard to the past; but it is not a certain method, for the ancestral spirits do not welcome being disturbed from their slumbers.

Hisdra lifted a bony hand. 'I have already consulted with the ancestors on your behalf, Dinbig. They told me nothing more than you now know.'

I nodded. The image remained large within my mind. Was

52

there a significance, an element of precognition in my dream, something that I had yet to fully understand? Or had Sermilio's note and the symbol simply stirred long-buried associations and brought them to the surface? I felt deeply unsettled, but could draw no conclusion.

At a signal from Hisdra the members of the Hierarchy, all bar she and Eldana, now withdrew. We three spoke for a while longer. Attention was given to my disguise and to the items I would be required to take on my journey to Anxau, such as the *gidsha* root and additional ingredients required in its preparation immediately prior to consumption. I was briefed thoroughly on the manner in which I was expected to conduct my investigations of Feikermun, but it did nothing to allay my fears. More than ever I realized that I was to be alone among enemies, at the potential mercy of fiends.

With dismal conviction a single thought persisted in my mind: I was a First Realm *Zan-Chassin* Initiate. I was useful. I was skilled, and I knew myself to be possessed of certain innate talents and wiles.

But I was also expendable.

That night I shut myself in my workroom at home and entered trance. In the way that I have been taught to do over years of training, I concentrated upon the objects in my chamber. I absorbed their forms, every detail that was available to sight, committing it all to subtle memory. Then I turned my attention to my physical self, every muscle, nerve, sinew and organ, consolidating and familiarizing. The *Zan-Chassin* call this process 'anchoring', establishing a contact with the world one is about to depart in order that one may safely find one's way back.

In fact my intention was not to journey within the Realms tonight, but rather to consult with my Custodian, Yo. With the first preparation complete, feeling myself suffused with spirit I dissolved the features of my chamber. I let go of the physical world and rose from my body.

I summoned Yo.

He was with me on the instant. 'You called, Master?'

'I have something important to tell you, Yo.'

'Do you wish me to take charge of your fleshly self, Master, whole you journey elsewhere?'

'No. Not at the moment.' I felt his disappointment. Upon binding him to my service there had been two main elements to our compact. In the first place Yo was to serve as Custodian of my flesh whenever I left the corporeal plane, for whatever reason. And in the second I was to provide him with a physical body through which he might explore the myriad unfamiliar wonders of the physical world.

For a Realm Entity it is a tremendous privilege to enter living flesh. They are easily seduced by the world and take every opportunity to acquaint themselves with the corporeal. I had elected to give Yo the body of a Wide-Faced Bear, a creature quite common to our lands. The ritual was complex, however, and required much preparation, which I had not yet had time to do. Thus, for the present, Yo remained unembodied other than for those infrequent occasions when he took custody of my own flesh. Plainly he had been charmed by the experience, despite the fact that his sole task was to keep my body perfectly motionless and ensure that it suffered no disturbance or discomfort. So I felt now a pang of guilt as he gently reminded me of my failure to provide him with flesh of his own.

'I am to embark upon an important mission,' I said, 'and have good reason to believe I may require your services. Be on hand, then, and alert for my summons at all times. My need may be urgent. Do not question anything I tell you, and be prepared to depart immediately at my word. I may be placing myself in danger by summoning you.'

'Will I be in danger too, Master?'

'Not directly. But bear in mind that my survival may depend upon the interaction between us, and that should my life be brought to a premature end I would be unable to fulfil my promise to you to provide you with a physical form.'

'That would be regrettable. I think I like your world.'

'I, too, am quite attached to it. I would not wish to take permanent leave of it just yet. Now, Yo, listen please. Your primary role will be as message-bearer between myself and those with whom I work. It is vital that all messages by relayed promptly and accurately.'

'I understand, Master.'

'Good. I shall speak with you again in due course.'

'Can I ask a question, Master?'

'You may.'

'Is this you that I see seated here? You do not appear to be yourself.'

I glanced down at the body seated below us. It was true: I was unrecognizable. The disguise Hisdra and Eldana had effected for me was far more thorough that I had expected. With the aid of profound raptures unknown to lowly initiates like myself, the very form of my face had been altered. My elegant fair-brown locks had been replaced by a shock of long black bristle. My whiskers, in which I took great pride, were gone, in their place the stubbly beginnings of a dark shadow of beard. My nose was fuller, fleshier; my chin broader. My body, too, had filled out slightly. In addition, fine clothing had been replaced by rough travelling leathers and fust. The transformation both reassured and chilled me. I did not resemble myself. And I thought again: that other person, out there somewhere – *how was it that* he *did*?

'It is I, Yo,' I replied distractedly. 'But you are right, I have changed. It is for a purpose. Now you may go, but be alert for my summons at all times.'

'I am your servant, Master.'

Yo was gone.

I returned to my flesh and remained deep in thought for some time. Hisdra, the Chariness, had denied that it was possible to create a perfect imitation of someone through magic. But, when I had first seen myself after she and Eldana had completed their work upon me, I had asked again, concerned.

She shook her head. 'What you see here as you view yourself in the mirror is a mock-up, albeit one that others could not achieve as effectively. It is a random alteration of your own features. We have made no attempt to have you resemble another: we have simply made you unrecognizable as yourself.'

Eldana added, 'We cannot create perfect representations of a specific face. We might make you resemble another person, but the disguise would be shallow. It would not fool anyone to whom that person is well known.'

'But to effect the disguise you have employed magic. Feikermun is said to be sensitive to magic.'

'The magic is employed only in the making. Once it is complete the magic is finished. There is nothing, therefore, for Feikermun or anyone else to detect.'

I had had little choice but to be satisfied with these answers.

My eyes came to rest once again on the chunk of green amber on my desk. Once again I lifted it and gazed at the tiny creatures trapped within its glassy depths.

Wirm of Guling Mire. I wondered at the coincidence of his having sold me the piece then having claimed more recently to have seen me in chains in Anxau, and to have knowledge of my execution.

Did he play any part in this strange business? Guling Mire, I knew, was a small settlement in western Putc'pii, lying close upon the Urvysh Plains in marshlands south of the Great White River. It is no great distance from the border with Anxau, and a detour there would not add much more than a day to my journey. Perhaps it might be expedient to pay Wirm a visit. There was no guarantee of finding him at Guling Mire, but I could make enquiries en route.

I stood, and upon a whim took the amber and wrapped it carefully in strong cloth, then slipped it into the pack I would carry on my journey.

5

MY FIRST STOP was Riverway, in Putc'pii. The journey there took a little more than a day. Bris met me early on a fresh spring morning outside Hon-Hiaita's Sharmanian Gate, called by a messenger I had sent to him at dawn. He arrived on his chestnut gelding, garbed in padded leather and a lamellar cuirass. A longsword in a battered scabbard slanted back from his belt; a smooth-helved battle-axe hung from his saddle; upon his pack was strapped a bow and a quiver of arrows. From experience I knew Bris to be a stout-hearted and more than capable weapons-man, and felt greatly reassured by his presence, though I did not anticipate particular danger between here and Riverway. It would be in the later stages of my journey, where Bris could not accompany me, that I would need reassurance most.

Affecting a hoarseness, my hand raised to my throat as though it pained me to speak, I introduced myself without embellishment as Linias Cormer. I faced Bris full on at a distance of little more than arm's-length, for I wanted to determine at the outset the efficacy of my disguise. His features remained easy, and though I watched him carefully I saw no indication that he suspected any duplicity.

Of course, Bris was an astute and intelligent fellow. I would never have permitted him to occupy a position of such responsibility and trust had that not been so. It may well have been, then, that he had something of an inkling that perhaps all was not quite as it appeared on the surface, but he knew better than to ask questions. Most importantly, I remained convinced that he did not suspect that the man with whom he travelled was actually myself.

We rode on our way into the bright morning. The road, Water

Street, leads south across Sharmanian Meadows, following the course of the River Huss south as far as Hoost's Corner. Here there is an intersection of ways. The southern route runs through Morshover Vale, climbing and twisting into the Red Mountains and Sommaria beyond: east it runs deep into the central provinces of Khimmur and, eventually, the great forested land of Vir and the plains of Ashakite. Our route was west on to Wetlan's Way, through the hills and woodlands of the *dhoma* of Beliss.

The woods lay in dappled sunlight, the ground brightly coloured with fresh spring flowers. The clear air chimed with birdsong, and small creatures scurried on the earth and busied themselves in the trees. One could almost imagine the world to be an untroubled place.

Two hours into our journey the breeze brought a slight taint to our nostrils. Bris raised his hand, slowing his mount. 'A rankbeast.'

We proceeded with caution, the horses nervous. The rankbeast is a lumbering monster, dangerous if aroused, but it does not by choice or habit roam close to men. It can generally be avoided without great difficulty, as its tough, armoured skin exudes a noxious substance which gives off a powerful stench, providing ample warning of its proximity.

Briefly we heard the creature crashing in the woods further up the slopes. From a highpoint on the road we saw the sway and shudder of strong saplings as it lurched through, and just once caught a glimpse of its huge, sweating back. The rankbeast's passage bore it away from the road and we passed on unmenaced.

With the sun a little way beyond its zenith we reached the Guardian Sisters, ancient twin watchtowers which, facing into Putc'pii, flank the road at Khimmur's border. A fascinating tale surrounds these twins of stone. They were built at a time lost to the memories or written records of men, but are said to house the discorporate souls of a pair of giant sisters named Egathta and Mawg. Aeons ago these two fell in love with a young human noble called Draremont who ventured into their homeland, Pansur. The land of Ravenscrag, Draremont's home, had fallen under the influence of a bane. His family, his people, the very lands upon which they dwelt were threatened with ruin and destruction unless a means could be found to quell the bane's evil power. Draremont was engaged upon a quest to save Ravenscrag, and believed that the ancient giant race of Pansur, the Thotán, could help.

Upon his arrival the giants treated him as a welcome and honoured guest in their community, but sadly were unable to offer him any assistance. He returned home, believing that Ravenscrag was lost.

The two sisters, Egathta and Mawg – who were alike in feature, thought and action – had become fascinated by this man Draremont. For many generations the Thotán had lived in isolation, far from human dwellings, and Draremont was the first human the sisters had ever laid eyes upon. They were enchanted by the tragic nature of his quest, and wanted to know more about him. His departure saddened them, and for days they moped and mourned as though stricken by some mysteriously debilitating illness.

Confiding only in one another, the sisters found themselves impelled to follow Lord Draremont in the belief that somehow they might aid him. So, foolishly, one night they stole from their huts and left the village of the Thotán, seeking Ravenscrag and Lord Draremont and intending to return only when their task was complete.

But they became lost, for they had never before been far from their home. For days, then weeks, they wandered hopelessly. Occasionally they came upon human settlements, but the people fled them in terror or, worse, attacked them with axes, spears and flaming arrows. Word spread through the land of a pair of marauding giants attacking villages and towns, and one day Egathta and Mawg came over a hilltop to find an army confronting them. Great catapaults launched massive stones and flaming barrels of oil at the two sisters; platoons of mounted knights charged them from all directions, hacking and stabbing at their thighs, bellies and buttocks; archers in their scores fired upon them from the cover of rocks and trees, until their skins bristled with arrows and the blood streamed from their massive bodies.

The sisters fled, howling in pain and distress. Everywhere they went the tale was the same: men reacted with panic and violence. Egathta and Mawg were driven further and further from their homeland. They did not know where they were or how they might return. They wandered in terrible distraction, utterly lost, hopelessly calling out in the night the name of the man they wished to save: Draremont.

But a year passed, and another, and they did not find Ravenscrag or Draremont. Nor did they find their way home. And though they came upon many races and many men, no one would help them.

On a cold, rainswept evening the huge twins arrived at the bank of the Great White River. They waded across and found themselves upon the northern edge of the lonely Putc'pii Plains. Exhausted and terrified they made their way vaguely east, avoiding anyone they saw, until they came to a low hill. Upon its gentle crest they sat down, side by side, too tired to continue. Egathta gazed west across Putc'pii's chill grasslands; Mawg gazed east into the bare wintry woodlands that would one day be Khimmur. And together they sang a song, a disconsolate chant, a forlorn dedication to the human they loved, for whom they had unwittingly sacrificed so much.

'Draremont,' they sang, and their sad voices carried upon the bitter winds. 'Draremont, Draremont, Draremont, Draremont . . .'

And there they died. Much later men found their bones and raised two towers over them in celebration of the deaths of the evil giants who had terrorized their lands. The towers still stand, but the bones have long gone, taken as talismans, souvenirs, relics, and distributed who knows where. But within the towers the souls of Egathta and Mawg remain, so it is said, ever gazing in hope of one day seeing the man they love. And the winds sometimes still carry their mournful lament, bearing it east, west, north, south, seeking ears that will never hear it.

For many years, so I understand, the twin towers remained empty for fear of the vengeful giants' souls within. But at some undetermined time a Khimmurian king elected to use them as prisons. Criminals convicted of heinous crimes were incarcerated within and left to rot. Much later magic was employed to subdue the two sisters' tormented souls, and eventually the Guardian Sisters became the watchtowers they are today.

The Beliss sentries, Lord Mintral's men, hailed us as we approached, and we halted for a short while to rest our horses and gather any news relevant to our journey and the road ahead. The woodlands had begun to thin half a league back, and from the Guardian Sisters we gazed now upon the wide, gently undulating grasslands of Putc'pii, a hundred shades of green, shadowed by fluffs of quick white cloud and rippling like a swelling sea in the breeze. Then Bris and I moved on, refreshed, and for the remainder of that day travelled in near-silence, meeting no one.

An hour past the border the road cuts northwest for Riverway. A body lay there, half-concealed in the grass.

Bris dismounted and cautiously approached.

'It's a man, dead these past two days or more. A solitary traveller, I would guess. Murdered and stripped of all possessions.'

We scanned the countryside as we rode on, seeking signs of the perpetrators of that evil deed. We would stand little chance against a brigand band; our one hope would be to try to outpace them. But it appeared the murderers were long gone, for we passed unmolested.

At dusk we were only a few leagues from the town, and the fine weather had held. I chose to make camp in a bushy hollow close to the road, for there was a serious risk of laming a horse by pushing on in bad light. We ate dried meat and bread and drank watered wine, kindling no fire for fear of attracting folk we would rather avoid.

We came into view of the town the following morning. It was a welcome sight, bathed in full sunlight, the wide river glittering at its back and a single cog plying east towards the inland sea. On the far shore we could see the old Kemahamek township, now virtually untenanted. The heavy scow manned by Stanborg the ferryman was hauling its way out from Riverway's muddy bank, and looked to be crowded with livestock.

I chose to stop at a hostelry on the edge of Riverway, and there paid Bris and bade him depart. I could not have him accompany me to The Goat and Salmon Pool for fear that his presence and association with Ronbas Dinbig would draw attention. But I assumed Bris would go there for an hour or so to refresh himself and fill his belly before starting back for Khimmur. I was prepared to wait until he had gone before entering the inn myself, and asked that he make no mention of having ridden with me.

I was wrong. Upon receiving his payment Bris bowed to me and wished me good fortune, then took his leave, pausing only to replenish his water-sack. I watched through the window as he went outside, climbed upon his mount and rode off at an easy pace back along the way we had come.

A good man. The best. I was proud and grateful that such a fellow should be in my employ. I wondered again about the wisdom of letting him go. With Bris at my side, watching my back, I would feel far more confident about riding into Dehut. But I fought down the impulse to ride after him and bring him back, knowing that I was deluding myself. The risk was simply too great. I made my way on to The Goat and Salmon Pool.

Riverway had been a bustling town at one time, commanding the sole ferry across the White River within many leagues; in the drier months the river is also fordable here on horseback. More recently the town has fallen somewhat into decline, for folk abandoned the area on the Kemahamek side of the river through fear of the Gneth which still roamed wild across the Hecranese border. Gneth did not in fact stray into Kemahamek, but the fear was always there, fuelled by memories passed down and no doubt embellished over generations – memories of the war years of the Great Deadlock, a century and a half earlier, when Gneth were instrumental in driving the Kemahamek from Hecra.

The roads in southwestern Kemahamek were used less and less, other than by military units assigned to guard the border and herders driving their stock north to the market towns. Riverway no longer bore signs of burgeoning prosperity. Numerous homes and commercial premises stood empty and derelict, and the place held a general air of neglect. But a handful of hostelries and sundry establishments still survived, deriving passable business from itinerant merchants, travellers and local farmers and herders. The Goat and Salmon Pool, always the most popular of these hostelries, was still noted for its good serviced, fine food and strong wines and ales.

Hirk Longshanks, the landlord's son, stood behind the counter as I entered the common-room. He was as tall as his name suggested, lean and hanging, his tow-coloured hair almost brushing the cobwebs from the cedar rafters. He glanced my way and nodded briefly, but his gaze was drawn to a more beguiling prospect: the serving-girl, Lanna, as she swished between the tables. Lanna, at fifteen or so, was a buxom lass with long, lustrous chestnut hair and deep green eyes. Her manner was bright and engaging, and she wore her newfound womanhood with knowing pride. I could well understand Hirk's fascination, for I felt my own blood stir at the sight of her.

I set down my pack before the counter and ordered a flagon of good dark ale and a dish of stewed goatsmeat, potatoes and corn. The inn was doing fair business. Casting my eyes around I recognized a number of faces among the clientele, and spotted one or two potential candidates for my employ. I engaged Hirk Longshanks in conversation, maintaining my façade of unfamiliarity. That is, I tried, for he was a man not greatly given to speech.

'I am Linias Cormer, of Chol. I am on my way to Dehut and hope to hire a couple of sturdy, honest men to ride with me as a deterrent to robbers and cutthroats who might regard a solitary traveller as an opportunity for illegal gain. Indeed, I have seen only yesterday convincing evidence that these roads can be perilous. Do you know any here who might be looking for this sort of work?'

Longshanks nodded slowly, easing forward his chin. The bulk of his attention was still on Lanna, who had returned to the counter to refill a wine pitcher. 'Hmm . . . possible, aye.'

'Perhaps you would be good enough to point them out to me?'

'There's Morden Halcamel, over there.'

I turned to look in the direction of his nod. Four Putc'pii were seated at a table, engrossed in a game of dice.

'Morden Halcamel. He is one of those four, is he?'

'Aye.'

Hirk Longshanks was not a deliberately difficult fellow, but

63

the art of supplying information was rather a stranger to him. 'Which one?'

'The big fellow, second from left.'

'And what of the others?'

'Well, next to him is Do Farness. Then there's young Albo. He's a good lad. And Romo Gorflock.'

'And all of these men you would deem suitable?'

'It's possible, aye.'

'And the others, over there?'

'That's Holf and Gilmut. They're herders, but one of them might be able to get away. And Stanborg's boy, Jerm.'

'These are all local fellows, are they?'

'Aye.'

Lanna had moved closer, clasping the brimming pitcher. In a conspiratorial voice she said, 'Not Jerm, you can't trust him. You know that, Hirkie. And Holf's too daft. All he knows is sheep.'

She giggled behind her hand.

'What of the two over there, in the corner?'

'They're Kemahamek,' said Lanna. 'They've been here a couple of days. I've seen them before. Don't know much about them, do you?'

Hirk shook his head. 'They've made no trouble.'

' "They've made no trouble",' repeated Lanna, mimicking his sober tone. 'That's all he cares about, isn't it, Hirkie? As long as you make no trouble you're all right as far as Hirk's concerned. That's so, isn't it, Hirkie?'

Hirk nodded sheepishly. 'S'pose.'

Lanna stood close to him and laid a hand upon his waist. 'Do I cause trouble for you? I don't, do I?'

'No, not you, Lann.'

'A good job you said that.' She squeezed his ribs, making him grunt and writhe, then moved off with a knowing laugh, tossing back her long hair.

Hirk Longshanks busied himself wiping a mug, smiling happily. I addressed him once more. 'I am also hoping to make contact with a trader who I believe passes through here from time to time. His name is Wirm, hailing from Guling Mire. Do you know the fellow?'

'Aye. He was here just recently.'

'Bound for where? Do you know?'

'I think he said home. Lanna, do you recall?'

Lanna, having delivered the wine to her customers, was making her way back. 'Home, thence Dehut. So he said. You'll probably find him at one or the other or somewhere in between.'

All roads led to Dehut, it seemed.

I took a seat at a vacant table while Lanna brought my meal. As I ate I struck up conversation with some of the men she and Hirk had named. The two Kemahamek were keen to hear what I had to say. In the end it was they whom I hired, for they professed themselves ready and willing to start out immediately for Anxau, and appeared to have more than a passing knowledge of Dehut. The others, though in several cases wanting work, were typical of the Putc'pii in being unable to commit themselves without further consideration and consultation.

Moreover, I recognized one of the Kemahamek. He had ridden guard before now for a business contact of mine, who had himself been working for my friend Viscount Inbuel m' Anakastii. The Kemahamek's name was Jaktem, and I reckoned him a relatively safe bet. He was a tall, quietly spoken man of about twenty-five. Robust of build and self-assured, he hailed from Twalinieh, Kemahamek's capital, and gave the impression of being useful to have around in a fight. His companion, Illan, was from Hikoleppi, Kemahamek's second city. Both men were adequately armed and accoutred, and had their own mounts. So, with the terms of their employment agreed, I finished my meal, paid Hirk Longshanks, and we set off upon the road to Anxau.

I was undecided whether to ride directly to Dehut or to make the diversion to Guling Mire in the hope of finding Wirm there. By Lanna's account there was a good chance of my encountering him in Dehut. But Wirm might change his mind, go elsewhere, delay his journey . . . anything. I still had little more than an odd coincidence to link Wirm with my business, anyway, and I harboured doubts that he would be able to provide me with any information of real value. Though I was uneasy about the fact that his name had cropped up twice, his involvement was, by all indications, quite innocent. He had simply sold me the green amber – which had no connection at all with my journey, but happened to have come out of Anxau. And he had seen, or claimed to have seen, my double being led in chains by Feikermun's beasts.

But for that latter reason alone I felt, on further consideration, that Wirm was worth seeking out.

So we travelled for the remainder of that day and into the next, riding deep into the grasslands of western Putc'pii and the semi-independent land known as the Urvysh Plains. We camped at the wayside, and then the following morning left Wetlan's Way and cut north across country, making for the settlement of Guling Mire. The truth is, the diversion served more than one purpose, for it helped ease – at least for a while – a weight that preyed upon my thoughts. I was postponing the inevitable, the moment when I must enter Dehut and establish contact with the crazed warlord Feikermun. And the longer I could keep that moment at bay, the better.

Darkening rainbellies which had begun to muster on the horizon before us now loomed closer as we rode across the wide ocean of grass. The sun faded and a bitter breeze sprang up, pushing directly into our faces, numbing cheeks and fingers. Before long we felt the first big splashes of sleeting rain, which developed into a series of harsh showers. It was a clear reminder of the season and the mercurial temperament of the elements.

We came in sight of Guling Mire as dusk closed in. We were cold, wet and miserable, wrapped in our capes, our spines curved against the driving rain. In the circumstances the settlement was a welcome sight, though ordinarily there is little to recommend it. It is a sprawl of buildings – some wooden, some stone – set around the uncertain edge of a dank primordial marsh. Some homes have been built in the marsh, mounted upon stilts sunk deep into the dark water and seeping mud. Others, generally those of the more wealthy inhabitants, crown the proximal low slopes. The marsh itself covers a vast area of creek-ridden lowland on the south shores of the Great White River. Guling Mire township grew up on outcrops of firmer ground at the marsh's southernmost rim.

The place gave me the shudders, for I have never been comfortable around large amounts of water. Guling Mire, with its slurping, sucking muds and ever-lapping pools, its swirling streams and gurgling, unpredictable eddies, comes straight out of my worst nightmares. We smelt the wet stench of its ooze even before we set eyes on the town, and my heart quickened. I began to wonder at the wisdom of choosing Guling Mire in preference to Feikermun.

A high defensive rampart of stone and clay stands upon the solid ground before the settlement. The only approach to its single gate is along a natural narrow causeway flanked on either side by bog. No more than four mounted men may ride the causeway abreast, and it is devoid of defensive cover. Hence Guling Mire is amply protected against assault.

One might ask why anyone would wish to attack such a horrible place. Indeed, persons unfamiliar with the region might well wonder what possessed anyone to found a settlement here in the first place. Guling Mire stinks; it is regularly subject to flooding; respiratory problems caused by the foul vapours that rise from the marsh are common among its inhabitants, and fever and disease are rife. Fearsome and deadly creatures inhabit the depths of the marsh, frequently making a meal of livestock, hounds or unwary humans, and wraiths are said to arise from the slimy waters on moonlit nights to weave among the narrow streets, slipping soundlessly through unsecured windows to smother sleeping infants in their beds. Yet more than a thousand people had chosen to live here – people of erstwhile nomadic stock, whose forebears had roamed the plains for generations, pitching their camps where the grazing was good and moving on as the need arose. They had relinquished their traditional lifestyle for settlement on the mire.

Why?

The answer is simple, if not obvious:

Eels.

The flesh of the young Grey-backed Twiner is a delicacy prized for its distinct and memorable flavour, and is believed by some to have invigorating properties, promoting longevity and the powers of the virile member. Thus it is relished by certain folk and regularly graces banqueting tables in wealthy homes, fetching a very respectable price.

Cultivating and harvesting the elver flesh in order to bring out its finer qualities is a meticulous business, so I understand. It demands particular care and attention, for the creature is quick to know distress, which can seriously disrupt its breeding habits and impair its flavour.

The only known breeding place of the Grey-backed Twiner is in the clogged creeks and marshes around Guling Mire. How this was first discovered is not known. It was a comparatively recent find, for the township of Guling Mire had been established for less than a quarter of a century. It's true to say that every inhabitant was linked in some way to eels, but one family in particular had found its rising star among the wriggling beasts. The House of Wirm, of which the merchant Wirm was head, had grown affluent on elvers. Under its auspices Twiner flesh had become available in many forms: fresh, dried, preserved, marinated or pickled; as paste, pâté or potage; in gelatin, oil, aspic or syrup; peppered, salted, sweetened or flavoured with herbs . . . the variations exceed my capacity to tell. Eager consumers were happy to take it in any of its recipes, and none but the scions of the House of Wirm knew the secret of its cultivation.

Some years earlier there had existed a rival House in Guling Mire, but it suffered misfortune and fell in time into ruin. Its wagons came under frequent attack, and so murderous were the assaults – leaving none alive to identify the assailants – that House Gorpen found difficulty in hiring reliable guards. A consignment of Grey-backed Twiner flesh delivered by House Gorpen to a noble Sommarian household was found to be tainted, causing acute inconvenience to the Sommarians and their guests. There were no fatalities, but the incident did guarantee the death of House Gorpen's reputation.

At approximately the same time House Gorpen suffered disaster on a personal level. Two family members drowned in the marshes in close succession; a third vanished. Suicide due to failing fortunes was deemed the most likely explanation, though the circumstances were never entirely clear. The two bodies were in fact not properly identified, having been stripped of much of their flesh by schools of hungry Twiners. House Gorpen collapsed; its remaining members packed their bags and departed, and the House of Wirm went on to prosper as sole purveyor of the slippery delicacy.

The open marshland behind the settlement was a network of eddy-pools, lagoons and tanks, bobbing with pots and traps and accessed by long wooden jetties and rafts. The eels were assiduously husbanded by dozens of low-paid workers, and armed guards kept watch day and night. Wirm employed a private army of more than two hundred disciplined men to maintain order in the settlement and discourage intervention from outside. Wirm himself dwelt in a formidably fortified manse on a low slope above the marsh.

When I arrived with my two Kemahamek companions before the settlement's main gate we were immediately challenged. The gate had been closed for the night. In the watchtower overhead the dim forms of a pair of guards could be made out, their faces illumined by the orange glow of a brazier. Other sentries stood close by upon the rampart, peering down curiously at the unexpected visitors.

I announced myself, having already decided upon the line I would adopt. 'I am Linias Cormer, from Chol. I seek an audience with your master on a matter of hopefully mutual advantage. Will you permit us entrance and perhaps point us to some hostelry where we might pass the night?'

'What is the precise nature of your concerns with Master Wirm?' enquired a harsh male voice.

'As I said, I have a proposition which I believe he will find interesting.'

I was gambling on Wirm's curiosity. He had a shrewd if ruthless intellect, and was not one to allow a possible commercial opportunity to pass him by. And, aside from that, Guling Mire was an inhospitable place, offering little in the way of diversion. Few people came here by choice, and so great was the fear of unwanted outside interest in the elver industry that those who did were carefully watched and not made to feel welcome. Such an attitude was effective in preserving Wirm's business, but it surely made life rather dull, if not oppressive. It seemed to me that Wirm, if he were at home, would welcome a break from his routine. He might be wary, but we were only three, after all, and with Wirm's henchmen flexing muscles in every niche and cranny we could hardly pose a threat.

There were muted mutterings in the guardtower, and someone gave way to a fit of coughing. I shivered, pulling the hood of my cape up further, for the rain was running in at the neck and wetting my clothing beneath. I was beginning to think I might be wrong, that we were to be turned away after all, when the gate gave a shudder and drew laboriously open, just enough to allow us through.

Four guards in dripping capes stood within. Their sergeant, a beefy fellow in stuffed leathers and dented pot helmet, gestured across the way. 'Apply to the inn yonder for a place to sleep. You will receive Master Wirm's response in due course.'

The inn, named The Leaping Twiner by some inspired soul, was a rickety grey building of half-timber construction. Its external walls were flaking and its eaves were sagging and bowed. It was one of just two establishments in Guling Mire which accepted foreign guests, and it appeared empty when we arrived. I took a chamber with three pallets. We were shown to it by a wheezing landlord who built a fire in the hearth and departed. There were a couple of leaks in the ceiling; a chamberpot and an old tin bowl had been positioned beneath to catch the drips. A fierce draught blew through a gap where the windowframe had rotted away. But otherwise the place was relatively serviceable, and as I had asked the landlord for his best accommodation I saw nothing to be gained by complaining.

We were changing from our wet clothes and warming ourselves before the fire when we heard the clomp of heavy footsteps in the passage outside. There came a heavy rap on the door. I opened it to face two soaked soldiers, dripping puddles onto the wooden floor. One of them addressed me. 'Master Wirm requests that Master Cormer join him at his home.'

'Ah, good. Are you to accompany me?'

The soldier nodded.

'Excellent. Just allow me a moment.'

I quickly finished dressing, donned my cape again, took up the small bundle which contained the green amber, and joined the two guards.

I was led through dark, winding, slippery streets up the slope

70

to Wirm's manse. It was a sizeable three-storey building set behind solid walls of wet grey stone. Guards were everywhere: tough, surly-looking men who eyed me darkly as I passed. My escort took me to an opulently furnished chamber, and I noted the many fine ornaments that adorned the place and the quality of the furniture and decoration. Wirm showed himself to be not merely wealthy but a man of some taste, a quality I had not expected.

'Slippery' is a word that springs readily to mind when describing Wirm. 'Eely' might equally well apply. He was a ropily thin, rather pale-fleshed individual aged somewhere in his thirties. Though less than half a head taller than I, his long limbs – somewhat out of proportion to his pinched torso – gave an impression of overall length. He seemed incapable of remaining still for more than a moment, comporting himself with quick sinuous movements and rapid shifts of stance. His face was narrow, sallow and deeply lined, with a prominent wedge of a chin. Wispy strands of pale brown hair fell past his ears but revealed much of his lumpy skull. His eyes were dark brown and incessantly mobile, travelling over you with short rests in unexpected places, as though he were constantly assessing your value in portions for varying purposes – a disquieting sensation. There was a faint oily sheen to his skin, and he had an unpleasant habit of touching you as he spoke, feeling your clothing – and even the flesh beneath – between thumb and fingers. This not only reinforced the feeling of being assessed, but also – in my case, at least – left me with a barely resistible impulse to look down at the place he had touched, half-convinced I would find a patch of slime glistening there.

'Master Cormer, is it?' said Wirm, rising, almost leaping, from a green divan as I entered. He came forward and slid his hands around mine, smiling. 'Welcome, welcome to Guling Mire.'

As he let go of my hand I found myself reflexively moving to wipe it clean on my trousers.

'Allow my man to take your wet cape, sir. Will you have wine?'

I thanked him and handed my cape to a servant. Wirm poured a ruby liquid into a silver goblet, then ushered me towards a

71

carved oak chair laid with soft blue cushions and positioned before a blazing hearth.

We were not alone. Another man lounged upon a second divan to one side of the room, near a window. He was a short, sloppily dressed individual with a bulging paunch and glowing red cheeks. Wirm introduced him as Vecco, but did not enlighten me as to his status or reason for being there. As Vecco made no contribution to our conversation I was none the wiser when I left.

'You have come from Chol, I am told,' said Wirm. 'Purely to see me? I am honoured.'

'Certainly I have ridden to Guling Mire with the sole purpose of seeking you out, Master Wirm. However, it would be untruthful to say I have come directly from Chol. Rather, I am lately out of Kemahamek, and am en route for Dehut, in Anxau.'

'Ah, so.' He appeared to give this a moment's reflection. 'And you have a proposition, is that not the case?'

Wirm had seated himself opposite me, lifting his legs to lay them upon the green divan and supporting himself on one elbow. My own position placed me with my back to the silent Vecco, a situation that did not put me at my ease.

'I am employed by the family Maille-Orchus,' I said, 'members of the Chol aristocracy with close links to the Royal House of Chol. My master, Lord Olmin Maille-Orchus, has sent me forth on private business to Dehut, but bidden me pay equal heed to a second task, that being to purchase choice samples of the famous Grey-backed Twiner flesh of which he has heard so much.'

I saw the gleam in Wirm's eyes, and a smile flickered suddenly upon his thin lips. He sat up and his free hand, the one that did not hold his goblet, roamed across the divan, long fingers lightly pressing, plying, pinching the short green pile. Plainly I had struck the right chord. To my knowledge twiner flesh had not been exported as far east as Chol, due largely to the fact that access to that remote land was severely restricted. But the potential now to introduce his goods to Cholian aristocracy, and even royalty, was something Wirm found too tempting to dismiss.

'Are you intending to take the Twiner meat back with you, Master Cormer?'

'That would be my hope. But it will be samples only, at least for the present, for I can carry no more. My master, however, has asked me to make enquiries in regard to establishing a regular supply, should he find the meat as palatable and efficacious as its reputation suggests. Do you have that facility, Master Wirm?'

'I have been working on it.' Wirm rose quickly and began pacing back and forth. 'Access to Chol is not easy, as you must surely know. The White River is perilous and indeed impassable in many areas. The lands to its south are inhospitable, due to terrain or hostile inhabitants or both. Likewise with the north, though perhaps marginally less so. Yes, conceivably that is the route I would use: from Kemahamek through Tanakipi, Pansur and Miragoff, utilizing both river and land. Yes, yes, I see no reason why it cannot be done.' His manner became a little cautious. 'However, the distance and extra expenses involved would be bound to have an effect upon the price.'

'That is understandable. I am sure we could arrive at terms acceptable to both parties.'

'Yes. I shall have to make calculations and advise you. Of course, if your master wishes to purchase in bulk, prefers to make his own conveyancing arrangements, or is able personally to introduce me to other interested and influential clients, then the price would reflect accordingly.'

'Good. Well, this sounds most promising. My master will be delighted. I think we can discuss the details later, perhaps after you have advised me of your basic price.'

'Are you intending to take your samples with you now, Master Cormer?'

'I think upon my return from Dehut will be most convenient. I will be less encumbered then.'

'Do you expect to be long in Dehut?'

'I do not think so.'

Wirm now stood close, inclining his head and torso over me. His eyes were on my left shoulder and one hand was poised as if he were about to touch me there. 'Would it be impertinent of me to enquire as to the nature of your business in Dehut? I

73

have many associates and very good friends there; perhaps I might be able to assist you in some way.'

I sensed that his interest was more than casual. 'Ah, no. It is a personal matter between my master and a former associate of his who is now resident in Anxau. But I thank you for your offer.'

The fingers of Wirm's hand, which had descended to feel the cloth of my tunic lightly, now withdrew. He clasped his hands together and straightened, stepping back a half-pace and surveying me. I could almost hear the clamour of his thoughts as they skeltered along two parallel courses: how he might establish a sure and profitable trade route into Chol, and how he might learn more about my business in Dehut.

I was pleased; my deception seemed to have passed off smoothly. I was now a dignitary in Wirm's eyes, someone to be accorded goodwill and respect. I offered him a path to greater wealth and influence. I felt I could now broach a stickier matter without risk of arousing his suspicion or disfavour.

'So be it,' said Wirm, his eyes for some reason on my shins. 'But if there is anything I can do to assist you, sir, please do not hesitate to ask. I am travelling to Dehut myself in a few days. Perhaps, for added security, you might prefer to accompany me?'

'You are most generous, Master Wirm, but with all respect I feel I must leave early tomorrow. I am already somewhat delayed due to harsh weather and one or two unavoidable incidents along the way. I am therefore keen to be done as quickly as possible and begin my journey home to my beloved Chol.'

'Quite so.' He gently pinched his upper lip between forefinger and thumb, his eyes glassy, then said, 'I shall have a price for you before you leave, and will make sure that the very best samples of twiner are made available for you upon your return.'

I drained my goblet and rose as though to leave, but at the same time took up the cloth bundle which contained the chunk of green amber. 'Before I depart, there is one other matter on which I would like to ask your opinion, if I may, Master Wirm.'

'I am at your service, sir.'

74

I displayed the stone. 'Can you tell me anything about this? I understand it was bought from you.'

Wirm's face registered mild surprise as his eyes fell upon the piece. 'Where did you get this?'

'From a Khimmurian merchant, Master Dinbig of Hon-Hiaita. I had hoped to acquire more like it, for I have seen nothing that quite resembles it. Master Dinbig was unable to help, other than to advise me to contact you should the opportunity ever arise.'

I was aware suddenly that Vecco had arrived at my shoulder. He gazed with waxy eyes at the amber, then looked up at me. He grinned unpleasantly, his lips, purple and pulpy, parting to expose darkly stained, gappy teeth. He brought his goblet to his mouth, tipped back his head and emptied it noisily. He looked again at the amber, then returned without a word to his seat.

'I'm afraid I can't really be of any service to you,' said Wirm. 'It is true I sold the amber to Master Dinbig. I picked it up in a village in the mountains, just across the Anxau border. The peasants find such things from time to time and are generally happy to exchange them for something or other with any passing trader.'

'Do you recall the name of the village?'

He shook his head vaguely. 'I asked about other pieces like this, but they had no more. I feel you would have a wasted journey even were you to find the right village.'

'Ah, well, I must content myself with just the one, then. No matter.' I returned the amber to its cloth. I was fairly sure that Wirm was, understandably, simply protecting his own interests by not revealing the name of the village. But he was probably right that I would find no more amber like this there. I said, 'I have heard that Master Dinbig no longer walks among us. Some sad business in Dehut, I was told. It's a pity; he seemed a genial fellow.'

'Yes, that is so,' agreed Wirm.

'I believe you were one of the last to see him alive.'

'Indeed. I was in Dehut when he foolishly committed his crimes. I subsequently saw him in the hands of His Excellency's men.'

'His Excellency?'

'Feikermun the Illustrious.'

'I was told that Master Dinbig was tried and executed.'

'Yes, I was there.' Wirm squirmed, kneading his hands – not with embarrassment or discomfort, I felt; more out of satisfaction. He was barely able to contain his rising pleasure. It chilled me. I tried to sound casual.

'You were present? At his execution?'

'I was.'

I had not expected this; Lord Mintral had made no mention of it. The implications were suddenly many. 'Are you in close association with His Excellency then, Master Wirm?'

'I am.'

Yes, of course. Feikermun had no doubt developed an appetite for twiners, encouraged by Wirm, who was the sole supplier. Wirm had wormed his way firmly and securely into Feikermun's favour – as secure as anything was with Feikermun, that is.

'Then you actually witnessed my – *ahem*! – you were present at Master Dinbig's end?'

Wirm drew in a quick breath, turning slightly away. He spoke through clenched teeth. 'It was a cruel death.'

Again I sensed his arousal, though he tried to disguise it. I fought down my revulsion and growing anger. Why should he feel such pleasure at my death? It could hardly be personal – we barely knew one another. He was, I could only conclude, perverse.

'What were his crimes? I have heard variously that he sold substandard goods to Feikermun and that he seduced one of Feikermun's favourite concubines.'

'Both are probably true,' said Wirm. 'Dinbig was a fool – something I had not previously taken him for.'

'How long ago did this execution take place?'

Wirm waved a long hand vaguely. 'Oh, *pph*, a month past, perhaps longer.'

'Are you certain of that?'

He looked at me curiously. 'Quite sure, Master Cormer. Why do you ask?'

'Oh, only that it seems less than a month since I bought this amber from him. But no, thinking back, it was longer than that.'

But my friend Inbuel had been positive in his account. He had spoken to me – to my double – in Dehut less than a month past.

I let the matter drop; to pursue it further might well arouse Wirm's suspicions. I glanced across to the silent Vecco, whose unpleasant gaze continued to appraise me quite brazenly. I was relieved that my business here was done for the present. Wirm summoned his servant to fetch my cape, and the guards to escort me back to the inn.

The rain had ceased when I came from Wirm's manse. Dark, angrily fringed clouds scudded southwards. The moon was high. Its light glistened on the waters of the foul marsh below, throwing up tortured phantom forms out of trees and the shadows of trees. Long lines of upright stakes, sunk into the mud, and weighted nets linked by cork floats marked the individual eel-tanks and man-made lagoons. Narrow wooden jetties thrust across the surface, spindly and crooked. I shivered, and wrapped my cape around me.

Yet again I was visited by the sensation that the ground was giving way beneath my feet. In Guling Mire, of course, this was quite literally true. The low hill upon which I stood was little more than an island floating on primordial sludge. If I took only a few dozen paces in any direction I would almost certainly find myself in soft, wet ooze, being sucked into the earth's dark and foetid depths.

As we made our way back down into the township I went over all that I had learned, tonight and on the previous days. Nothing seemed to quite come together; time and events seemed to have lost all sensible correlation. My mind swam with the strangeness of it, but the fact was that the real strangeness was only now about to begin.

6

SOMETIME IN THE night I was awoken by a persistent shaking sensation. I opened my eyes, not knowing where I was. The room was in near-darkness, pale moonlight revealing blots and outlines and little more. There was a figure crouched over me.

I was seized by the dream I had had in Hon-hiaita, of assassins in my double's employ stealing into my room to murder me. I panicked and made to strike out at my assailant. A strong forearm blocked my blow, fingers locked around my wrist.

'Master Cormer! It's me, Jaktem! Master Cormer!'

Jaktem . . . Jaktem . . . At last I put a face to that name, and all then fell into place.

'Jaktem, what is it?'

Jaktem released my wrist. 'Something's happening. Outside.'

He moved away, across to the window. Now I made out Illan's still form in the darkness, pressed to the wall beside the window, peering out through a gap in the shutters. I left my bed and stole towards them. Jaktem, crouched now by the sill, motioned caution with his hand.

The partially opened shutter allowed a view down into the street. We were on the first floor of the inn, at the rear. Our chamber overlooked a twisting alley with buildings close on the other side. The sloping, tarred wooden roofs of the inn's stables and storerooms were immediately beneath our window.

I could see nothing below but dark shadow, vaguely illuminated here and there by patches of weak moonlight. The cluttered rooftops spread away, all jutting, ramshackle angles, and beyond, at the furthest end of the alley, I could just glimpse the glistening marsh, black trees rearing in sinuous postures.

'What is it?' I whispered again.

'Wait,' breathed Illan, and pointed down into the alley. 'Watch there, between the houses.'

I concentrated my gaze on the area he indicated. Still I saw nothing but deep shadow. The harder I peered the more impenetrable it seemed to become, shifting as my eyes tried to remain focused upon it. And then the moon came from behind a cloud, throwing a ghostly wash of light on to the street, and – just a glimmer – was it? Yes! Something *had* moved, deep within the shadow.

'Did you see?'

I nodded.

'There's another positioned on this side, hidden by the stable roof.'

'Who are they? What are they doing?'

Jaktem shook his head. 'Don't know, but there are more gone round the front. Master Cormer, I think you should dress.'

Both my companions had garbed and armed themselves. I quickly moved away, stuffed my legs into trousers and boots and pulled on my tunic, then belted sword and dagger to my waist. I checked the inside of my belt where a length of garrotting wire was secretly stitched. A faint sound from beyond the room caught my attention. I moved to the door and pressed my ear against the wood. I heard the sound again: someone was moving downstairs.

It might have been the landlord or his staff, or even a guest if there were any, stirring from his bed to relieve himself, but my senses were sharpened and I feared the worst. I motioned to Jaktem to join me. We heard a muffled thud, then another. Then came the creak of a foot upon the stair.

Jaktem released a grim breath. 'They have entered through the front.'

I thought quickly. Whoever was out there was almost certainly not coming to pay their respects. I caught the stealthy footfall on the stairs again, a little closer now.

'How many went around the front?' I said.

'Five or six. Hard to be sure. Master Cormer, unless you know something different, I think we're in danger.'

My heart raced. What should we do? I could go out and speak with these men, try to reason with them, but I doubted

79

that reasoning was on their agenda. The furtive, organized manner of their approach declared them dangerous. Somehow I was convinced that their intention was to ensure I did not see the light of the next day.

Beside me Jaktem moved with sudden decisiveness, lifting the latch and opening the door.

'What are you doing?' I gasped.

'Give me a minute,' breathed Jaktem. 'Stay at the door and be sure to let me back in quickly.'

He was gone. My fear intensified. I did not know Jaktem. Were he and Illan in on this? Was I betrayed? I took some heart from the fact that I had just had time to see the glint of a pair of long daggers in his hands.

I glanced across to where Illan still stood at the window, eyes on the alley. He seemed intent on his task. I slipped into the doorway and peered along the corridor in Jaktem's wake. It was pitch dark; I could vaguely determine the outline of Jaktem's bulk as he moved towards the stairwell. He moved silently but to my surprise, as he drew close to the stairs, he began to sing, a wordless, thumping melody in a low voice. I listened, dumbstruck.

Suddenly Jaktem's tune was cut short. There came a grunt, a couple of bumps, and I heard his voice raised in surprise. 'Ho! What's this? Good eve, sir. I am sorry, I did not see you there.'

There was a moment's silence, then a curtly mumbled reply. 'Good eve.'

'I hope I did not hurt you,' said Jaktem. 'But what is this? You seem several, lurking here in the dark upon the stairs. By the devils, announce yourselves before I call the guards! Who are you? Are you here with dark intent?'

Again, brief mumbles. I could just about glean Jaktem's silhouette at the head of the stairs, cast in a dim orange light. Someone on the stairs was holding a lamp.

The intruders recovered from their initial surprise. Another voice spoke harshly. 'We seek Master Cormer. He lodges here.'

'Master Cormer is asleep, as are all respectable folk at this time. What do you want with him that cannot wait until morning?'

80

The voice hardened. 'Make way, man. Our business is not with you.'

'You shall not pass until you have answered my question. What is your business with Master Cormer? You have weapons drawn, by thunder! Who are you?'

There was a curse, then a gruff call from below. 'What are you waiting for? Take him!'

Now came sounds of a scuffle. Cries, a groan; confusion. There was a clatter on the stairs, more shouts; the lamp was doused. Suddenly Jaktem was back, panting, pushing me into the room.

'Quick, block the door!'

As he rammed it shut Illan and I grabbed pallets and a table to barricade the door.

'What happened there?' I demanded.

'One is dead, or at least he should be. A second took my boot in his face. They fell back down the stairs. But they are six at least.' Jaktem ran to the window. 'Quickly, it's our only chance.'

Even as he spoke I heard them in the passage. They were still confused, not sure which was our chamber. They kicked in doors regardless now, all pretence gone.

Illan was through the window, lowering himself quickly on to the sloping stable-roof below. Sword drawn, he half-ran, half-skidded down the roof and leapt into the alley.

'Go!' urged Jaktem. I grabbed my pack and followed, working my way towards the edge more cautiously than Illan. I heard grunts and the clang of metal on metal below, but could see nothing. I reached the lip of the roof. Now I made out Illan almost directly beneath me, fighting furiously against two assailants. I knelt, leaned over the roof and swung my sword-blade down hard upon the head of the nearest man, slicing his skull in two.

'He's there!'

I glanced back. Someone was outlined in the windowframe of the room I had just left. A lamp was lit at his back and I could see that the chamber was full of men. I saw, too, that Jaktem was on the roof, pressed up flat against the wall beside the window. As the first man began to climb through in pursuit

81

of me, Jaktem brought the pommel of his sword hard around into his face. The man toppled backwards. Jaktem stepped around with a whoop and stabbed into the window. There was a shriek from within, then Jaktem was running helter-skelter down the roof.

'Come on, Master Cormer!' he yelled as he launched himself into space. I followed, dropping over the roof into the wet mud of the alley.

Illan had finished off his man. Jaktem grabbed my arm. 'Quick, this way!'

We made off into darkness. I could hear feet clattering over the stable-roof in our wake now, and there were shouts from around the building to our left. I ran on blindly, aware by their hoarse breathing and the squelch of their boots in the mud that Jaktem and Illan were with me.

Figures came at us out of the darkness to our left – I could not tell how many. I heard Illan give a bellow as he threw himself among them. There was a horrible thudding sound and a whimper close by me.

'Up here!' came Jaktem's voice and he thrust me – I presume it was he – hard into a narrow snickelway between two buildings. The moon slid behind dark clouds. Now in utter blackness, with no light at all to penetrate the shadow, I was forced to slow my pace for fear of colliding with something. I could hear the noise of conflict at my back, then running feet somewhere a little way off to one side.

I weaved away from the sound, not daring to speak to Jaktem for fear of giving myself away. Then I realized I could no longer hear the reassuring sound of Jaktem's or Illan's breathing, nor their feet on the earth. I sensed too that the buildings had fallen away; I was on relatively open ground.

This alarmed me more than I could say. The moon remained obscured. I could see nothing at all. There were sounds close at my back, off to one side: scuffling, heavy footsteps.

'This way!'

It was not a familiar voice.

Another voice: 'No, over here!'

'Listen! There's someone over there!'

They were edging closer. I moved on, away from them, my

heart pounding from a fear as great if not greater than the fear of murderers in the night. By my calculations I had come a hundred or more paces away from the rear of the inn. I had left the buildings behind. I knew that in this direction there was no protective wall. There was no need for one: nobody could approach the settlement from any direction but the southern causeway, not even by boat, for all was hideous wet marsh and mire. And with every step I took I brought myself closer to that marsh.

I kept going, slowly, taking heart from the firmness of the ground beneath my feet. Suddenly I was aware of laboured breathing close upon my flank.

'There's someone there!'

'Jaktem!' I whispered. 'Illan!'

'Here! Here!'

The voice rang out loudly, so close I could almost have touched the man from whom it came. It was plain he did not call to summon aid for me. I lifted my sword and swung wildly at the dark. It bit hard into something both yielding and solid.

'*Aaargh!*'

He was down, but his screams rang an alert into the night. I swung again, but this time my blade chewed into earth.

'*Aaaargh!*' I could hear him slithering and thrashing on the ground, struggling to move away from the lethal blade he could not see. But neither could I see him, and I heard others converging upon his noise. I plunged away before I became the victim of someone else's invisible blade.

Now several voices, hushed and excited, spread in a rough arc to my rear. I had no choice but to push on, away from them. I glanced skywards; black cloud still hid the moon, but it moved swiftly and I could see that a break approached. The moonlight it permitted would almost certainly be sufficient to enable me to gain a rough grasp of my whereabouts, but it would also reveal me to my pursuers.

The man I had downed had ceased his screams, presumably reassured by the arrival of his cronies. I could hear him moaning still, and someone barked a curt command to take him to safety.

The ground beneath me had become spongy. It gave with every step, as though supported on springs, and I felt the cold in

83

my feet as water gathered around my boots. My fear mounted. I was surely heading directly into the marsh. Yet I lived, and if I turned around and went back I could confidently say that this would no longer be the case. These men were not looking for a prisoner: they had been sent to take my life.

Suddenly, with one lurching step, I was up to my knees in soft, bitterly cold slurry. I halted, gasping, utterly afraid. I did not dare take even a single step more for fear that I would sink completely into the stinking mud. But there were voices still behind me, moving towards my position, albeit slowly and cautiously.

I bent at the waist and leaned forward, stretching my arms, groping for something – anything. My fingertips touched only cold wet mud.

And then, as I swung to one side, they brushed against a clump of grass. I edged gingerly towards it, grasped it in my hands, pressed. It did not give – seemed rooted in solid ground. I lifted one foot, freeing it of the mud, and planted it upon the grass. Half-pulling myself, I dragged the other foot clear and hauled it from the muck.

And then the cloud broke.

'There he is!'

I glanced back. The moon's pallid glow showed half a dozen men spaced out some twenty paces to my rear. Behind them were the dark angles of the settlement's buildings. Ahead lay swamp, choked with dense undergrowth and trees, some top-pled, strewn with torn curtains of moss and creepers.

It seemed that the turfy land I was on extended some distance further into the undergrowth. It was the only way open to me. Even as I considered it I heard a strange hissing sound and something splashed into the mud close by.

I looked back again. Two of my pursuers had crossbows.

I was on my hands and knees. I pushed myself into a crouch-ing run and made off. Another bolt split the rotten stump of a fallen tree to my left. I weaved slightly, not daring to verge too far to either side. Then, mercifully, the moon slid once more behind a cloud and I was no longer a visible target.

But nor could I see.

I had fixed my sight upon a certain point where a gap presented itself between the tangle of branches before me. Towards this I raced unveeringly in the blackness. The ground continued to support me – in fact, it felt surer now. Perhaps there was some hope – perhaps I might yet find a path through the swamp, back to the town where I could lose my pursuers.

It was a desperate and irrational hope, but it was all I had to cling to. Twigs brushed suddenly across my face, stinging my cheeks. I ducked, slowing instinctively and raising my hands before me. I could no longer hear anything other than the sound of my own breathing and the soft thud of my feet. Had my pursuers given up, or were they waiting, listening to better determine my position?

I paused for a moment to regain my breath. A twig cracked! Somebody was less than ten paces away. A glance at the sky showed the moon about to reappear. I would be seen!

I pushed myself away, trying not to make a sound. Fortunately the ground no longer squelched with my every step, though my wet, mud-clogged boots seemed to make a noise almost as loud. I collided with something hard, banging my knee. My fingers traced the wet, rough curve of a fallen tree trunk, festooned with lichen and moss. As the moon came from behind the clouds I threw myself over and lay motionless on the other side.

'D'you see anything?'

'No. He's around here somewhere, though.'

The voices were hushed, a fair distance off but too close to allow me any respite. I watched as another black cloud approached the moon – assessed the way I would go next.

'We'll wait. If he comes back this way we'll get him; if he doesn't, the mire will.'

The ghostly moonlit marsh faded. I got to my feet and moved off, following a path held in my mind's eye, keeping low, one hand raised before me to avoid overhanging branches. Now I made good progress; the ground was firm and I could just about make out the lie of the land and the trunks and undergrowth immediately around me. I weaved between the trees, putting distance between myself and those at my back, and began to feel that all was not lost after all.

And then the ground turned to liquid beneath me.

I was thigh-deep in mud, almost toppling headlong as the forward motion of my legs was arrested. I sank deeper, then my foot came to rest on something firm. I thrust my weight forward, relying on the apparent solidity. But it fell away like sponge beneath me and I sank to my chest.

The shock of the thick, ice-cold mud, and the utter terror that immersion in water aroused in me, took the breath from my lungs. I could hear my hoarse, high-pitched gasps as I struggled to draw air into my body, but I seemed to be apart from it, somehow isolated, numb with terror. I think I would have called for help had I been able, hopeless though it was; but I had no voice. My arms swam on the surface of the slurry, my fingers seeking something, anything, to grasp on to. And I sank deeper.

I pushed myself forward – half a finger's length, another. The thought came to me to discard my pack, which hung over one shoulder. It was not particularly heavy, but any weight I could shed would surely help. But my fingers could not find the strap. I scrabbled helplessly, sank a little more.

The the tips of my fingers touched a branch which hung down into the muck from somewhere overhead I curled them around it and hauled, tentatively lest it break. It bent towards me, but seemed to take my weight. I drew myself up, forward, seeking the larger bough from which this branch sprouted.

I had dragged myself free to my waist, clinging with every atom of strength I could command, when the branch came away with a dull snap. I sank inexorably, falling forward on to my face. My fingers remained locked to the branch, which floated now, only half-submerged beneath the ghastly mud. I threw my arm around it, spluttering, managing to keep my head and shoulders from going under.

But my strength was going. I was cold, so cold. Only half-conscious, I pulled my way along the branch, slowly, slowly, feeling my muscles drag, the cloying mud sucking at me, drawing me down. With my free arm I flailed wildly, seeking something else to grab hold of.

A creeper offered a moment of hope, then that too came away in my grasp. Above me, outlined against the sky, I could just make out a long, twisting horizontal limb. I stretched upwards, but though my nails scratched against its underside I could find no purchase. And I was sinking now, praying, panicking, overcome with exhaustion. My fingers no longer touched the bough. The cold, deadly sludge rose over my shoulders to my chin.

I cannot properly describe what happened next. That is, I know what I thought happened, what *seemed* to happen. Yet even after what I was subsequently to learn, I remain unsure.

The moon reappeared. That was my interpretation, anyway, for quite suddenly I could see. And what I saw, clearly, was the heavy limb above me, slipping away as I sank to my death, and my mud-coated arm waving helplessly over my head. And higher overhead was a latticework of branches, starkly outlined against the dark sky. And everything was held in a soft, unworldly light.

There was something upon the bough. A figure, crouching, looking down at me. It was pale, vaguely human in form, I think, yet not like anything I had ever seen in my life. It sat in a hunched position, and it was watching me with a forlorn, puzzled expression, its head cocked slightly to one side.

And I gasped out: 'Oh help me! I'm drowning!'

Two enormous dark eyes slowly blinked, then the creature leaned towards me, nimbly extending its torso, and reached down. Warm fingers locked around my wrist and it hauled me free, single-handed, from the mud, drawing me up on to the branch beside it.

That is how I saw it; that is how I experienced it. Barely alive, I hooked my knee over the bough and dragged myself the last few inches, still held by the strange creature. I laid myself exhausted along the wide limb. I heard my rescuer's voice: 'Remain here. Do not move until morning. You will be safe now.'

I lifted my head, nodding in gratitude, seeking words to express my gratitude – but the creature had gone. I was alone on the bough.

Yet there was nowhere it could have gone to.

I gazed all around, raising myself into a half-sitting position. I could see clearly into the nearby marsh. There was nobody, Nothing.

I remained there for a few moments more, dazed, confused. Then I dragged myself along the mossy limb to the more secure platform of the massive fallen tree trunk from which it grew. There, with my arms curled for support around a protruding branch, I let my head rest on the wet, half-rotten wood, and closed my eyes.

Sometime during the night I awoke, shivering. It was black all around. I could just make out the closet trees and a sallow gleam on the surface of the ooze beneath me. The marsh was silent.

There were figures moving between the trees. Vaporous, luminous things which seemed to float above the surface of the marsh. I saw five or six, moving soundlessly towards, as I reckoned, the settlement of Guling Mire.

Marsh-wraiths, they had to be, though I had not really believed them to exist. I peered hard at the nearest and made out vague features, eyes or eye-sockets, a mouthlike depression. But the shape changed even as I watched, like animate mist.

Had my rescuer been one of these? I believed not. Whatever it was that had crouched above me on the bough had had physical shape, had been solid to my touch, whereas these things had no sustained form and gave the impression of being no more solid than air. And I wondered: had I dreamed I'd been saved? Had it been hallucination brought on by the desperate plight of my own mind? It seemed almost possible, now, that I had dragged myself free of the bog.

I was too cold and too exhausted to concentrate. I watched a while longer, not daring to move, as the marsh-wraiths passed on their way and were lost to sight. And I lay there, frozen, waiting to see what the dawn would deliver.

7

FIRST LIGHT BROUGHT a pale grey illumination, revealing for the first time the mass of twisted ghostly trees, the primeval forest growing out of the sodden, watery earth all around. The marsh lay in low mist, silent but for the occasional call of a bird or the splash of a fish or small amphibian. I had awoken – for I had somehow slept again, at least lightly – shivering and stiff with cold. My clothes were wet on my skin and heavy with stinking black muck.

With difficulty I roused myself to a sitting position on the tree trunk and began to take stock of my situation. It was not hopeful. Looking around me, I could barely see the ground, such as it was, for mist. Beneath one end of my tree it looked solid enough, but it was impossible to determine a path in any direction. And appearances were deceptive anyway. What looked solid to the eye could well turn out to be a thin layer of grass or reed lying on little more than slurry. As I already knew, a single step could take me from safety into bottomless mud from which there was no hope of escape.

And if I left, where was I to go? Back to Guling Mire, to Wirm's men? I assumed my assailants had been in Wirm's pay. Who else could have sent them? Yet I was unclear as to why Wirm should wish me dead. Last night I had been convinced that my deception had worked. Wirm had seemed positively eager to make a good impression. Why had he changed his mind? Or had he seen through me from the beginning?

Whatever the answer, I could think of little now to enhance my prospects in Guling Mire.

Yet I was stumped for an alternative. I could hardly make off into the marsh. I would barely last a minute.

As I thought about it I realized that I had lost all sense of direction. The sky was overcast, the sun not visible, and I couldn't determine from where the dawn had come. I had no idea which way Guling Mire lay.

I recalled the words spoken to me in the night by the creature that had hauled me from the mud. 'Remain here. Do not move until morning. You will be safe now.'

Or had it been a dream? It seemed so unreal.

I sat there, numb with cold and despair, and felt far from safe. For all the good survival had done me, I felt I might just as well have drowned last night.

A while later, as the mist was thinning, I heard noises in the undergrowth some distance off – irregular sounds that hung in the still morning air, as if someone or something moved with no concern that they might be heard. Then there were voices, men in some number, spread out – moving, I thought, vaguely towards me.

My heart began to thump. I looked around me again, but there was nowhere I could go. I lay down, flattening myself upon the fissured tree trunk, sliding as far as I dared behind its curve. I was scarcely concealed. If they came within a dozen paces of me I would almost certainly be seen.

Moments later I spied them through the mist. One, then another, then more. I estimated a dozen at least. They advanced carefully, each carrying a long pole with which he prodded the ground in front of him before every step.

Someone called out. 'Master Cormer!'

I ducked my head down. The voice came again. 'Master Cormer! Master Cormer!'

'You're wasting your time,' came a second voice. 'He couldn't have survived out here.'

The first voice resumed, louder, 'It's me, Master Cormer. Jaktem. And Illan. It's safe! Can you hear me? It's safe now!'

I raised my head an inch and peered over the trunk. The nearest of the men was about twenty paces off. I could see Jaktem, though not Illan. He conferred with the others. Some seemed reluctant to continue. I heard doubts expressed about safety, and further observations on the improbability of my survival.

Jaktem turned to address another man further back, half-obscured by the mist. 'We must go on – a little longer. As long as there's the slimmest chance.'

I squinted my eyes. The man he had spoken to stood behind the others and appeared to be in charge of the operation. If I were not mistaken it was Wirm of Guling Mire.

This confused me even further. I listened on, my head swimming. Somebody said something about there not being a chance of even finding the body.

'Then you go back if you wish,' retorted Jaktem. 'But I and Illan will search on alone until we are certain.'

'You would not be safe,' Wirm said. He was clad in a long coat of silver foxfur to ward off the chill of the morning. 'We will continue a while longer.'

They resumed their cautious advance. My thoughts raced. If Wirm had not ordered my death, then who had? Or was this some elaborate deception designed to lure me in? I could only hope that it wasn't – I knew that if I remained here I would die.

I pulled myself up until I was kneeling upon the trunk, supporting myself shakily with one hand. I raised the other hand and waved.

'I'm here.'

A raft and ladder were required to bring me from that fallen tree, for there was nothing but quagmire all around. Had I tried to leave without help I would not have gone three paces. Wrapped in warm furs, I was transported back to Wirm's manse.

Later in the day he came to the chamber where I was recuperating. 'Master Cormer, are you recovered?'

'I have slept and eaten. I think my strength is restored.'

'Good.'

I was seated at a table talking with Jaktem and Illan, hearing their versions of events from the point at which we had become separated the previous night. Wirm leaned over me, his eyes seeming to find something of interest close to my left ear. 'As I have already said to you, I am shamed and mortified by what has happened here. I cannot adequately convey my apologies, but be sure that those responsible will pay the price of their infamy. In the interim, if there is anything I can do for you do not hesitate to ask. I mean it. I am at your service, sir.'

'You are very kind.'

Wirm wrung his hands. 'Justice will be done, sir. Do not doubt. The culprit who masterminded this shocking attack has been apprehended, and in order that you harbour no questions as to my sincerity I would ask that you accompany me as soon as you are able. There is something I would like you to see.'

'I am able now, and quite ready,' I said, rising. I was intrigued. I had learned from Jaktem and Illan how, in the darkness and confusion of the conflict, they had become separated from both myself and each other. Each had managed to fight his way clear of his assailants and had tried to relocate me. Failing, they had passed the night hidden. In the morning it became plain that Wirm's guards were out to apprehend the culprits and that my attempted murder had not been Wirm's doing. Jaktem and Illan gave themselves up, and once their identities had been established had been permitted – in fact, encouraged – to initiate the search which culminated in my rescue from the mire.

I was not sure what to make of this. Something, somewhere did not quite fall into place. But I did not know what. For my part I kept silent about my experience, preferring to let all believe that I had somehow saved my own life by dragging myself on to the bough.

With Jaktem and Illan in tow, I followed Wirm from the chamber. We made our way down into the township, an escort of four towering guards at our sides.

'Last night I saw what I believe were marsh-wraiths,' I said. 'Luminous, vaporous wisps that moved of their own volition across the marsh. Did they enter the town?'

'Not that I am aware of.' Wirm put the question to the sergeant of our guard, who confirmed that no wraiths had been seen. Jaktem and Illan, too, had seen nothing, and again I wondered whether it had all been a dream.

'Do they enter the town sometimes?'

'Increasingly rarely,' said Wirm.

We marched on in silence, passing along a couple of narrow, twisting streets, heading, by my calculations, towards the rear of the settlement and the lagoons and eel-tanks in the marsh. Wirm had begun humming to himself. His mood seemed buoyantly casual, as though nothing at all were amiss. I felt his stealthy fingers lightly grasp my elbow. 'Are you at all familiar with the habits of the Grey-backed Twiner, Master Cormer?'

'I cannot say that I am. I have eaten the meat on one or two occasions, but that is as far as my acquaintance goes.'

'Did you enjoy it?'

'I found it tender and pleasant to the palate, yes.'

'Mmh. Of course, to gain its most beneficial effects you need to consume the flesh on a regular basis. It is rich in goodness, providing it has been properly cultivated. Eaten daily it becomes quite life-enhancing. The rewards can be most salutary.'

He gave my elbow a knowing squeeze, smirking, his eyes almost upon my face.

'I have heard as much,' I said. 'Unfortunately I am a man of fairly modest means. Even were the flesh available in Chol, its price would preclude my enjoying it on a regular basis.'

'Then, when preparing samples for your master in Chol, sir, I shall provide you with an additional, complimentary sample from the House of Wirm for your private consumption. How does that sound to you?'

'You are most generous, Master Wirm. I am in your debt.'

'Not at all.' He lapsed into silence for some moments, then said, 'A fascinating beast, the Twiner. Do you know anything about its life-cycle?'

'Scarcely a thing.'

'The eels live for no more than two years, and, though they can travel quite far from the Mire at times, they always return here, to their birthplace, to breed. No one is quite sure why that is, but it is thought to be due to the presence of certain rare foods in the mud or plant-life here. A mature adult male can grow to a maximum of a cubit in length, though most are somewhat shorter. The female attains approximately half that. Their diet is particularly interesting. For most of their lives the eels eat plant-stuffs or minute insects or larvae from the water and mud. But for a short period once a year, at the time of breeding, an extraordinary change occurs. The female Twiners become voracious carnivores. Their mouths develop ridges of sharp, calloused flesh, capable of taking the meat off small fish, frogs, other Twiners or animal carcasses. Even small water-loving animals can fall victim, should they unwittingly swim into a school of Twiners which contains breeding females.'

'Do they turn upon one another?' I enquired.

'Not ordinarily, though under certain circumstances – the specific nature of which I have not been able to determine – a group of females will attack and partially devour a male, leaving him alive but in a condition in which life cannot be sustained.'

'For how long does this behaviour manifest?'

'Within a month they revert to their normal habits. The eggs are spawned, hatch, and a month later it is time to cull the young. There, Master Cormer, you have learned a secret known to few outside of Guling Mire.'

We had arrived at a wooden palisade set with a large gate and watch-towers. Beyond I could see the long wooden rooftops of the processing areas, with sodden grey and black trees behind. Guards bearing spears and swords were as much in evidence here as at Wirm's manse. There was a barked command from within, and the gate swung open to admit us. We passed through, crossed a small yard and entered one of the long processing sheds. The stench of eel flesh and entrails was overpowering. Ranks of drying eels lay on hundreds of racks hung from the roof. Huge wooden pails stood beside the long benches where the workers toiled, and into these the guts were thrown. Hearts, lungs and vital organs went into green pails; intestines and digestive tracts into grey. Nothing was wasted, though I did not know where the offal was destined.

Workers, women as well as men, paused in their labours to bow as Wirm strode past. I cast my eye over them, and over the guards who stood watch around the building. The workers appeared pale and hollow-eyed, docile, somewhat cowed. I knew they worked long hours for scant payment. Many were plainly sick. I thought they looked quite stupefied.

We passed from the shed, traversed a small area of open ground and stepped up on to a rickety wooden walkway which stretched out into the watery lagoon of the marsh. The sun had begun to push through the low cloud which had dominated the morning. Tendrils of mist still rose from the marsh; the air was almost motionless and, as yet, chill. The walkway extended for more than one hundred paces, with others branching off at crazy angles and themselves extending and breaking into further walkways, so that a whole network of jetties latticed the lagoon. Moored to wooden bollards here and there were rafts to enable access to the areas the jetties could not reach.

I glanced down queasily at the creaking planks beneath my feet. Between them the glistening liquid mud was uncomfortingly visible. The dull sun gleamed off the surface of the misted swamp all around. We seemed to be making for the very end of the long jetty. My unease increased and I suppressed a shudder.

'The breeding season has just begun, as it happens,' said Wirm aside as we approached the end of the jetty.

The water here was quite deep – how deep I could not tell. From this point access to the eel-tanks was gained solely by the use of rafts. The tanks were formed of rows of long stakes sunk into the mud, lashed together and hung with fine-meshed netting. Each tank measured perhaps fifteen cubits square.

In the nearest tank a naked man lay spreadeagled on his back upon a raft. His wrists and ankles were bound with rope secured to four stout wooden posts sunk into the muddy water. His mouth was bright red and he was shivering with cold. Standing on the raft, close to his head, was a guard, leaning on a long quant.

Seeing us standing above him the prisoner raised his head and fixed his eyes upon Wirm. He strained against his bonds and from his mouth came a garbled gurgling sound. Blood poured down his chin and jaw. I realized that his tongue had been torn out.

I realized too, with a feeling of sudden disquiet, that I knew the man. He was Vecco, who had been Wirm's guest in his manse the previous evening.

'Master Cormer, here is the villain responsible for ordering your murder last night,' announced Wirm.

Vecco rocked his head from side to side, his bestial voice rising as his stump of a tongue struggled hopelessly to shape once-familiar words.

'Are you sure of this?' I said.

'Oh, absolutely sure. He has confessed.'

'But I don't know the man. Who is he? What was his motive?'

'That is unclear, but I suspect jealousy.'

'Jealousy?'

'Of me. I have suspected a conspiracy to bring the House of Wirm into disrepute for some time now. Somebody has been endeavouring to learn the secrets of Twiner farming for their own ends. Last night Vecco tried to have you murdered so that blame would have fallen upon me. I would have lost the business with Chol – and, more, would have been looked upon with suspicion by others.'

Something didn't ring quite true. I stared down at the desperate Vecco. Beside me Jaktem said, in a tight voice, 'It would have been interesting to hear his version of events.'

I glanced aside at him, and saw that he was bristling.

'I have heard him, be assured,' said Wirm. 'His actions last night were just the culmination of a series of events. I had suspected him for some time, but had no proof. Last night he gave himself away. Now, to reassure you, sir, please witness that justice has been done.'

Wirm gave a signal to the guard on the raft, who leaned heavily to his quant. As the raft eased away, Vecco, secured to the posts, slid slowly from the raft into the water. He disappeared momentarily beneath the surface, then came to the top, spluttering and coughing, coated in green and brown slime.

'Stop this, please,' I said. 'I do not wish this. There is no need for further torture.'

I had no inkling of what was to come. Wirm shook his head. 'He has been found guilty of a gross crime. It is only right that he pay in kind.'

There was a small gate fitted into the tank-side furthest away from us, and the raft bumped against it. In the tank beyond I could see that the dark surface of the water was disturbed. The guard bent carefully and lifted the gate.

The disturbance on the other side increased, the foul water rippling and roiling. It began to flow through the gate, a tiny storm on the surface, signalling something below, something unseen, which surged directly towards the hapless Vecco.

Quite suddenly a growth began to form along Vecco's side. Thick, quivering tendrils like hanks of sleek, smooth hair, mottled slate-grey merging into dark olive-green and charcoal-black. Vecco threshed, roared. The hair began to appear all over him, on his legs, arms, around his head, imbued with its own fierce energy. He sank for a moment, but his bonds would not let him go far. When he resurfaced he was a mass of writhing, shuddering tentacles. Hundreds of them. Thousands. Vecco was no longer visible, had become a tormented marsh creature which churned and plunged and threshed, and then gradually grew still as the filthy water around it reddened.

Wirm watched with fevered eyes; the pink tip of his tongue slipped out and snaked along his upper lip. Jaktem beside me was stiff with unvoiced emotion. Illan was ashen-faced, trembling slightly.

'That was unnecessary,' I said between clenched teeth, but Wirm seemed not to have heard me. He was at the edge of the jetty, kneeling, gazing down into the water.

'Ah, my children, my sweet ones. That's better now, isn't it? That's better.'

I suppressed an urge to step forward and push him from the jetty. How then would he like his pets?

'I shall return, if I may, to my chamber,' I said. Wirm gave no reply, but the sergeant of the escort gave a nod. I looked for the last time into the eel-tank. What remained of Vecco still hung sagging in the thick, mucky water, bobbing slowly, held by its four ropes. A few eels continued to feed on tatters of ruined flesh, but most had eaten their fill and swum on. One of Vecco's near-fleshless hands quivered slightly and a ghastly breathy sound escaped the pit of his mouth. He was still alive.

No petition I might make would change anything now. Vecco's condition was, as Wirm had described it, one in which life could not be sustained. I just hoped that his agony might be short-lived. I turned away, leaving Wirm to his musings, and beckoning to Jaktem and Illan to follow. Three guards escorted us back down the long jetty, through the processing shed to the gate of the compound. From there we were allowed to proceed unchaperoned to The Leaping Twiner.

97

8

OUR CHAMBER HAD been ransacked, though there had been virtually nothing there to take. Money and other small items I kept secure on a belt at my waist, and when I had fled the chamber I had taken with me my pack which contained the green amber, the precious *gidsha* root and sundry accoutrements. Out of desperation I had endeavoured to discard the pack in the marsh, but by sheer good fortune it had remained with me throughout my ordeal. Jaktem and Illan, too, had left hardly anything at the inn.

This left me wondering whether it had been only my death that Vecco – I accepted for the moment Wirm's version of events – had sought. Might his intention also have been to relieve me of specific possessions? I had revealed the green amber at Wirm's manse in Vecco's presence. He had bestirred himself to look at the piece, and I remembered the curious look he had given me then. A whole realm of dark intentions seemed now, upon reflection, to have been contained in that look, yet I could draw no single conclusion.

Could he have been after the amber last night? Why? Or had he some inkling that I carried *gidsha*? The latter possibility held chilling implications. No one outside of the *Zan-Chassin* Hierarchy knew that I had the *gidsha*. Was it possible that I had been betrayed by one of my own people?

I calmed my thoughts, for I was close to entertaining hysterical notions. Reluctantly I had to accept that I would probably never know the real reasons for Vecco's attempt on my life.

The landlord of The Leaping Twiner demanded recompense for the damage caused to his property. I felt it was hardly for me to accept responsibility, but I paid him anyway rather than cause a row. A short while later there was a knock at our chamber door. I opened it to find Wirm outside with two guards. He produced a small leather scrip, gathered and tied at the neck, which he held out to me.

'Master Cormer, I am here with humble apology once again. I learn that the unprincipled fellow who runs this establishment demanded payment of you for last night's damage. Here – here is your money back. I have settled with him, in full.'

'There is no need.'

'I insist, sir. He had no right, and his action brings shame upon me. Please, do not refuse.'

'Very well.' I accepted the scrip and thanked him.

'Is all in order now?'

'I believe so, yes.'

'Nothing has been taken?'

'It seems not.'

'Very good. Now, one other thing. It was as I recall your stated intention to leave for Dehut this morning. Most unfortunately you have been prevented from doing that, and I do not imagine you still plan to leave today, do you? It is already past noon. Then let me repeat the offer I made yesterday evening, that you accompany me. I have revised my plans and will be departing early tomorrow. You will be safe in my company and, all things being as they are, I consider myself bound and beholden to attend to your welfare as far as possible. Would you do me the honour, then, of travelling with me? In Dehut I can introduce you to persons of influence, if you so wish, possibly even including His Excellency himself.'

It would have been quite unreasonable and therefore difficult to refuse now, though I did not savour the prospect of Wirm's close company. Personal feelings aside, there were obvious advantages to travelling with him, as he had so deftly pointed out. So I smiled and gave him my thanks and accepted his offer.

Wirm writhingly expressed his pleasure. 'Regrettably I must absent myself this evening as I have important duties to attend to. But please avail yourself of all that Guling Mire has to offer. Your account at The Leaping Twiner has been settled in full. Let us meet at the gate at dawn tomorrow.'

He nodded and departed.

So it was that four days later I rode into Dehut in the company of Wirm of Guling Mire, at the head of a train of three wagons escorted by a score of mounted guards. Wirm's cargo was, I assumed, elver flesh in some form or forms, plus diverse goods for which he had a market in the conflict-torn city. At one point during the journey I had questioned him about Vecco, hoping to learn something of the man's origins, his purpose for being in Guling Mire and his relationship with Wirm. But Wirm was hardly forthcoming, saying only that he had known Vecco for some time and that he deemed him a treacherous snake which the world was well rid of. I asked also about Wirm's connections with Feikermun, trying to build up a more accurate picture of Feikermun himself. But again Wirm was circumspect in his replies, and I learned virtually nothing that I did not already know or had not at least surmised.

We arrived at Dehut to find open warfare on the streets. Without Wirm, who knew the optimum route into Feikermun's quarter and was treated with some deference, I doubt that I would have entered unharmed.

The first thing I noticed was the smoke. It was visible from a good distance away. Tall plumes and columns leaned almost motionless in the near-breathless air, varying in colour from white to grey to soot-black, rising ominously from one area of the city. It was visible from the road which wound through the low hills that let on to the wide flat plain upon which Dehut had grown. The city itself spread like a scab across the plain, a mass of predominantly low buildings, many of wooden construction, sprawling in ramshackle, haphazard manner as though without plan. Here and there were grander edifices, the decaying palaces and turreted manses of Dehut's wealthier citizens. A high curtain wall encircled the inner city, but much of Dehut's population lived outside this, protected only by wooden palisades, ditches, dirt mounds or, as was often the case, nothing at all.

Wirm reined in his horse.

'There is fighting,' he said. He shielded his eyes with one hand and scanned the city. 'It appears limited to a section of the northeastern quarter, if the fires are anything to go by. Probably the Stonemarker district.'

100

He explained that Stonemarker in northeastern Dehut was a disputed area of control between Feikermun and Malibeth. It had been held originally by Feikermun, then wrested from him some months ago in a fierce battle with his renegade brother, Gorl. Feikermun had won it back again, but upon Gorl's demise and the rise to eminence of Gorl's deadly lover, Malibeth, it had again fallen under bloody contest. Stonemarker also lay on the primary route into Dehut from the east, along the Wetlan's Way extension.

'Such fools,' muttered Wirm. 'They should be paying homage if they hope to survive. The Excellency is so close now. They do not know.'

The words sent a chill down my spine. 'So close?' I enquired, as casually as I could.

Wirm nodded. 'He is to be Supreme.'

'The signs are that his adversaries share the same objective.'

'Ah, but they do not have his vision, sir.' Wirm turned to appraise me with sliding eyes. 'They have not access to the power. They cannot conceive of what His Excellency has in store.'

It was the strongest validation of the *Zan-Chassin*'s fears that I had heard. It implied, too, that Wirm was in some wise involved with, or at least party to some degree in, Feikermun's plans.

'What does he have in store?'

Wirm merely gave a taut, mute, weighted smile. His cold eyes travelled down my body, over my horse and out to gaze again upon distant Dehut. He signalled the captain of his guard forward and the two conferred briefly, then Wirm announced, 'We will skirt around to the west a little way and enter from the south. We will leave the main road in a short while. Be alert.'

A secondary way, little more than a cart track, led off into the woods further down. Along this we travelled for another hour, through rough country close to the base of the low hills, until we came upon another, better-maintained road which cut up from the south towards the city. Before long the first buildings began to appear, small isolated wooden huts and hovels, becoming denser as we approached Dehut's walls. The faintest

101

hint of a breeze blowing our way brought the reek of smoke to my nostrils; it coloured the air around us with a bluish haze.

Nearing Dehut's high main wall we entered a shanty town, a slum consisting of hundreds of lean-tos and motley shacks built with spare wood and sacking or tarpaulin and little else. People watched as we rode by. They were clothed in rags, their faces filthy and gaunt, apathy and hunger in their eyes. Some approached with their hands held open before them. Fleshless children ran alongside us, calling up for food or coin.

At the city gate a small queue of traffic had formed. Everything was under the scrutiny of Feikermun's guards. Wirm's captain urged his horse to the front of the queue, roughly barging people out of his way, and spoke to the sergeant at the gate. The man glanced towards us, then turned and barked an order. A squad of soldiers – clad in soiled and faded livery of red-and-blue check crossed with a jet lightning bolt – rushed forward and, with much shouting and jostling, cleared the waiting people and their carts and wagons from before the gate. The sergeant waved us forward. He saluted Wirm as he rode by, and we continued unhindered into the city.

Ahead I saw a strange and macabre sight. Three makeshift gibbets had been erected beside the road. They were smaller than average, perhaps three-quarter-sized, and from each the carcass of a dog hung by its neck. A little further on were two more, and more beyond that. By the time we had gone a hundred paces we had passed the bodies of no less than a score of hanging dogs. A few were only pups, but the majority were mature beasts. Some had plainly been swinging for several days; their cadavers were pestered by flies and gave off a stomach-turning stench.

'What is happening here?' I enquired of Wirm.

'What, this? The hounds? His Excellency issued a decree that they should all, to the last one, be slaughtered and their bodies displayed. Dehut is to be wholly rid of dogs. He does not trust them.'

'Does not trust them?'

'He was menaced one day by a wolfhound. He believes that it and all its kind are in Malibeth's employ. Their extermination will teach his enemy a lesson.'

I turned from the canine corpses to stare at Wirm. His face gave away nothing. We rode on.

'My destination is Feikermun's palace,' Wirm said, nodding along a dusty street, bordered with plane trees, towards which we rode. Beneath every tree stood a forlorn figure who watched us inexpectantly. 'What of you, master Cormer? Can I be of service to you? Recommend a place to stay? Make introductions? You said you had business with somebody in Dehut. Perhaps I can help in some way?'

'As it happens, Master Wirm, my main business is with His Excellency, Feikermun of Selph.'

There was a flicker of surprise across Wirm's narrow features. A slight frown furrowed his brow and his gaze settled on my clavicle with interest. 'Is His Excellency aware?'

'No.'

'You should have said earlier, Master Cormer.'

'When I first mentioned my business in Dehut I had no idea you were so closely connected with Feikermun. But if you are able now to use your influence to gain me an audience with him I would be placed firmly in your debt.'

Wirm scratched his cheek, his gaze intent. I sensed he could barely contain his curiosity. 'If I were able to indicate in some way to His Excellency the nature of your business it might greatly facilitate matters.'

'With great respect, Master Wirm, I am able to reveal that only to Feikermun himself. My master's orders. You understand. But I wholeheartedly believe it is something in which His Excellency will have more than a passing interest.'

Wirm compressed his lips; his stare went right through me. 'Very well. I will see what I can do.'

We rode on towards Feikermun's palace. It lay at the end of the street, a three-level edifice of ancient grey stone set behind a high fortified wall. Three squat towers rose from the main building. The inspection procedure at the main gate was thorough. Though Wirm was recognized as a personage of some distinction, and accorded due respect, he was not considered above suspicion. We were permitted through into a closed yard within the gate, which was barred shut at our backs; then obliged to wait while more soldiers inspected the wagons. I

103

watched these men: they were Feikermun's notorious beasts. Their devotion to their master, their love of fighting and their lack of compassion were well known.

Eventually a second gate was opened and we passed through into the outer ward. From there we were escorted to a service yard where the wagons were to be unloaded.

'I am to go within, hopefully to speak with His Excellency, if he can spare the time,' said Wirm. 'You may accompany me if you wish. I can guarantee nothing, but if an opportunity arises I shall put your name forward.'

A sloppily dressed steward had emerged to greet Wirm, and with him leading the way we entered the palace. We passed through dingy corridors to arrive at last in a bare antechamber where a pair of silent sentries stood before a double door. The steward asked us to wait and stepped through the door. We seated ourselves on a wooden bench to one side. Wirm seemed slightly ill at ease and made no attempt to engage me in further conversation, which suited me, for I felt little inclination to speak. Presently the steward returned and called Wirm through, leaving me alone with my thoughts.

It was an hour, perhaps longer, that I waited there. The sentries remained motionless beside the double door. I was a touch nervous, intimidated by their scowling presence, but tired too after the long journey. This, combined with boredom and the close, stuffy air in the chamber, served to subdue my senses. I dozed, woke, dozed. At last I heard footsteps beyond the double door. The steward appeared and fixed me with an impersonal gaze. 'You are Master Linias Cormer?'

'I am.'

'Please come with me.'

I was led along more passages. The character of the place began to alter now. Previously I had noted a rather austere and neglected air to the palace. Stone was crumbling, paint and mortar flaking; the floors were unscrubbed and there were noticeable odours of mould and decay. The area in which I now found myself was, by contrast, well tended. The ceilings were, in the main, high and vaulted, painted in bright and often lurid colours. The walls, too, bore brightly coloured scenes, or were hung with framed paintings or rich tapestries. Splendid rugs eased the hardness of the floor, and the flagstones or terracotta pantiles beneath them, where visible, were clean and highly polished.

I took note of some of the pictures decorating the walls. They depicted scenes of battle, of unmitigated savagery rendered in spectacular detail; elsewhere were scenes of celebration, of gruesome tortures wreaked upon helpless souls, and of mass orgiastic feasts. A faint, sweet, rather cloying smell hung in the air, which grew stronger the further we walked. From somewhere ahead I could hear the strains of harsh, rather dissonant music, and somebody – more than one person – was shouting.

The steward arrived before another tall double door, this one plated in figured gold and again guarded by a pair of sentries. He opened it and ushered me through. I stepped into a scene unlike anything I had anticipated.

I was in a large, high-ceilinged hall. A banquet of sorts was in full flow. There were perhaps forty people present, at tables or upon couches, or in many cases sprawled upon rugs and cushions on the floor. Most were in various states of undress, some entirely unclothed. Several were engaged in sexual activity, in twos, threes and fours, urged on enthusiastically by those who watched. All were plainly in conditions of high intoxication and excitement. To one side a group of naked men and women were clamped or fettered to frames of iron and wood. Others took liberties with them; several bore bloody marks of violence upon their bodies.

The air was thick and smoky, heavy with the mingled odours of food, sweat, semen and incense or smouldering herbs. Tables were piled high with food and drink. A quintet of musicians occupied a low balcony at one end of the hall. They played frantically upon horns, pipes and a drum, and theirs was the sound I had heard from outside. But to call it music is an exaggeration. It was formless, tuneless, a mad cacophony. The musicians appeared as drunk as everyone else present, and while playing their instruments were also engaging in sexual acts with one another and with members of their audience who scrambled up to join them on their balcony. The noise of their instruments augmented the cries, moans and encouragements of the revellers.

Several small langurs leapt and chattered in the midst of this.

They picked at scraps of fruit, squabbled with one another, scrambled nimbly over furniture and writhing bodies, scaled the walls and chased each other along the overhead beams. There were birds, too: red thrushes and other smaller avians flying back and forth. Three peacocks strutted about, indifferent to the activities around them, while a fourth roosted on a high beam. At one end of the hall a pair of jet-black panthers were on lengths of chain attached to iron rings set in the wall. One rested on its haunches, eyeing the carnage, while its companion paced to and fro at the end of its chain, its head low.

Armed guards – more of Feikermun's beasts – were ranged around the perimeter of the hall. They leaned upon their pike-staffs and leered lasciviously at the sights before them, occasionally stepping forward to prod or poke at human flesh with the butts of their weapons, none too gently. I noted Wirm lounging at the main table, semi-clothed, his feet up. He was feeding on a leg of roast fowl, which he held in one hand; with the other he fondled the buttocks and genitalia of a young woman who was bent naked beside him. Upon the long wooden table before him were two young men of athletic build whose pale skins, streaked with spilt drinks and foods, gleamed with sweat as they disported themselves amorously among the comestibles.

In the middle of all this depravity stood a fearsome figure. He was naked, squat and lowslung and incredibly muscular, with a huge hirsute belly. His body was painted from head to toe in bizarre motifs, serpentine forms or flame-like tongues, rendered in a clash of brilliant colours. His thick lips were deep blue, his beard green and grey, his eyes encircled in white dashed with purple and red. His hair was long and wild and dyed in numerous hues. He grasped huge swollen genitals, which were stained blood-red and veined in black. He looked like a devil.

Feikermun of Selph. I had met him only once before and at that time he had been clothed and devoid, as far as I could tell, of body art. But he was unmistakable even so. With him were four beautiful, ebony-skinned servant or slave girls aged between perhaps fourteen and eighteen years. Each was naked but for a golden cincture at the waist and a series of four or five pieces of coloured linen bound around each arm. Feikermun was stamping erratically to the mad music, fondling himself, throwing back his head and shaking it wildly. He laughed loudly and unrestrainedly, roaring threats, cajolements and jeers of encouragement at those who performed for and all around him.

He emanated a disturbing aura. It was almost tangible. I experienced a familiar prickling beneath the surface of my skin. There was magic here, of an unwholesome kind. Its exact nature I could not determine but I was sure it radiated from Feikermun, and I had not sensed it when I had met him before.

Feikermun lunged forward as I stood there, my mouth agape, and waded among the bodies squirming on the cushions. He slapped, punched, pinched, pulled hair, laughing all the while. A red thrush flew past his head and he lashed out, forcing it to modify its path. Scooping up a flagon of wine he took a deep draught, then poured the remaining contents over the copulating bodies around his feet. He danced and tittered and tossed the empty flagon aside.

'Come on! Come on! More! Don't stop. No one dare stop. That's it! More for Feikermun! More! More!'

He straddled the nearest couple, settling his full weight upon the back of the man, who was uppermost. He began beating the man's buttocks hard, then reached down and grasped him by the chin and hauled him off the woman beneath. Feikermun thrust him aside and fell upon the woman. Gripping his erect red member he slid between her thighs and began to couple frantically, his eyes wild, feasting all the time on the carnage around him.

During the first moments after I entered the hall I stood in a daze just inside the doorway, taking this all in. Gathering my senses, I was not sure what to do with myself. My instinct was to withdraw quietly; I had no liking for what I saw. But that would lose me the opportunity to meet with Feikermun, perhaps indefinitely. Worse, he might consider my departure an insult. He gave no sign of being aware of my presence, but I could hardly bank on that. I had been invited to the hall, after all. Somebody – almost certainly Feikermun – must have sanctioned my invitation.

To insult Feikermun was to dice with death, so I remained as I was, hoping I might be invisible. Then I noticed that Wirm was beckoning to me, and I made my way across the hall to join him, stepping carefully between the writhing flesh and taking pains to avoid passing close to the painted demon.

'Here, sir, be seated. Delight in the spectacle. Do you desire a woman, a man? Both? What about Ollen here? She is a vision of pulchritude, is she not? And her charms are more than ample for us both.'

The woman Wirm was fondling turned her head to smile at me. Her eyes were glassy and vacant; she was plainly drugged. I assumed just about everyone else here must be likewise. I shook my head. 'Thank you, but for the moment I think I will refrain.'

'It is your choice.' Wirm was amused. I imagined he had been in this position before and derived pleasure from my discomfiture.

It seemed an age that I sat there witnessing debauchery. The most humiliating and painful indignities were served upon certain members of the assemblage, most particularly those confined upon the frames, to the extent that in one or two cases I wondered whether they could hope to survive beyond the day. And Feikermun had now taken up a multi-tongued lash set with tiny metal shards at its tips, and was again moving among the bodies, this time letting fly with brutal relish, drawing blood and cries of pain.

But worse was to come. Feikermun paused to take stock, and his eyes, travelling the hall, alighted on me. I felt myself stiffen as he straightened, his brow creasing, then lurched abruptly towards me. The four dark-skinned girls followed. He climbed up on the table in front of me and sank to one knee, crushing a pewter platter of stuffed woodcock.

'Ah, you are Wirm's conquest!'

His voice was a roar, almost ear-splitting.

'I have travelled here with Master Wirm, if that is what you mean, Lord Feikermun. I thank you for receiving me.'

Feikermun swept wide an arm. 'Do you enjoy the sport?'

'It is an extraordinary entertainment.'

'Extraordinary?' Feikermun's mad, bloodshot grey eyes bulged. 'Yes. Extraordinary! It is! It is!'

He threw back his head and bellowed with laughter, his whole

108

body shaking. I could hear the fluids slopping inside his great paunch.

The two young men who had been copulating on the table were resting now. One was on his back, his eyes closed, his arms stretched above his head, a languorous smile upon his face. The other leaned on one elbow, eating a nectarine and listening with a smile of lazy rapture to our exchange. Feikermun swung around to face them. 'D'you hear? Extraordinary! Ha-haa! Haw!'

He raised a huge bunched fist and brought it down hard into the belly of the young man on his back. The man jerked up in sudden shock and pain, and doubled over, a great *whoosh* of air escaping his lips. Goblets and plates of food flew from the table. Feikermun leapt to his feet. He struck out with the handle of his lash, knocking the nectarine from the hands of the second man.

'Get to it, bastards! Enjoy! Enjoy! Be extraordinary, or Lord Feikermun will eat your balls!'

I winced as he let fly with a sudden kick. But the second man rolled adroitly, avoiding the blow. He grabbed his partner, who was still curled up and gasping with pain, and dragged him from the table. His earlier bliss was supplanted by an expression of stark fear as he leapt upon the winded man and began to simulate the motions of sex, his eyes on Feikermun overhead.

Feikermun turned scowling back to me. 'They don't understand. Feikermun gives them everything they desire, and still they are ungrateful.'

He squatted, massaging his testicles. In the relatively short time that I had been there he had coupled three times, yet his penis was fully erect. 'Who are you?' he demanded fiercely.

'My name is Cormer. Linias Cormer, of Chol.'

'Chol. Ah, yes. Did Wirm say you had business with Feikermun?'

'If you would be so good as to allow me a short audience, Your Excellency, I believe I have something which will interest you.'

'Speak! Speak! Feikermun is before you!'

'With great respect, Your Excellency, I feel that my proposition would be better couched in private.'

109

Feikermun drew back. 'Do you menace me?'

'My lord, I assure you I do not.'

His voice became a low growl. 'Be aware, Feikermun will not be menaced.'

Into my mind sprang an image of hanging dogs. I began to mutter a further assurance, but Feikermun leaned backwards and reached down over the edge of the table. He grasped the uppermost of the two young men by his hair and dragged him to his feet. His victim stood mute and taut.

'Observe,' said Feikermun to me.

He swivelled around and jumped down from the table. Still holding the youth by the hair, he crossed the hall, kicking aside a peacock which passed in his way, to where the two panthers were chained. With a thrust of his mighty arm he shoved the youth forward. The two cats at first drew back.

'Down,' ordered Feikermun, and the young fellow dropped obediently to his knees.

The cats were on him an instant later, tentative and almost gentle at first, licking, testing, teasing with claws and teeth, drawing the first blood. He curled forward, endeavouring to cover his head, and tried to crawl away.

Feikermun stood, feet apart, watching.

'Stay!' he commanded, and to my horror the young man grew still, his eyes upon his master, his face contorted with fear and pain, while the two cats continued to maul his flesh. Feikermun turned back to me. 'See! Feikermun's people love him. They think him magnificent! They will do anything for him. Anything!'

The man's buttocks, shoulders and back were deeply lacerated now, his blood flowing freely to the floor. The panthers' motions were becoming more determined as their lust for his flesh grew. He lay forward on his belly, covering himself as best he could, crying with pain and terror, but made no effort to crawl away until Feikermun at last screamed, 'You may go! It is Feikermun's word!'

Now the man began to drag himself towards freedom. The cats growled, trying to prevent him. One climbed upon his back. His body was flayed meat now, and I sensed he had little strength left. Feikermun, with great bellows of laughter, strode

110

forward and began striking savagely at the panthers with his lash. They drew back, spitting and yowling. The young man crawled beyond the reach of their chains and lay still. Feikermun walked over to him. 'You did well.'

He lowered himself on to all fours over the poor wretch, his eyes on the blood that streamed from his wounds. Then he inclined his head and slowly began to lick his victim's flank, his shoulder, his neck. He raised his head, stretching his mouth wide and spreading his arms, clenching his fists in transport. 'The blood! Oh, the blood!'

Feikermun slowly stood. 'Take him away.'

He swaggered back towards me. 'You see? Feikermun will not be menaced.'

I nodded. 'I assure you, Lord Feikermun, I come with only goodwill.'

'You do not look like a fool. Now, your business— But wait . . .' He paused. His eyes rolled upwards and his jaw dropped open. I could see his tongue swaying from side to side in the red cavern of his mouth. It slipped forth and he licked his bloodstained lips.

'Feikermun thirsts!' he yelled, climbing on to the table again.

Two male attendants rushed forward carrying a gleaming silver two-handled bowl and a ceremonial knife. One of the four dark-skinned slave girls dropped to her knees on the floor before Feikermun. She bared her arm and an attendant removed one of the coloured sashes that bound it. I noted several small wounds along the veins of her inner forearm. The silver bowl was placed beneath her outstretched arm and the attendant drew the shining blade across her flesh. Her blood, dark and rich, coursed forth and spilled into the bowl.

'Be quick,' shouted Feikermun, his eyes upon the bowl, then the woman, then the bowl. 'Give it to Feikermun!'

The slave had her eyes closed. She was beginning to shiver. Her blood had almost filled the bowl. Feikermun watched her feverishly, the tip of his tongue poised quivering on his lower lip.

'Now!' he declared. The bowl was whisked away and passed up to him. He brought it to his lips and tipped it back, arching his spine and drinking deeply as the young woman's wound was bound and she, almost fainting, was carried away.

Feikermun closed his eyes. He let fall the empty bowl. 'Aah, the blood. The *Source*.' He let out a long, ecstatic sigh. 'Soon . . . Soon, the power. Almost . . . Almost . . .'

His eyes half-opened and he drew his thick forearm across his mouth, wiping the blood from his lips and whiskers. He lowered his gaze until it settled drunkenly on me, his head swaying. 'Not now,' he slurred. 'We will talk later. Now is time for indulgence.'

He turned, stepping down off the table, and staggered away. The dishevelled steward who had guided me to the hall now came forward and spoke in my ear. 'You are to remain in the palace. Your chamber has been prepared. I shall show you the way as soon as you are ready.'

'I am ready now,' I said.

The steward had been about to withdraw. He seemed surprised. 'Are you sure?'

'Quite.' I believed, and hoped, that for the time being at least I was forgotten. Feikermun stood with his hands on his hips in the middle of the floor, observing the antics all around him.

'What next?' he called as I rose from my seat. He swung around and his gaze passed over me, and for a moment my heart fell. I believed he was about to call upon me, even demand my participation. But something else had claimed his attention. 'Ah yes!' he roared. 'The hogs and asses. Bring on the hogs and asses!'

As I left through the entrance by which I had come a portal was opened at the other end of the hall and a dozen or so squealing pigs and a quartet of donkeys were herded in. They were driven towards the mass of naked bodies in the middle of the hall. My last sight was of Feikermun bounding across the floor, scattering a pair of grey langurs and howling like a demented banshee as he hurled himself among the animals.

9

'Yo.'

'I am here, Master.'

'I must be brief. I require you to carry a message to the *Zan-Chassin*.'

'I am ready, Master.'

'Alert the Chariness. Tell her I have made contact. The situation is unpredictable. I have reason to believe the subject is on the verge of power, but I do not know what form. My opinion is that he is out of control. There is conflict in the city; I have not been able to determine its extent or full nature. I seek information on two men. The eel-trader, Wirm of Guling Mire, who is a close ally of Feikermun. And a man called Vecco, who was Wirm's guest. I am looking for connections. Have you got all that?'

'I have.'

'Then go, now, with all speed.'

'I am gone, Master.'

It was a calculated risk. I gambled that I would not be under close surveillance so early on. Feikermun's distractions would surely prevent his thinking clearly about anything other than his immediate gratification. I took it as given that I would be watched, but to scan for magic was another matter. And, as the Chariness had pointed out, a summoning of an entity does not leave the same residual aura as the casting of a rapture. As long as I was brief – and I had been – I had good hopes of remaining undetected.

I had been housed in a single-roomed apartment on the second level of Feikermun's palace. Somewhere below me the orgy continued. From time to time I heard the sounds of carousing,

113

shouts and cries, the braying of asses, the squeal of pigs, the mad music of the five drunken musicians, and Feikermun's demented roars. It had been hours now. There had been a lull for a time, and I'd thought the revels must all be over; but a short while later they had resumed. Now it was dark outside. From my window I could see, across the sprawling town, the glows of the fires I had spied earlier from the hill road. There appeared to be three currently ablaze, quite close together, about half a mile northeast of the palace. From time to time, when the din from below diminished sufficiently, I heard distant shouts carried on the light breeze, as of numbers of men in conflict.

I had been brought food and had eaten alone. I did not know where Jaktem and Illan were. The steward who had escorted me to my chamber had advised me not to leave until summoned. I decided to take him at his word so, having dismissed Yo, I prepared for sleep, there being little else to do.

It was about midnight, I would guess, that I was woken by a moving light in my room and the realization that I was no longer alone. A hand-held lamp glowed; I made out the form of a human figure moving towards my bed. Beyond, I saw a second figure bulking in the open door, silhouetted against the dim yellowish light of the passage outside. The shape of the head suggested a helmet, and I took him to be a soldier.

I reached silently for my dagger in its sheath beneath my pillow. The figure with the lamp moved closer to my bed, then halted.

'Sir, are you awake?'

'Jaktem?'

'No, sir, it is I.'

The lamp lifted slightly to illuminate an unfamiliar face.

'Who? Who are you?'

'I, sir, who brought you here.'

Gradually the blear of sleep passed from my eyes and brain and I recognized the sallow features of Feikermun's steward. 'What do you want?'

'You are summoned into The Excellency's presence.'

'What, now? It is the middle of the night.'

'That is so.'

I sat up on the edge of my bed. 'He expects me now, not in the morning?'

'That is correct, sir.'

I ran my hands over my face. 'Give me a moment to wash and dress.'

'I shall wait outside, sir. I would advise a degree of haste. The Excellency does not expect to be kept waiting.'

Moments later I was ushered into apartments on the palace's third level. Feikermun of Selph awaited me in the company of two cronies and Wirm. The Excellency lounged upon a plushly upholstered couch, his short powerful legs up, one laid loosely along the couch, the other crooked, the knee resting against the couch back. He was garbed in a slack-fitting open-fronted robe of rich purple silk, loosely sashed at the waist. It had fallen open enough to reveal him to be naked beneath, and still painted, though the pigments had smudged and smeared. He appeared to have made some attempt to clean his face, but the result was simply a ghastly blotch of random colour which accentuated his unhuman appearance.

Wirm reclined upon the floor before a blazing hearth on a rug of pure white bearskin, his thin, pale fingers tracing the rim of a golden wine goblet. Another man sat upon a carved wooden chair nearby. He was a short, bulbous fellow of middle age, with a shining dome that was completely shorn of hair. I believed I had seen him earlier at the orgy, administering torment to a man and woman confined on frames.

The other stranger was tall and sinewy, aged perhaps twenty-five, with long brown hair and flamboyant though somewhat unkempt moustaches. He wore a dented leather breastplate and had a sword buckled at his waist. His face was pitted with the scars of pox, and a dark leather patch covered one eye. There was a sense of brooding energy about him and his mouth held a cruel twist. He looked every bit the brigand leader or mercenary captain.

Upon rugs to one side three of Feikermun's naked slave girls lay sleeping in postures of arousing abandon.

'Cormer of Chol!' Feikermun raised a muscular arm to wave me in. 'Come! Be seated! Join the illustrious Feikermun and his comrades! Drink!'

115

I bowed, and approached. A naked servant boy ran forward to take up a gold pitcher and pour amber wine into a goblet. I took the goblet and seated myself cross-legged in the place Feikermun indicated, on a stuffed, tasselled velvet pouffe a little way before him. Wirm was to one side, the bald torturer to the other; the one-eyed fighter was standing next to Feikermun's couch.

I observed Feikermun, and was again aware of the vague, disturbing aura of uncertain magic that he emanated.

'You are comfortable here? Everything is to your liking?' he enquired.

'Very much so, my lord. Thank you.'

'Good. You are Feikermun's guest. Feikermun intends that all who sojourn here are treated in proper and fitting manner.'

'You are most gracious. There – *ahem!* – is one small matter, if I might mention it.'

'Yes?'

'I came here with two companions. I have seen nothing of them since our arrival. I was wondering what has become of them.'

'Ah, yes,' said Feikermun. 'They have been executed.'

I was struck dumb. Feikermun stared at me for some moments without expression, then his cheeks puffed out, his eyes popped almost out of his head, his shoulders shook and he was convulsed with a great bellow of laughter. Beside me Wirm sniggered. The bald fellow rocked noiselessly. The fighter stood tall and impassive, observing me darkly with his single eye.

Feikermun laughed uproariously. He beat the back of his couch and clutched his shuddering belly. He rolled back and kicked his feet in the air, and the tears streamed down his cheeks. I remained silent and bewildered, not knowing what might be true.

At length Feikermun's fit began to ebb. He raised himself on one elbow and leaned towards me, but no sooner had he focused upon my face than he broke up again. I waited unhappily, my heart in my mouth, as he gave vent to shrieks and bawls of helpless laughter.

'Put to death,' wheezed Feikermun when he had regained sufficient control of himself. He wiped the tears from his eyes, further smudging the madness of colours upon his face. 'Sent packing.'

I at last found my voice and said, my mouth suddenly dry, 'Might I ask on what grounds?'

'Didn't like the look of the bastards. Didn't like the reek of their sweat or the colour of their piss.'

Again I was lost for words. I could only keep my fury suppressed as the instinct for self-preservation took over.

'And they knew torment,' Feikermun continued relentlessly. 'Theirs were deaths they will not quickly forget!'

He laughed uproariously again, beating his thigh, then ceased suddenly and fixed me with a piercing stare.

'What do you think you should do about it?' he asked, and there was no mistaking the taunting challenge in his voice.

I fought again for my tongue, and my voice shook as I spoke. 'Sir, I can say only, if the deed has truly been done, that I am shocked and appalled. These were good men who had committed no crime, and I would wish to register my outrage.'

' "*If* the deed has been done"?' Feikermun frowned darkly, his voice rising. 'Are you doubting the word of Feikermun?'

It was impossible; the man was wholly insane. I struggled to control my anger. 'I say only, again, that they were innocent of any crime against you.'

'How can you know that? Were you party to their every thought, their every action? Are you intimate with the enemies of Feikermun?' He leaned towards me. 'How long have you known these scoundrels?'

I shook my head in exasperation. 'A short while only, but—'

'Then you can know nothing!'

'Your Excellency, these men were in my employ. They were my responsibility.'

I half-expected that at any moment Feikermun would give the order to end my life, or that he would simply slaughter me himself on the spot, with blade or bare hands. Such was his state that anything could happen. I endeavoured to choose my words and tone carefully, but suspected that my manner or responses would actually have scant bearing on events. Feikermun would murder on a whim, with neither sound reason nor plan.

117

'Then you are an irresponsible fellow to allow such misfortune to befall your employees.' He leaned back and picked a sweetmeat from a tray beside him, stuffed it into his mouth and chomped noisily. He offered one to me. 'They are quite delicious.'

I declined as graciously as I could. Feikermun tensed slightly and let out a long, loud fart, then grunted in satisfaction. 'Bondo,' he said to the bald man, 'what *did* become of this man's two companions?'

'I have no knowledge, Excellency. I would imagine they were quartered among the servants. Do you wish me to enquire?'

'Later, not now. Have them moved into a chamber adjacent to our guest. Would that suit you, Master Cormer?'

'They are not cadavers, then?'

'Manifestly not. At least, not by Feikermun's orders. Feikermun sported with you. He enjoyed the jest. Your face . . . to use your own words, "an extraordinary entertainment".' Feikermun grinned, swallowed the tidbit, farted again. 'Now, you spoke earlier of business.'

I took a few moments to calm my thoughts. I was relieved, angry, and still not entirely certain what to believe. Until I saw Jaktem and Illan before me I would be haunted by the possibility of their deaths. I said, 'Lord Feikermun, with great respect I would emphasize the personal nature of my proposition. You might prefer that it is not voiced in company, other than the company of those you would trust implicitly.'

Feikermun eyed me fiercely. I sensed that his joviality had passed. He said gruffly, 'Just speak, man.'

'Very well. I have at my disposal a quantity of the rare visionary root, sacred to the Tanakipi peoples, known as *gidsha*. This root has been acquired from a particular source and has been cultivated and prepared in ways unknown to others. The result is a purer form of *gidsha* than is normally found. Its potency is significantly increased and its mind-altering properties enhanced.'

Feikermun inclined his head and torso towards me. His eyes were wide and lit with a cupid gleam. 'Where did you get it?'

'It is the property of my master in Chol.'

'Where does he get it?'

118

'I regret, Your Excellency, it is not within my scope to answer that.'

'I could force the answer from you.'

'No torture known to man or god could draw that information from my tongue, for I do not know it. My master alone has access to the supply, and he does not reveal his secrets to humble servants such as I. He has sent me to you, having an understanding of your interest, with a small sample of the root for you to try. If it is to your liking – and my master believes fully that it will be – then I may establish terms with you whereby it will be made available to you whensoever and in whatever quantities you desire.'

'Do you have the sample here?'

'Indeed I do.' I reached into my bag and brought forth a small quantity of the pale, lightly hirsute root. 'I would emphasize that it is not ready for ingestion at this moment. A few final preparations are required.'

'Taking how long?'

'A matter of no more than an hour or two.'

'And are you conversant with the techniques of preparation?'

'I am.'

Feikermun tugged at his beard, his eyes upon the *gidsha*. He glanced over at Wirm, then back at me. 'The potency is increased, you say'

'That is so. I am assured that the visionary and ecstatic states it promotes are beyond compare. My master is satisfied that, once you have tasted the experience this root offers, you will never again turn to its paler sister.'

'And then your master plans to extort money from Feikermun to maintain the supply?'

'Not so, Your Excellency. My master seeks only to please you and establish good relations. The sample I have brought is yours without charge. If, as my master believes, you are then keen to obtain more, it shall be at a mutually agreed price, no higher than the price you currently pay, whatever that may be. It is for you to declare.'

Again Feikermun glanced at Wirm. Then he narrowed his eyes in thought. 'Is this what I have been waiting for?' he murmured. He turned to me. 'It is good. Let us try your root,

Cormer of Chol. Bring it to me this evening at sunset. We shall test the veracity of your claims.'

I bowed my head. 'It shall be so, Your Excellency.'

I realized at that moment that a newcomer had entered the room. In the dimness of a shadowed corner behind Feikermun stood a woman, watching us silently. She was of slender and shapely build, slightly above average in height, with long, lustrous golden hair, and was garbed in a pale grey robe which fell to her feet. Her age I could not determine. She was youthful, yet had a quality of maturity and womanliness which caused me to wonder. Her beauty was exceptional and extraordinary. She was quite possibly the most attractive woman I had ever laid eyes on. I stared, for the moment mesmerized by the sight of her. There was something about her – I could not say what – some entrancing, almost angelic quality. I felt that she gazed right at me and into me, that her gaze penetrated my outer self and alighted upon my soul. Had she spoken then, had she asked something of me, anything at all, I would have obeyed her. I knew in that instant of seeing her that I could deny her nothing.

I rose, involuntarily, my whole being arrested by the sight of her.

'What is it, Cormer of Chol?' demanded Feikermun. He shifted to stare over the back of his couch in the direction of my gaze.

The loud, grating timbre of his voice shook me partly from my reverie. I felt myself suddenly embarrassed and fearful, yet I could not bear to take my eyes from the newcomer. 'Your Excellency, I am sorry. Please, I do apologize. I am simply enchanted by the beauty of this lady. I have never seen anyone of such exquisite features. Please, I do beg you to forgive my impertinence.'

All were now looking towards the woman. Feikermun was agitated. He sat up erect, looked back at me, then to her again. 'You see her?'

'Here before us, aye.'

He rose abruptly to his feet. 'What do you see? Tell me? What is it?'

'The lady, my lord. I see the lady, that is all.'

'Where, curse your soul? Where do you see her?'

I felt my unease mounting. I glanced at the others. This seemed like madness. 'This lady, Lord Feikermun. She who has just entered, who stands in the corner there. It is she I refer to.'

'In this corner?' Feikermun moved around the couch and stepped towards her, but he halted after only a couple of paces. 'Here?'

He waved a hand vaguely in her direction, and as he did so the woman faded before my eyes. I blinked, stared. There were only shadows where she had been. 'Lord Feikermun, she is gone.'

'Gone? Hah!' Feikermun threw up his arms and stomped quickly in a circle, his face to the ceiling, grimacing savagely. Then he wheeled on me. 'But you saw her? You saw her? Describe her!'

I described the woman I had seen. Feikermun's agitation grew, yet it seemed mingled with an uneasy satisfaction, as though my words had confirmed something for him. He turned to Bondo. 'You saw her not?'

The bald man shook his head. Feikermun addressed the tall fighter. 'Nor you, Hircun? Wirm?'

Both men signified no. 'Yet that is she, as Feikermun has described her to you, is it not?'

'It is,' said Bondo, and looked curiously at me.

'My lord, did you see her just now?' Hircun asked.

Feikermun shook his shaggy head. He pointed aggressively at me. 'But you, Cormer, tell me again.'

I repeated my description.

'But she has gone now?'

'She has. Lord Feikermun, may I ask, what is this? Who is this woman who has the ability to appear and vanish like this?'

He did not answer me but paced back and forth, his head bowed in an attitude of deep thought. 'He has seen her. He has seen her,' he muttered to himself. 'What does this mean?'

He ceased pacing and glared at me. 'Are you in league with my enemies?'

'My lord, I am not. Be assured! Your enemies are unknown to me.'

He paced on. 'What can it mean? What can it mean?'

Just then there was a loud banging at the chamber door. It

was opened briskly by a sentry, and a young officer of the guard strode in. He gave a quick bow, then hastened to whisper in the ear of the one-eyed Hircun. Hircun in turn stepped forward to speak softly to Feikermun.

'Ah, the witch!' Feikermun expostulated. He aimed a minatory finger at the newcomer. 'Back, then! Keep the enemy contained. Your life and the lives of your children depend on it.' As the officer departed Feikermun spoke to his general. 'Well, Hircun, your assessment?'

'It is pleasing news, Excellency, although we have lost some of our men. Malibeth's fighters have advanced as we predicted they would. They have occupied a couple of streets in no great number and we have cut off their retreat. If I act quickly now with two score of your best marauders at my side, I will have the enemies' heads within an hour of first light.'

'Yes! Excellent! And Feikermun will accompany you. Let the men know that Feikermun fights among them.' He rubbed his hands together gleefully. 'Yes, let us indulge in a little light slaughter. My beasts shall have their day. And then soon, by all the devils, I shall make the mad Bitch rue the moment she first dreamed of opposing Feikermun!'

He turned and stormed from the chamber. The fighter Hircun followed.

I remained as I was, dazed. One of the dark slave girls stirred in her sleep and murmured something. I spoke to Wirm, who had risen from his rug. 'What is happening here?'

Wirm moved close to me, his normally pale cheeks dark, his mouth taut and bitterly twisted. His small eyes burned into me, focused on the vicinity of my cheek. 'Be warned, Cormer of Chol, you are meddling where you cannot be tolerated. Heed my advice carefully: leave here now and do not return. Ever. Fail and you will know the price.'

He snatched up his cloak, which lay on the floor beside him, and with a heated glance at Bondo left the chamber.

Bondo eyed me with harsh and amused interest.

'I am confounded,' I said. 'I understand nothing here. What is the matter with Wirm?'

Bondo puffed out his cheeks and gave a mirthless chuckle. 'You have seen what you cannot see; you have done what you should not do. Master Wirm is gravely piqued.' He patted his belly with both hands and rocked for a moment on the balls of his feet. 'Ah, well, this is the way of it.'

Then he too gathered his robes about him and strode from the chamber.

IT SEEMED LIKE madness. I felt I was losing my mind. What in the world had happened in Feikermun's chamber?

It was as though my consciousness had been tampered with, as if my mind had been hoisted high and shaken hard, twisted, bent, inverted until it had virtually disintegrated and lay now in fragments; spinning, twirling tatters and shreds. There was nothing to grasp hold of here. Everything felt dangerous and insubstantial, as friable as charred paper to the touch. I had been in Dehut just a few short hours, yet I had undergone such a relentless assault as to leave my senses reeling. The entire place and everyone in it seemed to be without reason.

I had been escorted back to my chamber on the second floor. I sat now upon my bed. My thoughts raced.

The woman, the strange apparition, who was she? Why had no one but I seen her? Feikermun had known who she was. He was mightily perturbed by my description of her. Plainly she had appeared to him on at least one other occasion. Yet he had not seen her tonight.

What was happening here?

Malibeth? Could she be an enchantress? Had she the ability to project herself, or an image of herself, through space? I could not say. As far as I was aware I had never laid eyes on Malibeth.

News of movements by Malibeth's fighters had come hard on the heels of the apparition's vanishing, but that did not necessarily imply a direct connection. But, if not Malibeth, who could she be?

I harked back, wishing to recollect my exact feelings when the woman had first appeared – that is, when I had first become conscious of her presence. It was possible that she had been 'there' for some time before I perceived her. My first sight of her

124

had completely disarmed me, thrown my senses into disarray. I felt that I knew her, yet did not know how. Her extraordinary beauty and the sheer power of her presence had drawn me to her. I could have wept, so strong was the effect she wreaked upon my emotions. I was aware of nothing but her, her face, her strange and powerful immanence. I was reeling.

She had worn a slight smile upon her perfect lips; enigmatic, beatific, and yet weighed with inexpressible sorrow. I had felt rather than seen the aura that she emanated. I had never before experienced such intensity. She had reached inside me and touched in the places where my most hidden and secretive self resided. I would have done anything for her, anything at all.

And then she had gone.

And I did not know who she was.

I did not know who she was.

Just for a moment I questioned whether the whole incident might have been set up. In truth, the others had all seen her. Feikermun had played a ruse in which they were each complicit, though I could think of no reason. But Feikermun needed no reason, other than his own perverse amusement. From the moment I had first entered and sat down he had been playing with me, delighting in my helplessness when he told me he had executed my men, revelling in the power he held over me. It was in his character to play such games.

But no. The woman had not withdrawn into the shadows or passed from the room. She had faded before my eyes. Could Feikermun command such magical effects?

I did not want it to be so. I realized this with a poignant tightening of the muscles of my heart. Not only did I fear what it would mean if Feikermun possessed such abilities, I could not bear the thought of her being a creation of his, or of anybody's. I wanted her . . . I wanted her to *be*. A profound, soul-wrenching sense of loss had begun to pervade my being, that she had come and I had glimpsed her and then she had gone.

For some time I was unaware of anything but my bewilderment and yearning.

At last I forced myself to look again at everything else that had taken place in Feikermun's chamber. I considered the conflict in Stonemarker which had sent Feikermun rushing to the fray. Neither he nor his general, Hircun, had shown particular concern over the news the young officer had brought. They seemed in control of the situation and went to battle convinced of victory. In their eyes Malibeth could be beaten.

It was plain that I would have to find out more about the conflict, investigate Malibeth and the forces she commanded. The indications from where I stood signalled that Feikermun was on the verge of securing power – a disturbing thought. And what about the third leader in this divided city? There had been no mention yet of him. The mystery of the Golden Lamb held good.

Now I wondered about Wirm and his bizarre behaviour during the final moments in Feikermun's chamber. What could have occasioned his sudden hostility? Wirm was not a friend, nor by any stretch of the imagination a man I would trust, but he had until that moment, presumably for his own ends, been genial and cooperative, even helpful. Like everything else his changed attitude made no sense but simply compounded the overall madness of this place and my situation.

I tried to link Wirm's volte-face with what had occurred. Was he angered by my vision? Did he know something about the mysterious woman? Had he taken offence at my being the only person privileged to see her. Or could it have been the news of the conflict that had troubled him? Surely it had to be one of these, yet the answer still eluded me.

I thought hard. We had spoken of nothing else during my audience with Feikermun, except for the condition of my two men, Jaktem and Illan, and the business of the *gidsha*.

The *gidsha*!

. . . By Great Moban's Knee, how could I have missed it? Suddenly it was so obvious!

I sat up, for I had been lying in bed in the forlorn hope of sleeping, and I let the fact of it hammer into me. Wirm was Feikermun's supplier not just of Twiner flesh: *he brought Feikermun the gidsha root!* And I had blundered in like an oaf in a blindfold and had whipped away his trade right there in front of him. No wonder his fury! I was fortunate that he had not stabbed me on the spot.

126

I struck my forehead hard with the heel of my hand, berating myself. I had made an enemy of Wirm here in the one place where his assistance had become almost invaluable. What a fool! What a perfect mooncalf!

How would he respond? Almost certainly he would get rid of me if he could. Would he risk it here, in Dehut? Yes, if circumstances arose such that suspicion did not fall upon him, but I did not think he would risk offending Feikermun. He would attempt to turn Feikermun against me, which might not be difficult to do. All depended upon the *gidsha*. I prayed that it was as potent and effective as the Chariness had promised. If it failed to impress Feikermun I would be finished. But, if Feikermun approved, then Wirm's influence would diminish – though not wholly, of course, for he still had his elver flesh with which to court Feikermun's favour. Whichever way it went, I had now turned Wirm into a very dangerous enemy.

I had a brief vision of Vecco's fate. I shuddered and made a mental note never to return to Guling Mire.

Lying back again, I invoked calming techniques to still my mind. I remained concerned over Jaktem's and Illan's condition and could only hope that they were, as Feikermun had eventually said, still alive. But anything was possible here; I could be sure of nothing other than that one fact: anything was possible.

It was still the middle of the night and there was little I could do but wait for morning, so with difficulty I slept. That is, I think I slept. But at some point I found myself awake and staring across the darkened chamber. She was there. There was no light, yet I could see her perfectly. And she stood as before, motionless, watching me.

'Who are you?'

'I cannot tell you.'

'Tell me.'

'You will not understand.'

'You must have a name?'

I rose from the bed and stood in my nightshirt before her. I was enthralled by her presence, and waves of emotion rocked me as I gazed upon her. She smiled and shook her head slightly. 'You cannot know. Not now.'

127

I stepped forward. I wanted to take her in my arms, to hold her. I was completely gripped by the spell she had cast over me. I felt that I knew her, and yet she was a stranger. I loved her, and was afraid. Never before had I felt this way. I was helpless before her, wanting, longing for her, but not to possess her, not even to make love to her. Just simply to be with her, and to know, to understand.

But she raised a warning hand and moved back. 'Do not touch. We cannot.'

'Why?'

She shook her head. 'You would not understand.'

Despite her words I reached out and grasped her hand. I had to know, was she ghost or flesh? The hand was warm and soft in mine. For some reason this shocked me. I think I had expected nothingness.

She pulled away quickly. 'No more!'

'Please tell me who you are!'

'You must come. Enter the Citadel.'

'What?'

'When you are invited, though it may seem an invitation to your death, do not be afraid. Do not spurn us. Enter the Citadel, seeking. I will be there. There your questions can be answered.'

'Where is the Citadel?'

'Just be aware . . . Be aware.'

She was fading. How? If she were flesh . . .

'Wait! Don't leave!'

'Please come . . . I will wait for you there.'

She was gone. The chamber was in darkness. I groped my way back to bed and lay awake in a fever.

Later I wondered whether it could have been a dream.

With the dawn I was up and pacing my room. My eyes were swollen and heavy through lack of sleep. My brain seethed with unanswered questions. A young woman brought hot water, soap and towels. I asked if I were permitted to leave the chamber; she shrugged and replied that she did not know.

When she had gone I opened the door. There was no guard posted there, though one stood a little way down the corridor. I stepped out; his eyes flickered my way but he neither made a move nor spoke. I went on down the corridor, away from the guard. Ahead of me a door opened. A tall man came into the corridor.

'Jaktem!'

'Master Cormer! We were told you were close by.'

'Where is Illan?'

'Gone into the town, at first light.'

'Why?'

'To see what there is to be seen. I am to meet him later.'

'You have not been ill-treated?'

'No, sir.'

'I am glad to see you again.'

'Where do you go, Master Cormer?'

'I am not entirely sure. I wished to clarify my status. I thought I might be confined to my chamber, but that appears not to be the case.'

'Master Cormer, this is a strange place. There is madness here.'

'Aye, you are right. But why do you say that?'

'Remember yesterday, when we rode into Dehut? The dogs?'

'The hanging corpses? I do.'

'Well, later we – Illan and I – walked a little way outside the palace. We passed people standing beneath trees. One man or woman or child beneath each tree that we passed. They appeared to be doing nothing, but after a while, when we had seen so many, I asked one why she was there. She told me it was to gather any leaves that fell. Feikermun has given orders that no leaf must lie upon the ground, upon pain of death to his citizens. He believes that his enemies, seeing leaves upon the ground, will take it as a sign of slackness and inefficiency. They will think him weak and distracted, and will attack in force to overthrow him. Hence every tree in Feikermun's quarter of the city must have someone beneath it to pick up any leaf that drops from its branches. The task is tedious, especially at this time of year when few leaves fall. Yet foot patrols pass frequently to ensure that his will is adhered to.'

I nodded. I remembered the inexpectant faces the previous day, gazing from the shade of trees as we rode towards the palace. 'It does not surprise me. Nothing does, anymore.'

Later in the morning I left Feikermun's palace with Jaktem and went into the town. We made our way at a leisurely pace along half-deserted streets, past hanging dogs and doleful tree-attendants, until we reached the central square where Culmet's Bazaar was situated. It was here, I recalled, that Inbuel m' Anakastii had met and spoken with the man he had taken to be me. I was no closer to solving that mystery nor, I realized, had I learned anything about the enigmatic note delivered to me from the unknown Sermilio.

A good number of traders, peddlers and merchants were setting up booths and stalls and opening their shops, though not as many as on previous occasions I had been here. I saw several faces I recognized, but no one, of course, recognized me. The atmosphere of the marketplace was somewhat subdued. The citizens appeared cowed and anxious, and there was soldiery present in some number – that is, if one could properly term Feikermun's men 'soldiers'. They fought for him, it was true, and did his bidding with relish and gusto. But they were thugs with little or no formal military training; lethal bullies who lived for blood and took pleasure in the suffering they could inflict.

Above the buildings to our northeast, smoke could still be seen rising into the blue sky. I thought it seemed less than on the previous day, but whether that was due to the fires having been fought down or the smoke's being dispersed by the fresh breeze the morning had brought I could not tell.

In an inn beside the square we met Illan. I ordered breakfast for the three of us and Illan told us of his intelligence-gathering activities. For the most part he had been endeavouring to learn more about the fighting at the border between Feikermun's domain and that of Malibeth. His understanding was that Malibeth's fighters had broken through Feikermun's lines to reclaim an area of disputed territory consisting of two or three streets and their surrounding buildings. Unbeknown to Malibeth, Feikermun's men had permitted her troops to advance into this area and had then moved in from two directions to cut off their retreat. Thirty or forth of Malibeth's men had found themselves trapped. With the first light Feikermun's beasts, led by Feikermun himself, had swarmed into the area. The battle was fierce and bloody, and still raging when Illan had withdrawn in order to rendezvous at the inn with Jaktem. But in Illan's mind there was little doubt of the outcome.

'They are fighting house-to-house, and it's a hazardous business. But Malibeth's men are divided into small isolated pockets. Feikermun is cutting them off one by one, then moving in hard for the slaughter from all directions. His tactic is to set light to the buildings in which they hide, to force them out. He has taken few losses, but the corpses of his enemies have been laid out in the road for all to see. It will soon be over, I think.'

'Is he taking prisoners?'

'I saw no evidence of that. Any who tried to surrender – and there were not many, from what I could see – were hacked down on the spot.'

His account accorded with what I had gathered from the meeting in Feikermun's chamber during the night.

'Have you learned anything else?'

'Little of value. The stalemate appears to endure between Malibeth and Feikermun. If anything, Feikermun has slightly gained the upper hand. But something seems to be brewing. Those I spoke to are convinced that Feikermun is on the verge of a breakthrough.'

'In what form?'

'It is hard to be precise. People are too afraid or too ignorant to say much. But I have heard it said by more than one person that Feikermun is about to become a god.'

I sat back, pushing aside the plate which I had cleaned of bacon and bread. 'By what means is he to achieve this apotheosis?'

'I do not know.'

'Do either of you know of a place called the Citadel?'

Both men shook their heads.

'Could it be Malibeth's fortress?' I wondered.

'Malibeth has no fortress, nor a permanent headquarters,' said Illan. 'For safety she keeps on the move, using a number of houses in her quarter.'

'The Golden Lamb, then?'

'The Golden Lamb bases himself in a well fortified barracks

near the western edge of town. I have never heard it referred to by that name.'

'Is this Citadel in Dehut, Master Cormer?' enquired Jaktem.

'I had assumed so, but perhaps I was wrong.' I supped thoughtfully at my ale. 'What can you tell me of the Golden Lamb?'

The two men exchanged brief glances. Illan said, 'Very little. He is securely ensconced in the Waterstrike district in the west, and his domain borders both Feikermun's and Malibeth's. Since initially establishing himself there he seems to have taken part in little offensive activity, but has strengthened his defences to guard against incursions by either of the other two. His strategy, it would appear, is to wait, perhaps in the hope that Feikermun and Malibeth will weaken one another sufficiently for him to move against them.'

'An unsound strategy, if what you say is true and Feikermun is about to attain the status and power of a god.'

Illan frowned and nodded to himself.

'You know nothing of the Golden Lamb's identity, or whence he has come?'

'He keeps himself shrouded in mystery. I have been told that he wears a mask or veil at all times. He commands disciplined troops in good number, and his area of the city is the least troubled. He maintains order, but through the implementation of discipline and law rather than terror.'

I finished my drink. 'I would like to visit the area of conflict in Stonemarker. Can you take me there?'

'Aye. I know of a good vantage point from which you can view almost the entire scene of battle. If Malibeth's troops have not yet been conquered you can observe for yourself Feikermun's methods.'

As we left the inn I heard shouting and cheering. A crowd was gathering beside the street at one side of the square. Curious, I pushed my way through the press of bodies to try and see what had drawn them. I arrived to find soldiers cordoning off the street, and a moment later several figures on horseback came into view.

First came a squad of six men-at-arms, ensuring the way was clear. The next rider was Feikermun of Selph. He was mounted on a dappled-grey stallion, and sat straight in the saddle, his head held high. He wore a ferocious grin on his face and his eyes blazed with triumph. Devoid of body art now, he was garbed in shining red armour. In one hand he held a sword aloft. Skewered on its tip was the head of a man, blood dripping from the ragged tatters of flesh and gristle which hung from its crudely severed neck.

Behind Feikermun came his one-eyed general, Hircun, and another officer. They too held swords aloft displaying the same grisly trophies, and behind them marched Feikermun's beasts, a column of about forty in four ranks. The first thirty or so bore pikes, upon each of which was mounted a human head. The remaining men carried pieces of armour, weapons, clothing, and in a few cases the severed hands of their slain enemies. They whooped and sang as they marched, shaking the trophies at the crowds.

The people cheered as Feikermun pranced past, but I noticed that the loudest cheers were prompted by the soldiers lining the route, who roughly poked and prodded the townsfolk with the butts of their pikes to invoke the desired response. As the gruesome cavalcade passed by I turned and walked back into the square. 'Plainly you were right,' I said to Illan. 'The day belongs to Feikermun.'

We made our way into nearby Stonemarker and the scene of battle which Feikermun had just left. The smoke thickened in the air as we drew closer. A number of fires belched smoke skywards, where much of it was being borne off to the east by the breeze. Illan stopped at a long two-storey building which had a low wooden tower projecting from the roof at one end. At his knocking a man appeared from within. They spoke briefly in low tones and I saw Illan slip the man a coin. We were admitted. The man, having closed the door behind us, made off into the depths of the building.

Illan led us through an empty storage area to where a flight of wooden stairs led up into the tower.

'It was from here that I witnessed the battle this morning,' he said as we climbed to a small room at the top of the tower. Narrow windows gave views in four directions over Dehut. The north-facing window looked out on to the killing ground. Illan pointed out the area where the battle had been fought. 'That street there, beyond the junction, and two others on either side of it. You can still see what's left of the bodies of Malibeth's men.'

There were a number of burned-out buildings in the area he indicated. Two still burned, smoke and flame pouring into the sky. In the middle of the road decapitated corpses had been laid out in neat rows. Several dogs hung from makeshift gibbets or the eaves of buildings, and here and there isolated figures were to be seen standing idly beneath trees. The scene was macabre and bizarre.

Further away I could see barricades erected at the ends of streets. They were constructed of wood and stones, items of furniture such as tables, chairs, pallets, bedsteads – presumably brought from the surrounding buildings – and barrels, boards, upturned carts, uprooted fencing, sacks of sand or earth . . . anything, in fact, all piled willy-nilly on top of one another. Feikermun's troops were much in evidence, either behind the barricades or glimpsed at windows inside the buildings or moving to and fro in the streets.

'Beyond is Malibeth's domain,' murmured Illan.

'And the Golden Lamb?'

'On the other side.' Illan crossed to a window in the western wall and gestured with a hand into the distance. 'His border meets Feikermun's over there, in a line extending roughly from the third tower on the city wall to that belt of trees in the centre. Further north it touches upon Malibeth's border.'

There was not much to see. I don't know what I had expected, but I felt rather flat. 'Is there open conflict between Malibeth and the Golden Lamb?'

'From what I know there was much fighting when the Golden Lamb first moved in. Since then things have been strained but quieter; certainly the major conflict appears to be between Malibeth and Feikermun.'

'But both must be highly wary of this powerful interloper.'

'I would guess that Malibeth and Feikermun have set their spymasters to work to learn what they can about him.'

I turned away from the window. Something caught my eye overhead. I looked up. A strange figure was squatting upon one

134

of the crossbeams in the room of the tower, observing me. I stared hard, my heart giving a sudden lurch, and even as I did so the thing vanished.

I looked at Illan and Jaktem, whose faces were both upturned, following the direction of my gaze.

'Is something wrong, Master Cormer?' enquired Jaktem.

'Did you see anything?'

He looked at me blankly and shook his head.

'Illan?'

'No.'

I glanced up again. There was nothing there. I started for the stairs. In my mind I still beheld the figure hunched upon the beam. I had glimpsed it for just a moment, but I was convinced it was virtually identical to the pale creature that had hauled me from the marsh at Guling Mire.

'Come,' I said to the two men. 'I have seen all I want. I have much to do.'

11

Yes, I HAD much to do, but I didn't know what. I had
established beyond any reasonable doubt that Feikermun
was on the verge of power, but I still did not know what form
it took, nor whence he derived it. Nor did I know how I might
discover these things. The answers would, if all indications were
to be believed, be apparent soon enough, but by then, with the
power in his hands, Feikermun would surely be unstoppable.

I had no way of spying on Feikermun other than by staying
as close to him as possible in the remaining time I had. That in
itself was virtually impossible. He was well protected, erratic
and dangerously deluded, and I had no connections here – at
least, not as Linias Cormer. Ronbas Dinbig had contacts in
Dehut, though they were not close to Feikermun and anyway,
as far as they were concerned, Dinbig had perished weeks ago
at Feikermun's hands. It would be inadvisable to approach them
now; a stranger asking about Dinbig, Feikermun or anything
else would be bound to arouse suspicion.

The desperate idea came that I should summon Yo, pass my
flesh into his custody and, disembodied, observe Feikermun. But
I might follow him for hours without learning anything useful,
and all the time I would be risking detection. If Feikermun
found me out . . . I shuddered and dismissed the idea.

It did not help that I lacked precise instructions from the
Hierarchy. Did they wish me to assassinate Feikermun? Not
feasible if I planned to live beyond the event. Was I supposed
to sacrifice myself for the greater good? I was not hugely
enamoured of the concept.

And what *was* the greater good? How could it be determined?
Removing Feikermun could well destabilize the region further,

passing control into the hands of Malibeth and the Golden Lamb. Both were unknown quantities, especially the latter.

Then there was Wirm. I needed to discover the extent of his influence and, equally importantly, the source and means by which he was procuring *gidsha*.

And still there remained the matter of my double. Even given his execution by Feikermun, I remained deeply curious to know who he was, what his designs had been, and how he had effected such a perfect disguise. Had my reputation or business suffered through his actions? Did his demise mark the end of the matter?

We were making our way back from the battle scene in Stonemarker when a sudden thought stopped me dead in my tracks.

'Master Cormer?'

Jaktem and Illan were looking enquiringly at me. I apologized quickly – 'A moment's distraction' – and we moved on. But I was far from easy in my mind. What had struck me was the thought that my double might somehow actually have discovered the identities of my contacts in Dehut. He could have spoken to them, gained information, struck deals that would rebound to my disadvantage . . . anything. It seemed far-fetched – there was no way he could have known about them – but the idea, once sprung in my mind, would not be dislodged. I felt suddenly impelled to make further urgent enquiries, no matter the risk.

And more: What of the Citadel? What of the ghostly woman who had appeared to me, and the pale creature or creatures who likewise seemed able to manifest and vanish at will? I was in danger of being overwhelmed by it all. Every step I took led me deeper into a morass of the inexplicable.

We were on a fairly busy central street approaching Culmet's Bazaar. I turned to address my two companions. 'I have business I must attend to. Meet me back at our chambers at three hours after noon.'

'But, Master Cormer, will you not need us? You will be unprotected,' Jaktem protested.

'Just do as I say. Find out anything more you can about the situation here.'

As I turned to leave there was a loud shriek ahead of me.

Fifteen paces away the air seemed to shimmer and crackle. People fell back in alarm. An indistinct shape began to materialize out of nowhere.

Suddenly something was standing there. A tall, beast-like living thing, larger than a man. It had long, ropily muscled legs and arms, with curling talons on its hands and feet. Its body was covered in sparse brown hair. Its head was broad, with pointed ears, a long tapering snout and two rows of savage, uneven teeth. A slender tail, longer than the body, lashed back and forth upon the ground. There was something rat-like about the creature as it half-crouched, darting a malevolent gaze about it as if in indecision.

Then it sprang.

People scattered. The creature's long claws ripped into the flesh of a woman too slow to get out of its way. She fell to the ground, crying out. The thing leapt upon her . . . and disappeared.

I ran forward. The woman lay in the throes of death, a great gash rending her open from shoulder to stomach and her face half torn away. There was nothing I could do for her. All around was pandemonium. People ran, shrieking and sobbing in terror; others gathered around the dying woman.

Three soldiers appeared. Several men and women, speaking at once, tried to tell their sergeant what had happened.

I backed away. Illan and Jaktem were still with me. 'Find out whatever you can,' I said. 'I will meet you later.'

Leaving them, I made off quickly down a sidestreet.

The man I had decided to speak to now was named Vastandul. He ran a business from a small premises in a street close to Culmet's Bazaar. Ronbas Dinbig had found him a useful source of information, given sufficient incentive, as well as being a knowledgeable trader with whom Dinbig had made a number of profitable transactions.

Vastandul traded ostensibly in spices and exotic foods. He sold grey-backed twiner meat among myriad other things. He also had many contacts in Dehut's underworld. Goods of dubious origin bound for even more dubious destinations passed regularly, if clandestinely, through his hands. His extensive network of agents and contacts ran throughout Anxau and else-where. I cannot say I liked him, but business is business and for any serious trader in Dehut Vastandul was an essential man to know.

The problem was that, while Vastandul was acquainted with Ronbas Dinbig, Linias Cormer was a complete stranger.

I entered his shop with an uncertain feeling in my stomach. The familiar, heady smells of hundreds of spices and herbs entered my nostrils and I breathed in deeply, for the odour was oddly comforting. Ranks of wooden cabinets and shelves lined the shop walls, holding jars, urns, pots and vases; elsewhere were boxes, sacks, amphora and bins all filled with spices, herbs, seasonings, dried fungi, powdered bones, grasses, flowers, grains and other foodstuffs. Behind the counter sat a young woman in a grey smock dress, plump and attractive with long dark brown hair and deep brown eyes.

'I wish to speak to Vastandul.'

'Who shall I say is calling?'

'My name is Linias Cormer. He does not know me. Tell him I have come from Khimmur.'

I was taking a risk. Mention of Khimmur might well generate the wrong kind of interest. But Vastandul was an astute man with an instinct for business. I gambled he would see me before deciding upon any course of action.

I was right. Asking me to wait, the young woman left her seat and passed through an arched doorway hung with a dark blue curtain. Moments later she returned and held aside the curtain. 'He will see you.'

Stepping around the counter, I passed through into a short corridor.

'The door at the end,' the young woman said, though I did not need to be told. I approached the door and knocked.

'Come.'

I pushed open the door and stepped into the subdued light of Vastandul's poky, untidy rear office. Vastandul sat behind his desk, before him a large hookah from whose bowl rose wreaths of thick, pungent grey smoke. He was a huge, corpulent man of about fifty, with greased black hair and a thin black moustache. He wore a dirty, off-white linen robe, clasped with hooks and eyes at the front. As I entered he removed the mouthpiece of the hookah from between his lips and surveyed me with a glassy gaze. He extended a fat hand, indicating a chair. 'Please, come in, be seated.' He exhaled, coughing slightly, and a plume of thin blue-grey smoke pushed its way through the fug already filling the room. 'You have come from Khimmur?'

'Word from an associate brings me to you, as a person to be trusted and who knows the value of discretion.'

'What is it you want?'

'Information.'

'On what subject?'

'On my associate, Ronbas Dinbig.'

Vastandul's eyes narrowed between thick folds of flesh. 'That is not a name that should be spoken of loudly around here.'

'Be aware that I am not here in an official capacity. I seek only to clarify a mystery. Dinbig mentioned your name to me. Recently I learned that he died here. The circumstances are unclear. For personal reasons I would like to know what happened.'

I took from my belt a small pouch containing several silver coins, and pushed it across the desktop. Vastandul did not even glance at it. He shrugged his massive shoulders, opening his hands. 'I had not even known he was in Dehut.'

'He did not call on you?'

'Nor on anyone known to me – and I know most, probably all, of Dinbig's contacts here.'

This was almost certainly true. I concealed my relief. My worst fears were unfounded, then. My double had not contacted anyone. In all probability he had not known anyone.

Vastandul returned the mouthpiece of the hookah to his lips and inhaled deeply, then offered it to me. I shook my head. 'Why was he killed? I have heard only second- and third-hand reports.'

'He was a fool, and I would never have thought of him in that light. From what I am told he sold inferior cloth to one of Lord Feikermun's aides – at an inflated price, what's more. And then at the palace he availed himself of one of the women currently favoured by Feikermun himself. His brain must have been riddled with maggots – there is no other explanation. One

140

does not play such games with Feikermun.' Vastandul paused. 'He suffered greatly before he died – as did the woman.'

'Were you present at the execution?'

'I?' Vastandul shook his head, and his fleshy jowls and pale dewlaps swayed.

'What was he doing at the palace? He had not been there before.'

'Had he not?' Vastandul eyed me sharply. 'You are sure?'

'I know only what he told me,' I said quickly, covering my slip. 'My understanding was that he dealt once with Feikermun, but that was some years ago and Feikermun came to the Bazaar.'

'Well, I did not know that Dinbig had contact with Lord Feikermun either, but . . .' Vastandul spread his hands again and gave me a look that said all things were possible.

Satisfied with what I had so far heard, I changed the subject. 'I am told Feikermun is becoming a god.'

Vastandul lifted his chins. 'He is playing with forces most men would rather leave alone, but he is Feikermun, so . . .'

'Do you know how he acquires the power?'

'Our illustrious leader knows his own way. The laws of common men bend for him. It is not for one such as I to enquire into his affairs.'

I nodded, understanding. Vastandul did not know me and my questions had begun to lead into areas where he would not venture with a stranger. To criticize or even discuss Feikermun in the wrong company could have terminal consequences. Yet the tone of his voice told me he had reservations in regard to Feikermun and his endeavours.

I rose from my chair. 'I thank you.'

Vastandul inclined his head. As I was about to depart I said, 'Oh, one more thing, if I may. I need directions to the Citadel.'

'The Citadel?' Vastandul's thin black eyebrows arched, then a quizzical smile played about his lips. 'What do you know of the Citadel?'

'Simply that I should go there, but I do not know how.'

Vastandul's smile broadened, though he lowered his gaze and slowly shook his head. 'Only Lord Feikermun can tell you how to reach the Citadel, my friend. And should he ever do so, which I surely doubt, you will wish that he had not. Now, I bid you good day.'

There was a tautness in the street outside. Word had spread of the manifestation of the rat-creature and the woman it had killed. People stood in small groups, stricken-faced. I could almost smell their fear: the thing had come from nowhere, out of the air. It could come again anywhere, at any time. What defence was there against something like that?

I moved on, into the bazaar and the inn where I had eaten earlier with Jaktem and Illan. I ordered aquavit and took a seat where I could watch the door and the people who came and went. Vastandul would almost certainly have me followed. He would want to know my business, where I was bound, who I knew. Would it matter if it was reported to him later that I had gone to Feikermun's palace? It would put him on his guard, but that would be all. I decided then not to put too great an effort into losing the tail he had assigned to me.

I had several hours to spare before I needed to return to the palace. It would take only a short time to prepare the *gidsha* root for my appointment with Feikermun at sunset. I sat there for some time mulling over my thoughts, unsure of what to do next. Part of my mind, almost unconsciously, kept note of what was going on around me. And it was this part of me that spotted something out of the ordinary and brought me with a jolt bolt upright in my seat.

It was only a glimpse, through the open door, of someone passing by. I wasn't sure, yet it was enough to set the hairs at the back of my neck prickling and almost to bring a cry of disbelief from my throat. I was up and out of my chair and racing for the door. Scanning the marketplace I spotted the figure again, between the stalls, anonymous, garbed in grey and walking away from me towards the edge of the square.

I ran, pushing rudely past anyone in my way. My quarry turned a corner and entered a street. I was only a few paces behind him. I moved up, suddenly half-paralysed with fear, and reached out and touched him on the shoulder. He turned, and I stopped dead, aghast, my worst fears confirmed.

He was me. He was I. He was Ronbas Dinbig of Khimmur.

His gaze was enquiring and perplexed. He did not seem to recognize me – how could he? – but I was astonished at what I saw: the extraordinary likeness to my true self. I was utterly lost for words, aware of my mouth opening and closing but emitting no sound other than a breathy, barely audible popping. He blinked, frowned slightly. His attitude was not hostile, nor did he show any fear of having been found out. Rather, he appeared unsure of himself, a little confused.

I found my voice at last. 'Who . . . who *are* you?'

His frown deepened, and now I saw a tension in his face – a challenge, a flash of indignation in his eyes. He stepped towards me; the air between us seemed to blur and shift. I felt something like a breath – a light, imploding gust of air against my face and torso. I reached out, but he had gone. Vanished.

I heard a loud gasp from someone. I stood still in utter exasperation. I had lost him. I should have grabbed him, held on to him. What would have happened then? Would he still have disappeared? Would I have gone with him, or would I have been left standing where I was now, holding nothing?

There was muttering around me. The street was fairly populated and several people had witnessed our brief exchange. My rushing to accost the man had drawn their attention. Among their number was a pair of Feikermun's soldiers, assigned to police the street. They marched up to me now.

'What happened? Where did he go?'

I shook my head.

'I saw his face,' said one. 'I have seen him before.'

The second one nodded suspiciously. 'I too. He reminded me of someone.'

I was too dazed to respond coherently. 'I don't know who he was.'

'You spoke to him.'

'I thought for a moment that I knew him, that's all. But you saw . . . we did not speak. He simply vanished.'

Two more soldiers had arrived. I sensed the nervousness around me.

'Come with us.'

'What was your business with this man?'

143

'I had no business with him as such, Lord Feikermun. I merely thought he was someone I recognized.'

'And was he?'

'I cannot say. I am confused. I have been told many times by numerous persons that the man I thought I saw is dead.'

I winced as a series of agonized cries rent the air and drowned my words. We were in the banqueting hall where the orgy had taken place the previous day. Feikermun sat before me at a long table, garbed in a puff-shouldered tunic of red-and-white silk. Flanking him were Hircun, the one-eyed warrior, Bondo, Wirm and another man I did not know. The heads of three of Malibeth's slain men had been mounted on silver platters on the table. They had been squeezed between their own mutilated buttocks, garnished with beds of green nettle and thornbush sprigs; their mouths had been stuffed with pigs' droppings so that their cheeks bulged, and the nostrils were blocked with the same; upon their crowns their severed genitals had been arranged to resemble grotesque, absurd little flesh bonnets. They had been positioned to face me, sightless and mutely inquisitorial, quite impervious to their final humiliation but blaring their warning of the possibility of mine.

Further down the hall a man in an iron cage was being slowly roasted alive over a brazier. The cage was suspended on a heavy chain which ran through an iron ring attached to an overhead beam, then down to wind around a winch bolted to a stone column. The cage was narrow and tall, allowing the prisoner minimal movement other than upwards a few fingerlengths. Its bars, however, were sufficiently widely spaced to allow him to squeeze his arms and even legs through. It had been raised so that it hung directly over the glowing coals of the brazier, which was attended by two burly, sweating men in leather aprons.

It seemed the torture had not long begun. The flat iron floor of the cage had grown hot and the prisoner, who was naked, was clinging to iron rungs which the heat had not yet penetrated, forcing himself towards the roof of the cage. Feikermun and his four companions had been idly speculating upon the man's plight when I was marched in between a pair of guards. I waited before them, my nerves frayed, trying to disregard the trio of dead faces before me and the desperate pleas and whimpers that came from my side. I was unsure of my status now. Had I been arrested? Was I a guest still, or a prisoner?

'Silence!' roared Feikermun as the man's shrieks cut through my words.

'My lord, I beg you! Please, have mercy! *Please!*'

I could not help glancing his way. He had forced his limbs out between the bars of the cage, but no matter what position he adopted he could not avoid the growing heat of the metal. He writhed, burned red in several places, crying out in agonies I could not guess at.

'Why did you approach him?' Feikermun demanded of me.

'For that very reason, my lord. I believed him dead – at your hands, in fact. The sight of someone who so resembled him startled me.'

'And then what?'

'I have no explanation. I approached him . . . Before I could speak he vanished. Your own soldiers can attest to that fact, for they were witness to it.'

'And who did you think him to be, Cormer of Chol?'

'I was struck by his resemblance to a man with whom I met but once, some weeks ago, a merchant from Hon-Hiaita in Khimmur, named Dinbig.'

Feikermun froze for a moment, staring at me, his fists bunching on the table. The huge muscles of his arms swelled with tension. Wirm leaned across and spoke conspiratorially into his ear. Feikermun's eyes went to the two guards. 'Is it true that you witnessed this event?'

'Yes, Your Excellency,' one replied.

'You saw the man?'

'Briefly, Excellency. He was familiar, though neither of us could place him then. Now that a name has been mentioned I would say aye, that is who I was reminded of strongly: the Khimmurian you had executed in this very hall some weeks ago.'

I repressed a shudder, my mind on the iron cage. Beside me the second guard gave a nod of affirmation. Feikermun's bloodshot eyes returned to me. 'Wirm says you made enquiries about this Khimmurian dog in Guling Mire.'

'Not enquiries, my Lord. I had earlier purchased an article

from him which I learned he had bought from Master Wirm. I simply asked Master Wirm about the possibility of acquiring more, similar articles.'

Feikermun tilted his head towards Wirm, who again spoke quietly in his ear. Wirm's cold, hard eyes stared shiftingly at me, moving from shoulder to belly to head, never settling on my face. He would say anything he could to damn me further, and I cursed again the shortsightedness that had led me to incur his hostility.

'Your interest was profound, considering that you claim to have met the unprincipled hound only the once.'

'As I said, your Excellency, I was surprised at seeing a man I believed to be dead.'

'The dog *is* dead!' Feikermun roared. 'It could not have been he!'

'No, my lord, I accept that it could not. I was in error, there can be no doubt. Though, as confirmed by your men here, I was not alone. And the inexplicable fact remains that the man I tried to accost simply vanished before my eyes and the eyes of those watching.'

Feikermun seemed discomfited by this. He scowled, rocking slightly from side to side, and chewed in agitation at his inner cheek.

'Lord Feikermun, might I add something more?' I said.

He gave a single, brooding nod.

'I was present not an hour earlier at another singular event, concerning which I have no doubt you have been informed. A creature of some kind materialized briefly in the street, coming out of the air itself, and slew an innocent passer-by, then vanished.'

'What do you know of the woman's innocence?' demanded Feikermun with sudden accusation.

'I know nothing of her. Nothing at all. I coined a casual figure of speech, that is all. I assumed—'

'You assume much, Cormer of Chol.'

'My lord, I meant nothing. My enquiry was in regard to the nature of the extraordinary event I witnessed, that is all.'

Renewed shrieks of pain came from the man in the iron cage. I looked his way and saw that he was a mass of burns, blistering,

146

weeping. His skin glistened, red and angry as he threshed in helpless agony. I forced my eyes shut, clenching my jaw. I had begun to shake. I did not know if I could bear any more.

Feikermun hammered angrily on the table with his fist. 'Be silent!' he yelled over my shoulder. 'Feikermun is talking! Do you wish your tongue torn out?'

I could not tell whether the prisoner even heard him, but his cries abated somewhat. Then I heard erratic rattling and a slow, rhythmic, metallic creaking. 'Ha!' ejaculated Feikermun, and stood suddenly, grinning and holding out a hand to the one-eyed fighter. 'Hircun!'

Hircun shook his head, compressing his lips in a resigned expression, half-smile, half-grimace. Several silver coins lay on the table before him, which he now pushed towards Feikermun. The mad despot gathered them up with an exaggerated sweep of his arms and looked in triumph at me. 'Hircun and Feikermun wagered on the time it would take for the prisoner to think of swinging. They vary greatly. To some it never occurs at all; others begin as soon as the coals are placed beneath the cage. Hircun believed this one would begin almost immediately, as soon as the metal began to grow hot, if not before. But I, Feikermun, said no! It will take time. The entire cage will heat up before he thinks of it.'

I turned my head. The prisoner was applying his weight back and forth to cause the cage to swing upon its chain. To and fro it went, slowly, in a gathering arc, while he screamed out his agonies.

'It makes little difference,' observed Feikermun matter-of-factly, seating himself again. 'The iron will not cool sufficiently. It merely prolongs their suffering. Strong men have endured for more than a night and a day in that cage.'

I stood stiff and impotent, trying to shut out the terrible sounds, fighting down my anger and the urge to do something, anything, to relieve the poor wretch's suffering. For there was nothing I could do, and the notion had occurred to me that it might be partly for my benefit, my instruction, my intimidation, that this inhuman spectacle was being staged.

'Cormer of Chol, Wirm says that the article you obtained from the snake-bellied merchant Dinbig of Khimmur, whose

147

very name causes Feikermun to gag' – Feikermun hawked and spat a great gobbet of discoloured liquid on to the floor – 'is in your possession now.'

I gave a nod. 'That is so, my lord.'

'Feikermun will see it.'

I still had my pack. I reached in and withdrew the green amber in its cloth, and passed it to Feikermun. Unwrapping the amber, he admired it for some moments, turning it over in his hands. The light gleamed warmly in its citrine depths, the tiny still insects a cloud at its core. 'It is an exceptional piece. No doubt you would wish Feikermun to have it, as a gift, a demonstration of your goodwill. That, presumably, is your reason for bringing it here?'

Cold smiles appeared on the faces of Wirm, Bondo and the other man. Hircun remained impassive. I gulped back my pride, knowing I was had. 'My lord, if it pleases you to have it, then it is yours.'

'You are kind.'

The prisoner's shrieks suddenly mounted once more. I found myself trembling, my whole body vibrating with helpless rage. Something rose up, angry and uncontrollable, from deep within me. Before I could stop myself I had blurted out: 'My lord, *please*, I must ask that this man be freed from his torment!'

With an expression of dark surprise Feikermun of Selph thrust himself back in his seat, his thick forearms and huge, loosely bunched hands resting on the table before. '*You* must ask? *You must ask Feikermun?*'

For a moment, as I stood firm under his stare, I believed I was about to die. Then, to my surprise he gave a peremptory nod, twisted his lips into an ugly smile and said, 'Very well.'

He left his seat and stepped around the table, beckoning to me. 'Come.'

I followed him across the hall to where the two torturers stood beside the swinging cage and brazier.

'Remove the coals and still the cage,' commanded Feikermun.

The two dragged the brazier to one side, then, with the aid of wooden poles tipped with metal hooks, grasped the bars of the metal cage and brought it to rest before us. There was a sickening smell of burnt hair and flesh. I gazed at the poor ruin of a man inside. He still squirmed and writhed in his impossible efforts to rid himself of the terrible heat of the metal.

'Take this wretch from the cage and put Master Cormer in his place,' said Feikermun.

'*No!*' The word had catapulted from between my lips before I could prevent it. I stepped back involuntarily, straight into the grip of the two guards.

'No?' Feikermun taunted me with mock surprise, amusement in his eyes, a cold, sardonic smile playing on his lips. 'No? But it is Feikermun's understanding that you wish this man's torment to cease?'

'That is my hope, yes, to which end I call upon your great compassion and mercy.'

'Ha-hah!' He leaned back and laughed uproariously, then was suddenly silent, his hands upon his hips, fixing me with moist eyes and an offended expression. 'Feikermun knows nothing of such things, but he offers you a choice. Save him. He can go free, this minute. His associates, too. But you must take his place.'

I knew the prisoner was watching me, knew there was wild, desperate hope in his tortured eyes. The world seemed to close in on me. My legs threatened to give way. I was faint; there was a roaring in my ears and no other sound but the deafening storm of my own breathing. I noted the word 'associates', and heard my voice as if from a distance, spoken by someone else. 'With what offence are this man and his associates charged?'

'That is irrelevant!' snapped Feikermun. 'It is not for one such as you to question Feikermun! Cormer of Chol, Feikermun says to you once more, for the last time, you may save this man, you may restore him to life and freedom. You have only to say the word. Take his place, and he will be freed.'

I cast my eyes down, despising Feikermun with every fibre of my being.

'Well?'

I could not respond.

He thrust his great head up close to mine. '*Well?*'

He would not relent. He would not let me off. 'Feikermun is waiting.'

I shook my head.

'Say it!'

'I cannot. I cannot take his place.'

'Resume,' said Feikermun to the two torturers.

The prisoner gave a great cry. 'Nooooo! My lord, I beg you, please! Sir, please! Help me! Be merciful!'

I had barely the strength to support myself. I turned away, swaying. Without the two guards holding my arms I would not have made it back to stand before the table with the others. The sound of the prisoner's screams as the brazier was pushed back into place slammed into my brain, reverberated inside my head, pierced to the core of my bones, damning me.

'Enough!' bellowed Feikermun with a sudden gush of temper. 'The entertainment pales. Kill him!'

I steeled myself, reaching desperately within to summon strength, though I knew I was incapable of resisting. But I was mistaken: it was not me he meant. Off to my side there was a clink of metal on metal, a short sigh, and the screaming died. I exhaled shudderingly, and closed my eyes. I felt his life. I felt it hover, accusing, then flee this world. It could have been me, but I had elected otherwise. I had made that choice.

I opened my eyes again, forcing myself to lift my head to face Feikermun once more. He was watching me, his head above that of one of his mutilated victims. His smile taunted and sickened me, then vanished.

'Cormer of Chol, why did you go this morning to Stone-marker?'

I took several deep breaths, instilling calm into myself. The three severed heads seemed now to gaze upon me with reproach. I was dead, I knew, unless I could persuade Feikermun that I was indispensable to him. 'It was largely out of curiosity, Lord Feikermun. I hoped, in fact, to catch a glimpse of your enemy, Malibeth, for I am curious to know whether it was she who appeared to me in your chamber when we met during the night.'

'Malibeth? No, oh, no. That one, she is not the mad sow Malibeth.'

'Then, my lord, might I ask who she is?'

His unease was evident. He drew back, scratching at the side of his nose, seemingly indecisive. I realized I might easily over-play my hand, for with someone as unpredictable as him it was impossible to know where the boundaries lay. Yet the line I was adopting, though not to Feikermun's liking, was the right one, I was almost sure. It angered him that the woman had appeared solely to me. He was jealous, even. But he was insatiably curious, too. On this I gambled. I had been made special in Feikermun's eyes, though it profoundly irked him to admit it.

He failed to answer my question, so I pressed forward. 'I was also trying to gain directions to the Citadel.'

Feikermun started visibly and his eyes bulged. I sensed tension in the four men seated around him. The one I had not seen before leaned across and said something.

'What do you know of the Citadel?' demanded Feikermun.

'Only that she told me I should go there.'

'She? You have seen her again?'

'She came to me in the night, my lord.'

He stiffened, then vented a loud blast of air through his nostrils. 'What did she say to you?'

'That I should go to the Citadel. That is all.'

'Nothing more?' He didn't quite believe me.

'Nothing. Not an indication of where it lies or how I might find it.'

Feikermun pushed himself abruptly out of his seat once more and strode across the hall, gripping his bearded chin. At the far wall he wheeled around and pointed at me. 'To whom have you spoken about this?'

'I asked one or two persons in the street for directions.'

'What was their response?'

'Nobody I asked had heard of this place.'

'Piss upon you all!' He stomped back across the hall, then altered course and came directly at me. He stood in front of me, fulminating. I smelt his sweat and the odours of stale food upon him; his breath reeked of sweet wine. He was almost a head shorter than I, yet he was broad and mightily muscled. He was quite capable of tearing me apart with his bare hands.

'Cormer of Chol,' he breathed, 'where is the *gidsha*?'

I raised my pack. 'Here.'

'Is it prepared?'

'No. I was about to return to the palace to commence preparation when I was arrested by your men.'

151

'Go. Prepare it, now. Bring it to me when you are done.'

He walked away. Prompted by the guards, I turned and left the hall.

Outside we were met by the sloppily garbed steward who had escorted me earlier. 'Is there anything you require for your preparation?' he enquired.

'Only clean water. And a mortar and pestle.'

'They will be brought.'

The world seemed a blur. I was weak and sick to my core. The muscles in my back and neck ached with tension, and I was half-numbed by what I had experienced. I felt that I walked in a place where I did not truly exist, where I should not exist, for to exist here was an obscenity – beyond contemplation. It was as though I had become complicit in all I had witnessed. I was gripped by a heavy, impotent rage and an anguish of the spirit that threatened to crush me.

As I was marched on towards my apartment on the second floor I asked of the steward what crime the man in the cage had committed.

'His wife's third cousin was heard to speak of His Excellency in uncomplimentary terms.'

'His wife's third cousin? But was he directly implicated?'

'By association. His Excellency arrested the man's family, every relative that could be found.'

'What has become of them?'

'They have all been, or will be, executed.'

'In that cage? Even women and children?'

'Not the women or young girls, of course not. The Excellency does not cook women, for he requires their blood. It is the Source, after all. The Blood of Life. They are gone now, but their blood has nourished him.' We arrived at my door and he bowed his head. 'I shall attend to your request.'

I entered, closing the door behind me, vaguely aware that the guards remained outside. I crossed the room unsteadily to the open window, pushed my head out and retched, violently and uncontrollably. When I had done and my stomach could heave no more, I left the window, trembling from head to toe, and threw myself upon the bed and wept.

12

THE PREPARATION OF the *gidsha* root was not difficult. It was largely a matter of pulping, as the root is hard and fibrous and almost indigestible, and of disguising its natural flavour, which is bitter and thoroughly disgusting. There were one or two specific treatments the Chariness had instructed me to carry out, but even these could be mastered by almost anyone of reasonable intelligence, given a little time and patience.

It was important, however, that Feikermun believed otherwise. My continuing survival depended upon his unshakable conviction that he needed me. At some point I would have to hand over the last of the *gidsha* I had brought; at that time, if not before, Feikermun would demand to know the techniques of preparation. Once he had those he would still require me (as he thought) to maintain the supply of the specially cultivated root, but I would not be needed close at hand.

In many ways that would have been my preference. I could leave Dehut and its insanity and violence, ostensibly to acquire more of the drug. Once clear of Dehut, Linias Cormer could cease to exist and I could return to Khimmur and become Ronbas Dinbig once more.

But I was deluding myself with this thought, for I had yet to complete my task here. I had made virtually no progress so far, and I could not return to Khimmur with unsatisfactory results without incurring the Hierarchy's displeasure. I might even be instructed to return here – the last thing I wanted.

And, on a more immediately personal level, I was far from solving the mystery of my double, whom I had now actually *seen*, and the new enigmas of the ghostly beauty who had appeared to me, the bizarre manifestations that were occurring here, and the mysterious Citadel. Something was happening in

Dehut, something extraordinary and terrifying. With the lunatic Feikermun at its head, though not necessarily in control, it threatened to spread chaos and terror beyond Anxau's borders. But what was it? What was this power that would transform Feikermun into a living, vengeful god? And how could it be stopped?

I felt impotent, knowing so little and with only the vaguest notion of how to proceed. And as I in fact had no lasting supply of the *gidsha* my remaining here would be an ongoing game of bluff and evasion, with my life suspended in the balance.

The steward brought clean water, in a tall earthenware pitcher, and a mortar and pestle as requested. I enquired of him as to the whereabouts of Jaktem and Illan.

'It is my understanding that they are in their chamber, sir,' he replied.

'I would like to see them.'

He hesitated a moment, considering. 'I have no specific instructions in that regard, but His Excellency awaits you, and that is your priority.'

'Quite so. But the ritual preparation of the root is not a quick procedure, and the first stage requires that I allow it to soak untended for some time. I can do nothing while that process continues, and would prefer to spend the time constructively with my employees.'

I was bending the truth here somewhat, but it seemed to have an effect. The steward puckered his lips and said he would see what he could do, then swivelled upon his heel and departed.

It was Jaktem who came to me a little while later. The steward entered with him, presumably having applied to Feikermun or one of his deputies for instructions.

I thanked him and waited, hoping he would leave, but he simply nodded and remained as he was.

'I won't be requiring you any further,' I added.

'I am to remain with your man and escort him back to his apartment when you are done, sir.'

And to listen to our exchange and report, no doubt. I turned to Jaktem. 'Did you learn anything after I left you?'

He shook his head. 'No one knew what had happened. It was just confusion and terror. The only thing I did learn is that

154

nothing like that had happened before – at least, not in a public place.'

He was plainly not wholly at ease with the steward present, but from his face and manner I gathered there was little or nothing else he wished to add.

'The creature did not reappear?'

'No.'

I was baffled, and fearful. The threat was plain: murderous creatures appearing out of thin air to wreak mayhem and death. When I'd mentioned it to Feikermun he had changed the subject. He was uncomfortable with it, I could tell. Did he know what was happening? Was he responsible for it?

'Where is Illan?'

'In the town. He will be coming here in a short while.'

'Have you been placed under any duress, suffered any restrictions since returning here?'

'No, sir. Though I note there are now guards in the corridor outside our chamber.'

'That is perhaps not unexpected, given the circumstances. Jaktem, I hired you to escort me here and have, albeit unwittingly, subjected you to no little danger. Your work and Illan's has been exemplary; I made an excellent choice in taking you both on. But it would be wrong of me to expect anything more from you. You are therefore free to leave, with my thanks and full remuneration for your service, if you so wish.'

'Master Cormer, my understanding was that we were hired to see you to Dehut and out again when your business was done.'

'That was my original intention. But it is obvious there are dangers here that none of us could have foreseen. You may quite understandably prefer to remove yourselves, and I will not think worse of you for it. Your association with me is casual, after all. That being so, you may go now, with my blessing.'

'If it's all the same to you, sir, I would rather stay and see you through. And I know I speak for Illan, too.'

'Are you quite sure of this?'

'I am.'

'Then I retain you, gratefully. But should either of you change

155

your mind I will not hold you to anything. As for now, the next few hours are to be taken up with business for Lord Feikermun. I don't think I am likely to need you again before morning.'

'Very good, sir.'

He nodded his head, turned and left the room, the steward following. I hoped the steward had taken note of my speech and would report back to Feikermun the fact that Jaktem and Illan were casual employees, not regular henchmen. Should things turn bad for me they might at least have some small hope of escaping his wrath.

I turned my attention to the *gidsha*. First I lit some sweet-smelling joss, then cut the root into small cubes which I placed in the mortar. I added a little water and ground the cubes into a mash with the pestle. Into this I sprinkled several generous pinches of fragrant spices and herbs to disguise the root's foul flavour, and sweet honey to counter its natural bitterness and acridity. I tasted a tiny sample on the tip of my tongue. It still had a pronounced pungent quality which scoured my palate and offended my tastebuds, but that is the nature of *gidsha*. Its inherent flavour can never be wholly suppressed; at least my concoction disguised the worst of it. I washed out my mouth thoroughly, keen to ensure that no trace of the potent drug entered my system.

Now it was time to add those most vital ingredients given to me by the Chariness. The first was a spoonful of powdered *muss* gum, which I carried in a small phial stitched into a secret pocket in my money belt. *Muss* is a narcotic which dulls the senses to induce a pleasant, floating numbness. It is quite easily obtained and widely used, though like *gidsha* it is addictive. Then I added a few droplets of a tincture of Blue Joy, a juice with powerful stimulant properties, extracted from the bark of the bird-apple tree and suspended in an alcoholic base. Lastly came a secret ingredient, a peppering of a fine dust of green, white and violet motes whose identity I did not know. The Chariness had been precise in her instructions in regard to adding these final three ingredients, and I adhered to her words meticulously.

All done, I sat before the prepared root, cast a rapture of Purification and invoked a ritual chant. An hour later I was finished. Outside the sun had hardly begun to set. I waited nervously, uncertain whether I was expected to deliver the preparation forthwith or keep to my original appointment with Feikermun at sunset. I preferred to wait as long as possible, simply to put off the confrontation. Feikermun would no doubt send for me earlier if he wanted me, but quite possibly sunset was his chosen, ritual time for ingesting *gidsha*.

The sky was staining blood-red, the light in my chamber becoming subdued, and I had just lit the candles when the steward – I never did discover his name – returned for me.

'Are your preparations done?'

'They are.'

'Then come. His Excellency commands that you attend him now.'

Feikermun awaited me in the private chamber where he had received me the previous night. Again he was surrounded by his cronies: Hircun, the soldier; the plump, bald Bondo; Wirm; and the other, unnamed man. Feikermun's lips and the whiskers around his mouth were wet, stained bright red. I assumed he had been drinking blood. Female blood. Two of his dark-skinned slave girls rested upon cushions at one end of the chamber, coloured bandages concealing the wounds upon their arms. In one corner a huge grey ape squatted, tethered to the wall by a chain attached to a collar around its neck.

'Cormer of Chol, you have brought the precious *gidsha*?' Feikermun's eyes were fixed feverishly upon the bowl I carried in my two hands. His intonation was a little slurred. He sat, head and torso forward, on a carved seat before me, his knees wide apart, hands thrust upon thighs, elbows akimbo. His lips were drawn back into a taut grimace; one muscle-bolstered knee bounced rapidly up and down. He was quick, jerky, tense. I sensed his need for the root. And radiating from him was an energy that almost set me back a pace as I approached him. It was wild, violent, unpredictable. It had a quality of near-palpability, and it virtually reeked of unharnessed magic. It was as though something were striving to burst from Feikermun, and it broiled the very air about him.

I held forward the bowl. 'It is here, my lord.'

157

He gazed greedily at the mass, which had turned a deep green from the ingredients I had added, then frowned. 'This is *gidsha*?'

'Prepared, my lord, as I said, in a special manner. Enhanced for your delight.'

The others craned their necks to see.

'There is sufficient here for how many applications?' asked Feikermun.

'That will depend upon how much you are in the habit of ingesting at a time. By ordinary standards I would reckon this would suffice for four separate doses.'

He nodded, and leaned back. 'Good. Then eat.'

'My lord?' I gaped at him in horrified disbelief. 'I?'

'Yes, you, Cormer of Chol. You.'

'But Lord Feikermun, this is rare, valuable root, prepared for yourself. *Gidsha* of this quality is not easily obtained. And I do not – that is, I have never—'

A spasm passed across Feikermun's face and his whole body shook. '*Eat*, Cormer! Let Feikermun see it pass down your gullet, or by the gods he will force it down with his own two hands.'

It was a test, of course. He was not to know that the preparation was not poisoned. I was caught. I had never ingested this drug, and never wished to. I knew of the horrors, as well as the wonders, that it could inflict. I knew of its addictiveness. There were well recorded stories of unwary people trying *gidsha* and losing their minds, becoming gawks, loobies or berserks. And yet it had been obvious that Feikermun would not be so unwise as to place his trust in me, a complete stranger. Why had I not foreseen this?

I took up the spoon which rested against the edge of the *gidsha* dish and scooped up a small amount of the mixture. With a glance at Feikermun, and seeing no comfort there, I raised the spoon to my mouth, took the mixture in, and swallowed.

'More than that. More,' commanded Feikermun. 'There is enough for four in the dish, you say? Then eat a quarter, now.'

A quarter! I stiffened with horror at the thought of what that amount would do to me. 'My lord, I have never taken this before. This amount is for one who is used to *gidsha*'s effects, who has built up a resistance in some respects. I could suffer—'

'Excuses! Bah! What cares Feikermun for your suffering? Eat, damn you, then Feikermun will take you to the Citadel.'

'The Citadel?'

Feikermun rose, his face dark. The thick, hairy meat of his shoulder twitched. '*Eat.*'

I gagged as I forced the green mush down. Even with the added spices and flavourings it was bitter, sour, corrosive on my tongue and throat. All eyes were fixed upon me as I struggled to eat it, every spoonful a new ordeal. At last I was done. I replaced the spoon in the bowl and faced my tormentor. Feikermun had reseated himself. He regarded me with grim satisfaction. Beside him Wirm made no effort to hide an eely smile. I waited, wondering what was to come, how long before the effects would begin to manifest.

Feikermun leaned forward and snatched the bowl from my hands. He gulped down a portion of the mash, then smacked his lips, the green of the *gidsha* mash mixing with the blood around his lips to stain them a lurid brown. He belched, closed his eyes, and issued a long sigh, his hands upon his great bulging belly. Then he stood, taking up the dish, and crossed to where the ape sat tethered.

'Do you dream, Cormer of Chol?' Feikermun shouted.

'Dream, my lord?'

'Dream. Do you have dreams?' He was spooning more *gidsha* from the bowl and feeding it to the ape, who accepted it with apparent relish.

'I dream sometimes, yes. In my sleep.'

Feikermun tossed aside the bowl. He went to the nearby wall and unhasped the ape's chain, then wrapped the end about one of his wrists. 'Good,' he said. He moved over to the ape, making grunts and murmurs, and tugged twice upon the chain. The ape eyed him quizzically, baring its great teeth, then stood on feet and knuckles. Beside it Feikermun, even with his wads of muscle, was a dwarf. But he showed no fear.

'Feikermun dreams,' he said, and walked towards me, extending a hand almost amicably. The ape came alongside him, snuffling, its brown eyes, deepset beneath an immense beetling brow,

159

looking around mistrustfully. Feikermun grasped my hand. 'Feikermun dreams.'

His eyes were glazed, aimed at me but unfocused. I could think of nothing to say.

'Are your dreams more potent than Feikermun's?'

'I would not know, my lord. But I doubt it.'

He nodded to himself. 'Well, let us see. Come. Enter the Citadel!'

He lurched forward suddenly, pulling me with him. The ape came too. Feikermun was running so that I was also forced to run, and the ape lolloped along at our side. Feikermun was laughing: wild, raucous laughter. He ran with us around the chamber, then out through the door. 'The Source!' he yelled. 'Ha-ha! The Blood! The *gidsha*! The Source!'

We ran on, faster and faster, along corridors, passing sentries and staff who hardly gave us a glance. We passed through a gallery, along an arcade, crossed a wide patio where fountains played, entered more passageways. I began to feel tired, my lungs burned. We were running faster than I had known I could run. Feikermun's mad laughter reverberated along the passages. I felt light-headed. Walls flew by. Surely I could not go this quickly? I was not tired now. I felt nothing. Feikermun's voice was a colossal distant echo. I could no longer feel the floor beneath my feet. The light was changing. We swerved around a corner, raced up a flight of stairs, twisting, winding, then into another long corridor. We ran on, on. I could hear music, a woman singing. The laughter. A balcony ahead of me. Running. Roofs of Dehut. Pigments of sunset. All playing for me. So many colours. The palace had passed away. I was in the air. Then nowhere. Everything was changing. Quite suddenly, a vast open space, a ravishing sunset. Objects forming, things moving, vanishing. Then I was falling, terrified, crying out.

And I heard someone shout: 'The Citadel! The Citadel!'

And then there was nothing.

13

'AM I DYING?'
Yellowness. Deep, bright, burning. Yellow. Orange.
Amber. Nothing else but a pulsing intensity, a conviction of
engulfment, loss of body, loss of being. Fear.

'*Am I dying?*'

Where was I? *What* was I? How had I come to be? Was this
it? The end?

Such pounding intensity. A jungle of sound, of perception,
like nothing I had experienced. The yellow-orange. Shapes
above me, unmoving, all around, suspended. And a darkness
beyond, so black, so black. A dream? The fear rising again.

'*Help me!*'

I was soul, at last, nothing more. But nothing of me. An echo
of crazed laughter somewhere. No longer I. Just receding, and
all closing in.

'*Am I dying?*'

'No,' a voice whispered. '*You have just been born.*'

She was standing before me. I glimpsed her for a moment; then
she had gone.

'*Please come back!*'

Just the strange yellowish-orange light and the engulfing black
far overhead. And the figures suspended everywhere, a blur. I
could not make them out.

'*I need you!*'

My voice was swallowed by the emptiness of it all.

'*Where am I?*'

'*Here.*'

'*Where?*'

'*In the Citadel.*'

I heard the cry of a tiny babe. Then the sweet, tender song of the mother, crooning softly and joyfully. The peal of bells far overhead, resonant out of the blackness, the nothingness, waiting, before the world began.

'Where?'

'In the Citadel.'

I opened my eyes. The face above me, vast, tender, the eyes huge and filled with love. The mother, her song a paean in the spheres, a hymn of the universe, nurturing, comforting, reaching into my new soul. And so far to go. So far. So long.

'What is it?'

'The Citadel.'

'I don't understand!'

The cry of the baby. The road before, stretching into a fathomless distance over a bare, bare landscape. The figures, in the sky, in the orange, the amber, the yellow, suspended, everywhere.

And there was I, standing facing me. Ronbas Dinbig, in grey tunic, hose and hood, standing motionless on stone steps, looking across at me. He moved.

'Wait!'

He was gone.'

'*Do you dream, Cormer of Chol?*'

'I do not know?'

'Where are you?'

'In the Citadel!'

'Yes! But what is the Citadel?'

'What is it?'

'You do not know?'

'I know nothing. Help me!'

The laughter, far away, mocking.

'Ah, you do not know.'

'I do not know.'

'It is the Citadel.'

'But what is the Citadel?'

'Selph, Cormer of Chol. It is the Citadel of Selph.'

Selph?

Feikermun. *Feikermun of Selph.*

It seemed then that I slipped into unconsciousness, as though that word contained a power in itself, had been propelled into my mind like a great stone into a lake, drawing my thoughts to it and pulling them down beneath the surface. When next I returned to any form of awareness it was with a clamouring feeling of hope and dread. Hope in the form of a vague memory, a suggestion that somewhere there existed a normality, a world of familiar, comforting things, a place I could relate to, where not everything was utterly strange. And dread that this might not be so. That this place, this dream of a place, of a world, was just an illusion, that I had invented it out of my madness, or that, if it had ever existed in any form other than within my own deranged mind, then it no longer did so. There was only the utterly strange.

The yellowness persisted, toning into areas of deep orange, burnt umber, shades of green. The suspended shapes were clearer now, humanish figures – men, women, children, as many as three score or more – all with wings of black and gorgeous crimson, held in the air in the strange light, all around me, inert, frozen, as far as I could see, up into the profound, all-engulfing blackness beyond.

The nearest was just a short way above me, but beyond my reach. She was a young winged woman wearing a long white sleeveless gown of light linen or cotton. The gown shifted slightly under the play of a breath of breeze, but she was fixed and unmoving, one hand extended before her and her mouth open, eyes questioning and a little too wide, as though she had been caught in a precise moment of enquiry, her sudden surprise having scarcely had time to form itself upon her features. I could not tell whether she, or any of the others, was alive.

A little way off across the dust-strewn road was a building like a small temple, open to the sky, at its front seven tall stone pillars set at the top of a short, wide flight of stone steps. Beyond, towering over it, I could see – or thought I could see – the hulking outlines of other buildings: walls, battlements, turrets, towers. But they were vague, shadowy, indistinct; as my gaze tried to focus upon them they seemed to shift out of vision, and I had the impression that they weren't there at all.

I gaped about me, overawed and confounded by it all.

'*Do – you – dream, Cormer of Chol?*'

Had somebody asked the question aloud, or had it been spoken in my mind? Was there a difference?'

My vision swerved; the world slewed. I staggered backwards and sat down hard.

'What do you know?'

'I know nothing.'

'Nothing?'

'Nothing. Nothing at all.'

'That is good.'

And then she was before me.

'Don't go!' I cried, afraid more than I could express that I would lose her again.

She smiled, standing erect in a pale green dress, her feet and arms bare, her golden hair cascading about her shoulders. 'I told you I would be here.'

I scrambled to my feet and stepped towards her, reaching out, wanting her, wanting to hold her, needing her. She moved back a step. 'No.'

'Why?'

'I cannot explain, not yet. You would not understand. Soon you will, I promise, if all goes well.'

'And if it doesn't?'

She gave a slight, sad shrug. 'It will no longer matter.'

'But who *are* you?'

'My name would mean nothing, but if you need a name for me you can call me Aniba.'

'This place . . .' I said, gesturing around me.

'You are in the Citadel.'

'The Citadel of Selph?'

She nodded, studying me, her gaze clear and candid.

'It is Feikermun's home?' I enquired. For some reason I had never thought of this before, nor could I recall any other person making reference to it. Feikermun styled himself 'of Selph', and I had simply assumed it to be a town, city or region of which I knew nothing. I imagined it to lie somewhere north or west of Anxau, in lands I had barely visited; or even to be an obscure and formerly insignificant hamlet somewhere in Anxau's hinter-

164

land. Only now, when I was told that I was within its Citadel, did the question occur to me: exactly where in the world *is* Selph?

Aniba lowered her eyes, slowly shaking her beautiful head. 'It is his home, in a sense; it is also a place that is utterly alien to him. It is somewhere he has ravaged almost to destruction, yet his soul, what remains of it, resides here.'

'It is not a natural place. It seems not real.'

'Oh, it is real, in its way. Do not doubt that. It is here that all that might come to be resides. Anything that could precede any action that Feikermun might initiate can be found here. That is why it is such a dangerous place.' She looked at me again. 'I can see by your expression that you do not understand.'

'. . . It all makes little sense.'

'I know, you believe you are a stranger here. But think,' she said, 'what is it that precedes any action that you or any other person might perform?'

I considered for a moment, but had no answer.

'Raise your arm.'

I did so.

'What happened first?'

'You commanded me.'

'And then?'

I shook my head.

'You *thought*. Before any action comes the thought, and that is what we are facing here. Feikermun's thoughts, his dreams, his fantasies, his nightmares, impulses and obsessions, his instincts. Do you understand? Selph *is* Feikermun! You are within him now. You have taken the *gidsha* and through its agency have entered his inner world. It is another world, a madman's internal world, but it is real, as real as the world you have just left.'

I struggled with this. It seemed like lunacy. Everything seemed like lunacy. Yet everything I had experienced – it felt as if it had been for so long – seemed like this.

'What have I been brought here for?'

'To perform a task. We believe you can save us, all of us. We are threatened – our world is threatened, and yours too. By Feikermun. And we want you to save him.'

'Save him?'

'From what he does.'

'This is all meaningless to me.'

'I know. I want to explain further, but there is so much that you are not yet ready for. I am not the one to explain it all, but I can say that Feikermun has tapped into something, a power of unimaginable potency. He has found a key to open doors within himself, hidden doors within the Citadel. But the chambers to which he has gained access contain manifestations that he can never control. He will unleash them, believing he can. Some are already beginning to break free. If he is successful, if he is not stopped, he will release carnage, and the world you know will become a place of misery, changed beyond anything we can recognize.'

I looked around me at the strange, bleak, uncertain landscape, then back at Aniba. 'Am I to kill him?'

'No! That is precisely what you must not do. Understand that utterly: *Feikermun must not die!* Just now, though he strives to gain access to what resides within the chambers whose doors he has opened, he is prevented. At the same time, that which is within strives to break out, but Feikermun resists. That small part of him which remains human, which still contains an iota of goodness and rationality, holds back, knowing he tampers with forces too great. If he dies then that resistance dies too. The doors will remain open, the gates will be open, and everything the Citadel holds will be set free.'

'Then . . . what?'

'Feikermun must be overcome, subdued, led away from the path he has set out upon. And the doors must be sealed again.'

I almost scoffed. 'Impossible! Do you know what you ask? The man is a lunatic. He cannot be "led away".'

'That is why you have to confront him here, in the Citadel. In the Citadel of Selph, Feikermun may be found in all his aspects, all his personalities, all his possibilities and potentialities. You have to pursue him, explore this place, discover what it holds. There are secrets here, and danger. It is a place of wonders and horrors – but here, if you can find the right way, you can conquer Feikermun. But be sure of one thing: outside the Citadel, in the world that you know, Feikermun must not be allowed to perish. If necessary, at any cost, you must be his protector.'

I looked away, beyond her, shaking my head in disbelief. 'This is not right.'

Aniba was patient. 'When you truly understand what he has done you will know why it has to be this way. But I cannot show you everything. Somewhere else, deeper within the Citadel, Sermilio awaits you. He will explain more.'

Sermilio!

I stared hard at her. Was I dreaming? I had taken *gidsha*, *gidsha* that had been specially treated. All this, then, was not real, but a product of my hallucinating mind.

I said, 'Who is Sermilio?'

'It is better that he tells you himself,' Aniba said softly.

'Then take me to him, or have him come here to me.'

'I cannot. The laws of this place do not permit it.'

'There are laws?' I was surprised.

'Of a kind. The laws of paradox, if you like, of Chaos, of randomness. We who dwell here, though we do not understand them, all, must abide by them.'

I shook my head. 'Why me?'

Aniba half-smiled. 'How many folk, in moments of dilemma or distress, have made that same plea? I am not sure: that is the true answer. But in one sense it is because you were already here.'

'What does that mean?'

'Feikermun chose you, Dinbig.'

She knew my name!

Plainly my face revealed my shock, for Aniba smiled and went on: 'We did not know for a long time who it was. But you encountered him once before, did you not?'

I nodded.

'You made an impression. Something attracted him, made you noteworthy in his eyes. Perhaps he had some subliminal inkling of your knowledge of magic, your *Zan-Chassin* training. It was what he most sought. So Feikermun took you into himself, into the Citadel, though he did not know that he had done so. There – here – you grew, and, as Feikermun played with powers of which he really knew nothing, he opened the way which allowed you to escape. You were not entirely yourself – who knows what you were? You had been transformed, for part of you was Feikermun. But once free you made the mistake of insulting Feikermun, and suffered the price.'

'I was told I had died.'

'You did not die, as such. You were returned to the Citadel. And it is as well that this was so for, had Feikermun not recaptured you, you would have returned to Khimmur, and there come face-to-face with yourself. Think about what that means, for these are the kinds of forces we are dealing with.'

'That was not I! It was my double, someone or something impersonating me,' I protested.

She shook her head again. 'It was you, be sure of that. He was you following a course you might have chosen. And you reside here still, within the Citadel, striving like others to escape. This is something else that you must confront here.'

The conversation was extraordinary; I could not take in what I was being told. I felt that my mind was ready to burst into fragments.

You have taken gidsha I told myself. *You are under its influence.*

'What is all this?' I asked, gesturing to the winged people suspended in the coloured air all around and above us.

'This is what is really happening here, in Selph,' said Aniba. 'This is what Feikermun has done, though again he does not truly know it. Ask Sermilio when you meet him.'

Her voice had taken on a hollow quality. Her form was not as definite as it had been. I realized she was fading. 'Don't go!' I lurched towards her with sudden fear.

'I will return to you,' said Aniba. 'But at this point you must make a choice, alone!'

'No!'

My protest was futile, for I was on my own. The road stretched before me – so long, so far – a light breeze blowing dust across its breadth. I began to walk, not knowing where it would take me, not knowing what lay ahead.

It seemed an age that I walked, and then I found myself upon a wide drive, strewn with white gravel and lined with fir trees, which ran through formal gardens beside an ornamental lake.

On the far side of the lake was a pavilion built of grey-brown stone, a wide portico at its fore, floored with an alternating pattern of triangular black-and-white tiles. There stood Feikermun beside an altar-like table or slab of solid grey stone. Upon this was a woman, naked, and as I watched Feikermun raised a gleaming knife above her body, intoning inaudible words, his face turned to the orange-yellow sky. He brought the blade down and slashed across her neck. He bent over her, putting his lips to the mortal wound, and drank her flowing blood.

'He does not understand.' It was Aniba's voice, as though she stood at my shoulder. 'Since the beginning men have never understood. So much bloodshed, so much needless sacrifice, all through an eternity of misunderstanding.'

'I must stop him.'

'Yes, but first you must understand him, understand what he believes, so that you and others like you do not fall into the same trap.'

'What are you telling me?'

'Sacrifice, Dinbig. Blood sacrifice. Feikermun believes he drinks the blood of life. Others sacrifice men, women, children, animals, for their blood. They have always done so, to appease their gods, garner personal power . . . They worship the blood as the sacred, creative source of life. Feikermun drinks the blood of women, craving power over life, but it gives him nothing, for the belief is seeded in ancient ignorance.'

As I watched, Feikermun climbed upon the body of the woman on the altar slab. He seemed to change, his body coming to resemble a great grey ape. Yet still he was Feikermun, both Feikermun and ape at the same time. He grasped his swollen genital member and inserted it between the woman's limp outspread thighs, his mouth returning to the red wound at her neck as he began the frenzied motions of lust.

'In the early days men worshipped the blood,' said Aniba's voice, 'the blood that was uniquely of women, for it was perceived that this alone was the source of life. To primitive minds men played no part; it was woman's blood that created new life. The blood was worshipped, feared, revered. The belief has persisted over millennia, corrupted into myriad, often unrecognizable forms and transmutations as men and women have

169

striven to bring life out of blood. This is tragedy. So many sacrificed; a world founded on mistaken belief, on terrible misunderstanding. A myth, no longer even known, yet its rituals endure and are rarely questioned. But the blood is not the source; it bestows no power.'

'Yet Feikermun gains power,' I said. 'Terrible power. He is being transformed into a god.'

'He does not know where the power comes from. It is within and beyond, but it is too much to bear. He will not control it.'

Across the lake Feikermun eased himself off the pale body on the altar and stood, breathing heavily, still huge and simian. He glared across the water towards where I stood, and grinned madly, smeared with blood, though I could not tell whether he saw me.

'*Cormer of Chol, do you dream?*'

'I do not know.'

The scene had passed away; I was in another *where* now. All around me were the winged people. I drifted between them, moving backwards with a volition that was not my own. More of them. And more. So many, utterly motionless in the yellow-amber air.

'What is happening to me?'

'Seek Sermilio.'

I gazed upwards and saw my mother's face, heard her sweet voice sing, so full of joy and tenderness and love. The baby cried and the bells began to ring. Upon the steps a man stood garbed in grey, facing down a long and empty road.

And the blackness came down, taking me, and I wandered blindly, not knowing, in regions of nothing that were all that existed before the world began.

'*Am I dying?*'

'No,' a voice whispered. '*You have just been born.*'

14

A DULL, POUNDING thunder yammering through me, racking my body with pain. Dry, so dry; craving liquid; my tongue a cracked pebble; the roof of my mouth carpeted with sand. The merciless throbbing *shriek* inside my head, and the noise outside – people shouting somewhere, I thought, but a meaningless babble, far off and too painful . . . and I could not open my eyes for the light stabbed into them screaming . . .

Where was I?

I rolled over, sickeningly, a massive effort, my eyes screwed tight shut, shielded with an arm. I think I cried out: the pain and nausea were more than I could bear. I had to open my eyes. Gradually, still shading with my sleeve, I allowed the light through.

At first strange and unfamiliar, yet not wholly alien. Slowly blinking, waiting for order in my thoughts, and then recognizing the fixtures and furnishings of the apartment in which I was lodged in Feikermun's palace. I was sprawled upon the bed. How long had I been here? I recalled sunset, leaving this chamber. Now bright daylight streamed through the narrow window. I did not know what had happened in between – or did I not want to?

The *gidsha*. Was I still under its influence? Was I here in this chamber, or dreaming it? How could I know?

Do you dream, Cormer of Chol?

That echo in my memory. I shivered as the images ranged before my mind's eye. The Citadel. I saw it, and yet knew more had happened than I remembered now. So much more than I could grasp.

What was all the shouting outside?

I sat up slowly, the world slewing, my head ringing with

171

vicious pain. A pitcher stood beside the bed. I reached out and grasped it, watched my fingers close like claws around the handle. Ignoring the wooden cup at its side I raised the pitcher to my parched lips and gulped down the cold sweet water in greedy draughts. It helped, a little. The searing dryness of my mouth and throat abated, and even the wild pain in my head seemed to lessen slightly. I splashed water on cheeks and forehead, then sat on the edge of the bed, hands nursing my head, trying to remember, trying to understand. Something just below my consciousness, tugging at me, a voice, urging me to hear.

Yo!

'Master, I am here.'

I groaned. I was in no state to deal with him.

'I have an urgent message from your Chariness, Master.'

'Be brief then, Yo. I am unwell.'

'Can I be of assistance?'

'No. Impart your message and leave. Your presence may be detected.'

'In reply to the message I relayed on your behalf, the Chariness states that the eel-trader, Wirm of Guling Mire, is known to be a close associate of your target. He has connections in dark places and should be treated with care. The other man, Vecco, is a bastard-child of a Tanakipi kin chieftain and a villain of the lowest order. Beware him also.'

Tanakipi? There then was the *gisha* connection. Had Vecco been Wirm's supplier? Almost certainly, if Vecco had clan-links with influential Tanakipi kin-members, he could have smuggled the root out. But then why had Wirm had him killed? And why had Vecco come after me?

I was hardly enlightened. The Chariness gave me little that I had not already discovered or surmised. But Yo's words now, as he completed her message, were another matter.

'Feikermun is judged to be in a highly dangerous condition,' he said. 'He cannot be allowed to continue. You are ordered to take whatever steps are necessary to end his life at the first opportunity. Consider this your priority.'

'No!' I blurted out as the echo of another voice whispered urgently: *Feikermun must not die!*

Aniba. But could I be sure that she was real? Was what she

172

had told me real, or had all of it been hallucination induced by the specially prepared *gidsha*? The Citadel – was it anything more than fevered imagination? I had been there, had seen what it held. *I had seen myself!* But how could I know I was not the victim of my own delusions?

'Yo, I cannot prosecute that command. Inform the Chariness that there have been changes. I cannot kill Feikermun, not yet. I cannot explain now – it would take too long, and every moment that you remain here increases the risk of detection. But Feikermun must not die, not under any circumstances, at least until I have learned more.'

'The Chariness was adamant—'

'*So am I!* Go, now, and tell her what I have said. Until I know more, Feikermun must live. Now leave me!'

'I am gone, Master.'

My head spun. To disobey a direct command from the *Zan-Chassin* Hierarchy, on the strength of words spoken to me by a phantom while under the influence of an hallucinogenic drug? Had I lost my senses? I lay back on the bed, my blood pounding in my ears. I had to find out more, but the only way to do that was to re-enter the Citadel, and for that I would have to take more *gidsha*. The thought unnerved me. Was this how it achieved its insidious grip, luring men and women into mindless addiction through the power of its visions?

I tried to stand then, but a wave of pain and nausea pitched me back on to the bed. Still I could hear the shouting from outside: many voices, men. A shaft of dazzling sunlight stabbed through the window. I coerced myself gingerly to my feet and crossed the room unsteadily, one hand clasping my agonized brow.

As I arrived at the window I was startled by the sudden appearance of a shadow, accompanied by a scuffing sound immediately outside. A hand appeared near the top of the window, curling around the stone surround to grip with white-knuckled fingers. Then a booted foot slid on to the sill beneath. A moment later a figure filled my vision, blotting out the sun.

I stepped back, alarmed, before recognizing the visitor. 'Jaktem!'

Jaktem eased his bulk through the window space, dropped to

the floor and stood before me, flushed and sweating with effort. 'Master Cormer, are you all right?'

'A touch the worse for wear, but otherwise fine, I think. Why? What is happening? Why this unorthodox entrance?'

'It is the only way I could get to you. I am confined to my chamber. But a narrow cornice runs along the outer wall, linking our two windows. I made good use of it to check on you.'

'Where is Illan?'

'He managed to slip out before we were placed under confinement.'

'What is all this hullabaloo outside?'

'Malibeth's forces have attacked Feikermun's quarter in strength. They are at the palace walls. Feikermun was taken completely by surprise by the ferocity of the attack and the numbers thrown against him. He is sorely stretched to defend himself.'

'By the gods and devils!' I pushed past him to the window, my pain forgotten. Sure enough, I could see Feikermun's beasts upon the battlements, firing missiles into the streets below. Several buildings blazed and there was much activity beyond the walls, opposing forces blockading the streets and firing arrows from windows and roofs. All this I took in in a moment. I glanced along the wall as I turned back, half-consciously noting the slender ledge along which Jaktem had clambered. I marvelled at his courage and surefootedness.

'Is Feikermun in danger?'

'I don't know, but I think Malibeth may have used a catapult to smash the outer wall at a second point of attack, to the southeast, and gained at least limited ingress to the palace grounds.'

'Then it is serious! Jaktem, conceal yourself quickly – behind that armoire.'

As he did so I crossed to the door and flung it open. A sentry was positioned outside, barring my way with a halberd. 'I must see Lord Feikermun.'

The man curled his lip. 'You will stay here. His Excellency will see you when he chooses.'

'No. It is important. I have to speak to him.'

He shook his head. 'When Lord Feikermun chooses.'

He was a column of meat and no brain, and too fearful of his master to disobey orders. 'Can you get a message to him?' I asked.

He hesitated. I produced a silver coin and his eyes brightened. 'Just tell him that I must see him. It is urgent. Tell him,' – I was suddenly inspired – 'tell him I have spoken to the woman.'

If that did not arouse Feikermun's interest I did not know what would. I recalled how unsettled he had been at the revelation when I had first seen Aniba, in his chamber. And again, later, when I had spoken to him about her. But how long might I have to wait until Feikermun agreed to an audience with me? Clearly he was tied up with Malibeth's assault upon the palace. It could be hours.

The sentry pocketed the coin and I turned back, closing the door.

'I could overpower him, Master Cormer,' said Jaktem in an undertone, coming from hiding.

'No. There will be others out there. For now the best course is that you return to your chamber, if you are able, so that no one is aware we have communicated. If I leave here, I will try to find a way of letting you know. Until then, wait and do nothing to endanger yourself. But if you learn anything significant, come here by the ledge again, if you can.'

Jaktem nodded and climbed back on to the windowsill. He waited a few moments, scanning the castle walls, assuring himself that he was unobserved, then eased himself out on to the ledge. I watched him as he inched along the wall, marvelling again at his nimbleness, until he disappeared through the window of his own chamber.

I had no clear idea of what I was going to do. If Feikermun responded to my summons I did not know what I would say to him. I was still feeble and racked with head-pain, and the notion that I had to safeguard Feikermun when I despised him so utterly, had to contravene a direct order from the Chariness, angered me. I could not be sure of anything, and the only way to find out more was to return to the Citadel of Selph. What were its secrets? What would it yield up to my enquiries now? Could I journey there alone, or did it require Feikermun to guide me, as before? The only thing I was certain of was that

I could not re-enter the Citadel without the agency of the *gidsha*. So I applied myself once more to its ritual preparation. I was not certain whether it was safe to take it again so soon – whether my sanity would be able to bear it – but I pushed these considerations from my mind so that I might concentrate upon the task.

When the *gidsha* was ready I sat back and took stock. There was no word from Feikermun. Outside the battle raged still. From what I could see it had become a pure exchange of missile-fire, with neither side appearing to have gained the upper hand. But my view was limited. I had no way of knowing how things were going to the southeast where, according to Jaktem, Malibeth had breached the outer wall. Should I take the *gidsha* now, alone? Here in Dehut, anything might happen while I was in the Citadel. Feikermun could be slain, the palace fall to Malibeth. What would that mean?

'Aniba, tell me what I should do.'

She did not appear. Instead there was a loud sound of rushing, beating air; I felt its wind against my skin. Towards one corner of the chamber a figure half-appeared: a youth of androgynous aspect. I had seen him before in a dream. Upon his back were a pair of gorgeous black-and-crimson wings. They beat wildly and his hands clawed and struck at something unseen. But his face turned towards me, just momentarily, and he spoke: 'Come. Please come now. We need you.'

And he was gone. I hesitated in a moment of indecision, then took up the *gidsha* bowl and ate a portion of the green mash, about as much as I had taken the first time. I went to the door and opened it. The sentry stood outside.

'Did you go to Lord Feikermun?'

'I sent a messenger.'

'Has there been any reply?'

'The man returned to report that he had delivered the message to His Excellency.'

'And was there any word?'

'None.'

'Then, should His Excellency come here, please tell him I have gone to seek her. He will understand.'

The sentry tensed. 'You may not leave.'

'Do not be alarmed. I will be here in this chamber. Just give Lord Feikermun that message. He may wish to accompany me.'

I closed the door on the baffled man and stood for a while in the centre of the room, absorbed in keen and nervous anticipation. I did not know how long it would take for the drug to begin to work its effects, but I recalled that on the previous occasion Feikermun had made me run. Did the running stimulate the onset of the drug's effects? Unlike the corridors through which I had pounded with Feikermun and the ape, this chamber did not offer me sufficient space to run, but I began to jog on the spot, slowly at first, a little self-consciously – then, as I found my rhythm, more energetically.

Nothing happened. I ran on, working up a sweat, drawing great draughts of air into my expanding lungs, enjoying the sensation but thinking that perhaps the *gidsha* was not going to work this time. I watched the stone wall opposite. It was hung with various objects: a rectangle of tapestry, a round wooden targe, the mounted head of a slain doe. I was engrossed by the fine grain of the stone, which I had not noticed before, but which glittered in the subdued light, a million minuscule facets of tiny crystal which I saw now for the first time with extraordinary close-up clarity.

Then the walls around me were obliterating before my eyes. It didn't surprise me: it was the most natural thing. They fell apart; the floor dropped from beneath my feet; I rose, passed into the wall, between the myriad particles of stone, into a blackness filled with silent, moving shapes.

Bodies were flying by me in all directions; a rushing wind; the sound of many beating, flapping wings. The winged people in their scores, stricken-faced, struggling in the air, thrown here, there, unable to help themselves. And I passed through them, avoiding collisions as though I were a ghost. I heard their voices crying out in the darkness, in panic, raised in unison, distorted as they tumbled and twisted, blown by some force they could not comprehend. I moved on, not knowing where I was going or what impelled me.

Then there was stillness.

I was upon the road, the long road, and the winged people were held unmoving in the amber air all around. And I was a child, a babe. I heard my cry, and my mother's sweet song, and the tolling of the bell. I began to walk, so heavy, unfamiliar as the body settled in, and far away along the amber road a figure stood, its back to me, gazing out upon a sunset.

It seemed an eternity that I walked; then I stopped and turned and looked back. A man stood upon the steps, in grey, watching me. He was I, Ronbas Dinbig. Watching me, watching me, as I watched him also and knew that he was I and I he. The tears, the beauty of it, stung my eyes. I turned again. I had no choice but to continue on my way.

Sermilio's face, when at last I stood beside him, was rapt and beautiful as he gazed upon the glory of the sunset. The light stained his skin. He was youth and woman and man and bird, and something other. He was Avari, I understood that now, as I understood that all those others who were held in stasis in the air around us were Avari. The Tutelary Spirits, the Companions of the Soul. Perhaps Sermilio spoke into my mind and told me this, or perhaps I intuited it. What I did not know was *why*.

I spoke as one speaks in a dream, not knowing what I was going to say, yet saying it, and hearing myself saying it, knowing that I could have said nothing else yet thinking that there were other things I might have said.

'Why do you wait here?'

He raised his arm towards the glorious light. 'It is the beginning, and the end. It is everything.'

'Everything?'

'That which precedes whatever might become. Everything.'

'But why do you stand here?'

'The choice is not mine. I am waiting, we are waiting.'

'For what?'

He paused. 'For the world to begin.'

'You called me here.'

'We needed you. We still need you. But you have not brought what I asked you for.'

'What was it that I was to bring?'

'The amber,' Sermilio said. 'The Amber of Selph.'

I felt a moment of terrible misgiving. The Amber of Selph. Was this the amber I had brought with me from Hon-Hiata, that I had purchased earlier from Wirm of Guling Mire, that I had now passed into the hands of Feikermun? The amber that held the cloud of tiny creatures with red and black wings? I stared around me again at the bodies of the Avari suspended in the strangely coloured air, and strove to deny to myself that it could be this that Sermilio referred to.

Sermilio turned and smiled, but his eyes were sorrow-weighted.

'Is it the rare green amber that you speak of?' I asked. 'The amber that holds the winged creatures?'

'The winged creatures. The Avari.' He gestured mournfully at the frozen figures. 'Us. It is we who are trapped within.'

Feikermun of Selph had trapped the Avari. He did not know that he had done it, though had he known he would have rejoiced. His probings into the workings of magic had taken him deep into the mysteries hidden within the Citadel of Selph, and there he had stumbled upon the first layers of all potential, the seething immensities that underlie reality, pure, unformed, unchannelled, unconscious thought, Chaos, the immeasurable fathomless stuff of pre-Creation. And there dwelt the Avari, assigned to maintain the order of the world, to ensure that the unlimited power that existed in the hidden domain of Selph was contained for the protection of all, that the universe might unfold in its proper manner, learning as it grew, as near as possible harmoniously, in balance. The powers of Selph, unleashed without control, would overwhelm it utterly. Forestalling this was the task of the Avari, assigned to them for all eternity from the beginning of time.

But there also dwelt the Scrin, the Avaris' immortal foes. They strove to unhinge the balance, disrupt the unfolding and allow Chaos and randomness and ultimately evil to flood Creation, destroying for destruction's own sake all that had come to be. The conflict between the two had persisted through-out time, but the Scrin, though relentless, had never succeeded in overcoming the Avari, and the unfolding of divine Creation had continued more or less along its natural course.

Until now.

In his obsessed probings Feikermun had succeeded in pen-

179

etrating further than any man before into the dark and secret labyrinths of Selph. Fuelled by *gidsha*, his mind crazed with the lust for power, he had stumbled upon the immeasurable reservoirs of raw potential, the teeming energies, the Chaotic streams of yet-to-be or never-to-be.

Probably only half-guessing at what he had found, he sensed something of the power he had uncovered and plainly believed he could command it. He experimented, played, struggled; and the forces of Selph began to stir. With Feikermun as the unwitting conduit they began to see through into the formed world.

Feikermun brought disharmony. The Avari perceived this, and the immense threat these premature stirrings of Selph represented. They moved to prevent him. But such were the energies he toyed with that, by a single thought, a single wish, Feikermun stopped them. His blind, furious impulse caused time to cease for the Avari. They were frozen in stasis, and in the same instant that he had formed the wish, his instinctive response to their intrusion, Feikermun had departed Selph. He returned to the formed world and Dehut. But, as he propelled himself from the Citadel, the idea of stopping the Avari was carried out also, crystallized, a physical thought: the green amber, the Amber of Selph.

These things Sermilio told me as we stood beside the road in the blaze of a glorious and melancholy sunset which outshone the amber light all around. And the black simultaneously overhead, confounding perception and defying possibility, seemed to draw me upwards, into an unknown reach, an unfathomable nowhere.

'I brought the amber,' I said, and Sermilio looked at me with surprise and hope. 'I received your note, though I did not know to what it referred nor who had sent it. And I came here for, as I thought, inescapable reasons. I brought the amber without knowing its significance.'

'Then you have it?'

'I had it. Feikermun took it from me.'

Sermilio's face fell. 'Feikermun has it? Where?'

'Somewhere within his palace, I believe.'

He clapped his hand to his brow, then swept back his long

180

fair locks. 'This is disquieting news, but perhaps not all is lost. When he took it from you, did he display unusual interest, excessive covetousness, excitement?'

'He regarded it as a beautiful object which he desired to possess, I would say. His intention was to humiliate me. He gave no indication that there was anything more than that.'

'That is good.'

'Is Feikermun aware of the existence of this artefact, or of its true nature and origin?'

'No. We must be thankful that he does not know what he has done.'

'Does anyone?'

'I believe not. When the amber was cast into your world it did not pass with Feikermun. It went' – he spread his hands and hunched his shoulders – 'somewhere. Randomly.'

'And Wirm came upon it, and then sold it to me.'

'It is curious that an associate of Feikermun's should stumble upon it. Perhaps not entirely coincidence. But fortunately he did not know what it was he had.'

'When I brought the amber back to Wirm I was attacked. Not by Wirm, but by the henchmen of a man named Vecco, who was Wirm's guest. At the time I did not know why he attacked me, but he had seen the amber. Could it be that he knew what it was?'

'Vecco . . . Vecco . . . He may have been an agent of the Scrin.'

'The Scrin know of the amber?'

'Oh, yes,' said Sermilio. 'And they seek it, for with it they would hold us forever prisoners in their grasp. What was Vecco's relationship to Wirm?'

'It is hard to say. I believed they were confederates, but following Vecco's abortive attempt to murder me, Wirm had him executed.'

We had begun to walk slowly along the road, side by side. Sermilio's head was bowed, deep in thought, his fabulous wings swaying upon his back, rustling softly. I glanced back over my shoulder. No longer could I see the temple-like structure or the figure in grey who was I, watching me. And no longer was I a babe, clumsy-fleshed, nor a child. I had come a long way along the road, though I still did not know where it led. Ahead I saw a cluster of buildings materializing in the bleakness.

'In Dehut,' I said, 'there have been strange manifestations. Feikermun seems on the verge of power, mooted to become a god. There is tremendous conflict. His enemies have attacked him in force. I saw a creature appear out of the air, a savage, rat-like humanish thing which attacked and killed a woman, then vanished. Was this the Scrin?'

Sermilio gave a half-smile. 'Almost certainly. Feikermun has inadvertently opened the way out of the Citadel. Though there are still barriers, the Scrin are discovering ways of breaking through. Feikermun has no control over them. If they are not stopped they will soon break through in force. Then they will unwork the very fabric of Creation, reduce the cosmos to primordial Chaos where no aspect of life or intelligence can exist.'

'Then surely they also will cease to exist?'

'The Scrin do not wish to exist. Their sole purpose is to destroy – everything, including themselves. They exist only for as long as others exist. When all else is gone, the Scrin die.'

'The creature I saw – do the Scrin always take this form?'

'The Scrin take whatever form you perceive. As do we. This is hard to explain, but we exist only as you imagine us, whether you are aware of having imagined it or not. Somewhere in your mind you have perceived the Avari as winged humans, fair and attractive to the eye. Therefore, that is what we are to you. The Scrin—'

'I had barely heard of the Scrin until now.'

'Yet somewhere within you was an image, and this you saw when the Scrin creature manifested. We do not truly exist within the scope of your experience; we are things of an *other* order, an *other* reality. We do not even have a name, except that you have given us one.'

'Many humans believe in you as guardian spirits, put into the world to guide mankind.'

'In a sense this is true. In a sense, you are also us. You descend into substance, we watch over you as best we can, for in substance you lose virtually all awareness of what you truly are. At the end, when your flesh decays and you can no longer hold the substance, we who are not substance guide you back.

You are absorbed then, all of your experiences are absorbed, back into the One Mind – that which underlies all Creation, that which *is* Creation. This way It learns, It grows, It unfolds, and gradually, after an infinity has passed, It will perhaps come to understand Its nature and purpose. I speculate only, for such things cannot be known by beings such as we.'

'But if Feikermun succeeds, if the Scrin succeed, everything will end.'

'That is so.'

'Then what is to be done?'

'Firstly the amber must be brought back here, into the Citadel, in order that we can be set free to confront the Scrin.'

'How?'

'That is for you to determine, Dinbig.' Like Aniba previously, he called me by my own name, letting me know that he was party to my duplicity. 'You say Feikermun is under assault?'

I nodded.

'He must not die. If he does, access to the Citadel will be lost to you. You must protect him from his enemies, discover what he has done with the amber, take it from him without his knowledge and return with it here. Whatever happens, you must not let it fall into Scrin hands, nor allow anyone to destroy it. If it is broken, we are lost . . . all is lost.'

We were among the buildings now. It was a small village, by all outward appearances uninhabited. I had been here before, in a dream; I could not tell if this was a continuation of the dream.

'I may not be here when you come,' said Sermilio, 'so I will tell you now what I can. Not everything, just enough. That way, should things go wrong, you can tell our enemies little. You are to bring the amber here.' We turned and walked down a narrow path at the base of which was a low glade backed by dark trees. In the centre of the glade was a well. 'Bring the amber here, to the well.'

I approached the low circular stone wall which rimmed the well, and peered over. Below me, far down, ringed by twisting tendrils and brown and black leaves, was a perfect circle of water which reflected my own image. But it was not Cormer of Chol who gazed back at me; it was my true reflection, that of

Ronbas Dinbig. As I contemplated this the water rippled and stirred as though something beneath had disturbed its surface. The image slithered away. There was a rustling sound, and threshing, splashing. I heard a baby cry, then silence. I straightened.

'You must enter the well with the amber,' said Sermilio. 'That is all I can tell you.'

'Enter it?' I felt a chill.

He put a hand reassuringly upon my arm. 'Remember, this is not the world you know. Do not expect or anticipate, for nothing will be as you are accustomed to. You are in the Citadel, and this is the Well of Selph. From here all things come, and it is to here that the amber must be returned. If you achieve this, you will know what to do next. But do not shrink, do not merely drop the amber in. You must bring it and then proceed. If you succeed, then we may be released.'

I looked up to the sky, to the hanging winged figures diminishing into specks in the high dark distance. 'Why are you at liberty, Sermilio, when all the others are trapped?'

'There were a few of us who were not caught when Feikermun formed the amber. A very few. We are all engaged in the work of bringing you here, safely, with the amber.'

I recalled my experience in the marsh of Guling Mire, when I had been rescued from certain death by the pale creature on the fallen bough. I mentioned this to Sermilio.

'He is one of us,' he said.

'He was not like you.'

'He was, as I said before, as you perceived him.'

'And again, in the tower in Stonemarker.'

Sermilio nodded. 'There were enemies nearby. You could have come to harm. You were not supposed to see the Avari, but Chaos is manifesting. We have little control now.' He stepped back, spreading his wings suddenly. 'I can stay with you no longer. Remember, you must bring the amber and enter the well. You will be helped if it is possible.'

He rose from the ground, effortlessly, the great coloured wings beating back and forth, and passed into the reappearing sunset, until he was no more than a black, familiar shape against the light, and then, nothing.

184

15

I MOVED AWAY from the wall, suddenly terribly aware that I was alone. The bodies filled the air all around. The blackness above, the amber light and the sunset – I cannot explain, but I saw all these things at once, even though the one form of light should have excluded the others – the sunset cast its glow upon the land so that everything was stained: the buildings, the ground, the trees, the motionless Avari, the sky itself. Blood light, not glorious now, but deathly. An ocean of blood. Blood, the Source, the Life, misconceived and now spilled and wasted. Death, red mantling all.

I climbed the sloping path to the little cluster of apparently untenanted buildings, then stood at their edge looking out across a bleak plain. The road ended here, I realized for the first time. I gazed back along it, filled with remorse. I could see little; so much was obscured. But I knew now that the well was my death, just as the road had been my life. No matter what I chose to do, or thought I chose to do, I would come here in the end, inexorably. And if I acted wrongly I would return here again and again until I found the right way.

There was movement out on the plain. A terrible sight. I was upon a low ridge, gazing across a wide landscape. Before me Feikermun rode upon a woman's shoulders, beating her with a many-tongued lash as she staggered forward, so that the blood ran down her back and over her buttocks and legs. He was charging into battle, laughing maniacally. He hacked with a sabre at men, women, children cutting them down, carving a gigantic swathe through humanity's hordes, fleeing before him. Beside him came his beasts, raping, pillaging, mutilating for the sheer perverse joy of it. And behind them loped and lurched the demonic Scrin, gorging upon the ruined flesh, eating the wounded alive. They had no need to do anything more – Feikermun did their killing for them. Blood rained from the skies; the rivers ran red, clogged with bloated corpses; the roads were choked with those trying to flee. But the world was small and there was nowhere to run.

I watched in helpless despair.

What can I do? What can *I* do?

Feikermun twisted upon the woman's back and saw me. He grinned and raised a bloody fist. 'Ha-ha-ha! Do you dream, Cormer of Chol? Do you dream?'

I stepped back. The dreadful scene was fading. The air was filled with bodies, rushing by, but I saw nothing. I heard the frantic beating of many wings, the watery threshing; smelt the blackness, the wet; heard the screams; so many screaming and nowhere to run.

'*Do you dream?*'

Do I?

The water parted, just for a moment, and I looked up and saw Wirm standing on the jetty above me. He gazed down, pitiless, a cold smile upon his lips. And, yes, there were others beside him. There was Jaktem, and Illan. And there was I, watching me die.

And I sank back, threshing, my arms and legs held by the ropes, and the eels devoured my flesh, smothering me, and all was a red blur, Wirm seen through a film of clouding water, the slippery shapes, the water entering my lungs, eels burrowing into my eyes, my mouth, my innards, and my tongueless roars became gurgles and the mouths tore at my dying flesh.

'*Do you dream, Cormer of Chol? Do you dream?*'

'I do not know. *Help me!*'

'Bring the amber to the well.'

'I cannot. I have died.'

'Yes, many times, and many times more until you do what must be done.'

I cried. My mother sang. The bells rang overhead. I was waiting for the world to begin. Aniba stood before me.

'No, we must not touch!'

'But why? I need you. I want you.'

'I am not what you think.'

'Then what are you?'

She was silent.

'I want to understand. I want you.'

'Bring the amber to the well.'

'I am dreaming.'

'*Do you dream, Cormer of Chol?*'

'I am dreaming that I have died. Or am I dreaming that I have lived?'

'Bring the amber, or all will end.'

I was falling, and I saw my tiny body stretched upon the floor far below, waiting for me to arrive.

'Speak! Tell me what she said!'

The world rang with shocking pain. Still all dark. Resounding. Cudgel-blows smashing that which was I from side to side. And I was trapped, not knowing where, except that flesh was my prison.

'Tell me, curse you! What were her words?'

Again the blow, the stinging, shattering pain. And the thirst, the shrieking in my mind, my mouth and throat a harsh desert of fine grit.

'Her name, Cormer of Chol! What is her name? Speak it, or you will be roasted alive!'

Her name!

I was being shaken roughly, no more blows on my face. My eyes opened for a moment, caught the savage image of Feikermun towering over me, eyes fierce and mad, mouth a grimace, red hair matted and wild.

I have been inside your mind, I thought. *I know your soul. You do not know what you have done.*

His hand rose, a blur above my face, and he slapped my cheeks, one, then the other, forcing me back to awareness, out of the *gidsha* dream, through pain.

'Her name! What is her name?'

'Her – name – is – Aniba.' I could barely speak the words, my mouth was so parched and swollen.

'Aniba! Aniba!' Feikermun thrust me back and rose. Only

187

now was I aware that he had been holding me up in a half-sitting position, his fist bunching my tunic beneath my throat. I hit the floor hard and the world swirled and spun.

'Aniba! Aah, Ani-iibaaa!'

I could feel the thud of his footsteps upon the heavy floorboards. With difficulty I forced myself up on one elbow. Feikermun strode around the room, his hands clasped beneath his chin, his face upturned, repeating Aniba's name again and again, enraptured. I realized then that he loved her, if such a man was capable of love; that he was wholly infatuated by her – but he did not know her.

There were others in the chamber.

'Water,' I rasped. Someone moved, took up the pitcher, brought it back, tipped some of its contents over my head, then knelt and put its rim to my lips. I drank greedily and nodded my thanks. It was the nameless steward. He withdrew from my vision.

'Aniba, Aniba. Oh, my Aniba!' Feikermun halted suddenly, wheeled and rushed towards me. He dropped to one knee, his great gurgling belly almost smothering me. A brutal hand gripped my chin and forced my face to look into his. 'Who is she? What did she say to you? What does she want?'

'My lord, she said little.' My mind was racing. The fact that I had spoken to her gave me power over him, of a kind. But he was insanely jealous, so I walked a fine and precarious line. He wished me alive to find out what I knew and how it was that I could gain access to her, yet his temper might at any time gain the upper hand so that he ended my life on a raging whim.

'She is Feikermun's. Do you understand, Cormer of Chol? Feikermun will have her, and no other will touch her!'

His fingers squeezed my jaw so hard I thought he would crush the bone. I nodded, somehow. What was I to say to him?

'Who is she? Where does she come from?'

'She dwells within the Citadel, my lord.'

'In the Citadel?' He looked surprised, even disconcerted at this. *Yes, she is within you, somewhere*, I thought.

He released my jaw. 'Then Feikermun must return. She is the one woman. She must be Feikermun's.'

He rose again, and I wondered, *What if he finds her there*? I

188

already knew. He would destroy her; he was incapable of anything else. No matter how he desired her, he could do nothing
except destroy. It might be partially inadvertent, as with the
Avari, but he would destroy nonetheless.

What would that mean? I could not say; I knew only that I
had to do all in my power to ensure that Feikermun never
found Aniba.

'The *gidsha* is good, Cormer of Chol. You were right. Is there
more?'

'A little,' I said, fighting hard to recall, for my memory was
a blur. 'I can acquire more.'

'Then you will do so. Feikermun commands. We will return
to the Citadel. You will lead Feikermun to Aniba.'

I said nothing, wondering if there was a way to bend this
circumstance to my advantage. Feikermun stared down at me.
'Now, tell Feikermun everything she said.'

'My lord—' I began, and was interrupted. A door had opened
and a man swept into the chamber. I recognized Hircun, Feikermun's one-eyed general.

'My lord, they have control of the outer barbican,' said
Hircun. 'My men have been forced to fall back to defensive
positions within the inner ward.'

'I piss on the mad Bitch!' railed Feikermun. He kicked out at
a stool, sending it flying into the wall, then screamed at his
general. 'Does Malibeth think she can overthrow Feikermun so
easily? Hircun, are you a mouse? Why have you not crushed
her forces? They cannot match the beasts of Feikermun!'

'Lord, their numbers are—'

'Silence!' Feikermun shrieked. 'Don't bring excuses!' He
raised his fists above his head. 'Malibeth! Malibeth! Feikermun
will drink your blood yet! So close, you do not know. You
think to overthrow me, but I have the power! Yes, and you will
see, very soon, what it means to cross swords with Feikermun.
I am the scourge of my enemies and I will treat you until you
howl to die!'

I looked from his wrathful face to that of one-eyed Hircun,
and instinct told me that Hircun had the more realistic grasp
of the situation. He was worried. Feikermun too, I guessed,

189

despite his bravado and bombast. But what was I to do now, for my role was to ensure that Feikermun did not fall to Malibeth.

And the amber. How was I to find it in this beleaguered madman's den?

There was beating in the air, coloured wings in the corner of the chamber – then gone. And no one but I saw them. Feikermun stormed out, head down like a charging bull. His last words to me hung harshly. 'Cormer of Chol, we will go together, and this time I will not leave you. You will take me to her. Prepare the *gidsha* now!'

I lay back as the footsteps of the others passed from the chamber. I had not seen who else had been here with Feikermun. The door slammed shut, tossing me like tortured driftwood on an angry sea. I settled slowly, my ears ringing. The thought of entering the Citadel again so soon was too much to contemplate. I wanted to sleep, only sleep.

'*No, you cannot!*'

'Please.'

'*We depend on you! We need you!*'

'I have no strength. I am but one man.'

'*But you are not alone!*'

'Who will help me?'

'*I will.*'

'Aniba!' In pale blue raiment, she knelt beside me. 'I cannot do this.'

'Without you we will die. We will all die. And the world and all that has ever been will follow. Nothing will remain, not even that which has not yet been.'

'Are the Scrin truly so powerful?'

'More than you can guess. You have seen of the Scrin only what your imagination can conceive. But with the Avari held captive and the gates to the Citadel of Selph thrown open, the Scrin will surge forth in ways and forms you cannot imagine. They will make monsters of all men, turn you all one upon the other, and then they will follow behind, annihilating all that remains until all that is left to annihilate is themselves, which is what they seek.'

I closed my eyes, trying to summon strength from somewhere within. 'Feikermun seeks you.'

'If he finds me he will destroy me. That is all he is capable of now.'

'Yet you want me to keep him alive.'

'You know why. If he dies we cannot close the gates, nor the doors to the chambers within. Feikermun is your only access to the Citadel; no one before him has brought it so close to the surface. If he dies it will sink again beyond your reach, but with its gates still wide. The Scrin and all of its contents will still be able to pour forth.'

I gazed up into her eyes, so tender, so full. I reached up, aching to touch her and draw her to me, but she pulled back and shook her head with a solemn smile.

'Don't leave me!'

'Bring the amber, Dinbig.'

'I do not know where it is.'

'Ask Feikermun, then watch. Let him show you.'

She was gone. I sat up. Much of my pain had passed. I felt clearer, stronger. I brushed my wet hair from my face, drank again from the pitcher, then stood and went to the window. The sun hung low in the afternoon sky. The scene around the palace walls had changed little. Feikermun's troops lined the parapets, and I could make out Malibeth's fighters from time to time beyond the wall. Buildings still smouldered, but there seemed to be a lull in the fighting – here, at least. There were sounds of battle further south, uncomfortably close. I wondered, *Does Malibeth have any inkling of what is at stake here, or is it coincidence that she has struck now?* Almost certainly she was aware of Feikermun's imminent accession to power, and had made her move now to pre-empt him. But equally I would have wagered that her intention was to kill him, thinking this would end his reign. She was ignorant of what it would ulti- mately mean.

I turned away from the window, mindful of Feikermun's last words. Once again I commenced the preparation of the *gidsha*.

I had barely finished when the steward, accompanied by two guards, came for me. 'Lord Feikermun summons you now.'

It was growing dusky. I had been on the verge of lighting candles. My mouth and cheek were painfully bruised from Fei- kermun's blows, but I realized suddenly that I was faint with

191

hunger. How long was it since I had last eaten? I mentioned this to the steward, who replied that he would arrange for food for me, but that there could be no delay in taking me to Feikermun.

'I must speak to my men next door. They have ingredients that I ran short of for this preparation,' I lied.

The steward looked dubious. 'How long do you require?'

'A moment.'

'Very well.' He led me, with the guards, up the corridor. Inside the chamber Jaktem sat alone. He rose quickly as we entered, his face registering shock when he saw my bruising.

'Has Illan returned?' I said in a low voice, though it was virtually impossible to communicate without being overheard.

Jaktem shook his head. 'He is probably prevented by the fighting.'

I nodded. 'I am being taken to Feikermun again. I require something of yours.' I cautioned Jaktem with a glance and a raised finger, then went to his saddle-pack and, my back to the steward, pretended to remove something from it and put it in my pocket.

'Let me see!' demanded the steward. I took from my pocket the phial of powdered *muss* gum which I had secreted there before leaving my own chamber, and showed it to him. He gave a curt nod. 'Very well. Is that all?'

I nodded.

'Then let us go.'

'Jaktem, I would remind you once more that you are under no obligation to me,' I said loudly. 'You have performed the duties for which I hired you, and you are free to leave my service at any time.' I spoke to the steward. 'This man and his partner owe no allegiance to me. They were employed for a specific task, that being to accompany me to Dehut. They should not be held against their will.'

'That is for His Excellency to decide. Come!'

I was marched quickly back to my chamber, where I feigned mixing the *muss* powder into the new *gidsha*; then we left smartly. Squads of soldiers, their faces grimly set, rushed along the corridors, heading for battle with Malibeth's intruders. Through a window I saw injured men having their wounds

192

tended in a courtyard. Beyond the nearest buildings, smoke rose ominously into the reddened sky, which had now begun to cloud darkly. We ascended to Feikermun's apartments on the third level. He was absent. Guards stood at the door, within and without, and by the windows, which were drawn with drapes. Torches and candles illuminated the chamber. A pair of grey langurs chattered on a table and began leaping about excitedly as we entered. The steward pointed to the remains of a meal upon the table: meat, bread, olives, cheese, some green salad and fruit. 'You may help yourself while you await His Excellency.'

He swivelled on his heel and left. I needed no further bidding, but crossed to the table and fell upon the food. There was wine and water also; my preference was for the former but, with my system already drug-intoxicated and enfeebled, reason bade me chose the latter.

Feeling moderately better, gnawing upon a rib of pork, I crossed to a south-facing window to assess the extent of Malibeth's advance from her new breakthrough in the southeast. Instantly a guard moved to block my path, features hard-set, a surly challenge in his eyes. He motioned me back with his weapon. I returned and seated myself at the table, watched by the guards and langurs, idly contemplating the bowl of *gidsha*. And then I remembered the amber. I cast my eyes quickly around the chamber, but there was no sign of it. I made to move, better to survey the place, but a guard stepped forward, pike crossed before his body, and indicated that I should remain where I was.

Presently I heard Feikermun's voice in the corridors outside, yelling orders in tones of wrath. He grew louder. 'I want her head! Bring me her head! No! Better! I'll have her alive! By morning, d'ye hear me, dogs? By morning, in my hands, or you'll all die. Ha-ha! Let her know what it means to defy me!'

Notably, once more, he employed the first person in reference to himself, in contrast to his accustomed usage of the third person. I wondered whether this was significant, a measure of his stress and the threat he found himself under – then my thoughts fled as he crashed into the room.

He rammed through the heavy door, almost taking it off its

hinges as it flew back and hammered into the wall behind. I jumped violently. The monkeys leapt in terror. Feikermun was a fearsome sight, garbed for battle in red steel breastplate over a mail shirt, mail leggings and vambraces and gauntlets. His genitals were encased in an exaggerated codpiece of figured red iron, and his head was stuffed into a stylized horned helmet with peak and neckguard. With his wild hair contained, the head appeared diminished upon the immensely broad shoulders. His face had been painted in a mad array of colours, similar to when I had first seen him in the Banqueting Hall. Unconsciously I rose from my seat, my heart hammering in my chest.

'Cormer of Chol, let us go!' Feikermun strode threateningly towards me, his eyes flashing to the *gidsha* bowl. 'Take me to her, now. She is the last. Her blood is all I require, and then I will return to deal with Malibeth!'

Aniba's blood! He believed, had somehow persuaded himself, that this was the final key, the last barrier to his acquiring the power he sought so frenziedly. Love her or not, he desired her life.

'My lord, it is not—' I began. Feikermun lashed out, a shocking, brutal, upswinging blow that caught me on the side of the head, lifted me off my feet and knocked me headlong across the table and on to the floor on the other side. Foodstuffs, goblets and plates showered around me. Stunned, I raised myself shakily to knees and elbows, head ringing, world pounding, Feikermun's voice a roar of outrage. 'Do not offer opinions, oaf! Feikermun did not ask, he commanded!'

I was yanked to my feet. Feikermun had me by the shoulder of my tunic. He lifted me single-handed and thrust me on to the table, threw himself on top of me, his face contorted above mine. 'The *gidsha*, piss of a dog!'

I was almost crushed by his bulk. I nodded dumbly and he eased himself off. I heard the slosh of liquids in his great gut. I sat up and reached for the *gidsha* bowl, took up the spoon beside it and ate the green mush as Feikermun watched. As soon as I had taken enough he snatched the bowl from my hands and devoured half of what remained. Then he strutted across the chamber, taking the bowl, and disappeared through a side-portal in an alcove at one end.

I sat on the table's edge, nursing the bruises on my face, looking around again for the amber. The main door opened and Wirm came in. He wore a longsword and a breastplate of studded cuir-builli. His features hardened when he saw me. He glanced about the chamber and, seeing that we were alone but for the guards, advanced upon me, pushing his thin face close, eyes staring past mine, and hissed, 'I warned you there would be a price to pay if you did not leave. You have ignored me. Do not think I will let it pass.'

Feikermun re-entered, towing his ape on a chain. The ape, like he, was garbed in war gear, and its pelt and skin, where visible, had been dyed in vividly coloured figures. Wirm turned, spreading his hands and bowing from the waist with an obsequious smile. 'My lord.'

'Are your men assembled?'

'They are. Below.'

'Take them to the South Wing to support Hircun on the ground level. That is where the mad Bitch's whelps have broken through. Go, now!'

Wirm bowed again and left the chamber.

'Now, Cormer of Chol, we must travel,' declared Feikermun. 'And quickly. I shall bring back a surprise for sweet Malibeth.'

He seized my arm and yanked me from the table. 'I am coming!' he screamed. 'Aniba, Feikermun comes for you now!'

There was little time. I had to find the amber now, before the *gidsha* took effect and we were transported again into Selph's Citadel. '*Ask Feikermun. Watch him,*' Aniba had said. What did she mean? Surely I could not simply ask and expect him to reveal its whereabouts?

'Lord Feikermun,' I said, 'I have a boon to request of you.'

Feikermun started and blinked as if he had received a swinging slap on the cheek. 'What did you day?'

I repeated myself. Feikermun stared at me as though unable to grasp my meaning. 'A boon?'

I pressed further. 'Do you recall the piece of rare amber that I presented to you yesterday? I was wondering if I might see it once more.'

I watched his face carefully, partly to see whether his features betrayed him by revealing that he had gained some inkling of

195

the importance of the amber. I saw mounting indignation, irate disbelief, but nothing that would indicate Feikermun's having grasped the full scope of the situation. But I perceived something else – just a flicker of his eyes, a tiny reflex motion of the head, off to the side in the direction from which he had just come. This was it! He had told me, as Aniba had said he would! *The amber was over there somewhere.*

But how to get to it?

Feikermun turned almost purple as he struggled to come to terms with the outrageous, the unpalatable, the incredible fact that I had had the temerity to ask something of him. *He*, the illustrious, the untouchable, the soon-to-be god. Under different circumstances he would have struck me down instantly, taken my life on the spot without so much as a thought, but now he needed me, or believed he did, and he fought hard to contain his emotions.

Finally something burst from him, a great splutter of pent-up spleen. 'You—You *ask*? You *wish*?'

The last word was a roar. At the same time he released my arm, brought his arm back and around and cuffed me hard about the head as though I were an intransigent child. The blow sent me sprawling to the floor.

Feikermun shifted to and fro, two steps one way, two the other, still struggling to find a way to come to terms with the outrage. The ape lifted its huge arms and brought them down with a colossal thud upon the floor close by my head. I lay still, not sure I was going to survive the next few moments.

Then there were yells in the corridor outside. I heard the door fly open and a man's voice, raised in alarm, 'My lord, she is here!'

'What?' Feikermun spun around.

'Malibeth, Excellency. Her men. They have entered the private apartments and are at the south stairs. We are holding, but we must pull back. Excellency, for your own safety you must vacate your apartments until we have them secured.'

'Let me see!' bellowed Feikermun. He charged from the chamber. I lay still, half-dazed. I felt warm breath upon my cheek. The great ape had laid its head close to mine, was staring at me with curious mindlessness, its huge, flat leathery nostrils delivering short blasts of air into my face.

I had moments, if that. I got up and, unnoticed by the guards – their attention was on the conflict outside – moved across the chamber. In the alcove was a wooden seat. I shifted cushions, opened a small cabinet. Nothing. To my side was the door to the room from which Feikermun had brought the ape. I stepped across and quickly through. I was in a bedchamber dominated by a huge four-poster bed, its covers adrift, filth upon the sheets. By one wall stood an ornate chest of carved black wood, and upon this rested the amber.

I crossed quickly, picked up the precious rock and stuffed it inside my tunic, then returned to the main chamber. The guards were unaware of me. I could hear fighting – it seemed so close. Feikermun's belligerent yells, even closer, dominated all. I felt a moment of concern, that he would hurl himself into the fray and be slain by Malibeth's men.

Then he was returning, making his way back to the chamber. I steeled myself, wondering what would happen next.

16

WHAT ACTUALLY HAPPENED was that the world went insane.

As if it had not already been.

It was inevitable, given all that had so far transpired, and I should have foreseen it. In many ways perhaps I did, but I lacked the means to predict the form the insanity would take. It is the nature of madness, I suppose: one can sense its approach, be aware of the signals and indications which blaze like angry beacons on high hillcrests, but its onslaught cannot be stemmed. It is monstrous but indistinct, clutching and slippery, never to be contained, reasoned with or subdued. It ravages, and does not even know that it does so.

Feikermun stormed back towards the chamber where I waited. The door opened, but slowly, in complete contrast to what I had expected. Feikermun's voice still yelled, his feet still pounded, but into the chamber came perhaps the last person I had expected to see.

I stood rooted to the spot in utter astonishment. 'Lady Celice!'

She stood in the light of candles, in all her beauty, the ravishing young wife of the Orl Kilroth of Selaor in Khimmur. The tips of the fingers of her hands touched one another lightly before her and she gazed at me calmly, her eyes clear, her lips slightly parted, her bosom rising and falling beneath a thin, low-cut green gown. Despite everything, I felt the first irrepressible quickening of my heart and the surge of blood to my loins.

'What are you doing here?'

'I had to find you. I was worried for you.'

I was utterly confused. She stepped towards me, and I saw now that the smile was false, the calmness a sham. Her beautiful face was an unconvincing mask which failed to cover her strain. Feikermun's guards watched her like famished men.

'Celice, what is the matter?'

'We must talk. Dinbig, there is something we should discuss.'

'Sshh! Don't say that name!' I glanced in alarm at the guards. By Moban, she was about to give me away! Mercifully none seemed to have heard, or, if they had, did not make the connection. But then the thought came: how does she know me? She had never seen the disguise I wore. She could not have recognized me, unless . . . unless someone had betrayed me.

I fought down my panic. There was something unutterably strange going on here, something I could not fully grasp.

'You have used me, that is all,' said Celice. She gripped her hands tight before her bosom and I saw that tears had started to her eyes.

'Used you?'

'For your own ends. I mean nothing to you, do I?'

'That is not true.'

There was a beat of wings, a glimpse of flurrying red and black, a waft of air upon my face.

'Is it not? Then why . . .?'

'There are others,' I said. 'Not only I. What about Mintral?'

'Mintral? Lord Mintral?' She almost laughed, but her anger and hurt showed uppermost. 'Is that what you think?'

'I—'

'Mintral is a friend, nothing more,' said Celice. 'Which is more than I can say of you.'

'But the Orl, your husband. You married him, and then—'

'*He* married *me*! Do you think I was consulted, was given a choice? I was a child, the marriage advantageous to my parents. It was arranged years ago, without my knowledge, without reference to my feelings or wishes.'

'I see.' I was stunned, not by what she was telling me – there was nothing so unusual in that – but by the fact that she was here, now, telling me under these extraordinary circumstances. 'Celice, what is happening? You have never spoken like this before.'

'You did not wish me to. You have never wished to know who I am, what my hopes and aspirations might be. You seek

199

to gratify your needs, and then you are gone. That is all I represent, Dinbig, isn't it?'

'*Do not speak that name!*'

The ape snorted at my shoulder. My hair prickled on the back of my neck. *How could she know?* Celice put her hands to her bosom and tore aside her gown to expose her naked breasts. I caught my breath. She continued to tear the gown down to its lower hem so that it rendered in two. Beneath it she was completely naked.

'Here,' she said. 'Tell me this is not all I am.'

'This is unjust,' I said, reaching for her. 'You participate as eagerly as I.'

I took her, irresistible, bent my head to kiss her shoulder, her neck. As I did so she smiled. '*Take the amber to the well, Dinbig.*'

My lips touched chill metal; I drew back, and faced a nightmare. Celice was Feikermun of Selph, clad in coloured mail and plate, his lips curled into a malevolent grin as I recoiled.

'*You are not so different from I.*'

'It is not true!'

'*I exist within you.*'

'No!'

'*You cannot fight Feikermun. Feikermun is greater than you.*'

'I will fight you.'

'*But you cannot kill me, for what will it mean?*'

'I will find a way.'

He shook his head. '*I know who you are.*'

Something else was happening. The beating of bodies, the gasping of wings. I stared up through the bloodied water and stared down and watched myself die. I cried out as I groped upwards in the dark for a bough that was beyond my reach, as I was sucked down slowly into the foul oozing muck. And slowly the room returned.

The guards watched the door. I could hear Feikermun approaching, bawling curses, threats and obscenities. I blinked and shook my head, then patted my midriff, felt the amber there. The guards snapped to attention; the door flew back.

'Cormer of Chol, accompany me!'

He snatched up the ape's chain, seized my arm and half-dragged me from the chamber into the corridor. The place was full of shouting. He veered left, and I glanced back over my shoulder. At the far end of the corridor, at the head of a flight of stairs, Feikermun's men were hacking with swords at others below them. From around the angle of a wall a figure suddenly appeared, dropped to one knee, raised a crossbow and let fly at us. The bolt went wild, chipping into the wall some way off. A palace beast swung with his blade, almost decapitating Malibeth's crossbowman, who slumped to the floor. More of Feikermun's men came running to drive back the foe from the stairs.

I was shocked. Malibeth was so close. We rushed on, guards closing in to guard our backs. The floor felt warm beneath my feet. Why was I naked? From somewhere far away, an unknown, unknowable distance, I heard a baby cry. I clutched my middle again. Yes, the amber was there, beneath my tunic. I was not naked and we were fleeing along the corridor – Feikermun, the ape and I – as behind us the battle raged for the palace, for Feikermun's life and for ultimately so much more. I heard shouts as men died. I smelt the smell of fear strong in my nostrils, and realized it was my own. I saw the walls split asunder, then cement themselves together again. And then I saw Illan.

He was in the square, Culmet's Bazaar, talking to someone I did not know. How had I got there? I did not recall leaving the palace. Illan failed to notice me, though I stood close by. He concluded his business and the man he was with, a pale young man with light golden hair, made off across the square. Illan turned and, still ignorant of my presence, walked by me and entered a nearby tavern. I was curious, and chose to follow the man he had spoken with.

He led me through the marketplace, his shoulders slightly hunched, posture a little stiff, as though nervous, self-conscious. Leaving the square, he turned into a sidestreet. I followed, pushing through the crowd, and had gone but a few paces when I felt a hand upon my shoulder. I wheeled around. Before me stood someone I knew, a man who did not exist. He was Cormer of Chol, perplexed, flushed. He was I, Ronbas Dinbig, disguised.

201

He struggled for words, as did I, but he found his voice first. 'Who . . . who *are* you?'

I felt suddenly, through my fear, my horror, an irrational heat. I wanted to strike him down, for he could not be I, not even disguised. He was an impostor, imitating me, wearing a mask. But why? And I thought, *How can I recognize him if I don't know who he is?* The notion angered me further and I stepped towards him, not quite sure what I intended. The air shimmered and blurred. There was a flash and the world fell away. I stood in another street, a loose knot of people around me, falling back in fear and dismay. A little distance off I acknowledged the presence of three men I knew: Jaktem, Illan and the man disguised as Cormer of Chol. But I gave them no thought for uppermost came my wrath, my hatred, and I sprang as women and men screamed in terror. My claws ripped randomly into nearby flesh, opening a middle-aged woman with one long tear. As she fell I leapt upon her, ready to pull the meat from her living bones, but she was gone and I was falling through nothing, crying out in panic, 'What is happening here?'

The carcases of dogs. The leaves not falling from trees beneath which men, women, children waited to ensure they could not litter the ground. And Dehut burned. Dehut was riven with strife.

Feikermun still gripped me by the arm, and we ran, his soldiers at our backs, his breath loud in my ear and his chinking armour and the chinking chain of the great ape that grunted, lungs like bellows, at his side. We descended to the second level, then the first. Lurid frescoes of battle scenes and orgies, celebrations of cruelty masked as heroism, the walls alive with obscene tortures and pleasures. An ass stood beneath an arch, watching stupidly as we approached, and Feikermun's roar dominated all: 'Aniba, I am coming! Malibeth, I am coming!'

My breath was short, searing my lungs. I clasped the amber to me, afraid that it would fall. There was a humming in my mind, and the filthy, bloodied water parted again and I saw us all before I died.

'Aniba, help me!'

'Aniba, I am coming!'

Shouts from the side. Ten or so of Malibeth's men were rushing to intercept us across a yard which opened on to the passage in which we raced. Feikermun vented a great cry and swerved to confront them. He had acquired a huge double-handed axe from somewhere and he launched it at the first of the enemy, swinging in a great arc; the wicked blade bit clean through leather, flesh and bone, taking off shoulder and arm in a single blow. Malibeth's fighter stumbled forward to his knees, gaping as his blood fountained forth and his limb dropped to the ground, still clutching a sword. He crumpled forward in his death swoon, not yet believing he had died, and Feikermun charged on.

But he was outnumbered. More men were coming from the left; flames and black smoke leapt high from behind a wall, crackling and roaring. Feikermun's guards leapt to his aid. He swung at another of the enemy, cackling insanely. The man sprang back, lunged with his sword. Feikermun dodged nimbly, swung again and took him hard in the flank.

Another darted at him, and another. His guards intervened before he might be overwhelmed, but I could see that he could not hope to survive unless he withdrew. I was without a weapon. The great ape leaned upon its knuckles beside me, indifferent to the affray.

'Lord Feikermun!' I yelled 'You must withdraw. We go to the Citadel, to Aniba!'

Feikermun failed to hear, or ignored me – I could not tell. He and his men were all but surrounded now. Two of them had been cut down. I ran forward, seized a fallen sword and rushed at one of Malibeth's men, thinking, *Moban, I do not want to kill this man. He may not be my enemy!*

His back was to me. I might have run him through, but I hesitated. Another saw me, bawled a warning, and suddenly I was facing two. I backed away, rueing my hesitancy. I am no expert swordsman, and these men were fierce, trained fighters. One thrust forward. I parried his blow, but the other leapt at me with a yell, sword descending towards my head. I dodged, went down on one knee. There was a bloodcurdling bellow and suddenly the first swordsman was lifted high from the ground. Feikermun's ape hurled him against the wall.

203

The second soldier backed off, but the ape loped away towards its master. The soldier turned back to me but I was already swinging with my sword. The blade bit deep into his thigh and he staggered back with a groan, blood blossoming wetly. I rose, stabbed, pierced his lung and ended his life.

I stood for a moment regaining my breath, panic seizing me in paralysing waves, cold sweat drenching up clothing. More of Feikermun's troops were arriving, hacking their way towards their crazed master. Malibeth's men began to fall back. Feikermun was suddenly free of the mêlée.

'Lord Feikermun, the Citadel!' I cried, afraid he might yet be cut down.

He heard me this time, and turned and grinned, then raised both hands above his head, gripping the axe-helve, and performed a brief victory-dance before striding towards me, one hand cupping his jock.

'The Citadel! Aye, we are there, or is it here?' He thrust me roughly back to the passageway and we ran on. 'It is mine! Aniba, it is mine!'

I was not sure whether what he said made any sense. I wasn't sure of anything. As I said, the world had gone insane. I realized there was Scrin among us. Towering, rat-like, predatory, part-manifested, a phantom altering the air, swiping with claws but striking nothing that I could see. Then it was gone, as if it had stepped through a veil.

'The Citadel is here!' cried Feikermun, laughing.

We passed into the banqueting hall, a white peacock with blood on its back flapping aside as we rushed in. It seemed that Malibeth's troops had been held for the time being. Feikermun paused, leaning upon his axe-helve to regain his breath, his painted face streaked with sweat. A number of his fighters were with us; they moved to check exits. I gazed about me at the hall. There was something strange about it, about the way its walls stood around us, its high vaulted ceiling over our heads. It was not quite real; it seemed superimposed, as though something else lay unseen behind it, or perhaps, conversely, it lay behind something not seen but sensed or half-inferred by a subtler perception. I could not be sure that I was here, but, if not, where else was I?

A langur leapt across a long table and then vanished as though swallowed into nothingness. Aniba stood near one end of the hall, her body stiff, her beautiful features strained and tormented. Her posture, her look, reminded me of Celice.

Celice! How had she been here?

I caught the flurry of wings, black-and-red-banded, feathertips almost brushing my face. Rushing air. The cries of the trapped and slain. And I glimpsed the weird amber light, the winged bodies suspended and the black overhead, the bleak plain and the fabulous sunset, a small far boat on still water, one person within, gazing up, waiting, waiting for the world . . .

'Aniba, what is happening?'

'It has broken through! Feikermun barely resists – his last defences are falling. The Citadel is here, now. The gates of Selph are wide. All its horrors, all its perils, will be unleashed upon the world.'

'What must I do?'

Before she could answer I was conscious of Feikermun's bulk charging past me, head jerking wildly from side to side. I had half-noted how he had straightened suddenly when I called out Aniba's name, how his eyes had wildly searched the room. It had not occurred to me – it should have – that he still could not see her. And I had inadvertently given her presence away.

He strode forward in the direction of my gaze. 'Where? Aniba? Where?'

Aniba drew back, then moved a few paces to one side. Feikermun saw nothing. 'Aniba, come! Feikermun needs you. Your blood, give Feikermun your precious blood!'

He looked back at me, perceived the new direction of my gaze and stepped towards her blindly. Aniba moved back.

'Do you see her?' he yelled at his beasts. I watched their faces as they turned; it was plain that none saw.

'What must I do?' I asked again.

'Bring the amber, as before. But now it will be harder. You will walk in two realities at the same time, both torn with conflict. I cannot predict—'

'Where is she, Cormer?' snarled Feikermun, his eyes bulging, his wrath and jealousy almost palpable.

Aniba said as she passed into invisibility. 'Let him believe that he needs my blood. It is a fallacy, as I have already explained, but if he believes it he will continue to seek it. It may, just this once, serve you.'

'*Where is she?*'

I shook my head. 'She is no longer here.'

'You lie!'

'No, Lord Feikermun, it is not a lie.'

She had gone. I felt bereft, abandoned, wanting to call her back, needing her presence, lost and alone and afraid.

'Bring her back!' yelled Feikermun, trembling with emotion, spittle flying from his lips. 'Bring her back!'

'I have no control over her.'

'I need her. Her blood, she brings it for me. It is all I need now. Aniba's blood will give me the godhead!'

I stared at him, wordless, detesting him to my soul, fighting down the urge to take the sword I still carried and slay him – for he had turned his back to me now: it would have been an easy matter to step forward and plunge the blade into his unguarded flesh. I would die, yes, but he would be gone forever. I would have carried out my task, the orders of the Hierarchy, the *Zan-Chassin*. So tempting, to ignore everything else. Cut him down. End his life. Give Dehut into the hands of Malibeth. She could be no worse.

But it could not be. The Citadel was real. Selph was real. Sermilio, the Avari, Aniba, the Scrin. The amber against my belly. Feikermun was turning back to me, mouth twisted, discoloured teeth bared, face framed by the helmet gleaming with colour. 'What did she say?'

I shook my head. 'She did not speak. I asked her, for guidance, but she was mute.'

'If you lie . . .'

'I do not lie,' I lied.

I heard my mother sing, so far off, so sweet, and I cried out as I gulped my first air. The road lay before me as my body settled in, heavy, heavy, my mother's face above me. Aniba, Aniba . . . Far away in the bloodset distance Sermilio waited, gazing outwards, and the bodies of the Avari specked the sky. His voice, sorrowful, filled with wonder, 'Oh, the beauty of the light upon this world. Don't let it end.'

He spread his wings and rose into the blood, and the man on the steps, clad in grey – who was me, who was I – watched and waited as the world began to die.

Feikermun turned from me. Hircun, the one-eyed, had entered the great hall and was conferring with his master; his pocked face shone with sweat, was smudged with black grime and blood. I overheard some of their words and gathered that the situation was continuing to deteriorate. Malibeth's troops were still edging forward and had gained important strategic positions, though they had been forced to withdraw from the palace's inner compound. Hircun was mooting the possibility of evacuating the palace altogether, at least until the foe could be driven back to the outer wall.

'Impossible!' snapped Feikermun, almost insensate with rage.

'But, my lord, we could be overrun. If we pull back and regroup, we can launch another assault from three sides as her troops try to enter. The south corridors are perfectly designed for an ambush. We could—'

Feikermun puffed his chest and thrust forward his bearded chin, his upper lip curled. 'Feikermun will not abandon the palace, Hircun. Kill my enemies – that is your job. Do it now. Drive them away, and bring me the head of the Bitch.'

'My lord, many buildings are fired. This hall might yet burn or come under assault.

'*Do it!*'

His scream was hysterical, dangerous. Hircun stiffened, then bowed and hurried away.

I tried to look at Feikermun, but my vision would not stay fixed. He was the ape, he was Feikermun, he was me. There were creatures emerging from beneath his feet – slimy, crawling things. His eyes bulged, burst in a shower of vile jelly and gave birth to shrieking, tapering monstrosities that ran amok in their scores, scattering monkeys and peacocks and other birds. Feikermun crouched feasting upon the flesh of a dead Avari.

I put my hands to my face to try and shut out the horrors. *What was happening here*? We were inside the Citadel, but the Citadel was here, also. The Citadel *was* Feikermun, Feikermun of Selph, and he could not control what he had brought forth. The gates of Selph and all its hidden chambers were thrown open; the Scrin poured forth upon Dehut and the world, and Dehut waged war with itself.

And I, too, waged war, for somewhere here amid all this carnage my double existed. Conjured out of Feikermun's thoughts, inadvertently set free, recaptured, executed and now free again. Who was he? *What* was he?

He was you following a course you might have chosen, Aniba had said. I was filled with a murky, nebulous fear. A course I might have chosen. *Feikermun took you into himself, into the Citadel, though he did not know that he had done so. There – here – you grew . . .*

What was I now, then? If I had grown in the mind of a madman, and now was set free? What had I become?

And another shocking realization rocked me to my roots. My mind recalled the nightmare I had suffered before leaving Hon-Hiaita in Khimmur, the nightmare in which my double had brought himself to Hon-Hiaita and had successfully passed himself off as me. He had stolen everything that was mine, taken my place among my associates and friends, and then he had come for me, sending his assassins in the dead of night to remove me from the world.

What if he were now making his way to Khimmur to achieve just that while I remained trapped here in Dehut, in the Citadel?

He looks like me! I thought. *And I do not! He is me, to all intents and purposes, and I am someone else, a man, Linias Cormer of Chol, unknown to anyone, for I do not in truth exist. I became Cormer in order to seek out the person who claimed to be me. It is I who am now the imposter!*

The blood was rushing from my brain, from my extremities, laking in my centre as my ears roared, my lungs refused to draw breath. Red and black. The wings fluttering weakly as if in their final throes, everything fragmenting, the beginning of the end of the world.

Waiting . . .

Harsh voices pushed through; the double door of the banqueting hall flew open and a man strode in. I blinked, shook my head, discovered I was on my hands and knees on the cold flagstones, particles of sawdust pressing into my palms. But I looked up and recognised the newcomer. It was Wirm.

He strode towards Feikermun as I got to my feet. Behind him came two of his men holding the arms of a woebegone figure who half-sagged between them, his clothing torn, his head hanging low upon his chest, blood upon his leg and neck, legs and feet tottering forward as if boned.

'What do you want?' growled Feikermun.

'We found this man trying to gain entry to the palace,' replied Wirm, arching a cold glance at my hands. 'His actions were furtive. He tried to avoid us, and when caught insisted he brought a message for your ears only. My first inclination was to execute him, for he is clearly a spy, yet I hesitated, for words he then spoke to me suggested there might be something of value in what he wishes to tell you. I have brought him here that you may judge for yourself.'

Feikermun scowled at the prisoner. 'Well, speak, if you plan to live another instant.'

Wirm's soldier grasped the prisoner by the hair and jerked his head erect. His face was badly bruised and bloody, one eye swollen and almost closed. But I recognized him, and almost staggered. It was Illan.

He looked dazedly my way, then back to Feikermun. 'I have a message,' he said, his words slurred and pained. 'From my master.'

Feikermun turned to look at me with indignant surprise. I remained blank, baffled. Feikermun frowned and said, 'Why do you come to Feikermun in this manner when your master is already here?'

Wirm's eyes were upon me, fixed for a moment, hard, hostile, Illan shook his head. 'Master Cormer is not my master.'

'You work for him.'

'Employed by him for a few days, but employed by another to bring him here.'

Feikermun peered forward, then aslant at me. Wirm nodded slowly, displaying a thin smile of satisfaction, for the shock on my face must have been evident.

'What other?' demanded Feikermun.

'One who stands against you.'

'Malibeth?' Feikermun bustled, gripping his axe-helve tight. 'You are Malibeth's man?'

Illan twisted his head. 'No, not Malibeth'. He grinned with pain.' My master is the Golden Lamb.'

17

THE GOLDEN LAMB! I had, for a time, all but forgotten this other mysterious player in Dehut's fortunes. I stared at Illan in a daze. What treachery was this? And why?

Now we were striding through the northern corridors of Feikermun's palace, or further into the depths of Selph – I could not tell, for the world was a barely recognizable place. I was here, I was there, without consciousness of having moved. My mind went over and over what had just occurred in the banqueting hall. Illan's words had struck me dumb, and what he had told Feikermun next left me reeling, my mind rebelling as it clamoured against the notion that I had been betrayed on all sides.

Illan, and plainly Jaktem too, had been assigned by the Golden Lamb to bring me here. No matter that they had saved my life in Guling Mire when Vecco's men had attacked me; their true motive had been undeclared. They had brought me to Dehut under false pretences as part of some scheme into which I had no insight. Who were these two whom I had come to trust? And what was in the mind of their unfathomable master?

In the hall Feikermun had been an image of apoplexy. He had almost risen from the ground when Illan declared himself an agent of the Golden Lamb. He, like I, was initially dumbfounded by the revelation, and when he eventually found words it was only to stammer, 'Wh – what do you say?'

Ordinarily I think he would have killed the Kamahamek outright, but Illan with some finesse trod the same slender line as I had done before him, gambling that the information he possessed was too important to Feikermun to permit the madman the luxury of yielding to his immediate impulses. Even so, it

211

was indeed a gamble; Feikermun's grip on himself was minimal at best.

Wirm, close by, was also stock-still, his small eyes unusually still, glued now to Illan. A breathless silence held the hall. It was as though mention of that name, the Golden Lamb, had cast a spell; even the fighting outside had fallen momentarily silent.

'My master sends you cordial and respectful greetings, Lord Feikermun,' said Illan, standing without assistance now, proud, conscious that he commanded the attention of all, though his body was twisted with pain. 'He charges me to give you notice that he is aware of your plight—'

'*Plight?*' Feikermun fairly shot the word into the room.

'—and that you risk being overwhelmed by Malibeth's surprise assault upon you—'

Feikermun's grip tightened further upon his axe-helve and he quivered with rage. He could still not admit that he had been taken unawares and that his adversary might be stronger than him. The words that Illan delivered were an insult he could barely tolerate; I could see the supreme effort he was making to hold himself back, avid to hear the remaining words issued by a foe of whom he, like all others, knew so little.

'—My master therefore proposes a meeting between the two of you—'

'Bah!' ejaculated Feikermun. 'Why would the great Feikermun seek intercourse with a devil who will not even show his face?'

'For those reasons my master has defined, which I have just related to you, my lord: namely that you risk being overthrown and thereby placing inordinate power into the hands of Malibeth.'

Feikermun thrust himself toward, pressing the axe-blade to Illan's throat. 'Stay your words, piss of a whelp, or Feikermun will take your head!' he roared. Illan twisted his head away, bracing himself and closing his eyes tight for an instant as if believing that he had gone too far.

'I give you only the words of my master, which he bade me convey to you exactly, Lord Feikermun. I am but a servant.'

Feikermun chomped and seethed but eventually he drew back,

darting a fiery glance my way, then said, 'What are the terms of this meeting?'

'That it takes place at a venue of my master's choosing, to which I am charged to take you, and that it be for the purpose of arriving at a peaceful and equitable solution to the current crisis.'

'Feikermun is being taken for a fool, a rabbit who will hop readily into the lair of a wolf, is that it? Your master wishes to trade insults? Then tell him this: he underestimates Feikermun. Feikermun has the Source, the power, and he will smash your Golden Lamb. But first he will bring him to his woolly knees and hear him bleat for mercy!'

'My lord, I think you are misconstruing my master's words. He seeks ways to bring this affray to a conclusion without further destruction, and is willing to work with you to achieve that end. But I am charged also to say that your refusal to at least meet with him will be deemed deliberately obstructive, and therefore an act of war. My master will be left with no choice but to align himself with Malibeth and throw his full weight against you, crushing you utterly.'

I have to admit, no matter Illan's duplicity, I admired him then. It took pluck to stand before a monster like Feikermun and utter those words. Feikermun's eyes bulged; the veins pulsed in his neck; he spluttered, almost inflating with anger as he battled further with the immense, unfamiliar pressures of keeping himself in check.

Illan added, hastily, 'Equally, any act of violence of vengeance against myself or my companion Jaktem will he held an act of war and will be met in the same manner, as will any similar act against Master Cormer of Chol.'

Feikermun used the reference to turn upon me. 'What is your part in this, Cormer?'

'My lord, I am dumbfounded. Until a few minutes ago I was unaware that this man had any connection with the Golden Lamb. I believed him a casual employee whom I had enlisted purely at random to accompany me here. I have never had contact with the Golden Lamb and know nothing of him. Why he should make reference to me in any way, or why he should assign his agents to bring me to Dehut, is an utter mystery to me.'

'The other one!' Feikermun suddenly yelled. 'The other one! Bring him to me!'

An officer with a detachment of guards ran off to fetch Jaktem.

'Who is your master?' demanded Feikermun of Illan.

'I have told you, my lord. He is the Golden Lamb.'

'I know. But *who* is he? Where has he come from? What is his aim?'

'That I cannot tell you.'

'You will if I choose to make you, be sure of that.'

'Lord Feikermun, I do not have the information you seek. That is why I was sent. Neither I nor Jaktem have had direct contact with our master. We work for him only through intermediaries. I can tell you nothing of his ultimate intentions, for they are not revealed to a servant as lowly as I.'

'Who are these intermediaries?'

'Again, their identities are unknown to me in advance, and it is never the same person twice.'

'Then how do you communicate? How do you know one another?'

'By coded signals indicating whether it is safe or not to proceed.'

Feikermun stared long and hard at Illan whom, as if interpreting his thoughts, spoke again before he could say anything. 'My lord Feikermun, those persons with whom I met are no longer within your domain, he assured of that. And my work is now finished. There are to be no further rendezvous. I am charged to deliver my master's message and to bring you to him, nothing more.'

'When is this proposed meeting to take place?'

'My master awaits you now. If by midnight tonight at the latest you have not come, it will be taken that you do not intend to, unless I, in company with Jaktem and Master Cormer, am able to present to my master convincing reasons why he should wait a little longer.'

Feikermun nodded to myself. I had doubts that he would accede to the Golden Lamb's proposition, yet plainly he was

214

intrigued, and desperate. He was distracted, also. The *gidsha* dream had him fast in its grip, as it did me, and all around us the Citadel of Selph continued to spew forth its contents into the world. I discerned shapes moving in the hall, indistinct and almost formless. Were others aware of anything? I could not tell. Did the Golden Lamb know anything of what was really happening here?

Wirm loudly cleared his throat to draw Feikermun's attention, then spoke quietly in the lunatic warlord's ear;. Feikermun nodded several times, then addressed Illan. His tone now was quieter, more thoughtful. 'We shall go, yes. Feikermun will give audience to your master. Let us see what he has to say.'

'Do we depart at once?'

'Where is the place he has chosen to meet?'

'I have not been told to reveal it in advance, simply to take you there.'

'Feikermun assumes he is not expected to come alone?'

'My master invites you to come in whatsoever company you wish, though the meeting itself will be held in private.'

So we waited a short while longer, until Jaktem was brought. He entered under guard, a look of relief upon his face when he saw Illan. His eyes then met mine, but failed to hold my gaze.

In the meantime both Feikermun and Wirm had despatched messengers from the hall. I assumed precautionary measures were being taken to safeguard Feikermun's passage and make secure, or as secure as possible, this meeting with his mysterious foe. I assumed also that he was hatching a plot, and wondered how wary the Golden Lamb was, how well he knew his adversary. Officers came and went and in due course, at a moment chosen by Feikermun, we left the banqueting hall.

Now things turned awry again. It was as though the tension of Illan's arrival, his confession and the message he had brought, had focused my attention, partly breaking through the *gidsha* dream, holding back Selph's assault. Everything had been almost clear and I had been in strange attunement; nothing had seriously intervened. Now that was ended. We went to meet the golden Lamb – I do not know where – and quite suddenly everything changed again.

I was in another place. Feikermun was there; so were Jaktem,

Illan, Wirm, a score of Feikermun's beasts and the ape. I was aware of the palace walls and of the open air, that we had stepped on to a wide parade-ground and were skirting its perimeter, hugging the walls, moving towards a portal on its far side. The dusk had descended and the sky – overcast now, with fiery ribbons and glowing stains of vermillion, blood and molten rose visible low in the east – had begun to let fall a steady, light rain. From behind us the glows of burning buildings cast restless shadows across the rooftops, and columns of dark smoke towered high, lifting twisting embers into the twilight.

But all of this was secondary, a reality lying at the back of the *gidsha* reality into which I had been cast. I was within the Citadel of Selph, or Selph was within the world – the distinction meant little. The winged bodies were all around, hundreds of them, more than I had imagined, as far as I could see. Between them moved the tall shadowy forms of the Scrin, an army of phantom things, heading . . . where? I could not tell. Had they access to Dehut, or did they still haunt only their own domain?

And animals hung, dogs – strangled, garrotted – and pigs and monkeys, some of the corpses putrefying. There were cries in the air, tortured and not-human, and I could not tell where they came from. Feikermun marched ahead of me; he looked back and laughed. 'Do you dream, Cormer of Chol?'

Something was wrong. We reached the portal; one of Feikermun's beasts was drawing it open. A crossbow-bolt *zinged* off the stone ground a short way off, then another, and another. There were shouts from somewhere behind. Turning, I saw men in silhouette rushing along the parapets. Malibeth's men, being met by Feikermun's. Metal clashed; a body fell from the wall. A tall dark shape formed suddenly, fell upon the body, ripping at its flesh, then disappeared. I only glimpsed it, and it was like nothing I had seen before; but I knew what it must be.

The Scrin take whatever form you perceive . . . do not truly exist within the scope of your experience . . . things of an other order . . .

We crowded towards the portal, Illan leading, then Jaktem, both chained. I pushed through, glimpsed Wirm, his eyes flickering on me. Was he waiting for his moment, a chance to slip

216

a blade between my ribs? Feikermun shouldered past, almost knocking me to the ground, toting his axe high.

'Aniba, be here! I am coming!'

I knew that I had to get away. Could I risk abandoning Feikermun? I considered his position. He was as well protected as he could be under the circumstances and, as he had said himself, in going to meet the Golden Lamb he was hardly likely to hop like a rabbit into the lair of a wolf. Malibeth's forces were behind us and, in the main, held back. If they pushed through, Feikermun could lose his palace but he, by my assessment, was presently out of Malibeth's reach.

Nothing was certain, of course, and there still remained the Golden Lamb. His proposed meeting might be a genuine attempt to resolve the crisis by one means or another, but the means could take any form. He was an absolute unknown. But I could not see that any contribution I might presently make would help preserve Feikermun's life. The madman was surrounded by his beasts, men who would protect him to the bitter end, and I had little doubt that many more of his troops were watching and following us. And he was on the verge of being unstoppable. Better, all things considered, to absent myself from the company and find my way with the amber to the well.

And then?

I did not contemplate it further. Most immediate was the problem of actually leaving Feikermun's company undetected. And if I achieved that I would be alone in the Citadel of Selph, in the *gidsha* dream, the nightmare that Dehut had become. The thought petrified me. *Aniba, will you be there? Will you help me?*

I let myself drop back a little way as we trotted on, leaving the palace behind, keeping to the dark of a built-up street. The rain had by now soaked my hair and shoulders. I waited, watchful, seeking an opportunity to break away and lose myself down an alley. But I, too, was being watched. Feikermun's beasts jogged close to me, giving me no space to dart between, and Feikermun looked back over his shoulder and leered. 'Cormer of Chol, are you taking me to her?'

'I thought you wished to meet with the Golden Lamb, my lord.'

217

'In time. In good time. First I must have what I need, then the Golden Lamb will be of no consequence.' His eyes hardened. 'Take me to her, man!'

Did he think I had some control over Aniba's movements? 'Lord Feikermun—' I began, but the look on his face silenced me. He shouldered his way brutally back through his men to confront me, scowling, his eyes blazing. We had all come to a halt. Wirm moved up close into my field of vision; his tongue snaked along his lips.

'Bring her to me, Cormer,' ordered Feikermun. 'Bring her now.'

'I have no power over her.'

'But she comes to you.'

'I do not know why, my lord. But she has appeared to you also, has she not?'

'In the past,' he said, abruptly wistful, then snarled, 'But she did not speak!'

'I am sorry, my lord. I do not know how to summon her.'

Feikermun raised his great axe. 'Perhaps she will intervene when she sees that I am about to end your life!' He turned his brutish, painted rain-streaked face to the dark sky and bellowed, 'Aniba, come to me! Come, now, or this wretch will end his miserable days here, on this wet spot, with my blade cleaving his skull!'

There was nowhere I could run, crowded by enemies. Though I had a sword I could not hope to defend myself against so many. I reached desperately into my mind, trying to summon a rapture. I was but a lowly First Realm Initiate and knew nothing powerful enough to stop a force like Feikermun and his beasts, but I might possibly distract him for an instant. Long enough . . . to do what?

It seemed that time was suspended, that I stared for an age at that monstrous axe-blade poised above my head, and at Feikermun, squat and powerful, his agonized features turned upwards past mine, tortured by the unearthly glimmer of clashing realities, the water splashing off his face, running through the chaos of paint. The ape hulked at his back, a solid flesh shadow, its own face turned upwards, sifting the air with a brooding semi-intelligence, disconsolate as though seeking something it lacked the faculty to comprehend.

Feikermun's cry cut through: 'Aniba! Aaaaaaaannnnnnnnnnn iiiiiiiiiiiiiiiiiiiiiiibbbbbbbaaaaaaaaaaaaaaaaaa aaaaaaaaaaaa!'

The yell cracked the air, rent the world, spiralled away from us, splitting and purpling the sky, piercing me, and a faint wet light, the glistening raindrops on the hovering blade, a stir of feathered wings, the suspended, the cries of the dying Avarai as Scrin moved among them, strode purposeful things on their journey from the Citadel, perhaps not yet quite certain of the way into the unfamiliar world, but conscious that the way was open, Selph unleashed, the world, the cosmos, exposed, for which they had striven through countless eternities, theirs now to plunder and rive and finally destroy, so fervid were they for their own end.

For they cannot die while anything else exists.

Had Sermilio said those words? I could not remember. Something like them. That was my understanding. I did not know. The axe hovered, I stood upon the rainswept road, its end just before me if I made that choice, and I could see no further.

'Aaaaaaaannnnnnnnnnniiiiiiiiiiiiiiiiiiiiiiiiibbbbbbbbbbbbbaaaaaaaaaa aaa aaaaaaaaaa!'

I stared with tears in my eyes at the sunset, brought to my knees. The beauty of the light upon this world.

Don't let it end!

The cry of the baby, some distance now behind me, and the bells ringing far above. The mother sang, her voice so sweet, so strong, so pure, filled with joy and wonder, and sorrow and fear for what the future might hold.

Don't let it end!

'Do you dream, Cormer?'

'I don't know!'

'Have you brought it?'

Whose voice was this? Sermilio's? Yet I could not see him.

'Have you brought it?'

'The amber?'

'Yes.'

I felt the rough stone beneath my tunic. 'It is here.'

'Go, then. There is so little time. Take it to the well.'

219

I stepped out onto the road, heavy, heavier than before. The familiar strange buildings stood before me, burnished by the light, their shadows long and blacker than was natural. The well lay just beyond.

'Aaaaaaannnnnnnnniiiiiiiiiiiiiiiiiiiibbbbbbbbbbbbbbbbbbbaaaaaaaaa aaa aaaaaaaaa!'

The axe was above me, filling half the sky, a vast deadly tarnished silvery blade, struck with crimson raindrops, poised to fall, to cleave through the bodies of the winged ones, inert to their death agonies.

Don't let it end!

'Take it now! Hurry!'

I dragged myself on. I was between the first buildings now, entering those black shadows. I felt ... so *aged*, my body enfeebled, nothing before me, too weary, too saddened to carry on. Nowhere to go.

The well. I could see it, down the little path. dark trees swaying behind it. But I was on my knees, the amber an unbearable weight, something pulling me down, into the mire, all far too much effort and no will any more to continue. I wanted to close my eyes and sleep forever.

'Am I dying?'

Silence, but for the soughing of the wind in the dark trees.

'AM I DYING?'

'Do you dream?'

I could not go forward. the well was beyond my reach.

'Tell me!'

Silence. It was the end.

Don't let it end!

18

She lifted my head then, turned me to her breast and gave me succour. Her voice soothing and sweet, her arms holding me safe, the closeness of her, the smell, the warmth, her song. Safe. Don't let it end.

The blood-specked blade was falling, cleaving the sky, dropping through eternity to sever me, its song a terrible keening that chilled the soul. I was somehow climbing to my feet, unsteady, clutching the amber in both hands, stumbling down the little stony path to the strange well.

At the rim I looked down. Far below I looked back at me looking down.

'Go now! Don't hesitate!'

I threw myself over as the axe-blade howled, as the god Feikermun's blade smashed the earth.

Falling, slowly, endlessly, towards myself and whatever else waited below.

'Am I dying?'

I could not understand where everyone had gone. I had been with them, a prisoner, waiting for the axe to fall, and there had been no escape. Now I was alone, still descending, and the reflection I saw below me shifted, the surface of the water stirred and I fell on, passed through it, feeling nothing – on, on, down the perpetual black tunnel, the Amber of Selph held precious to my belly, the shadows of Scrin beginning to materialize then dissolve around me.

I had died! I was certain of it now. This was my death. Was I too late?

A light shone ahead, bright and blinding, dilating, rushing now towards me, flooding me. I cried out, but made no sound. I looked up into her face, so huge above me, smiling, eyes filled with joy and wonder, the first face I had ever seen.

'You are my mother!'

'Now do you understand?'

'I don't know. It is too much to ask.'

She smiled, slowly shaking her head, then began to sing softly to herself, to me whom she held so close and safe. The bells rang far overheard, and I knew then she was everything.

'Have I died?'

'That is not the question.'

'Am I dying?'

'You do not know?'

'I think, perhaps, I understand.'

'Then say.'

'You are my mother?'

'Then . . . what?'

'*I have just been born.*'

'Aaaaaaaaannnnnnnnnnnnniiiiiiiiiiiiiiiiiiiiiiiibbbbbbbbaaaaaaaaaaa aaaaaaaa!'

The spell was broken. Fear and violence darkened the world.

'He has followed me here!'

She replied, 'I knew he would. He has come for me.'

'And if he finds you?'

'He will take my blood. It will give him nothing, of course, though he will believe otherwise.'

'Can he do it?'

'Here he can, yes.'

'And then?'

'There will be no "then". He has already set Selph free, though it hesitates for an instant, part-blind, a little unsure of its power. If I am gone it will hesitate no longer.'

'Then your death does give him power.'

She shook her head. 'No, for it will be the same if I live – except that, while he seeks me, he will continue to believe that he needs me. I cannot prevent him now. I never could, though I tried.'

'Then who is he?'

'You still do not understand? He is Feikermun. He is your brother.'

'*No!*' I could not grasp that. I could not have it.

'The Citadel is his home, it is he, as it is your home, as it is you. It is Selph, that is all. You are here now, like he is, following paths you might have chosen. And whatever remains, if anything remains when all this is done, will be the path of the future. It can be decided now, or it can all end.'

'But it is not my choice!'

'Then whose? You came here—'

'*I had no choice!*'

'Think that if you will, though it is not so. Choice is yours now.'

'But what must I do?'

'Dinbig,' she said, and her smile was warm and filled with intense sorrow and such love, 'you must choose. Remember, what comes before any action? Act, then, and understand what your actions will mean.'

I stood dumb, aware that everything was changing once more.

'We are waiting . . .' she said.

'For it all to end.'

She was no longer with me, only her words, floating: 'Or begin.'

The bodies were imperfectly still in the strange light, the gorgeous wings spread in many cases as though arrested in flight. I had brought the amber but nothing had changed, and I was at the beginning of the road once more. Why the beginning?

I have just been born.

Must I walk it again? There was no figure in the distance standing rapt before the sunset. There was no sunset, just darkness and rain, imbued with that queer illumination which gave me vision.

I turned and saw the young man in grey upon the steps. He stepped down and came to stand before me, his feet stirring spumes of yellowish dust upon the road, despite the rain.

223

'Give it to me now,' he said, holding out his hands for the amber.

I looked at him long and hard. His face was mine, the real me, familiar, but I shook my head. 'I have brought it here. I must keep it.'

'What for?'

'Until I know.'

'You should know. I am telling you. You must give it to me now.'

'No.'

'You do not even know who you are.' His smile held a hint of scorn. 'How can you know what you must do? Give it to me. It is proper. That is what you brought it for.'

I was afraid. Was he right? Should I allow him to take the amber? What then?

Who was he? How could I trust him? He was me, but then who was I? How could I trust myself?

'You do not even know who you are,' he said again.

I gazed past him, out along the road. 'What will you do if I give it to you?'

'Take it to the well.'

'I have done that. That is why I am here.'

'No, I must take it.'

Something glimmered in the far distance, beside the road, a red movement. The glint of light on metal, and a figure, two figures, one low-slung and strong, one immense, just glimpsed for an instant. Feikermun! He waited there, the ape towering at his side.

'No!' I drew back. My double, the true likeness of myself, seemed amazed.

'You are not you!'

I stood firm. 'You will not have it.'

'Then what will you do with it?'

I could not say. Far away, Feikermun had stepped out on to the road. My brother? How?

We are of the same source, each and every one of us.

He watched us, clearly visible now. I sensed his consuming hunger. I said, 'You have to die.'

224

'Or you.' My double smiled. 'But which is which? And what will remain?'

Feikermun's voice reached my ears. 'Cormer of Chol, give it to him. Give him the amber.'

Did he know now what it was? Who I was?

I was afraid, but I shook my head emphatically. Feikermun bellowed with rage. Viciously he swung his axe at the nearest of the Avari, but his reach was not enough and the blade missed. Feikermun began to run, pounding down the road towards us. 'Where is she, Cormer? Bring her to me!'

Bring the amber to the well, Sermilio had said. *You will know what to do next.*

But I did not know. I knew only that I could not let it fall into Feikermun's hands. I stepped down, alone now, and crossed the road, then mounted the temple steps upon which my double had stood. I passed between the seven tall stone pillars, aware of Feikermun drawing closer. Behind him were phantom shapes – tall, slashing, numerous. *The Scrin are with him now!* Panic was rising within me as I entered the temple.

But there was no temple. I was in the rain-soaked streets of Dehut. A little way off stood a group of men – soldiers. In their midst was a figure in red armour, beside him a huge painted ape. The armoured man held a great axe above his head as though about to bring it down and splinter the skull of a bruised man who stood before him. The bruised man was afraid. He was Cormer of Chol, but he was not who he claimed to be.

The armoured man bawled out into the night. 'Aniba! Aaaaannniiiiibbbbaaaaaa!'

And I roared, for my anger and hatred was such that I wanted only to destroy everything I saw. That was my purpose, to destroy, to murder, to revenge, that I myself might at last be destroyed.

The men before me turned as one, alarm and terror on their night-stained faces. They reached for weapons, their stances betraying their uncertainty. Attack me, or retreat? I knew no fear, only lust to tear their flesh, to annihilate their souls; for when they were gone I could be something other, could extinguish all that remained. This, and nothing else, was my purpose, for which I had striven for so long.

225

Feikermun's eyes were wide. He strode forward, bellowing at me. 'No! Back! Feikermun commands! Your master commands!'

My master? It had no meaning. The Scrin know no master.

'Obey! I brought you here! *I set you free!*'

I cared nothing for his words. I threw myself at the foremost of his beasts. Their weapons scoured and stung, but I fed on the pain, swiping, slashing, biting, my perfect fury mounting. I saw Cormer of Chol seize the moment and slip away. Why did that bring me satisfaction and yet increase my anger?

'Back!' screamed Feikermun. 'It is Malibeth you seek, not Feikermun! Back! Begone!'

I would have laughed, but we do not know how. That he should have the arrogance to think . . . I ripped flesh, scattered to sullied atoms a screaming soul, and then . . . it all shimmered. I was gone.

Breathless, I leaned against a wall in the black of an alley. I had put distance between myself and Feikermun and his beasts and that *thing*. I could no longer hear them. The glows of the fires were visible in the sky, the billowing columns of smoke opaque; the cool rain dashed my burning cheeks.

What had happened there? Something . . . I had seen . . . I forced it back. Did not want to face what it meant. Madness. The *gidsha* dream.

You must take the amber.

But haven't I already taken it? I did enter the well.

My fingers closed around the hard rock in my tunic and I was confused. So much happening. Where was I now? What was I to do?

I knew Feikermun was searching for me again. How could I know this? How could I be certain that he had not been killed by the Scrin back there? I shook my head, unsure, unwilling to think because the answer was too shocking. But I knew. I *knew*. I pushed myself away, stumbling in the dark, wondering where I might go next. And was so afraid, caught up in this dementia, this nightmare over which I had no control. The *gidsha*. Let it end. Let it end.

Don't let it end!

I am dying. I am dead. I have just been born.

226

He is your brother.
No, not that. Never that.
Oh yes. In the eyes of the cosmos.
I cannot go on.
You have no choice.
I HAVE A CHOICE!
Then make it.

Is it a dream. Cormer of Chol?

No, it was no dream. I ran on down that alley, further, through the corridors of Feikermun's palace, scattering animals as I passed. No leaves fell. A child stood beneath a tree, waiting.
We are waiting . . .
The Avari hung, waiting.
We are . . .
I am.
I cried out: 'Anniba! I am coming! Wait for me!'

Two figures stepped out, one on either side. They roughly grabbed my arms and brought me to a halt.
'Be still and do not cry out or you will die!'
They were soldiers. there were others with them. I did not think they were Feikermun's beasts, nor Wirm's men.
'Come. Don't struggle.'
I was led away, down many streets, unsure of where I was, panic beating in my breast. And all the time the world was changing, changing, the wings beating close, visions of the Avari, the Scrin, a sudden conviction that I was still within Feikermun's palace, or that I was falling, falling, into the well, that I stood beside the road and gazed upon the glory of a sunset, that I was entering the temple . . . But the rain, more forceful now, splashed upon my face; my clothes were soaked and clinging cold; strong hands guided me forward; the sky was black overhead, with just the faintest reddish wash above the hills.
'Where are you taking me?'
'Be silent!'
'Are you Malibeth's men?'
'Be silent!'

227

We passed through wide puddles and mud, then we passed beneath an arched gate and were in the darkened courtyard of a pale-toned villa. An oil lamp glowed above a fortified door. We entered, marched along a richly appointed corridor, down stairs then rough steps, into musty cellars, through a hidden door, and on. We were below the streets now, I was sure. Up again, through several small rooms and then into a wide, dimly lit hall.

A man sat upon a wooden chair placed on a dais at one end of the hall. That is, he had the body of a man, strong and athletic, and his bearing, even seated, was relaxed and assured. But his face was hidden. The whole head was contained within a carefully figured helm, wrought in gold or golden metal. The helm was moulded into the form of an animal head: a lamb. There was an element of extreme menace in that image: so harmless, timid, innocent a creature transformed into something golden and sinister upon the shoulders of a human being.

Below the helm he wore a long surcoat of blue and yellow lozenges, with mail shirt and leggings and leather boots beneath; there was a longsword buckled at his waist. Half a dozen guards were posted before him, clad in mail and helmets, clasping halberds erect. The soldiers who had brought me in remained close; they conveyed the impression of being well drilled, disciplined and highly efficient.

The helmed figure on the dais surveyed me in silence for long moments. When he spoke his voice was hollow, dull and metallic.

'You are Linias Cormer of Chol.'

'I am.'

The golden head moved slowly from side to side. 'No, you are not.'

A spasm of fear clutched my heart. 'I assure you, sir, that is who I am.'

'No.' He spoke with absolute certainty. I could scarcely doubt that I was uncovered, but how could he know? I would admit nothing until he had proven his assertion. But his next words chilled me utterly. 'You are Ronbas Dinbig of Khimmur.'

I felt the blood drain from my face. 'No! I am Cormer, Linias Cormer of Chol!'

The Golden Lamb eyed me in silence, one finger crooked beneath his metal chin. 'I have the means to expose you. It might save your life; on the other hand, it might condemn you to death. But now is perhaps not the time. Let us talk, but before we do let me warn you. You have magic at your disposal. Do not think to employ it. If you do my men will strike you down instantly. Do you understand?'

I said, 'Sir, I have no magic.'

He waved a hand dismissively. 'Enough. Just remember what I have said. Now, I require information of you. Strange events assail us. Dehut is in bloody turmoil, but something else is happening beyond the ordinary. There have been manifestations, fearsome creatures appearing in our midst, then vanishing; other inexplicable disorders. What do you know of this? Is it Feikermun's doing?'

'Feikermun believes he is achieving godhead,' I replied. 'In fact he is unwittingly achieving something of far greater reach, something which must be stopped. But surely you are aware—'

I hesitated. How much should I reveal? Did the Golden Lamb know anything, anything at all, of the Citadel of Selph? If I told him more, what use might he make of it? I recalled that neither Jaktem nor Illan had claimed to have heard of the Citadel, yet – treacherous dogs! – how could I give credence to their words?

'Go on,' said the Golden Lamb softly. His voice was strange – not only distorted by the helm but of an unnatural timbre.

My anger boiled over. 'Why did you assign your men to me?'

'For your protection.'

'Protection? *Pah!* I trusted them. I believed in them. I even *liked* them, and they have betrayed me. And now you mock me!'

'I do not mock. Have you need to change your feelings? They have done you no harm. They worked well for you. They helped save your life.'

'At your behest! Why? *Who are you?*'

The Golden Lamb was still. I half-sensed that behind the mask there was a sardonic smile. 'I am as you,' he said. 'Someone who has good reason not to reveal a true face.'

'What purpose do I fulfil in your scheme? I do not know

229

you—' I stopped, thinking back. Malibeth's lover, Gorl. She had slain him after he took power, or so it was believed. Was it possible that he had not been killed? Had he escaped her, or had the whole thing been a ruse between the two of them? Why? So little was known. Could this be he? Did he work secretly with Malibeth against Feikermun, or was he alone against the two? But if he were Gorl, how could he know about me? And what part did I play?

And then another thought came: this masked, helmed enigma, *might* he *be my double?*

My mind could not follow so many paths that whirled and twisted before it. I was spinning in the unknown, on the edge of delirium.

'You were saying,' said the Golden Lamb. 'About Feikermun . . .'

'He has unleashed a power, an immense destructive force. The manifestations you have witnessed are elements of it, but there is more. Much, much more. Feikermun labours under the misapprehension that he controls this force. In fact he has little control. He has spawned it; that is, it has come through him into this world. But it will destroy him and all else.'

'Can it be stopped?'

'I— I do not know.'

'Feikermun must die, then.'

'No! It is he who has opened the way to the Citadel, and he must be allowed to live at least until the way can be closed again.'

'The Citadel?' The Golden Lamb inclined his body forward.

I had said more than I'd intended, but there was no simple way to stop now. From his attitude I took it that the Golden Lamb knew nothing of the Citadel, or of Selph. But that might be a ruse. *Who was he?* 'It is a realm of potential, a place that lies beyond the world of our normal perceptions. It is the domain of pure, unformed thought. I can explain no further than that, for I truly know little.'

'But it is from there, this Citadel, that the destruction emanates.'

'That is so.'

230

'And we are to be its hapless victims. Are you saying that there is nothing that can be done?'

'The one thing that can be done is to keep Feikermun alive. As long as he lives there remains a hope that the gates to the Citadel can be closed.'

The Golden Lamb eased himself back in his seat. 'An interesting notion. Advantageous from Feikermun's point of view.'

'If you believe I work for his benefit, you are wholly wrong. Surely your two agents have made that plain to you.'

'Quite so, yet there is intrigue here within intrigue, duplicity within duplicity. How can any of us be sure of anything? After all, we do not even know ourselves.'

In my heightened sensitivity that statement seemed laden with import. Perhaps it was, but my mind raced and the world blurred and shifted and I knew only that I had somehow to get away from here and return with the amber to the Citadel of Selph. It struck me that I might yet enlist the Golden Lamb's aid.

'You have been there, have you?' enquired the Golden Lamb. 'To the Citadel?'

I nodded.

'How?'

'Sir, believe me when I tell you that I do not really know. The truth is I have been there, and I am there now even as I am here before you. The Citadel is here also. I can make it no clearer than that.'

'Then might I also enter it?'

I paused. 'I do not know. I entered it, as did Feikermun, with the aid of a drug.'

'What drug?'

'*Gidsha* root, specially prepared.'

The Golden Lamb absorbed this. 'Do you have access to this drug?'

'In a very limited amount. But the preparation is specific and takes time. Even were you to consume it, I could not guarantee the result. I do not understand it myself. Moreover, it is possible that the drug is now redundant, as the Citadel is here, with us.'

'Yet I believe you perceive more than I do.'

I gave no reply. The Golden Lamb sat in contemplation for

some time, then said, 'What of Feikermun now? He is seriously threatened by Malibeth and comes here to meet with me?'

'That is my understanding.'

'He is not coming without having taken precautionary measures. Possibly he intends a trap.'

'I am not party to his plans, but he was suspicious, I can say that.'

'My two men, Jaktem and Illan, are they with him and in good health?'

I answered in the affirmative on both counts. 'Sir, if you do meet with Feikermun I would implore you, do not kill him. Not yet. Take him prisoner if you can, but hold him safe. He may be your enemy, but he holds the only key to withstanding the Citadel's assault.'

'I will take due note of your words. Now, tell me, what is this thing that you clutch so carefully to your belly?'

I cursed myself. In my distraction I had forgotten the amber.

The Golden Lamb extended an arm. 'Bring it to me.'

One of his soldiers marched up to stand before me, and I had no choice but to relinquish it. He took it to the dais and the Golden Lamb held it up, regarding it for some time from behind his mask. 'It is intriguing, and strangely beautiful. What is it? A magical artefact of some kind?'

'Sir,' I said, feeling that all was about to collapse about me, that everything had been in vain. 'Sir, trust me when I say that piece of amber is of vital importance in this matter. It is of the Citadel, was somehow cast into the world, and must be returned. That is the business I was engaged upon when your men intercepted me.'

And I thought: *Why do I still have it? I took it to the well – now I am here. Why?*

'You brought this with you from Khimmur, did you not? Why?'

How could he have known that? I stammered, 'it – it has been in my possession for some time. I had no idea of what it was. I brought it in the hope of learning more about it and perhaps acquiring others like it.'

My words sounded feeble and inadequate. I was confused I could hardly even recall how I had come by the amber, or what

232

I had planned to do with it. And now, after everything, it was lost. Given into the hands of one who might well know its secret or, if not, might like Feikermun choose to take it into his own possession.

To my surprise the Golden Lamb passed the amber back to his guard, indicating that he should return it to me. 'Take it, and go.'

'Go?'

'You are free, at least for the present. My men will escort you back to the streets. We will meet again, Cormer of Chol, or Dinbig of Khimmur, or whoever you are, and it will be very soon. And when we do, be sure I shall test you and I shall know you. And if you fail the test I will kill you. Now go, and do what you are assigned to do. And be very certain of your motives. Be clear of who you are behind your mask, and be wary of who you pretend to be.'

Again it was as though he uttered words that meant more than I could presently comprehend. He rose as his soldiers moved to escort me, and stared down from the dais, an imposing figure. Perhaps I imagined it, but I had the distinct impression he was weighing something in his mind, as though wondering whether to say more.

But all he said, eventually, was, 'Go.'

19

SHAKEN BY THAT meeting and by what the Golden Lamb appeared to know about me, I found myself abandoned in the deserted backstreets of Dehut. The rain still fell; the glows of burning buildings in the southeast pulsed low in the night sky, silhouetting high towers and the peaks and angles of rooftops, and faintly the shouts of battle reached my ears. I was lost again, clutching the amber. I had done all I had been told to do, but nothing had been achieved.

Or had I? This was the *gidsha* dream, I remembered. I could not be sure of anything.

With startling abruptness I was cast back to a dream I had had in Khimmur – it seemed long ago, but its details were as vivid as if I had lived it yesterday. My first glimpse of the androgynous winged youth, Sermilio, whom at that time I did not know, standing gazing into the sunset, then pointing me to the cluster of buildings, saying: 'Go to the well. From the well all things come. Out of the well comes the truth.'

And I remembered my feelings then, of not understanding what it all meant, of being so close, as if . . . if only . . . if I could just break through, I would understand. That feeling came upon me now, so powerful I felt my soul would burst from me, for I was almost there, almost seeing, almost knowing . . .

Don't let it end!

I DON'T KNOW HOW TO PREVENT IT!

I saw the water running in tiny coloured rivulets about my feet. I stared, enraptured and at the same time struck with horror. Reflected in the water were the images of the Avari, unmoving, their stillness more terrible than ever before. The emptiness and silence – I no longer sensed even the remotest beating of wings.

I looked up: they were not above me. They were solely within the dark pools and rivulets of rain at my feet. I dropped to my knees, impelled by that image, the reflection that did not reflect. I sank into it, into the strange light, pulled or falling ... ... and now I was among them – they were all around, in the air, above, about, in their hundreds, as far as I could see. And I looked at the amber light and the amber in my hands, which somehow contained the winged host. Nothing had changed. The swarm of tiny bodies within, which I had once thought to be minute insect forms, were as they had always been. Though I had entered the well carrying the amber, nothing had changed.

There was a shift of place. I sped above the road, between the buildings, to arrive at that small glade where the well stood. I saw Sermilio sprawled upon the ground before me. His head was propped against the well's low wall and his wings spread lifelessly upon the earth. I knelt at his side, deeply afraid. His eyes were closed but I saw that his chest rose and fell faintly.

'What has happened? Are you dying?'

The eyes opened, lids fluttering, his look glassy. 'Where ... have you been?'

'I came,' I said. 'I brought the amber. I entered the well. And now ...?'

His eyes rested upon the green amber in my hands and his expression changed, became intense, filled with urgency and enquiry, seeing it for the first time. 'You ... must ... go again.'

'Again? But why? Why has nothing happened?'

'It has.' He gripped my arm. 'You do not see it, but it has. Now there is one thing left to do. Go once more, I implore you. Quickly, before it's too late.'

'*It is already too late!*'

I spun around, rising. Behind me were Feikermun, the ape at his side, and my double, Dinbig of Khimmur. At their backs towered a colossal creature, its shape indefinable – for it appeared to be many shapes at once, altering as I stared, never staying still, never quite solid, yet present, fearsome, real. It held aspects of everything I could conceive, and more that I never could. I knew it was Scrin.

'It is already too late,' repeated Feikermun, a grin of savage gloating on his lips, his eyes aflame with mad challenge. His face was a mess of colours; water glinted on his red armour. 'Look.' He spread a muscle-distorted arm to indicate the Avari. 'They are dead now. It is over. Give Feikermun the amber.'

I looked uncertainly from one to the other, then down at Sermilio. His pale eyes were open, fixed upon Feikermun. A trickle of blood ran from between his lips. 'It . . . is not over . . .' he rasped, struggling to rise. 'Not . . . yet.'

'Oh, but it is,' replied Feikermun tauntingly. 'It is. All that remains is for Cormer to give up the amber.'

He knows what it is! I thought. Feikermun was holding out one hand. At the same time my double stepped forward, his own hands extended. Sermilio was almost on his feet. I glanced aside at him; he seemed barely able to hold himself up. I wondered, *If it is truly over as Feikermun says, why does he want the amber?*

'Go, Dinbig!' commanded Sermilio.

'Dinbig?' A flicker of uncertainty on Feikermun's face. He glanced uneasily from me to my double, then back. At the same moment Sermilio threw himself past me with a sudden yell. He had drawn his stiletto-like blade, was lifting it high, and plunged it into the breast of Feikermun's ape.

The ape vented an agonized bellow as a fountain of blood gushed forth. It staggered back, clubbing at its assailant. Sermilio had fallen face-down on the earth. The ape roared dismally and wilted on to one massive knee, it head tilting, teeth bared, eyes filled with sudden sad reproach. Feikermun gave forth a stricken cry, 'Nnnoooooooooooooooooo!'

My double stepped towards me, reaching for the amber. I jerked back. He came at me again, his hands upon the amber. I pulled away and without thinking threw myself over the low wall.

Once more I was falling, down into the Well of Selph. This time there was no reflection of myself looking up at me. This time my double came after me, almost with me, hands outstretched for the precious yellow gem.

We fell together. Perhaps we were one, yet we fought, fought for that glassy stone in which the fate of the cosmos was sealed. Why did he want it? What was his aim? Did he work for Feikermun? Yet Feikermun had tortured and executed him.

Then why? Perhaps I would never know; I knew only that he fought me and that he hungered for the amber. His was a path I might have chosen, and if I did not subdue him now I might still find myself thrown upon it. Fail to defeat him and it would be my end. I would be gone; he would remain, would be me, to pursue his own ends, choose his own path, whatever it might be.

We fell – we fought – but I held fast to the amber and he could not wrest it from me . . . and when we ceased falling he was no longer there.

Nothing was there. I had entered emptiness. The end of the world.

Or the beginning.

Don't let it end.

Infinite paths stretched before me, leading away into nowhere. All possibilities. Any one of them mine.

I could not choose.

'*You cannot stand still.*'

'But if I take the wrong one?'

'*There is no "wrong" one, there is only what you choose. That is the way you must go.*'

'But I do not know where.'

'*Then decide now.*'

'I am afraid.'

'*Use your fear. It is yours. Make it work.*'

'It drowns me.'

'*Then rise. You must not let it end.*'

'Why me?'

'*That is not the question. Why anything? It is so, that is all. It is the way of it.*'

'Yet I cannot choose.'

'*Wrong. You have already chosen. You acted after thought, whether you knew it or not. Now you are here. Think only what you have come here to do.*'

I looked at Aniba. She lay upon a bed, hardly recognizable, her frail body beneath a white sheet, her hands on the surface by

237

her sides, her head resting on a pillow. She was ancient; she was my mother; her eyes were closed; she barely breathed. She was dying. It was her time. She had done all she had come to do.

I sat by her bedside and took one of her hands in mine. Her fingers gave the tiniest pressure; she knew my presence.

'*Am I dying?*'

'Yes,' I said. 'You are moving on. You will soon be born. Let go now, in your time. It is all right.'

The smallest smile flickered at the corners of her pale lips. '*Do you understand now? Do you know me?*'

'I love you,' I replied. 'I always have.'

'*But do you understand?*'

'Yes,' I said. My eyes stung with tears. I lifted her hand to my lips. Sweet, unknowable mystery. 'Will we ever meet again?'

'*We may, I cannot say.*'

'You will live again. Will you know me?'

'*I will.*'

'But how will I know you?'

'*You will know the love you feel one day when you look into a stranger's eyes.*'

'It will be you?'

'*It has always been.*'

I opened my eyes – just once, for a moment, for the first time ever – and I saw her face above me, smiling, and the love in her eyes, and I heard her sweet song, filling the sky, succouring my soul. Safe. Forever, as the bells began to ring.

And I heard my cry. Then a single bell.

'*There is one thing more.*'

I nodded. I did understand now, though I did not know how. I took the amber and placed her feeble hands around it, laid it upon her breast.

She smiled. '*I take his thought. He did not even know he had cast it, nor the damage a single thought could cause. Learn from that, Dinbig – the incalculable power that precedes any action.*'

I nodded, blinking back the stinging wetness in my eyes. 'It is all right. Go now. It is done.'

She looked so peaceful lying there, so trusting. There was

silence. And then the bell. I knew she had gone. Moving out into darkness. There came a sound of wings, from a distance, then closer, a rushing air, beating coolly past my face, breathing upon me. Gone.

I sat for an long time. Far away a bright, flat ocean, stained with the colours of the sunset beneath which it lay, revealed a tiny boat with two figures seated within. The boat's drift took it further and further, until it was a dot, and at last no longer visible.

Then I saw something that made my heart kick: a dark cloud – I thought it was a cloud – beginning to form above the red horizon. It was growing, quickly, reaching into the sky and coming closer, almost blotting out the glory of the setting sun. As it drew nearer, I began to make out what seemed to be particles within it. A multitude of individual tiny particles making up the mass of the cloud, all moving together yet freely and independently, as if with life of their own.

The cloud came closer, closer, and higher, shadowing the earth on which I stood, and now I saw the forms, so many of them. The air was loud with their coming. And I gasped at the sight, for they were clear now and properly defined. They were not particles, nor dust nor anything like it. They were people, or spirits, in their thousands and thousands. Each of them was winged. They were the Avari, more than I could have imagined, soaring upwards to fill the sky, pouring out of the sea beneath the fabulous sunset, a great wind rushing before them roused by the beating of their many wings. They flew free at last, as I wept.

They were all around me now, passing in endless random procession. I gazed in wonder until I found myself looking down at the frail body that lay before me, at the thin veined hands clasped around the green amber. Gently I unclasped them. I held up the amber and gazed within.

It was empty.

And, as I held it there, a lick of wind from the passing Avari host lifted it and broke it apart. It crumbled into powder, which was whisked away and dispersed in the stirred air.

A solitary figure detached itself from the passing mass of the Avari and began to descend towards me, wings outstretched.

239

Against the red sky it made a familiar shape. Sermilio alighted beside me.

'You are not harmed?'

He shook his head, smiling calmly. 'It is different now. We are free again.'

'Is it over?'

'Far from it. We go to do battle with the Scrin, to drive them back, close the gates of Selph and seal the Citadel again from the world of men.'

'Can you succeed now?'

'If we can close the gates – and I believe we can – your domain will be safe at least until another human finds access to the Citadel. The war with the Scrin will rage on, as it always has done, but the Avari will be here to watch over the souls of humankind.' He looked upward at the departing host. 'I cannot rest here. There is too much to do.'

He took my shoulders, smiling, and squeezed them. 'Farewell. You have done well.'

Sermilio rose from the ground, his wings outspread, then sped swiftly in the wake of the free Avari.

'What of Feikermun?' I called after him, but there was no reply.

I grew conscious again of the tears streaming down my cheeks. I felt overwhelmed, both with the joy of accomplishment and the grief of loss and incomprehension; delight and sorrow, a deepening sense of ineffable mystery. I turned, beginning to retrace my steps, not knowing where I was going or from where I came, yet somehow certain that beyond what I knew to be myself was something other, something eternal which was part of all that existed, had ever existed and was still to be, and which understood.

The amber light had faded, the sunset had passed. I looked up into blackness and cool rain spattered my cheeks.

'*Where is she, Cormer?*'

'She has gone, my lord.'

'No! Bring her now! Make her come! *Aaannnniiii-ibbbbaaaaaaaa!*'

I shook my head, so certain now as the axe was poised above me, ready to descend and sunder me from this world. 'There is nothing I can do. Nor will she come to you, nor will you ever find her now. She has gone.'

There were tears in Feikermun's eyes – I think he knew that what I said was true. But he could not or would not accept. The tendons of his neck stood out like cords and his features contorted with rage. 'Then you will die!'

There was nothing I could do to save myself – nowhere I could run, crowded by enemies, Feikermun's beasts and Wirm's men, and no rapture I could summon that would change anything. Yet I felt no fear, and simply waited for what must come next.

Dehut's night was split by an earshattering roar which drowned out even Feikermun's agony. His beasts turned as one, and he too spun around, arresting the fall of his blade, deflecting it from me. The beasts cried out, yelling in terror and alarm, and drew their weapons to confront the monstrous Scrin that had materialized just yards away. They were unsure; the creature eyed them for a moment, swiping and slashing at the air, ravenous with fury.

'No! Back!' bellowed Feikermun, thrusting himself towards the thing. 'Feikermun commands! Your master commands!'

And I remember thinking: *My master? The Scrin know no master.*

Then the creature hurled itself at Feikermun's men and I took the moment to duck away, slipped into a crack between nearby buildings and ran quickly, in near-darkness, veering into alleys, around corners, putting distance between myself and the shrieks, howls and roars behind.

When the sounds had died away behind me I paused to regain my breath, leaning against a wall. Looking back and upwards I could see again the glows of the fires in the night sky and the tall, opaque columns of billowing smoke. My skin burned, the rainspots welcome on my cheeks. I thought about the Scrin: *They are however we perceive them.* Had each of us, then perceived the same monster in our midst, or did we see individual, differing interpretations of whatever it was that had broken through?

Something disturbed me deeply about that encounter, something I could not quite identify. I pushed myself away from the

241

wall, thinking: *I have taken the amber. The Avari are free. Yet the dream, the nightmare, continues.*

Feikermun would be looking for me now, I was certain of that. I did not know how I was so sure, yet I had in my mind a vision of winged people appearing in the Dehut street and driving back the Scrin that tore into Feikermun's beasts. And an image of Feikermun, confused, raging at the Avari, who likewise vanished in the wake of the monster. And when he turned and found me gone, he roared his vengeance into the night.

I stumbled on in the dark, wondering where I might go next. The *gidsha* dream. I was possessed by a strange conviction that I knew what was about to happen. I thought, *Somewhere close by soldiers wait to intercept me. I am being taken to meet the Golden Lamb.*

I was right.

I was also wrong.

A short way further on I was hit suddenly by a stench that made my stomach roll and my skin crawl. In almost the same moment something slammed into me, hard. As I slipped in the mud my fingers closed on hair and cold skin, something slightly and horribly *giving*. There was a loud, angry humming noise. My senses reeled, rebelling against the stink, and I fell to the floor, the thing on top of me.

I rolled, half-crazed with panic, believing I was about to be torn apart. In the darkness everything was abruptly still, bar the pattering rain. I waited, hardly breathing, thinking the thing was still close, searching me out. My heart hammered against my ribcage. But nothing happened, and presently I found the courage to edge forward, my eyes better adjusted to the dark now.

I saw the thing a little way in front of me, a dense blot in the wet mud, its gut-churning reek still living on me. It did not move. I thought I knew what it was now. With one foot I stretched forward and prodded. It gave slightly with my pressure but showed no volition of its own. I pushed again, harder, and at last allowed myself to relax.

A carcase. One of Feikermun's hung dogs, half-rotten, fly-

242

infested and crawling with maggots. I had collided with it and pulled it from its makeshift gallows when I fell.

I moved away, half-consciously wiping at my clothes and skin as if that would remove the stench. And just ahead, somewhere – this way, that way – the Golden Lamb's men waited.

Or was it different now? I no longer carried the amber. I had been here before but it was not the same. And what if I should take another path? Deliberately or by chance, what then? Would it change things? Was the pattern already cast? How would I ever know?

Did I really have that choice?

I became aware suddenly that there were figures moving past me in the darkness. Creeping stealthily by, several of them, their feet squelching in the mud and the light creak and jangle of leather and metal . . . Before I had time to conceal myself and take stock I was grabbed by rough hands. A hand was clapped over my mouth. A figure loomed beside me, pressed a blade to my throat.

'Do not move! Do not cry out!' My sword was taken away and I was dragged back into the lee of a building. 'Keep your magics to yourself or you will die!'

A helmeted face was close to mine, a pale blotch enlivened by the dark gash of a mouth and two hollows for eyes. The pressure of the hand upon my mouth eased a little. 'Make not a sound.'

The hand slid away, though the blade remained at my throat. 'You will come with us.'

I had been here before, but it was all different this time. I risked a hoarse question. 'Who are you? Where are you taking me?'

'You will know soon enough. Now be silent!'

They marched me away – not far. There were squads of soldiers moving cautiously in the opposite direction, and others assembled in the backstreets. We arrived at a tall villa with a familiar fortified door; we entered, passed through the cellars and came eventually to the hall where I had been, or thought I had been, not long earlier. The Golden Lamb occupied his seat upon the dais. He was garbed virtually as before, and his guards were alert around him.

243

'You are Lineas Cormer of Chol?' he asked sternly from behind his metal helm.

I felt a chill run down my spine. This was all so familiar. 'I am,' I replied.

The golden head turned slowly from side to side. 'I would dispute that.'

'I assure you, sir—'

'Then you are not Ronbas Dinbig, the merchant, secret representative of Khimmur and man of numerous and sometimes dubious talents?'

My gut turned hollow. He seemed to know, or suspect, so much. What trap was this? My mind sped this way and that. I tried to force myself to calm. 'I am not. As you yourself know – for your own men brought me here from Riverway in Putc'pii.'

The Golden Lamb surveyed me silently and nodded slowly to himself. 'We shall see.' He clicked a finger. 'Bring the other!'

A guard strode to a portal in one wall beside the dais and pulled it open. There was a brief movement from within and then a man was brought into the hall, flanked like myself by two guards. Perhaps I had experienced too much in too short a space of time, for when I saw him I felt hardly a thing. Not shock, not surprise. It was as though I were incapable of feeling anything more. I simply saw him and recognized that it was he – that it was I. He was my double.

He was brought forward to stand before the dais, somewhat obliquely to me. I eyed him; he eyed me. Now the uncanniness of the situation began to strike me again. I felt that my nerves were stretched to their rawest, furthest limit, that the world spun slowly and soundlessly around me. The blood roared sickeningly in my ears.

The Golden Lamb stood and came to the fore of the dais to address the newcomer. 'You are Ronbas Dinbig of Khimmur?'

'I am.'

And now I felt truly, truly threatened. I had denied myself; he did not. This was my worst nightmare. If I were found guilty of fraud and he were declared to be me, then he might leave here, as me, and return to Khimmur. What would become of me?

Should I confess? But it might all be a trick, an elaborate

244

ploy designed to force admission from me. And what then? I would be forced to confess my mission, the secret plans of the Hierarchy and everything else.

Who was the Golden Lamb? Could he be in league with Feikermun? No, it seemed impossible. But why such an interest in me and my role? Who *was* he?

I drew a deep, shuddering breath, and said, 'It is not true. I am Ronbas Dinbig.'

'No! He lies!' My double made to step forward but was restrained by his guards. 'He is not Dinbig! You can see! Look at him! He is a fake, an imposter!'

The Golden Lamb stood with his hands on his hips, feet firmly planted. 'This is most interesting. Cormer, or Dinbig, or whoever you are, why do you suddenly change your tune? A moment ago you were vehement and convincing in your denial.'

'Sir, I did not know what you planned. I came here in secret, partly to discover the identity of this . . . *person* whom I had learned was impersonating me.'

'But as you yourself have just admitted, you were escorted here by my own men. They know you as Master Cormer, hailing from Chol.'

'But that is not, truly, who I am.'

'He lies!' sneered my double. 'Have him prove it.'

'Can you do so?' enquired the Golden Lamb.

'Not here. Not now,' I said, my fear mounting again. 'I wear a disguise, but it is not one I can remove, nor you. Experts in Khimmur must do it.'

'Pah! Blatant poppycock!' spat my double. 'I am Dinbig! See, look at me! Ask me anything! Then you will know!'

A rage began to grow within me, coupled with a sense of total helplessness. What a path I had followed; what a deadly, vicious trap I had allowed myself to walk into. For he spoke the truth. He *was* me. Like the amber that had held the Avari, he had been spewed forth out of Feikermun's madness. He was Feikermun's conception of me, drawn from a more or less chance encounter some years ago. He was 'I' following a path I might have chosen in other circumstances, given other motiv-ations, other impulses. He came from Feikermun, and I shud-dered to think of the damage he might do.

245

I said, hardly convincingly, 'Likewise, you may ask any question of me. If you know anything of my life and background you will know that I am speaking the truth.'

But my double also spoke the truth, I realized. Almost certainly he had been spawned with 'my' memory intact.

'Is it possible,' mused the Golden Lamb, 'that you would *both* answer correctly any questions I might ask you? Ah, well, it does not really matter, for there is a simple test I can conduct which will prove beyond any shadow of a doubt which one of you is lying and which is telling the truth. The matter will be done, then, to everyone's satisfaction. Are you both willing to participate in this little exercise?'

'Do we have a choice?' I asked.

The Golden Lamb turned his head to me, and I sensed that behind the mask he smiled. 'To be perfectly honest, no.'

I shrugged. 'Then I agree.'

'Excellent. And you, sir?'

My double remained mute and tense, but gave a single brief nod.

'There is one last thing,' added the Golden Lamb. 'When the test is complete only one of you, the one who reveals himself to be telling the truth, can be permitted to live. The imposter I shall execute on the spot. But it is probably hardly worth my mentioning this. The test must be conducted and, as I have said, you have no choice but to participate. Let us proceed without further delay.'

20

THE GOLDEN LAMB seated himself on the edge of the dais, his legs hanging loosely over the front, hands resting upon the lip. He appeared casual, but I noted his men shifted their stances almost imperceptibly, the better to intercede should either of us think to take a lunge in his direction.

'Now, is this not intriguing?' he began. 'Here are we, uncertain of one another, seeking one another out. You wonder who I am; I wonder who you are; perhaps you each wonder as to the true identity of the other. We are each, for reasons perhaps even we are not entirely sure of, disguised. We each wear a mask of differing type, but the effect is essentially the same in each instance. I find myself pondering this with a kind of fascinated glee.'

He allowed a moment to pass; neither I nor my double spoke. The Golden Lamb said, 'Ah, well, as I said, it is time for the test. It is very simple, ludicrously so, and will cause you no pain, though I repeat that whoever fails must necessarily perish. And should you both fail – not impossible, given the queer nature of what is happening here in Dehut – then you will both die, under summary law, exposed as frauds, liars and who knows what else. Do you wish to say anything?'

I hesitated a moment, then spoke up edgily. 'I am suspicious. You claim infallibility for this test you intend to conduct, but I do not know you and I can conceive of no test or exercise that could guarantee the result you seek.'

'Of course you can't. Your ability to do so would render the test null and void. As for knowing me, the test, by its nature, might be illuminating for he who survives it.'

'What is my significance in this?' I demanded, feeling the heat of sudden indignation. 'I am not of Anxau, have little more than casual interest in its affairs. Of what importance can I possibly be to you, unless . . .'

'Unless?'

'Unless you work somehow with or for Feikermun of Selph.'

The Golden Lamb uttered a short bark of laughter. 'I do not, I assure you. But, I say again, the test will prove illuminating to the victor, if there is one. Now, we are wasting time and there is much to do. After all, fortune is in the air, so I hear.'

He sat motionless, silent. I could not see his eyes within the golden helm, but I sensed that they shifted from one to the other of us. His attitude was expectant, I thought, but could not fathom why. I looked to my double, whose face remained as blank as mine must have been.

'Well?' said the Golden Lamb.

I was baffled.

'I am waiting,' he said.

'For what? I do not understand.'

'Have you nothing to say?' His voice was loud, if muffled, and there was a tautness in his posture now.

My double spoke. 'What . . . what are you asking of us?'

'An answer!' declared the Golden Lamb. He jumped down from the dais and stood before us, hands upon his hips. Then he turned and began to pace back and forth. His helm was tipped slightly back; he seemed lost in thought. He stopped pacing some distance across the floor, and spun around to face us. 'Nothing? Are you sure?'

It was surely a strange and cruel game. I was dumb; my double also. The Golden Lamb said, 'You have both failed. With regret, then, I must sentence the two of you to death.'

'Failed what?' queried my double. 'This is madness. Do you play with us? What have we failed? Where is the test?'

'I say once more, fortune is in the air, so I hear.' The Golden Lamb advanced upon us, then halted. I sensed that he scrutinized us both minutely, and he must have seen something in my expression, for he leaned towards me. 'Yes, Cormer, or Dinbig, or whoever you think you are? Yes? Have you something to say?'

I was groping, suddenly, desperately seeking, striving to

dredge something – I did not know what – from my memory. What was happening here? I could not work it out – and yet . . .

I stared at him.

I had it! And he saw that I had it. By Great Moban, I almost laughed out loud. I was disbelieving, stunned, could hardly fathom it, and doubted even as I did.

'Impart it not in the hearing of the other!' commanded the Golden Lamb. He strode away, his back to us. 'Speak into my lieutenant's ear, and he will convey your words to me.'

My guards pulled me back. I glimpsed fear on the face of my double. The Golden Lamb's lieutenant moved up close to me, and now I found myself floundering. For I could not remember the response. I was so shocked, so overwhelmed, flooded first with incredulity, then relief, then, again, fear – for I was about to fail. *Fortune is in the air, so I hear.* I could not remember how I should reply!

The lieutenant's heavy-lidded eyes narrowed, his face hard. I struggled with my memory, urging it to come, damning myself. But I was empty. 'I cannot remember,' I cried out at last, 'but I know now who you are!'

The Golden Lamb turned, observing us, then said slowly and levelly, 'That is not enough.' He turned to my double. 'What say you?'

The other Ronbas Dinbig looked at me, green eyes flashing. 'He is an impostor who seeks to trick you. He knows nothing.'

'But do you?' asked the Golden Lamb.

'I know as much as he!' the man blurted out.

'It is not enough!'

'No, he cannot know,' I said. 'Ask him. He cannot know.'

The Golden Lamb was sombre. 'No. It is just possible that he could, or you could. It cannot suffice. There are too many possibilities, too many risks. It must end here, then.'

He gave a signal. Two of his men drew swords and stepped forward from the dais.

'This is unjust!' cried my double.

'Give me a moment, please,' I cried. 'I am trying. I simply cannot remember.'

'I ask only that you be certain of yourself,' replied the Golden Lamb. I looked at him – there was something in his intonation, his inflexion. An image flashed into my mind, a word, a combination of words . . . And then . . .

I remembered. He had given me the final clue, the last vital aid to recollection, to help me see the words written before me as I stood in the parlour of my home in Hon-Hiaita only – how long ago was it? Two weeks? Three? More?

Go well and safely and be certain of yourself.

'Well?' said the Golden Lamb. 'I see something in your face. But if you have words to say, I repeat, do not speak them in the hearing of the other.'

I nodded. Still hardly daring to believe, I whispered into the lieutenant's ear: 'With every breath comes change.'

He straightened, wheeled about and marched across to his master, who bent his head, listened, and then, saying nothing, came to me. He took my arm firmly and led me aside. My two guards came with us, but he gestured them back. I stood with the Golden Lamb in the portal through which my double had entered under guard, out of hearing-range of all others, including the Golden Lamb's men. 'I believe you are Ronbas Dinbig of Hon-Hiaita in Khimmur,' he said in a subdued voice. 'But there is one last element to the test, by which I can be quite certain. Tell me, who am I?'

'I can scarcely believe it,' I replied, 'and even now half-believe that I may be the victim of some monstrous trick. But if that is not so then you can only be my friend and oftimes confederate, Viscount Inbuel m' Anakastii of Kemahamek.'

'Kill him!' shouted the Golden Lamb.

'No!' I protested. 'No, wait! I implore you!'

The two soldiers with swords had moved instantly to my double, who shrank back now in dread. But they hesitated at my outcry, seeking confirmation from their master. The Golden Lamb raised a hand, his unsettling reflective face turned toward me. 'Are you sure?'

'Hold him still, but let me explain.'

The Golden Lamb motioned with a nod to his men. He took my arm again and drew me through the portal. Once more guards made to follow and he signalled them away.

'Inbuel, is it really you?' I said when the door had closed upon the hall.

He lifted his hands, unfastening straps at his neck, and raised the golden helm. He tossed back his head, freeing the dark curling hair which had been flattened by the helm to his crown and brow, and grinned. 'Sir Dinbig! Well met, I say! Well met indeed! How are you?'

He clasped my shoulders as I clasped his, still too shaken to gather my thoughts or respond in any way, and we embraced. Inbuel laughed, drew back, wiped sweat from his brow. 'It is hot in this great helm. Now, you are bruised and the worse for wear, but not seriously harmed, I hope?'

I shook my head. 'A predictable consequence of spending time in the company of one such as Feikermun. But tell me—'

'No, tell me, first, why I should spare that sorry wretch in there. His antics have plainly served you nothing but ill.' With a glance to the door he lifted his helm and replaced it over his head, commenting softly, 'Apart from a select few, not even my own men know who I am.'

As he refastened the buckles I said, 'You are right, he has served me ill. But he is not truly to blame.'

'How so? His disguise is immaculate, I will say that.'

'It is not a disguise. You were wrong, Inbuel, when you said that we were each disguised, for he is not. Ironically, he is the only one of us who has openly displayed his true self, naked and without guile. Yet it is unacceptable.'

'I fail to understand.'

'That man who stands there beyond this door is not an imposter, Inbuel. He wears no mask. He is me, he is real, just as I am. He is dangerous, yes, undoubtedly so. But he was cast into this world unwillingly and unwittingly, as we all have been, but fully formed, an adult, with memories – *my* memories – intact. He almost certainly believes quite genuinely that it is I who am the impostor. And to my knowledge he has committed no crime. He exists, that is all, and is guilty only of that – which is to say that he is not truly guilty at all.'

'You will have to elucidate at greater length, my friend, if you are to convince me that you have not taken leave of your senses,' said Inbuel without harshness. So I proceeded to explain

251

what I could, detailing the essence of my discoveries since he and I had last spoken in Hon-Hiaita and revealing the extraordinary origin of the man who was my double. I told of the bizarre role that Feikermun had played in his 'birth', and spoke too of the Avari, the amber, the Scrin, and the Citadel of Selph, including my unwilling ingestion of the *gidsha* root. 'It is all beyond my capacity to embrace intellectually,' I said, 'and almost certainly the drug still exerts an influence upon my perception, but the facts are what they are nevertheless. You have personally witnessed something of what is happening here, and of the strange and powerful magics involved. I have experienced much, much more. I believe it may be almost over – at least in regard to Selph's influence – not that the Avari are free again. But not all is as it was.'

'And there are now two of you, where before there was but one,' Inbuel added. 'It may be that he is not an imposter, but neither can he truly be said to be you. My test has proven that much, if you were not already aware of it. You cannot both continue to exist.'

'To kill him out of hand would be an act of cold-blooded murder.'

'Then what would you suggest?'

'Hold him; give me time to think.'

'It may not be possible. Battle rages outside. We could be obliged to move from here at any time. It is a hindrance and a risk to carry him with us.'

'Let us speak to him,' I said. 'But first, tell me, what of yourself? I am beyond amazement that the Golden Lamb should be my old friend. Yet there are sides to it, implications, that disturb me somewhat.'

'Later,' replied Inbuel evenly. 'Let us deal with the matters most immediately at hand.'

We return to the hall where my double waited between his guards. Indeed he looked cowed and wretched now, and watched us with imploring, suspicious eyes. I felt a stab of pity for him – and as I thought again of who he was I was visited by a strange and unsettling emotion.

The Golden Lamb addressed him. 'Master Dinbig has explained something of your situation to me. He demonstrates unusual compassion, understanding and generosity of spirit in his words, and makes it plain that you are a victim of circumstances over which you had no control. He does not seek your death, yet both he and I are agreed that you cannot continue to live while he also lives – for you two are, in the truth of it, one and the same. An aberration, a paradox, an anomaly, an unreality that somehow has become real. We must find an answer to you.'

'You believe yourself to be me,' I said, 'and in many ways you are. But you are not. You are not of this realm of experience. You are the unconscious creation of a man who, for an instant, assumed the aspect of a god. A demented god who did not know what he did.'

I watched my double's face carefully as I spoke. Perhaps I wished it, but I thought that something of what I was saying struck home. Earlier fire in his eyes had faded; the challenge and defiance in his posture were gone. I saw a tiny, shy flicker of inconsolable illumination. He was downcast, and again, more powerfully, I felt sympathy.

'Feikermun brought you out of the realm of thought – his thought,' I continued carefully. 'He allowed you to manifest here. But he did not control what he had done, nor was he aware that he had done it. Do you recall committing misdemeanours against him? He imprisoned you, had you beaten, tortured, killed, yet you continue to live. He believed you to be me, and was incapable of knowing that he had in fact spawned you, that you came from the image of me he held in his mind.'

My double stared at me dazedly, swaying slightly. 'I remembered . . . his having killed me. I did not know why. I could not understand. Over and over I have tried to understand it.' He turned his head from side to side. 'I thought he had chosen to let me live again. I thought he was my father, and my god. Yet he despised me, did not know me or wish to know me.'

'Did you know him?'

'No. Only inasmuch as I have just said. I wondered . . .' He put his hand to his furrowed brow. 'It has been so strange . . .'

I nodded, studying him, and our eyes met. 'Aye, it has.'

'I have felt . . . I have not know where I belong. I have memories, yet no feeling of place. I exist as if in a dream. Here, there, cast back and forth, not knowing why I act, believing myself to be someone but not knowing who that person truly is.'

I looked aside at Inbuel, the Golden Lamb. His face, of course, was hidden, but I believed he must have been experiencing something of what I felt. I could feel no anger against this poor creature who stood before us. Kinship, rather, and empathy. *He is I*, I told myself again, *and unsure of who he is or how or why he came to be.* In that sense he was no different from any other born into this world.

But he had to go, to return somehow to the Citadel from where he had come. We could not both exist in the same world – and he was incomplete. Moreover, he was born out of Feikermun's mind; he undoubtedly carried something of Feikermun with him: a darkness, a craving, a capacity for cruel excess . . . I could only speculate, but the fact was that, though I pitied him, I still feared him – as I had from the beginning. Even in his acceptance and sad resignation he threatened me.

'What is to be done?' he asked, looking from me to the golden-helmed figure at my side.

The answer came to me. 'You have to return to the well.'

'I do not know the way.'

Neither did I. When I had gone there I had been drawn, without knowing how. And it had been under the *gidsha* dream. Did I still dream? I could not tell. I said, 'Do you acknowledge and accept the truth of what I have said?'

He hesitated for a moment, then nodded and said slowly, 'It fits, though it is so strange. After all that has happened . . . yes, I can, without too much difficulty, accept it.'

He might have been tricking me. He was held here by the Golden Lamb and had won only a nominal reprieve from a sentence of death. He had nothing to lose by going along, or appearing to go along, with my words. Yet in his eyes, and in my heart, I saw and felt that he was sincere. Could I be fooling myself? Could he? The doubts were ever-present, and there was still no answer as to how we should proceed, but I gave myself over to instinct, to intuition, trusting that it would not fail me.

'Then we must find the way back.'

The Golden Lamb lightly touched my arm and beckoned me aside. 'You spoke of the root, *gidsha*,' he said in an undertone. 'Would that open the way?'

'It might. I am not able to say.'

'Have you any?'

I nodded. I still carried with me a small portion of the root and the other ingredients.

'You think you are still under its influence.'

'I do not know, but it would seem likely.'

'But if he took it might it serve to return him to the place you have mentioned?'

'It might, but . . .'

'But what?'

'I cannot be sure. To know whether it had been successful I would need to accompany him. I do not know if I am strong enough for that. I have taken so much of the root already.'

I feared the root; I was also afraid, without being certain why, of returning to the Well of Selph. To do so, it seemed to me, would be to defy immutable laws. I had been there, I had been again, and I had done what I had been asked to do. The gates of the Citadel were closing now. If I went back to the well I might not return, for the well was my death, as the road that led to it had been my life. I understood that I had journeyed beyond, had been permitted a glimpse of an unknowable otherness so that I could return the amber and release the Avari. This had been vital to compensate for Feikermun's awful blundering, for he had turned the cosmos adrift and allowed Chaos to run amok. Feikermun had been where he should not have been, and I had been given the privilege of following in order to set things to rights. But to go there again . . .

I sensed its consequences in my bones, and shrank away.

'Is there something wrong, my friend?' enquired Inbuel softly.

'There has to be another way,' I said. I looked back at my double, who regarded me without animosity but with a measure of uncertainty in his eyes. I commanded his fate, and he knew it. He professed himself willing to return to Selph but, if it proved impossible and he remained here, then the threat of his existence still held. I would have to kill him, for if I did not he would kill me in order to become me.

I heard Inbuel's whisper, almost as if he read my thoughts: 'It might be simplest if I ended it now.'

'Could you do it? I cannot sanction it. I have told you it would be murder: he has committed no illegal act.'

'What of those he will commit?'

'Execute a man in advance for something you believe he may one day do?'

'That is not how it is in this instance, my friend. You surely know that. We can say with utter certainty that, if he lives on, he will be a threat. He can surely act in no other way. He has knowledge he cannot be permitted to carry. Your own people, if they knew of his existence, would be obliged to hunt him down and kill him. I say *if*, for let us look at his situation. To survive he must kill not only you but me as well. He would then *be* you; no one else knows his true identity. Thus I am willing to act now to forestall all risk of such a development.'

'He *cannot* be killed.' It came to me as if for the first time, with a terrible resonance.

'What do you mean?'

'I mean it is impossible. Feikermun gave him life, then executed him. But he returned. I have seen him, I have *been* him, and I have seen that he can be other things. He has no control, but he cannot die. Where did you find him?'

'My men came upon him in the backstreets close by. They believed he was tracking you.'

I looked back at my double. 'What were you doing when you were apprehended by these soldiers?'

'I do not know.' He looked woebegone. 'I found myself there. I came from . . . elsewhere. I don't know where. This has been the pattern of my existence.'

Again I felt for him. Whatever he was doing, whatever his goals might have been, he was acting without real choice, compelled to follow what must have appeared a pre-set course, and never knowing why.

'Were you looking for someone?' asked the Golden Lamb.

My double hesitated, then said, 'I think perhaps I was seeking my creator.'

It took a moment for that to sink in. 'But you say you did not know him,' I said.

'I did not, yet I knew he must exist, for otherwise how could I exist? So I sought him, not knowing who he might be. I wanted to know.'

'What of me?'

'I sought you as well, in a sense. I had a suspicion you wished me harm. Yet instead it is you who have told me who I am.'

And in a sense, I thought, *I too am your creator, for Feiker-mun could not have brought you into this world in such a form if he had not first held my image somewhere within himself. My brother; our creation.* The thought set my mind slewing; I felt I had almost seen something, almost understood, and that then it had gone, flitted away from me, elusive to my grasp, shy of my comprehension.

'. . . it is all such a blur. And I ask myself, what has been the purpose of it all? I have come into this world knowing nothing; have sought the answer, the reason for my being; have found it, perhaps; and now I am to return to not-knowingness. Why?'

'If you have found an answer, have understood the mystery of your origin, you have gained more than any man or woman known to me,' said Inbuel.

My double looked at him for a long time. 'But I do not want to die.'

'You have recollection of your existence before you entered this world?' I asked.

He gave a nod. 'Some, I believe.'

'Then it is not death that awaits you. It is, rather, the continuation of your existence exclusive of this particular realm, where you do not belong, where you cannot continue to be. It is not the end.'

'But will I know that I have existence there?'

'Did you before?'

'I believe . . . I am not sure. I recollect, but I cannot say whether I had knowledge of myself at the time. It is beyond me to know.'

'There are some questions that only the experience can answer,' I said.

We were interrupted then by a loud rapping upon the door through which I had first entered the hall.

'Come!' called the Golden Lamb, turning. A man entered, an officer, a sheen of sweat upon his face. Around one forearm he wore a bloodstained bandage. He marched forward, halted, tilted his head in salute, then strode to the Golden Lamb and spoke softly into his ear.

'Splendid!' came the booming voice from within the helm. 'Most excellent! Bring him.'

The officer returned to the door and beckoned to someone outside. Into the hall came several soldiers, bringing with them a sagging, sorry figure. They half-dragged him to a bench before one wall close to where we stood, and sat him down. He seemed barely conscious. His head flopped forward, chin upon his chest, hair adrift. He was weaponless, and much of his armour had been removed; his limbs and torso were smeared with colour, serpentine patterns, tongues of bright flame, as was his face. Saliva dribbled from the corner of his mouth, darkly streaking his beard.

'So,' said the Golden Lamb, standing before him, 'we meet at last.'

Feikermun of Selph made no response. His eyes were half-open but directed towards the floor, and his head lolled upon his wide shoulders.

'Tell me the circumstances of his capture,' said the Golden Lamb to the officer who had first entered.

'I can relate only in terms of what I witnessed, my lord,' said the man, 'for I do not understand them. We had been observing him for some minutes. We saw Master Cormer make his escape when Feikermun's company was diverted by a fearsome creature which came, as far as I could ascertain, out of the air. There was a furious battle – several of his men were killed, others were striving to escape – then quite suddenly the creature vanished. Feikermun began to search for Cormer; he had with him a gigantic ape. Something appeared, just for a moment: a winged youth, wounded it seemed, for there was blood around his mouth and upon his chest. He slew the ape with a single thrust of a slender sword, then he too vanished. At that Feikermun let out a great cry, clenching his head in his hands and falling on his knees as if in mortal distress. His men were in disarray. I saw our chance and ordered the attack. We had cut down a

258

number and Feikermun surrounded before they knew we were among them. A few fought on, hopelessly, and a large group melted back into the dark streets. We did not follow. Feikermun, throughout the skirmish, was slumped on his knees upon the ground, weeping like a child. He offered no resistance when we took him and disarmed him, and he came here meekly as though his very spirit had been taken from him.'

'His spirit, everything,' I said, gazing at him. 'He is a broken man.' I could not wholly grasp it, yet I understood something of the enormity of his loss. 'His belief could no longer sustain him in the face of what was real. He had no more delusions to feed on; I suspect he has seen the truth, and it is too much to bear.'

'Is this my father?'

I turned, as did the Golden Lamb. My double stared with hollow, questioning eyes at the squat figure of Feikermun. He made to step towards him. The guards barred his way but then, at a motion from the Golden Lamb, they let him pass. He came forward as if in a trance and gazed down at Feikermun.

'You are my father,' he said in a trembling voice. Then, louder, 'You gave me life. Do you know me?'

Feikermun's bulk shifted slightly, as though the words had penetrated his terrible stupor and echoed dizzyingly there. Slowly he raised his head, a great and intolerable weight. Blood-shot grey eyes settled on the man confronting him, and for an instant – no more – I thought I saw a spark of recognition, life returning, or something. Then the eyes lost their focus again and stared bleakly into a lost, perhaps treasured distance. The head slid slowly forward. One slack hand twitched slightly on a massively muscled thigh.

What happened next I shall never forget. It happened in a moment, almost too quickly for the eye to follow, yet I recall every detail as though it were being played out over and over again, slowly, before my eyes.

My double turned around, his eyes glassy, and looked from one to the other of us with an unreadable expression. Then, with a movement of unexpected suddenness and speed, he threw himself at the nearest guard. He pushed the man backwards with one out-thrust hand while with the other drawing the surprised guard's longsword from its scabbard. With a wild yell he lifted the sword in two hands, whirled around, and brought it down in a wide but certain arc. His strength confounded me, for with that single blow he took Feikermun's head from his shoulders.

In virtually the same instant that my double moved the Golden Lamb's guards reacted. Three leapt to form a defensive wall before their master, thrusting him back. Two more launched themselves directly at my double. As his sword-blow completed its arc and the first blood gushed from Feikermun's neck, a slashing blow severed both of his wrists where he gripped the sword. The hands dropped to the floor, still clutching the sword as it clattered upon the flags. A swordthrust from the second soldier pierced my double's back, the tip protruding for an instant from his chest.

He gave a groan, staggering as the sword was wrenched free, and brought himself around to face us. Blood sprayed from his wrist-stumps, falling on to Feikermun's shaggy head, which had come to rest between his feet, mouth agape, the eyes still open, staring up at its creation with an expression resembling disbelief.

My double's mouth opened, trying to frame words as his knees buckled. 'It is over,' he whispered. He tottered and fell, coming to rest across Feikermun's legs, his head tipped back to rest upon the crazed warlord's great bloodied thew. Feikermun's headless corpse remained seated, the shoulders slumped forward, and the lifeblood flooded forth, pouring down into the face and mouth of the man who rested beneath and his own, which gazed up from the floor.

My legs grew weak, and I heard the blood roar in my ears, the room rotating around that grotesque tableau and its image of grisly intimacy. I had the feeling that it was not I who stood there – that someone else had taken over me, an observer, a witness to my death, for I had died here. I had seen it. I had seen what would have happened had I chosen another path.

I knew there were voices crying out all around me, but I could not hear their words. I heard only that single bleak statement in my mind: *It is over.*

21

B UT IT WAS not over. It did not hit me immediately, but
Feikermun's death raised new dilemmas.

The hall fell quite suddenly quiet. The soldiers of the Golden
Lamb stared with blank expressions at the two disfigured
corpses whose lifeblood formed a rapidly dilating lake and
bright racing rivulets on the floor. Those whose weapons had
been used slowly wiped them clean and resheathed them. They
waited half-dazedly for a command.

The Golden Lamb said, in a leaden voice, 'Take these bodies
away.'

He walked to the dais, beckoning me to follow. 'I am not
sure of the implications of this,' came his voice, sombre and
muffled from within the helm. He rested his buttocks against
the lip of the dais and folded his arms on his chest. 'You say
this man, this other you, cannot die. I look at him now and
say that he is unquestionably dead. Are we to anticipate his
return, then?'

My thoughts were on Feikermun, and in my mind echoed the
caveat I had received from both Aniba and Sermilio: *Feikermun
must not die*. I looked back at Feikermun's corpse.

'He has killed his god, his creator. He was but an image or
a thought captured unknowingly in Feikermun's mind,' I said,
at the same time thinking: *He has killed one of his creators,
and then himself, so that the other, who is me, may live on.
Ronbas Dinbig is dead before me, and I am alive, and I am he,
both living and dead. Who or what is it that has perished*? I
closed my eyes for a moment, then added, 'If Feikermun has
died prematurely, the gates of the Citadel will remain open. My
double will then remain to haunt the world. But if that is so, it
will not be for long, I fear.'

261

'You fear?'

'If the way is open then we will have far more to be afraid of than the havoc he can wreak.' As I said it I realized I had little choice now. I had to know, and the only way to know was to return to the Citadel and the Well of Selph. Warily I reached into my clothing for the *gidsha* and the other ingredients.

'What are you doing?' asked Inbuel.

'I am going back.'

It was empty. No figure was upon the steps; the pillars of the temple cast no shadows. No baby cried; the mother did not sing, and no bell rang in the air above. The yellowness of the light, the amber clarity, had been supplanted by a toneless haze. There was not a breath of breeze to shift the dust, but overhead the great firmament of blackest black still hung.

The Avari had gone. The road stretched ahead of me for as far as I could see, no one standing at its side. The overwhelming feeling was of abandonment.

I did not recall how I had come to be here, nor did I know where I was going, except that the road was there and it was the only path I could choose. But I was heavy, so heavy, the body settled in, unfamiliar . . . and so far to go, so far, so very long. Eternity lay before me, obscured by my death which would cleave it from me, severing me but leaving all else. Yet I had seen it. I had understood.

How would I know? I could only trust.

Alone, seeking to know, but everything I sought was unknowable. Here was I, who was; here too was I, who might have been; and there was all else, held within me. I was part of it, and yet it was denied me. Such a very long way to go, and not knowing why.

I came at last to the small stone buildings among which I knew I had stood before. I was weary; it had taken so long and I remembered little. The blood-light of sunset stained the bare land, deepening the long shadows, altering the world over which I had come. *The blood engenders life, the light nurtures and sustains it. Not of woman, not of man, though we are born of the two. We are waiting . . .*

262

And not far ahead lay the little path that led down to the well, the dark swaying trees behind it. No further. There was nothing beyond – nothing that might be experienced by mortal flesh or perceived by mortal eyes or senses. There was only the well and all that it contained.

I turned around and looked back, perhaps to try and recall, or perhaps to reassure myself that everything I still did recall had been real – that I had not fooled myself, or that my memory or my imagination had not fooled me. The scene was almost as I had expected it to be, but the road had gone. This time I could not go back. Why was I so certain that I had been back before?

I moved on, passed between the little houses and the temple and down the grassy path to the well. I rested for some moments against the low stone wall of the well, and stared up at the empty, sheltering sky. Did the fact that the Avari had gone tell me what I wished to know? It seemed so; I was satisfied.

I sat upon the well's wall and, after a while, swung my legs over so that my feet hung above the infinite space beneath. Leaning forward a little I could see my reflection gazing back at me. And it was I: it was the face of Ronbas Dinbig looking up. It was only right. I had done what I had done, and this was the end. I had slain Feikermun, my father, my brother, my creator, my god. I had done so only when it was time, and it had *been* time. He had known me. How could we have come together had it not been so?

And I had let the other remain, which was as it should be.

I leaned forward then, gazing down into the depths, and I let myself fall.

And I fell as I had fallen before. I glimpsed the red and the black and heard the soft beating of powerful wings, and this time it seemed that not quite everything into which I descended was entirely strange.

Am I dying?
I heard my mother sing.
Am I dying?
I heard the bell far above.

263

Am I dying?
I heard the baby cry.

And a voice I had never heard before, but which I knew and loved so dearly, whispered: 'No, *you have just been born*.'

22

THERE REMAINED QUESTIONS to be answered. There remained old scores. There remained Wirm.

I had forgotten about Wirm. It seemed he had slithered away, probably wisely, seeing the pattern of events and knowing Feikermun's reign to be effectively over. Wirm would not let it end there, of course; I could be certain of that. He would wait, plot, seek his moment and his advantage, then reappear in Dehut to remind or convince whomsoever he chose of his indispensability. Wirm might have lost Feikermun, but he was a resourceful and resilient fellow, not given to capitulation or defeat and well practised in the art of extracting personal advantage from adverse circumstances.

So, yes, I had forgotten about Wirm, perhaps not even thinking him significant in the greater picture. But that was a mistake, for certainly Wirm had not forgotten me.

I do not remember leaving the Golden Lamb; it was inadvisable to have done so. But I know I took the *gidsha* again, hopefully for the very last time; and under the moot auspices of that uncanny root one quickly comes to accept that one is subject to different laws, different valences. One learns not to be surprised, that the dream commands the reality, that the world is nothing more nor less than a reflection of mind. Aniba had made me see that before the action is the thought, the concept, and had allowed me to understand that the same must apply to everything. Our universe, then, is the sum total of our experience, realized, actualized, but always a product of conscious or subliminal processes. The existence we know is that which we have made, all creatures, sentient and other, throughout time and across space. It is a common agreement, though we have no knowledge of having agreed, for we believe

ourselves individual; we consider ourselves unconnected, separated from each other and everything else. But we seek, and the
more we seek the more we discover there is to find, because in
the act of seeking we are endlessly creating – permitting to come
into being that which we may, one day far from now, recognize.
The mystery is our own, not yet to be known in its entirety, for
to know it will be the end of everything, a final consummate
union, and another beginning. Together then, innocently and
unconsentingly, we give existence to everything, including ourselves, including our gods. We are the urge and the spawn, and
our greatest secrets we are born to conceal, to hold deep in
places where we cannot – or should not – yet go. We *cannot*
know them too soon, for to be aware before the proper time,
the ready time, is to unleash the unimaginable. Everything is
but a dream. This is what the *gidsha* told me.

But, if the *gidsha* bestows insight, it also steals. It takes
memory as it takes reality; and when I opened my eyes it was
as though everything that had gone before had been a dream,
for, as with horror I recognized where I was, my first thought
was that perhaps I had never actually left.

It was a blazing bright greyness that pierced my eyes, forcing
them shut, my head twisting away. But my limbs did not follow.
I opened my eyes gradually, allowing the light in by degrees.
My arms and legs were oddly stretched and would not obey
my efforts to move. I was lying naked upon my back. I felt
warmth on my face, chest and legs, but a chilling, shifting cold
beneath and – though I rested upon something hard and ungiv-
ing – a sensation of gently undulating and rather sickening
movement.

I caught the reek of foul water in my nostrils before I saw it,
knew its touch as it lapped coldly at my skin. I went rigid as
the panic slammed into me, then began to struggle.

Futile. I was bound.

The water was all around me, black and scummy, and I was
supported low upon its surface by a bed of seeping wooden
planks. My wrists and ankles, outsplayed, were tethered with
fine rope to four stout poles which were driven into the mud.
Arching back my neck I saw, obscuring the overcast above me,

266

the shadowy bearded long-haired figure of the raftsman leaning musingly upon his quant, awaiting a word from his master.

'It is useless to struggle,' said Wirm. I raised my head and saw him standing flanked by henchmen above me at the end of the jetty. His mouth was twisted into a thin gloating smile, and his small bright eyes darted incessantly over me, gleefully triumphant at my fall.

I searched for words, anything, just to speak, for into my mind lurched another horror, a memory of a previous event witnessed from another perspective. 'How did I get here?'

Wirm laughed and wrung his hands delightedly. He looked at my right thigh.

I felt preposterous relief. I could speak. I had my tongue. Yet what was that worth when I was about to die anyway? Horribly. I could imagine Wirm's pleasure at hearing my screams.

'I brought you,' he replied, his eyes now on one of my out-stretched hands. 'Now, this is an interesting time. The Twiners are close to the end of their season. I suspect that already many will have lost their appetite for flesh, but there will be enough, I think. It means simply that your agony will be prolonged. My advice is that you open your mouth, let the water enter. It will be quicker that way. But I think you will struggle, no matter what, and fight until the last breath. They all do, like men in burning cages. It is the indomitable urge to cling to life at any cost, even to the last excruciating moment.'

'Wirm, I had no intention of robbing you of your trade with Feikermun,' I protested. 'I didn't know. I simply didn't know!'

'You ruined everything, you meddling fool!' he snapped. 'Feikermun was mine! Everything he had I would have controlled, and then you came along wanting to take it for yourself. Now he is gone. All my work for nothing. You will compensate me for this, Cormer of Chol. You will compensate with the spectacle of your death, but I will continue to despise you long after you have gone.'

Now it was clear. Of course, Wirm had higher ambitions than I had suspected. Through controlling Feikermun's *gidsha* addiction he had made Feikermun his virtual slave. He knew what Feikermun was doing, probably knew something of the power he sought. He had made Feikermun his puppet; Feikermun's power would have become Wirm's.

'No,' I protested bitterly. 'It was not like that. I did not know. I sought no control over Feikermun.'

'I warned you when you first announced your intention. I told you then to go. You could have lived, but you paid no heed. Ah, well, I shall enjoy the next moments, though they will not be enough. Far from enough for what you have cost me.'

He gave a nod to the raftsman. The raft bobbed slowly as he shifted his stance and leaned to the quant. The rope tautened about my ankles and I felt the rough planks begin to slide from beneath me.

'No!' I cried, in desperation, terrified as much of the water itself as of what it would bring. 'Wirm, wait, please!'

But Wirm stood fast, one leg quivering erratically, his eyes glued greedily to my face.

My legs were fully in the water, then my middle, my chest. Finally, gasping, my head slipped from the retreating raft. I clamped shut my mouth and eyes as the foul wetness washed over me, and struggled violently against the ropes securing my ankles and wrists. I came threshing to the surface, spat slime and muck which despite my efforts had somehow got into my mouth. Craning back, I saw the raft bump up against the side of the tank.

The water covered me again.

When I resurfaced, gasping, the raftsman had raised the gate in the tank's wooden wall. Did I see or only imagine the surge of disturbed water as the slithering carnivorous serpents came for me? I know I was crying out, sinking, held by the ropes, rising. I felt their maws upon me now, the first voracious feeders attacking my side. There was no pain, not yet – just the sensation, almost gentle, of little mouths intimately nudging and exploring . . . and the knowing. I sank, came back, saw Wirm and his cronies through the film of clouding water, devouring my plight. I sank again, coughing and spluttering, feeling the slippery shapes on my body and face, the eels which tore at my dying flesh.

And then there was somebody or something else on the jetty.

A pallid form, thrusting Wirm aside, springing from the jetty's edge. It passed above me. I heard the thud as its feet alighted upon the raft. There was a yell, then a splash and screams as the raftsman fell. I was aware of my blood colouring the water, the slithering on my flesh, and the frenetic surge of panic. But the raft began to edge towards me as the pale creature took the quant and thrust hard, then reached out and grasped my arm. I did not see a blade, but the rope gave, then the rope that held my other wrist. My head and shoulders were lifted, the raft sliding beneath. There were yells from above. The other ropes were severed and I came clear of the water. With swift movements, aided now by myself, my rescuer pulled the ravening eels from me.

'Wait,' came his command. 'Do not move.'

He leaped up suddenly from the raft to the jetty, where Wirm was screaming at his men. Two were levelling crossbows. The pale thing was among them, knocking them to the side.

Wirm had drawn a sword. He lunged at the creature. It blocked his blow with a mighty arm, then stepped in, lifted him and threw him struggling backwards through the air. He came down at the edge of the jetty, staggered, struggled for balance, arms windmilling. He gave a dread-filled glance over his shoulder as he toppled backwards into the thick swill of the mire.

Wirm disappeared beneath the surface, came to the top, hammering at the water, shrieking. The water churned. I saw the strands of sleek grey backs speeding towards him. He went under again, and when he next rose his face and arms were a mass of angry writhing Twiners.

More of Wirm's men were running towards the end of the jetty. Those already there, three in number now, were standing, swords drawn, before the pale creature which had for a second time saved me from the mire. But they positioned themselves well back and were hesitant about advancing upon it. From the far end of the jetty, close to the processing sheds, could be heard shouting. Glancing that way I saw many figures running back and forth; several appeared to be fighting. Others were pounding on to the jetty now. I took them to be Wirm's men again, then saw they were engaged in combat with some of those who had gone before them.

I was confused. The pale creature turned and launched itself from the jetty to land lightly beside me on the raft. It sank to one knee. 'Wait here. You are safe now. Those who come are friends.'

I looked into a face that was bland and almost featureless except for two enormous dark eyes, wondering. And as I looked I saw, as if through a pale mask. I gasped. 'Sermilio!'

His lips formed a smile but he said nothing.

'It was you!' I said. 'You who pulled me from the mire before.'

'Perhaps,' he said. 'That is a way of looking at it.'

'But this is not you. You are not Avari.'

'I have told you before, we are as you perceive us. We are as you *elect* to perceive us. You consider us disconnected entities, so that is how you conceive us. You imagine Avari being separate from you. You think of Scrin in the same way also. You are not yet able to conceive of us as all being one. You create us individually, and so that is the nature of the manifestation. Your own ideations. You cannot yet see that. We are aspects of Selph, but it is held secret, locked into the Citadel, where is held everything, all the evils of the world as well as all the good. For now you can be only as you are, growing slowly in the natural order of things, and the secrets must remain secrets.'

He smiled, seeing the bafflement on my face. 'Were you successful?' I said. 'Feikermun is dead. Did he die too soon?'

'Scrin remain in some small number within your domain. We will hunt them down if we can, but be alert. Wherever you hear of carnage without apparent reason, know that Scrin may be at work. It is a tragic fact that, were you only ready, all of you, you could end this with a single thought. But if you realized that power too soon you would become as they are, unable to contain it, enslaved by the need to destroy. We must wait, then. Now, farewell. I go.'

He leapt away, upwards, and as he did so he faded from my sight. Momentarily I had a vision – of the winged host, the Avari, rising in their thousands from the sunset ocean, their wings, crimson-and-black, filling the sky. Then that too was

270

gone, and I lowered my eyes, knowing there were some things I would never understand.

Wirm's men had thrown down their weapons. They were heavily outnumbered by those others pouring on to the jetty, and with their master gone sought only to preserve their own lives. But who were these others, and how had they succeeded in breaching Wirm's seemingly impenetrable fortress in the mire? The answer to the first part of that question came as a distant figure emerged from one of the sheds and stepped up to the furthest end of the jetty. I thought I knew him, though at this distance I could not be certain. He was large and ungainly, and walked with a slow, laboured, listing gait. His approach seemed interminable. He wore a mail surcoat and a silvered helmet, and carried a huge sword. A bodyguard of four soldiers surrounded him.

I waited, shivering, aware of the blood from the scores of tiny wounds inflicted by the female Twiners over most of my naked body. At last the man arrived and stood at the jetty's edge, hands upon his great hips, huge belly jutting forward. 'You are in a sorry state,' he said, and glanced across to where Wirm's mutilated and now abandoned remains floated in the water. 'Still, you have fared better than he.'

'You are a welcome sight, Vastandul,' I said, 'though your appearance leaves me mystified.'

'I came to help you,' he said. He spoke to one of his men, who threw me a rope. As I hung on to it my raft was hauled to the jetty. I climbed up by a wooden ladder which ascended from the eel-tank to the jetty. A blanket was brought and wrapped around me.

As I waited I looked down at Wirm's remains. His blood reddened the disturbed water. I saw a flicker beside one half-eaten eye, and shuddered. The eels had taken their fill and, as was their habit, left him alive but, to use his own words, in a condition in which life could not be sustained.

'Come,' said Vastandul. 'Let us go to the manse where you can be properly cared for. Can you walk?'

I nodded.

'How did you do it? How did you conquer Guling Mire?' I asked as I shuffled across the creaking boards. 'And why?'

'All in good time,' answered the huge man. 'Suffice it to say that I was not alone.'

He waved a fat hand towards the processing sheds, and glancing up I saw a figure standing there, facing our way. It was garbed in a yellow-and-blue surcoat, its entire head covered by a reflective golden helm.

The Golden Lamb raised his hand and I, bone-weary, managed to raise mine in return.

23

'A RARE DISGUISE INDEED, that can keep a man safe even from ravening Twiners,' observed the Golden Lamb with irony. He was seated upon the blue-upholstered carved-oak chair which I had occupied the last time I had been here, in the opulent reception chamber in Wirm's fortified manse. He was right: I should have died, for I had been in the water long enough before Sermilio intervened. The Twiners had had ample time to do to me almost as much as they had done to Wirm. But the false flesh moulded on to my face and body by the Chariness and her helpers to transform me into the fictional Linias Cormer had bolstered me against the first wave of hungry mouths. And it seemed the eels had not found it to their liking, for relatively few had sustained their attack. When Wirm had subsequently plunged into the water the Twiners had turned on him with a frenzy that matched the pitch of their unslaked ardour. He had proven far more palatable than I.

So I had emerged from the mire scoured by dozens of minor flesh wounds – without aid I would almost certainly have bled to death eventually – but none of them would leave a permanent scar. And I was alive, whereas Wirm was, I hoped for his sake, now dead.

The Golden Lamb, my friend Viscount Inbuel m' Anakastii of Twalinieh in Kemahamek, was watching me keenly, his brown eyes sparkling. 'You are unrecognizable now,' he said, the irony still prominent in his voice. 'A non-identity, neither Cormer nor Dinbig, yet with elements of both.'

It was true. I had seen myself in a mirror. My false flesh was half-eaten away. It and my real flesh littered my features in ribbons and tatters and deep uneven craters and scars, bloodless in places, raw and angry elsewhere. I was like a creature tormented by some terrible flesh-devouring pox. More appropriately, I thought, I resembled something that had returned from the dead, for in so many ways I had.

We were alone, the Golden Lamb and I. I was resting, weak and shaken but grateful for having survived and relieved in the knowledge that it was over at last. Almost. There was still some talking to do.

Jaktem and Illan had departed the chamber just a short time earlier. They had come to pay their respects, both keen to explain to me their part in the Dehut affair. I learned that they had received their orders a few days before my departure from Hon-Hiaita; they had been in Hon-Hiaita themselves, in fact, members of the entourage assigned to Viscount Inbuel during his brief sojourn. But instead of accompanying him back to Kemahamek they had been sent to Riverway in Putc'pii, to The Goat and Salmon Pool. Their instructions were to await the arrival of an anonymous personage who would be riding out of Khimmur en route for Dehut. They were to offer him their services as bodyguards – it was expected that he would be seeking such. But if unsuccessful in their application they were to tail him, doing all in their power to ensure his welfare, and once in Dehut to report to the Golden Lamb on his movements and progress.

'We are sorry we gave you cause to believe we had betrayed you, Master Cormer,' said Jaktem, looking uncharacteristically ill at ease, 'but as you now know, it was never that way. We worked for you at all times, assigned by another, and in ways that you could not understand at the time.'

'I see that now,' I agreed. 'And, if my memory serves, you have not yet received your due salary.'

'We have been paid in full for our service,' said Illan with a glance to the Golden Lamb.

'But not by me,' I said. 'I hired you on specific terms, and I shall see to it that the agreement is honoured. Unfortunately I have been stripped of all I had—'

'Your clothing and immediate effects have been found here,' said the Golden Lamb from within his ornate helm. 'Your other belongings we brought with us from Dehut.'

'Then I charge you two to apply to me later, certainly before you leave Guling Mire, and you will be fully paid. And I shall prepare references and endorsements also, for use in the unlikely event that you should ever find yourselves in need of work outside of your current employ.'

After the two men had left, the Golden Lamb crossed to the door and spoke briefly to the guard outside. Then he returned, closing the door, and seated himself. He removed his helm. 'It gets stuffy in here,' he said, shaking free his dark curls.

'Inbuel, are you not concerned that someone will enter and see you?'

'I have just passed precise orders to ensure against that. We will not be disturbed. Now, let us relax a little. It has been a tiring day.'

He poured dark amber wine into two silver goblets and brought one to me. I sipped the liquid, welcoming its vigorous bite as it slid down my gullet. 'Where is Vastandul?'

'He will no doubt he here later on. For the nonce he is too busy rubbing his hands as he contemplates his new properties.'

'New properties?'

'Guling Mire,' said Inbuel with a bland smile. 'Vastandul is keen to become an eel-farmer. In return for his aiding me here it was agreed that he would take over the settlement. There are conditions, of course. Largely they pertain to the treatment of his workers. Wirm used a workforce of near-slaves, kept docile by drugs and brutality. They worked long hours and lived in quite appalling conditions. That will end now.'

'Is Vastandul conversant in the techniques of Twiner cultivation?'

'What he does not know he can learn from his workers. I think he will make it profitable.'

'Can you be sure he will not go the way of his predecessor?'

'I believe so,' Inbuel sipped his wine. 'He is not entirely alone in this enterprise, you see. There is an invisible partner, a certain youthful and somewhat dashing noble of Kemahamek with whom Vastandul has done good business in the past. Vastandul has a number of interests in Kemahamek. He would not wish them compromised. There is room for a third partner, should you be acquainted with another trustworthy investor who might be interested. It is a tempting low-risk venture.'

275

'I can see it might have its attractions. Should anyone spring to mind I will let you know. For the present, though, I prefer not to think about eels or anything concerned with them.'

'Quite so.'

'A number of things intrigue me,' I said after a pause, and at Inbuel's bidding I set about trying to fill in the gaps of the previous days. By his account, soon after ingesting the *gidsha* root for the last time in Dehut I had fallen into a deep trance. Tentative attempts had been made to rouse me, but to no avail, and given the circumstances it was felt I should be watched but not disturbed. The description sounded familiar as I recalled my acquaintance with the Tanakipi people and their experience of the drug.

At about this time Feikermun's beasts, supported by Wirm and his men, had launched a concerted attack against the Golden Lamb's position in an effort to rescue their master, whom they obviously hoped was still alive. The Golden Lamb, being out of his own domain, had made the decision to with-draw to a more secure location rather than risk being sur-rounded and cut off in the building he currently occupied.

This was achieved, but somewhere along the way I, under close escort by two of the Golden Lamb's men, had come out of trance and announced my intention to seek an immediate audience with the Golden Lamb. The soldiers had urged me to wait: he and the bulk of his force were guarding the rear, and we would be obliged to backtrack some distance through the dark streets to find him. But I was determined to find him immediately, and my guards, acknowledging me now as a per-sonage of some importance, lacked the authority to restrain me by force. I set off, not knowing where, oblivious to any danger, and the guards came with me.

We ran into Wirm's men. There was a fierce skirmish during which I, painly still half-tranced, wandered away and was lost. When he learned of this the Golden Lamb, deeply-troubled, could do nothing but assign men to search for me, and wait.

Early in the morning he was approached by Vastandul. 'He had had a man tailing you for some days,' explained Inbuel. 'Apparently you had been to see him, asking questions that aroused his curiosity. Now he told me that his man had witnessed your capture by Wirm, who had immediately fled the city. He was believed to be returning here, to Guling Mire.'

'What made Vastandul approach you?' I asked.

'His man had reported that I had you in my custody, so he presumed an interest on my part. We had been in contact before – Vastandul had announced himself almost immediately upon my arrival in Dehut. He has no idea who I am, of course. He is a man with many connections – you know that yourself. It can be useful to cultivate good relations with him. Equally, he was quick to acknowledge the wisdom of courting the Golden Lamb's favour.'

So the Golden Lamb and Vastandul had debated the feasibility of rescuing me. Neither had any love for Wirm, and both were agreed that for Wirm to retain his currently powerful and growing status was of advantage only to Wirm himself.

Plainly, though, if they were to have any chance of saving me they would have to move swiftly. This engendered its own problems, for Wirm had a head start of several hours and, with the battle for Dehut still raging, the Golden Lamb was prevented from releasing a large force to Guling Mire. Moreover, there was the matter of entering Guling Mire once there, for as I have said before it was considered unassailable.

As it happened, Vastandul had been planning this moment for a long time. He believed he had a way of moving decisively against Wirm, even in his own wet fortress. So a deal was struck. Almost immediately Vastandul rode from Dehut with a small company of his own men, accompanied by the Golden Lamb himself and eighty mounted soldiers. The Golden Lamb's main body of troops retired to his own domain in the west of the city. Feikermun's beasts were in fact beginning to show signs of desperation as Malibeth made continuing encroachments from the east; with the loss of their leader their resistance lacked its earlier spirit.

At Guling Mire the conspirators gained entrance by a simple but effective ploy. Vastandul drove a single wagon to the main gait, accompanied by three mounted guards, and requested ingress. Word was sent to Wirm, who was too busy (murdering me) to greet his visitor immediately. But he knew Vastandul – he had, like most shrewd folk, dealt with him in Dehut – and was keen to retain his favour. So he commanded that Vastandul be escorted immediately to his manse to await him.

Vastandul had other ideas. The moment he was within the settlement's walls eight men sprang from within his wagon and, with his three mounted guards, took arms against Wirm's sentries. With the element of complete surprise they were able to hold the gate open long enough for the horsemen of the Golden Lamb to come pounding down the natural causeway and go into Guling Mire.

The gate was swiftly secured and the bulk of the Kemahamek troops swept on into the town. Wirm's men fought hard, outnumbering the intruders by more than two to one. But they were scattered and unprepared and, man to man, were no match for such seasoned and disciplined soldiers. In effect they were defeated before they really knew they had been attacked.

'We learned at the gatehouse of Wirm's whereabouts, and were able to move there rapidly and almost unhindered,' said Inbuel. 'Even so, we were fortunate to get to you in time. Sir Dinbig, how did you free yourself and put up such a fight? The odds were massed against you. Clearly the *Zan-Chassin* possess the most impressive abilities, even though you assured me you knew no magic!'

I let it go at that. Some things are better left unsaid. The truth was that in many ways I remained as mystified by my escape as he. I knew what had happened – that is, I knew what I *believed* had happened – but so much seemed part of a dream, a *gidsha*-induced hallucination. I was beginning to accept that there would be aspects which I would never be able to clarify.

'We must speak frankly about Dehut, Inbuel,' I said. 'Grateful as I am for the intervention of the Golden Lamb, the fact is that his presence there creates problems of a political nature on a grand and troubling scale. I have to report my discoveries to the Hierarchy and the king. I can do nothing else, and Khimmu will not take kindly to the knowledge that Kemahamek has been secretly extending her influence abroad.'

Inbuel nodded to himself and gave a wry smile. 'Ah, Sir Dinbig, what intrigues we create, eh? What webs we spin. The truth is that Kemahamek has no particular designs on Dehut, or Anxau. I was sent in for almost precisely the same reason that you were: my government had intimations of Feikermun's ambitions. I was there to observe him – and Malibeth – and if necessary intervene.'

'King Gastlan and his advisors may not view it in quite such a light. After all, in effect you now rule the city jointly with Malibeth, do you not?'

'In effect, yes – that is, assuming Feikermun's men's resistance has finally collapsed. I must return there quickly to oversee events. But when I report to my superiors in Twalinieh that Khimmur has, through enviably deft deployment of her expert spies, unearthed the secret of my identity – or at least begun strongly to suspect it – they will respond accordingly. I can guarantee it. Kemahamek will not willingly incur the disfavour of Khimmur and her neighbours, though of course we cannot be seen to back down immediately simply because you people breathe a peevish sigh. There will be formalities, high-level discussions, diplomatically worded protests from your government and even more diplomatically coded replies from mine. Such is the way of things. But the Golden Lamb will quietly withdraw. What else could he possibly do? If Khimmur made her knowledge known abroad we would be harangued from all sides.'

'Quite so. But this leaves Dehut, and by extension all Anxau, in Malibeth's hands.'

'Yes. But let us imagine a situation in which both Kemahamek and Khimmur are seen to be instrumental in removing the Golden Lamb from power in Dehut. Malibeth will undoubtedly be grateful, and will be at pains to show her gratitude, for she might well understand what the outcome would be were we both to turn our attentions to her as well. We will have lots more meetings and exchanges of official letters, of course, for we don't want to humiliate her. Far rather show an amicable, avuncular face, and a united front. Malibeth will not be slow to perceive that she holds power in Dehut only for as long as we permit, and our nations can make abundantly plain what we consider to be acceptable behaviour on her part. She will have to be watched – that goes without saying; she is a wily and resourceful woman, after all. But I don't believe she is a fool. No, I see this ultimately as an opportunity for our two nations to extend our joint influence while at the same time enhancing relations between us in a very constructive way. A happy outcome all round, I think. Yes, indeed, a very happy one. So let me refill your goblet and we will drink a toast. To mutual aims and future cooperation! Now, you look tired, my friend, and I have much to do as I must return to Dehut at first light tomorrow. I will leave you to rest.'

Later in the day I learned something of the mystery of Vecco. He had been, to some small degree, Vastandul's man. This I was told by Vastandul himself, who seemed to have eyes and ears in more places than even Dinbig of Khimmur.

'I employed him to keep me informed about Wirm's activities,' said Vastandul. 'His information was very limited, often little better than useless, and he charged highly for it. But I wanted him happy and in my line of sight; he was a weasel, up to no good. Regrettably for him he underestimated his opponents, went too far and paid the price.'

'But where was he from, and how did he influence Wirm?' I asked, pretending no knowledge whatsoever of the man.

'He was a Tanakipi,' confirmed the huge fellow. 'And a renegade, something rare in itself. He supplied Wirm with cultivated *gidsha* smuggled from his own people, but he had greater ambitions. From what little he let slip I built a picture of a man plotting a coup of some sort against Wirm – Vecco wanted Guling Mire and the access to the world beyond it that the Twiners offered. He would have seduced powerful folk with elver flesh, then later enslaved them with *gidsha*. He was trying me, wishing to learn where my allegiances lay. He could have become powerful indeed.'

When I mentioned this subsequently to Inbuel he nodded sagely. 'That would appear to bear out my own findings.'

'But he tried to murder me,' I said. 'And it may have been to acquire the amber, which has sinister implications.'

Inbuel nodded to himself. 'I suspect it was little more than honest cupidity. I think Wirm was wise to Vecco and set him up, using you to trap him. Let us assume that he persuaded Vecco that you were a danger to them both and suggested your demise might be advantageous. Perhaps he told Vecco that the amber was of particular value, and agreed that Vecco might have it. Then, when things went wrong, he arrested Vecco, cut out his tongue to silence him, and let you see that a certain kind of justice was being meted out. All this is conjecture to a certain extent, but it fits.'

'Except it means that Wirm lost his supply of *gidsha*.'

'By this time Wirm had gleaned as many secrets out of Vecco as Vecco had out of him. He had found a way of bypassing him to get the *gidsha* directly from Tanakipi.'

'Then there is still a source of available *gidsha*?'

'No longer. I reported my findings to Twalinieh some time ago, with the request that the source be kept open until I had finished investigating Wirm and Feikermun. Now that the business is closed, the Tanakipi elders will be informed. I do not imagine they will be slow to stem the leakage, or punish those responsible.'

'I suspect Vastandul would have given much for that *gidsha* supply.'

'We could not permit that. The root is far too dangerous. And my friend, be careful what you say to Vastandul. Remember he does not know who I am and will do all he can to find out. Similarly, he does not know who you are, though as far as I am aware he has no reason to suspect you to be anyone other than who you claim. One day, almost certainly, he will meet again with Ronbas Dinbig, will he not? There will be an interesting exchange then. I wish I could be present to witness it.'

The Golden Lamb departed Guling Mire at dawn the following day, as he had said he would. By this time I had contacted the *Zan-Chassin* Hierarchy, leaving Yo in custody of my corporeal self and journeying instantly to Hon-Hiaita.

'You have done well, Dinbig,' declared old Hisdra when I had given her my report. 'We are pleased. Remain now in Guling Mire. An escort will come to bring you home.'

'I am concerned by one thing, Sacred Mother,' I said. 'It is that I may yet crave once more, and then again, the visions that the *gidsha* gave me. The experience is profound, like nothing I have known. Even with its terrors it is seductive. I am afraid it may call me back, and I will be unable to resist its call.'

'It is true, you have ingested a great deal in a very short space

281

of time. More than most would. It is likely to have noticeable residual effects for a while: visions, hallucinations, memory lapses, distortion of your time sense and other experiences you may be at a loss to explain. There may be physical symptoms too: cramp and sweating, perhaps delirium. It is essential that you resist any craving to take the drug again. It will require will-power, but the craving will pass. We will be with you and will take steps to ensure your well-being. You have not taken enough for it to have claimed your soul.'

I slept well that night, and spent my remaining time in Guling Mire resting and keeping a low profile. Jaktem and Illan had remained behind with me, at the insistence of the Golden Lamb, but apart from them I saw little of anyone other than Vastandul, who was keen to have me join him at meal-times. His cordiality became a bore as I found myself parrying enquiries into my background, my impressions of the Golden Lamb, any thoughts I might have as to the Lamb's identity, and other issues relating to my business in Dehut and its consequences.

After three days my escort arrived, twenty armed and mounted Khimmurians, anonymously garbed and equipped to allay suspicions as to their origins. If Vastandul was curious as to how I had summoned such a handsome retinue in so short a time, he said nothing, and I rode from Guling Mire hoping I might never again lay eyes upon its awful ooze or smell its dank bogs and foul mists.

And that, really, is the end of this strange story except that it remains for me to tell of my last encounter with Aniba. For I did see her again, though the circumstances were unusual and, as with so much at that time, I will never really be certain that I did not dream.

It was early evening, soon after my return to Hon-Hiaita. I was seated at my desk in my study, mulling over in my mind the events of the previous weeks. The shutters had not yet been closed.

I remember gazing at the deepening sky over the hills beyond the harbour and pondering that other sunset above the primordial ocean within the Citadel of Selph, with Sermilio standing

282

there beside the road, looking out on that light, his features filled with sorrowful enthralment and his gorgeous plumage whispering lightly in the warm air. In my mind I saw the bodies of the Avari suspended all around, then Aniba lying before me, pale in death, her soul passing. And the cloud rose from beyond the watery horizon, the winged people surging free once more.

I looked out towards the sky, the real sky beyond my Hon-Hiaita window, and it seemed for a moment, just a moment, that I might even break through, that I was on the brink of looking through, in epiphany's embrace, so close to understanding what it all meant.

I had risen unconsciously from my chair and was standing at the window. The sunset glowed upon the slopes and was reflected in the shimmering harbour waters. I felt a sense of intense bliss. I was moved almost to tears, my heart swelling in my breast as I marvelled at the splendour before me, the soulful beauty of the light upon this world. I knew then that any amount of pain, any degree of suffering, was bearable for my being allowed to witness this. This sight alone, this single experience, was enough – was in fact everything. Life could offer no greater reward. And then the vision was gone, the moment dispelled. I had *almost* been there, but as always something remained hidden. Always, no matter how far we travel, there must be something beyond.

It was then I realized she was there. Behind me, waiting for me to turn. This I did, slowly, without urgency. She occupied the shadows at the side of the room, a light smile upon her lips. I felt again as I had done the first time I laid eyes on her, in Feikermun's chamber. But there was something more now, which I had no words for, and the love I felt for her grew and was more natural and more marvellous for that.

Her eyes went briefly to the window. 'You have gazed upon the face of eternity, and what have you seen? That it is as when you gaze into the face of another and know that it is your own.'

I recalled Sermilio's words – or had they been hers? Or had I imagined them? *We are as you elect to perceive us.* Did that apply to all things? Perhaps it had to.

Then my thoughts became confused, as though I had lost my

way. At first I could find no words, then eventually I said, 'I did not think I would see you again.'

'You should know better, Dinbig, after all you have experienced. I had to come, once more. Why else would you have called me?'

'Called you? I did not.'

Her smile quivered slightly. 'Then how am I here?'

'That is something I do not know how to answer. Why have you come?'

'To tell you two things.' She raised a hand before her, the first two fingers and thumb gathered and extended, and slowly traced a figure in the air: a stem surmounted by a pair of outstretched and down-turning limbs, in their crux an oval. It was an image of the figure that had been etched on the note I had received weeks earlier, signed by Sermilio, bidding me bring the unarmed amber. It was receiving that note that had launched me upon the strange journey to Dehut and the subsequent discoveries of Selph, and I still had it in a drawer inside my desk.

'I come to tell you of your new status,' said Aniba. 'Through your efforts you have become something unusual among men. You are now one of those who have entered the Arch of the Wing.'

The Arch of the Wing: the secret cabal which claimed exclusive knowledge of the ways of the Avari.

'I must tell you also that you have, out of necessity, been participant in things for which you are not truly ready. You have seen and learned things that cannot be communicated to others.'

'I understand. I will speak of my experience to no one.'

'You do not understand, Dinbig. It is not merely a matter of holding your silence. You cannot be allowed to recall what has happened.'

'But how can I possibly forget?'

'It is already done.'

I shook my head, baffled.

'It has to be this way,' said Aniba. 'But not everything will be lost.'

'But I recall,' I said. 'It is clear in my mind.'

'That is good.' She hesitated, then said, 'Lastly, I have brought you a gift. You will think it will help you remember, and that is important also. It is over now, Dinbig. Between us, together, as one, we have achieved. And remember, someday you will look into a stranger's eyes . . .'

'Don't go,' I said, but I spoke only to shadows at the edge of my room, shadows pierced by soft rays of roseate light, and I questioned whether she had been there at all.

Nothing had changed when I awoke the next morning. I remembered Aniba's visit and everything we had said. I recalled everything that had gone before; but I wondered about the gift she had mentioned. She had left nothing in her wake other than the memories she insisted I could not have.

I have the evidence of what happened, for I wrote it down. It is all as I recall. Had Aniba been correct, I could never have told this story. Unless, of course, my memory plays me entirely false, and I have only imagined it all.

Might this be so? Might it even be possible that I have imagined not only what happened, but the telling of it too? It is an unsettling thought, but it is also absurd, for you, my reader, whomsoever you may be, have surely just read it. Unless this story is something that you too have imagined.

No. I recall, and I have recorded it, and I will never forget.

I went to my study after breakfast that morning to finalize the drafting of an important document. I noticed then the piece of rare green amber that rested on my desk. I had bought it from a man of somewhat dubious reputation, a fellow named Wirm who is now gone from this world. He died in a coup organized by another man known to me, named Vastandul. The coup was clandestinely supported by my close friend Viscount Inbuel m' Anakastii. In fact I had played a small but significant part in it myself, though I have no wish to go into details here.

The truth was that Wirm had been up to no good. He traded in the flesh of the Grey-backed Twiner, an eel, and he used this business as a cover for other, darker enterprises. There were certain political complexities in the matter; it was far more intricate than might appear on the surface. But it was over now, and the document would secure my own investment in the

285

industry at bog-swamped Guling Mire. I was to sign this agreement later that day, in company with Vastandul and Viscount Inbuel, making us equal partners in Guling Mire's elver-flesh business.

I was pleased with the way things had turned out. It had been a tricky affair.

The amber, glinting in the sunlight, caught my eye. It was a fascinating piece, irregularly shaped and varied in tone and pigment. I found myself staring into its depths, and I wondered, for within it was contained a mystery: a single object which looked like a tiny feather, lustrous black and banded in deep red.

And I lifted the amber and turned it in my fingers. As I did so it appeared, through a strange trick of the light, that the red of the feather flowed like liquid, like blood, into a deeper region, a dark central core, a well in which I could almost see ... I could not say what I could almost see.

I set the amber down, dwelling upon that which I could never truly know. A breath of breeze from outside touched my face, and just for a moment I thought I heard a sound, a rustling, close to the window. The beating of wings? Why did that image come to mind? It seemed to stir something within me, yet I could not quite recall. I reminded myself that I had so many days past ingested *gidsha*, the sacred visionary root of the Tanakipi peoples. Its mind-altering properties are powerful and profound, and I had been warned to expect and be prepared for residual effects for quite some time.

So I put my quill to the paper and my thoughts to the task at hand.

Somewhere, not so very far away, I heard a baby cry.

APPENDIX

The *Zan-Chassin*

OUT OF THE shamanistic beliefs and practices indigenous to the regions of Southern Lur was born in the nation known as Khimmur a formalized, stratified system of applied ritualized sorcery, *Zan-Chassin*; 'Powerful Way', 'Path (or Ladder) of Knowledge; and 'Mysterious Ascent' are all approximate translations of the term. The *Zan-Chassin* cosmology held that the universe was created by the Great Moving Spirit, Moban. Moban, having created all, moved on, and Creation was left to do as it would without interference or aid (in certain mystical circles Firstworld is still referred to as the Forgotten Realm).

Numerous modes of being were conceived to exist within the Creation, not all of which were readily perceived by or accessible to human beings. In the normal state man realized two domains, the corporeal and that of mind or intellect. The power of *Zan-Chassin* adepts lay in their ability to transcend these and enter various supra-physical domains, termed the Realms, there to interact with the spirit entities active within them. Emphasis was also laid upon contact with the spirits of ancestors who had passed beyond the physical world to dwell in the Realms beyond, and who could be summoned to an ethereal meeting-place where they might provide advice and guidance to their descendants in the physical world.

Where *Zan-Chassin* practice differed from that of the shamen of many other nations was in its systematic and quasi-scientific approach. Understanding the nature of the Realms became paramount, resulting in the introduction of a set procedure whereby the aspiring adept, through precise training and instruction, might learn in stages both the sorcerous art and something of

287

the nature of the Realm of existence he or she was to enter, thus mitigating somewhat the inherent dangers. Previously the noncorporeal world had been conceived of as a single Realm of existence. Men had gone willy nilly from their bodies to encounter, with little forewarning, whatever lay beyond. The risks were considerable. Many perished or were lost or driven insane by their experiences.

The *Zan-Chassin* way revealed the Realms to be of varying natures, with myriad and diverse difficulties and obstacles being met within each. Just as normal humans might realize different 'shades' of existence, depending upon the development of intellect, organs of sense, etc., so could *Zan-Chassin* masters come to know and experience the differing natures of the Realms. Adepts were taught to subdue the spirit entities within each level of experience before progressing to the next, thus providing themselves with allies or helpers at each stage of their non corporeal wanderings. The dangers, though still very real, were thus diminished. Aspirants progressed from one Realm to the next only when adjudged by their more advanced mentors to be ready and sufficiently equipped.

Nonetheless, over time many of even the most advanced and experienced *Zan-Chassin* masters failed to survive their journeys beyond the corporeal.

Within Khimmurian society *Zan-Chassin* proficiency was a key to power and influence. Practitioners generally enjoyed privileged social positions, and indeed the natural constitution, such as it was, was structured such that Khimmur could be ruled only by one accomplished in the sorcerous art. A few *Zan-Chassin* chose the anchoretic life and lived beyond society, but they were in the minority.

To some extent the *Zan-Chassin* were feared by normal folk, who were much prone to superstition. Their magic was not understood; their ways were somewhat strange and wonderful. The *Zan-Chassin* made little effort to remedy this, it being useful in certain circumstances.

Women enjoyed honoured status within the *Zan-Chassin* hierarchy. They revealed a natural affinity with the concepts of noncorporeality and spirit-communication which few men were able to emulate. They were equally proficient in the exploration and 'mapping' of the furthermost discovered territories of Mobab's great and mysterious Creation. Thus the hierarchy remained matriarchal in character, withstanding efforts to reduce the feminine influence.